MIDNIGHT FOR JUSTICE

CHARLOTTE STUART

DON STUART

QUARTERMASTER PUBLISHING

Published by Quartermaster Publishing, Vashon Island, WA

Cover design by Chris Holmes

Interior design by Interbridge

ISBN: 979-8-9891529-5-7 (paperback)

ISBN: 979-8-9891529-6-4 (ebook)

For those who persevere in the cause of justice.

Are you not aware that there comes a midnight hour
when everyone must unmask . . .
Soren Kierkegaard

PART ONE

SUNRISE

"The darkness is at its deepest just before the sunrise."
Voltaire

Chapter 1

Tuesday, April 29, 1975
Saigon, South Vietnam
An industrial waterfront pier

A series of explosions flashed across the early morning sky.

But the workers on the quay did not look up. Wooden crates were heaved onto cargo nets and then hoisted, one by one, onto the waiting ship. An anxious crew supervised. "*Mau lên, Mau lên!*" they shouted, waving their arms to speed things up as mortars thundered in the distance, closer now.

On shore, a nervous crowd had gathered. They jostled each other for position along a high chain-link fence. Cargo loading was nearly complete and, on a signal from an officer on the ship's rusty bridge, two men opened a gate in the fence and began directing people across the wharf's cracked pavement and aboard the ship.

At first, everyone moved in an orderly line by twos and threes. But soon those behind began to push their way through the narrow gate. Fighting and yelling broke out as desperate people struggled to reach the safety of the gangway. Old men and women were pushed aside. Children at risk of being trampled were carried in their parents' arms or on their backs. People crowded up the gangway and onto the ship's deck.

There were still a few crates on the dock, but as conditions became increasingly chaotic, the nervous officer on the bridge finally signaled for the ship to leave. The crew ashore hurried to board. And, immediately after, the corroded stack emitted a puff of thick black smoke.

Cries of consternation exploded from the crowd. The fence began to sway under the press of bodies and finally collapsed as a mass of frightened people surged toward the ship.

Amid the ensuing chaos, the officer on the bridge directed his men to raise the gangway, but it was loaded with people and much too heavy to move. More people were still crowding aboard as a hawser splashed into the water when the stern line was cast off. The huge propellers began to thrash. The ship edged forward. As it strained at a bow line, its stern slowly began to pivot away from the dock. The air was pierced by screams as the gangway, still overflowing with people, fell into the river. Others were forced off the quay into the water by those pushing up from behind. Their calls for help were lost amid the cries of the crowd and the clatter of nearby gunfire.

The propellers stopped and then reversed. A thin, frail man still clung to the bow line, trying to climb the straining hawser to the safety of the ship. A crew member reached down to give him a hand, but the man was too far away and, as the ship began to back up, the line went slack. The man fell into the river without a sound. The crewman then quickly threw the heavy line into the water and the ship was freed.

With a look of stately but insulted dignity amid the surrounding turmoil, the deeply loaded ship backed away, stopped, slowly pivoted, and moved forward to join a throng of other vessels fleeing down the river to the sea.

Two years later
Mindanao, Republic of the Philippines
An old pier along the muddy shores of Sarangani Bay

Even the birds were voiceless in the midday heat.

It was a part of General Santos that was almost entirely maritime-industrial. Along with ship repairs and cargo handling, there were several commercial fish processing firms, some with recognizably American names. Most of the old docks and warehouses were still in active use, but some had been abandoned and were falling into disrepair.

One old ship that might once have been a local freighter lay quietly at her moorings, paint peeling. A rust stain ran orange down her side. Her hull was fouled with barnacles and seagrass. Her propeller and rudder collected the weeds and refuse that drifted up and down the inlet with the minimal tidal current. A relentless sun had baked her topsides to a uniform, featureless gray.

An old man sat on the pier in the shade of a dilapidated warehouse. He smoked a dark brown cigarette. There was work to be done, but he wasn't in any hurry. The ship had already been there for nearly two years. No one had said a word about moving her in all that time. Anyway, there was no work crew, just the old man with his cigarette and a couple of kids he'd hired as part-time guards. All they really had to do was keep watch, make sure no one went aboard or disturbed the ship or its cargo, keep some hatches ventilated, lubricate and occasionally operate some of the machinery, and, very occasionally, supervise a few local workers to chip and paint the exterior when the rust got bad.

The old man was happy. It was an easy job.

Chapter 2

Sunday, February 5, 1978
Sand Point Naval Station, Seattle
Enlisted Men's Barracks One

Steven Jerome's bare feet padded silently between rows of sleeping men and across a worn but brightly polished linoleum floor. The hard khaki shirt he'd pulled on to ward off the cool night air wasn't helping much. There was no choice though. He had to take a leak.

The heads were in a large, darkened, open room at the back of the barracks. As he passed a row of bathroom stalls, he could hear the sound of a running toilet. Then he heard another noise and caught a glimpse of someone entering the room behind him, silhouetted against one of the frosted moonlit windows that ran along the side of the building. He stepped up to the urinal and willed himself to ignore the other man and accomplish what he'd come for.

Jerome saw the flash of the blade and felt indescribable pain. But he remained blissfully vague about what exactly had happened to him as he sank slowly to his knees and as his blood seeped through his shirt, ran down his leg, and formed a widening pool on the tiled floor around him.

The killer quickly moved away. At the rear door, he took one step outside, then turned and leaned back into the building to shatter the night's silence with a piercing scream.

The sound echoed off the bare painted walls. Sailors stirred in their bunks. Sleepy voices mumbled questions.

As others awoke, Steven Jerome drifted off into his final sleep.

Outside, the killer ran around the corner of the building and sprinted up the frosty, neatly mowed strip of grass that separated this barracks from the next. At the front entrance, on the opposite end of the building, he paused, peered inside the door through a small wire reinforced glass window, then, when it was safe, slipped quietly back inside.

Chapter 3

Thursday, February 9, 1978
Sand Point Naval Station, Seattle
Law Center, 13ᵗʰ Naval District

There could be few illusions about the man's guilt. The paperwork made a convincing case. If Seaman Apprentice Arnie Beck had been framed, as he claimed, someone had done a damn fine job.

Even before he'd finished reading the Naval Investigative Service Office (NISO) summary, U.S. Navy JAGC Lieutenant Duncan Carmichael was already developing counterarguments. The matter would almost certainly end with a guilty plea. But that didn't keep his lawyer's mind from compulsively sorting through plausible lines of defense. If they had to make a deal, he wanted it to be the best one possible for his client.

The buzz of the intercom announced Beck's arrival. Carmichael was a tall man with very dark eyes, his natural authority enhanced by his crisp blue uniform. He stood and stepped over to open his office door. Flanked by two Shore Patrol guards, the young sailor was marched into Carmichael's Office. At Carmichael's request, Beck's handcuffs were removed, none too gently. Then the guards stepped into the hall and closed the door, leaving him alone with his client.

Beck didn't wait for an invitation to sit. He took the chair furthest from Carmichael's desk, the one nearest the door. There he slouched down, silent and watchful. Beck was average height, with a muscular build, a man who looked like he could handle himself in a fight. A steely stare followed Carmichael as he moved to the chair behind his desk.

"I'm Lieutenant Duncan Carmichael. I assume you know that I've been appointed by the Navy to represent you?"

Beck made no response. He continued to watch from across the small room.

Carmichael's ensuing careful explanation of their lawyer-client confidential relationship elicited a barely perceptible nod when Beck was asked if he understood. It was at least a start.

"You also need to understand your rights to counsel," Carmichael continued. "I've been appointed by the Navy to defend you at no cost to you. I am a lieutenant, a U.S. Navy Judge Advocate, and a fully trained and licensed attorney. I happen to also be a member of the bar in the State of Indiana where I grew up. If you want my help, I can assure you, I'll do my very best on your behalf."

Beck blinked but made no indication of his wishes.

"You also have some other options. If there is another Navy lawyer you'd prefer, you can request him, and if that person is reasonably available, the Navy must assign him to you. Finally, you can also retain a civilian lawyer at your own expense." He paused. "Do you understand what I've just explained?" Carmichael was starting to wonder if his prospective client was fully functioning.

"I understand perfectly," Beck said with exaggerated precision.

"Great. So, what would you like to do?"

"None of the above."

What the hell did that mean? "Are you saying that you plan to represent yourself on this charge?"

"Nope."

"You do intend to have a lawyer?"

"Yes, I do."

"Ah, I'm not sure I understand."

"I'm not going to need a military lawyer, Lieutenant. And I won't be hiring a lawyer either. I have a lawyer comin' from the ACLU."

Carmichael was more than a little surprised that the American Civil Liberties Union would be interested in this case, but he tried not to show it.

Beck waited, as if to savor the moment. "There's no way I'll get a fair trial from the U.S. Navy. This thing's all about politics. It's been all over the papers. People been calling me a racist. Talk like Jerome was some kind of saint."

Carmichael hadn't seen any press reports on this case. But Beck's claim was not that unusual. In this post-civil rights, affirmative action era, there'd inevitably been political pushback. He'd heard of cases in which the ACLU had actually gone to bat for people who were claiming "reverse discrimination." Maybe the organization was looking to appear impartial. Americans were looking for "equity" wherever they could find it—or at least that was the claim.

"I see," Carmichael said. It complicated things. In his experience, civilian attorneys didn't always do well with military cases.

"They're sending me some Seattle hotshot named Sid Warren." Beck's tone suggested he wanted Carmichael to know he was being replaced by someone better.

For Carmichael, however, it was all just another day in the office. He represented the people they assigned him. Didn't matter who they were. "Good," he said. "If you'd like, I'll arrange a time for you to meet with him here at the Law Center. It might be more comfortable than meeting at the brig. Keep in mind that if you and this Mr. Warren want my help on your case, you're welcome and entitled to it; whatever you prefer."

With that, Carmichael stood and went to the door. Beck also stood, his bearing more detached than military. Carmichael sensed a touch of hostility smoldering just below the surface. He called to the two Shore Patrol guards seated across the hall to come for their prisoner.

Beck flinched as the cuffs were squeezed tightly shut. The senior of the two guards, a first-class petty officer, took Beck by the arm and roughly propelled him out into the hallway. Carmichael had noticed that Beck's wrists were already blotched with red, presumably abraded by overtight cuffs on his trip over.

"What is your name, sailor?" Carmichael asked the guard.

"Masterson, sir," the man snapped out.

"Well, Masterson, keep in mind that this man is only *accused* of a crime. He has not been convicted of *anything*. Until he is, he is presumed innocent. That means you should show him some respect. You got that?" Carmichael didn't raise his voice. His authority was on his sleeve.

"Yes sir!"

Turning to Beck, Carmichael said, "I'll see that you and Mr. Warren meet together as soon as it can be arranged, okay?"

"Yes . . ." said Beck, and then added "sir" as an afterthought.

Chapter 4

Monday, February 13, 1978
Sand Point Naval Station, Seattle
Law Center, 13ᵗʰ Naval District

At just after three, Sydney Warren turned into the U.S. Navy base at Sand Point. A uniformed Marine guard waved her to a stop. He was helpful enough, pointing out the Law Center and advising her where to park. But she found his overuse of the word "ma'am" irritating. As was his rigid salute when she'd pulled up and again when she pulled away.

The Navy base was another world. Its closely trimmed lawns, neatly swept walkways, and ordered rows of identical, perfectly kept two-story brick buildings made her uncomfortable. Not even the abundance of maturing trees could disguise the stiff institutional atmosphere. The place felt like a hospital, a boarding school, or maybe a prison.

Even the Law Center seemed alien. Usually, she felt right at home when entering other lawyers' offices. They inevitably displayed the shared badges of the legal profession: a charming receptionist, rows of old law books, framed diplomas, the urgent clacking of typewriters, harried secretaries moving about with piles of official papers. A sense of organized purpose.

This, however, was just another ageing government office, functional certainly, but cold and anonymous. Its polished linoleum floors echoed as she walked.

The Law Center's reception desk had been a large sliding glass window over a Formica counter cut into the wall off the open entry hall —something one might expect to see in a dentist's office. Or at the Department of Motor Vehicles. The receptionist, a uniformed sailor, had called ahead and then given her polite and very specific directions upstairs to the JAGC lawyer's office.

Nobody had come down to personally escort her. Apparently, this Lieutenant Carmichael couldn't be bothered.

It was three-eleven when she finally stood before a closed office door marked with a slip-in, printed cardboard sign: "Lt. Duncan Carmichael, JAGC." There was a uniformed Navy man seated in the hall outside the door. He had a band around his arm with "SP" written on it in big white letters. She didn't like being late, but that was the way it was. She nodded at the man in the hall, straightened her tailored jacket, took a deep breath, and knocked decisively.

"Come in." It sounded as much like a command as an invitation.

The room was small, hardly qualifying as an office in Sydney's world. And dingy. She did pro-bono work for the ACLU, but she was employed by a prestigious downtown law firm and was accustomed to better. She looked around at the dreary accommodations—the gray walls interrupted here and there with faded military posters and a few unimpressive photos. She was reassured to see a framed diploma from Indiana University School of Law. Beside it, however, and also framed, was a Certificate of Completion from the Naval Justice School, whatever that was.

The uniformed man behind the desk could have been in an ad for the Marines with his short light brown hair and strong chin. When he saw her, he pushed back his chair and stood with the ease of an athlete and the confidence of a man used to being in charge.

"May I help you?" he asked.

She was confused. The young sailor downstairs had called ahead, hadn't he?

Then she noticed the other man in the room. He hadn't bothered to stand. Instead, as she came in, he gave her a slow, deliberate once-over, making her glad she'd chosen to wear a conservative suit.

Sydney stepped forward, brushed a few strands of long dark hair away from her face, and extended her hand to the officer at the desk. "You must be Lieutenant Carmichael."

He shook hands but continued to look puzzled.

"I'm Sydney Warren. I believe you were expecting me."

"Sydney?"

Out of the corner of her eye she saw the other man stiffen. She turned toward him and moved forward to shake his hand as well. "You must be Arnie Beck. The ACLU sent me."

Beck ignored her outstretched hand and turned to Carmichael. "This a joke?"

Sydney stood very still, looking from one man to the other. "You *were* told I was coming?"

"We were expecting a Sid Warren," Carmichael explained. ". . . a man," he added, apologetically. It was clear to her that not only had they been expecting a man, but that they would both have much preferred one.

It was far from the first time she'd been misidentified because of her name and discounted because of her gender. Her shoulder muscles involuntarily tightened, and she felt a flash of anger. But she forced herself to remain calm and matter-of-fact as she turned back to her client. "Mr. Beck. The ACLU said you needed a good lawyer. Someone with strong criminal defense experience. They sent *me*." To be honest, they'd had to do some serious convincing and to call in a favor to get her to take the case. It wasn't her usual pro bono fare.

"I don't want a lady lawyer."

She smiled tightly. "Who said I was a 'lady'?" As a joke, it fell on deaf ears.

As she looked around for some place to sit, Carmichael quickly pulled up a chair for her. An officer and a gentleman, she thought. No doubt also a chauvinist.

"Mr. Beck, there are a few things you might want to consider before you make a final decision on this." Turning to Carmichael she asked, "Have you explained to Mr. Beck the nature of the confidential relationship between lawyer and client?"

"You're not gonna be my lawyer," Beck said.

"Beck does have a right to counsel of his choice," Carmichael said.

Sydney held herself upright and remained matter-of-fact. "Mr. Carmichael, would you mind giving us the room. For just a few minutes?"

The JAGC officer hesitated, glanced at Beck, then shrugged. "I'll be right down the hall if you need me." He grabbed what looked like an empty coffee mug and stepped into the hall.

When the door closed behind him, Sydney turned her chair to face her prospective client. "Okay," she said, "Let's talk."

"We've got nothin' to talk about."

"Okay, then why don't you just listen. I'll talk. I need to explain who I am and why the ACLU sent me instead of some 'gentleman' lawyer." She smiled but did not wait for him to respond. "I'm a practicing associate attorney with a highly respected downtown Seattle law firm. Because I believe everyone has a right to a good and proper defense, I sometimes donate my services through the American Civil Liberties Union.

"It isn't something I have to do, Mr. Beck; it's something I *want* to do. We don't demand any payment in return—my employer allows me release time for this. Jeff, the lawyer your dad spoke with at the ACLU, is quite familiar with my professional capabilities and commitment. You may think he dumped on you by sending you a woman. But he actually did you a very big favor."

Beck had remained silent. It didn't feel like she was getting through, so she added, "Also, you may want to talk with Jeff again about this, but it was my understanding that I may be your *only* option. The ACLU doesn't have that many lawyers with my credentials who are available and willing to take unpaid cases of this nature. He told me you claim you're facing some kind of reverse discrimination as a white man charged with killing a black. We don't approve of discrimination of *any* kind." She couldn't keep herself from adding: "Even against women."

Then she paused and gave him a hard stare with her sharp blue eyes to let that sink in. "So that's why I'm here."

When his sullen silence continued, she made one final try. "Mr. Beck, the clients I've defended don't think of me as a woman. Rather, I'm the lawyer who saved their butts. I don't know if I can save yours, but I can sure as hell try."

After a brief pause, she continued. "I've seen the recent newspaper stories about you, and they don't look good. The Navy men who will be on your court-martial panel will have read those papers too. And they will be fully aware of the vigorous anti-racism policies the Navy has recently adopted. I do believe there may be some serious doubt whether a current Navy court-martial can be fair in a racially charged case of this kind."

She wasn't 100 percent certain about what a Navy court-martial would be like in this instance, but she definitely didn't trust the military justice system. That was one of the reasons she'd accepted the case in spite of her initial reluctance. She'd actually been looking forward to it, if only because it would help break up the monotony of her current daily grind at Steiner, Bentley and Waterhouse.

She sensed that beneath his angry glare he was wavering. "I'll do a good job for you, Mr. Beck. That's a promise. But you need to be okay with it." She paused, then asked, "What do you say?"

Beck leaned his hard chair back against the wall and made a helpless gesture with his hands. "It doesn't sound like I've got much choice." He was silent a moment. "What happens if I want both of you? Can I have both you and this lieutenant if I want?"

"We'll need to ask him, but it's my understanding that you can."

He gave her another once-over. "Well, you got good legs—I'll give you that much."

She laughed, despite herself. "Do I take it that's a 'yes'?"

"It's going to damn well have to be, isn't it?"

"I'll tell Mr. Carmichael it's settled then."

She found Carmichael just down the hall talking with another officer, a good-looking man of about Carmichael's age with short brown hair and lively brown eyes.

"Holding out on us, Carmichael?" the other officer said as he gave

Sydney a special "for-women-only smile." It was so blatant she almost laughed.

"Ah, Frank, this is Sydney Warren. She's the lawyer the ACLU sent for Beck. And this is Lieutenant Commander Frank Merrill. He will prosecute Beck."

Sydney knew that most Navy lawyers both prosecuted and defended cases. They undoubtedly shared a certain prosecution-defense collegial camaraderie that was rare in civilian practice. She thought that might have some advantages, but she was also skeptical of what appeared to be a comfortable friendship between these two men. They were colleagues, working for the same employer, apparently in adjacent offices. One big happy family. No wonder there were so many complaints about military justice. "Lieutenant Commander Merrill," she said sweetly, extending her hand.

Carmichael quickly herded her back toward his office. "Well?" he asked as they moved down the hall.

"He wants *both* of us."

Carmichael lifted his eyebrows in surprise.

"That's possible, right?"

"Entirely possible." He didn't sound pleased, but he could hardly say no. "Is it okay with you?"

"Yes, I suppose it has to be."

"Let's get to it then."

Beck was still seated in the same chair and didn't bother acknowledging either of them when they returned.

"Miss Warren tells me you're ready to discuss your representation..." Carmichael began.

"That's *Ms.*," Sydney interrupted.

She saw Beck and Carmichael share a look. "*Ms.*, right," Carmichael said.

"Okay, Mr. Beck," Sydney said. "Let's go over a few things just to make sure we all understand where we are."

"Yes, Mzzzz Warren," Beck said with a deliberate eye roll.

"You may call me Sydney."

That seemed to amuse him. "Just plain Sydney?"

"Just plain Sydney is fine." She could tell by the look on

Carmichael's face that he didn't approve, but it wasn't his call. "How about I call you Arnie? That okay with you?"

"Fine by me."

"Has Mr. Carmichael explained the nature of the confidential relationship between client and counsel?"

Beck nodded.

"Well, I'd like to go over that myself as well, if you don't mind. To make sure we're all in agreement."

"Wait a minute, Ms. Warren," Carmichael interjected. "I need to hear from Beck what he's decided about his representation."

Beck nonchalantly flicked a piece of lint off his pants. "I guess if I can have both of you, why the hell not. Maybe you'll keep each other honest."

"I think it's a good idea," Sydney said, addressing their client. "There are probably some ways Mr. Carmichael can make things easier for us, as an insider and as a Navy officer."

"I agree," said Carmichael. "But if he takes both of us, I do think he ought to put one of us in charge." He glanced meaningfully at Beck.

Sydney didn't much trust Carmichael; after all, he was military, but it was their client's decision. "What do you think, Arnie?"

Beck shook his head. "I don't care." He looked back and forth from Carmichael to Sydney. "What the hell, if I'm stuck with both of you, both of you can be in charge."

Carmichael looked disappointed, but he didn't argue with their client's decision. Turning to Sydney he shrugged and said, "Well, I guess we're in this fifty-fifty."

"That isn't possible." Sydney had always hated losing. She tried to catch Beck's eye, but he was busy studying a hangnail on his right hand.

"Beck, you *do* understand what you've authorized?" Carmichael asked.

"Look," Beck said. "You two just do what you got to do. Okay?"

"All right," Sydney conceded grudgingly. "If we have a problem with something specific, we can present it to you to decide. Now, where were we? Oh, yes, I was about to go over the nature of the confidential relationship. As attorney and client, we have a special privilege allowed by law. That privilege allows you to speak freely with the assurance that whatever you say to me, ah, or to Lieutenant Carmichael here, will not be revealed." She placed emphasis on the "Lieutenant" as a subtle reminder that her counterpart was a Navy officer as well as a lawyer. "It will remain just between us." Beck's eyes flicked over her, but he remained silent. "In addition, we need to be informed. We need to know whatever you know in order to properly defend you. You've got to trust us."

Carmichael suddenly leaned forward and cleared his throat. "What Ms. Warren is trying to say, Beck, is that you should give us your version of what happened."

"No, I'm saying more than that. Much more." She wasn't going to get sidetracked on this—it was too important. Beck looked up at the two of them, suddenly showing some interest. Perhaps even some amusement.

"I'm saying that you need to tell us the truth, even if you think it makes things look bad for you. If you hold out on us, we could go to court not knowing something that could have saved you."

Carmichael looked as though he wanted desperately to interrupt again. But he kept silent.

"So," Sydney concluded, "keeping all that in mind, tell us what happened."

Beck hesitated, then said, "What happened is, I was framed."

"All right," Sydney said. "Tell us what you recall from the night Jerome was killed. Where were you, what did you see, what did you do?"

Beck nodded. "There's not much to tell. I was asleep. I'm a sound sleeper. Next thing I know people are yelling about blood and bodies. The lights come on. Guys are crowding into the back room. I get out of bed and go back to see what's going on." He paused. "I was a little slow getting there because I don't wake up too easy. Never have."

"And . . . ?"

"And there was a group of guys standing around in their shorts pointing at Jerome laying there bleeding all over. The next thing I know they're all over me, yelling their heads off."

"They say you resisted," Carmichael said.

"Well, yeah. What was I supposed to do, stand there and let them take me down?"

"Did you realize why they were accusing you?"

"I thought maybe someone had it in for me or something. I didn't know it was my knife that had done the job."

"Describe your knife for us, Arnie."

"Well, it's a nice knife, a real nice knife." His lips turned up in a faint smile. "Handle's carved out of ivory to fit your hand. It's got perfect balance. It's a beauty."

"The other men in the barracks knew you carried a knife?"

"Yeah." He leaned over and patted the side of his leg. "Right here. In my civvies I carry it with me all the time. Got a leather sheath. Keeps people from messing with me." He frowned, seemingly at the fact that there was no longer any knife there. "They took it away from me. It's evidence I guess."

"What did you do with your knife that night?"

"I hung it on my bed, on the post by my head. Same as every other night. All the guys knew it. During the day, when I'm on duty, it's in my locker."

"And they also knew you're a heavy sleeper?"

"Sure. Probably."

"So, anyone could have taken it?"

"Yeah." He hesitated, looking from one to the other. "Will I get my knife back?"

"When it's over, maybe. If you're found not guilty."

Carmichael interrupted. "You have any idea who might have removed the knife from your headboard?"

"Nope."

"What about your shoes?"

"Somebody swiped my shoes. Like I told you, I was framed."

Sydney turned to Carmichael. "What about his shoes?" The summary she'd read hadn't mentioned any shoes.

"They were apparently wet. Had grass on them. There was frost on the grass outside the building that night."

"I see." Sydney felt a twinge of disappointment, but she immediately recovered. If he'd been framed, this had to be a part of it.

"Like I told you, I was asleep." Beck's tone had an edge as if warning them not to question his story.

"Where were your shoes, Arnie?"

"Under my bunk. Where else?"

"Then anyone could have taken them too, is that right?"

"Yeah," he quickly agreed. "Anyone at all."

Sydney glanced over at Carmichael who picked up the questioning.

"What about your fight with Jerome?" he said.

"I hit the bastard, so what?"

"Tell us about it."

"I hit him. He hit me. I hit him back. It was a fight."

"Why did you hit him, Beck?"

"He called me names."

"Such as?"

"Honkey bastard. Dumb cocksucker. Like that," said Beck.

"So you hit him."

"Damn straight!"

"Didn't he also warn you to stay away from his girlfriend?"

"Yeah, so what?"

"Were you sleeping with his girlfriend?"

"She's black. You know that, right?"

"I'm just asking."

Carmichael's questions sounded like cross-examination. Sydney felt like reminding him whose side he was supposed to be on but recognized that he was getting some useful information.

"Why would I want to sleep with some black slut?" said Beck.

"Come on, Beck. Did you or didn't you sleep with Jerome's girlfriend?"

Beck gave Carmichael a sly, man-to-man smile. "Okay, so I was curious what a little dark meat would be like. Sure, you bet, I screwed her."

What a guy! Sydney knew it was going to be hard for anyone to see this young man as a social victim, the product of a broken system. But it didn't matter. She'd agreed to take the case. She had her duty as a lawyer. He needed her help, and it was her job to even things out. So that's what she would do.

"You realize, Arnie," Sydney said, "the prosecution's going to claim you killed Jerome because of a fight over his girlfriend. It gives you a motive."

Beck suddenly flared up. "Look, they're gunna say whatever the hell they have to say to convict me. They're all up tight because some nigger got himself stuck. That's not supposed to happen in their '*new*' Navy." His voice got louder. "And they think they've got an open and shut case. But I'll tell you what . . . they don't have shit." His voice had risen to the point where he was almost yelling. Then, in another quick shift of mood, he shut down with his arms crossed and a rigid, silent stare.

Sydney exchanged troubled glances with Carmichael. Who was this kid? And why wasn't he the least bit deferent to his own lawyers who were there to defend him?

Carmichael got to his feet. "Okay, Beck. That should be enough for now." He glanced a question at Sydney.

"That's all I need for now." She was angry at herself for having said something to encourage their client's rant about black women. Carmichael was probably right to call a halt. But maybe if he hadn't been so hardnosed, Beck might have stayed calm. You couldn't expect someone who felt like a victim of the system to trust you right off. You needed to earn trust slowly by showing respect. It didn't look to her like much respect flowed downward in the U.S. Navy.

Carmichael went to the door and called for the guards. After Beck was gone, he returned to his desk, looked at Sydney, and said, "Well?"

"Well, what?"

"What do you think of your client?"

"What do you think of *yours*?"

"He's obviously guilty. But it doesn't feel like we'll be pleading this one out any time soon."

"We don't know he's guilty."

"You think he's innocent?" He might have been asking if she thought the world was flat.

"He could be. Maybe he *was* framed like he said. But that isn't the point, right? As his lawyers, aren't we supposed to be on his side?"

"What are you going to do if he tells you he did it but plans to lie about it on the witness stand?"

"Why should he do that?"

"They always lie. The only question is whether you know that for sure. You just told him you want to know the whole truth. I've never seen how it does my client any good to tell me the truth and force me to either keep him off the stand or withdraw from the case so he can testify —thus giving away his lie to the judge and prosecutor."

"We're supposed to give him the best defense possible. I can't do that if I don't know the truth. I think you're just trying to avoid facing some abstract ethical dilemma at the expense of a possibly innocent client."

"I don't see it that way at all."

"Well then, maybe you should consider withdrawing from the case." She stood up as she spoke, ready to end their discussion.

"Sit down." It sounded like an order. She didn't much care for it.

"*Please*," he amended. "Please sit down."

He did sound sincere. She sat, but on the edge of her chair, as a warning to him that she could leave at any minute.

"I'm in this with you fifty-fifty, remember? And despite what you may think, I intend to do my damn level best for our client. I too believe Beck has the right to a good defense. Whatever other differences we may have in approach, I'm sure we can agree on that."

"Just so we understand each other," Sydney said.

Carmichael laughed. "Oh, I think we understand each other, just fine."

CHAPTER 5

Thursday, February 16, 1978
Sand Point Naval Station, Seattle
Third Floor Hearing Room, Law Center, 13th Naval District

In the next few days, Carmichael and Sydney interviewed several men who'd been present at the time of the killing. They learned nothing inconsistent with what they already knew from the NIS report. Beck's fingerprints were on the knife, but none were in the blood. Several of the men had heard the killer scream, but no one could confidently state that they recognized it as Beck's voice. Beck's claim that he'd been framed was plausible while still seeming unlikely.

The pretrial investigation was convened the following Thursday morning. The Commandant of the Thirteenth Naval District, Admiral Clifford van Damme, had appointed a line officer from District Services, Commander Thomas Wells, as pretrial investigating officer. As the officer in charge, Wells would recommend whether Beck should be brought to trial, and if so, on what charges. Carmichael had only a passing acquaintance with the man but believed him competent.

There wouldn't be much chance of anything but a referral to general court-martial, so he and Sydney decided not to present a defense case in the pretrial. Why tip their hand? Not that they had much to tip. Still, there was no sense giving Frank Merrill a preview of coming attractions unless there was some reasonable chance it could affect the outcome of the pretrial hearing. They would use the hearing mostly for discovery of the government's case.

The small, cramped courtroom on the top floor of the old law center building was used mostly for administrative discharge hearings and the occasional special court-martial. It was a stuffy garret with a tiny window at one end and a back wall that sloped downward, conforming to the shape of the roof. It had been equipped with a large gray metal conference table and a number of wood chairs of differing vintage and design.

A Navy yeoman third class sat at a separate table to one side with a machine that recorded what *he* said onto blue plastic discs rather than on a magnetic tape. The reporter talked into the machine through a large rubber mouthpiece, repeating conversations in the room rather than recording them directly. The procedure was the product of an attempt by the Navy to be frugal in the cause of justice by using relatively untrained military personnel as court reporters. Carmichael always found he could hear the reporter's voice as everything said was echoed into the machine. It took some getting used to, having your words bounced back at you like that.

Sydney arrived dressed for the occasion in a severely tailored navy-blue suit. Carmichael couldn't help noticing that it actually enhanced her tall, slender figure.

Beck looked about the same as he had in Carmichael's office. Sufficiently military in the freshly cleaned uniform Carmichael had insisted upon, but somewhat smug yet wary, like someone spoiling for a fight. It was no wonder everyone automatically assumed he was guilty. If he'd truly been framed, he was the perfect scapegoat.

Predictably, the Navy's first witness was Radarman Third Class Peter Shields, the duty man the night of the killing. Shields came into the room and stood beside a chair near the commander and facing the court reporter. Frank Merrill was seated at the prosecuting trial attorney's table.

"You swear to tell the truth, the whole truth, and nothing but the truth, so help you God?" Commander Wells intoned the oath like he was offering a prayer.

"I do." Shields lowered his hand and sat down. He looked self-conscious. But he was well-groomed and respectful. He would make a good impression on a court-martial panel.

Carmichael looked over at his co-counsel. She was carefully studying the witness with her cool blue eyes. He wondered what she was thinking. Was she capable of putting aside her anti-military bias and assess this sharp young petty officer as he would be seen by the professional navy men who would be on Beck's jury?

Merrill noted that Shields had been on duty the night of the murder and asked what had alerted him to the fact that something had happened.

"I heard a yell from the back of the barracks. Then I saw several men go back there."

"And what did you see when you arrived?"

"Jerome was on the floor. I checked to see if he was alive, and he wasn't. I noticed that the back door was ajar just as Seaman George Brock came in and reported there was no one out there."

"What did you do next?" Merrill asked.

"I directed the men to stay inside and away from the body. I asked one of the men to make sure no one messed with the scene. Then I returned to my duty office at the front of the barracks and called for help."

"How long did all of this take?"

"I was away from my office no more than four or five minutes," Shields said.

"What made you think Seaman Beck was involved?"

"One of the men came to me and said that there was blood on Beck's knife. It's always hanging on his bedpost, so I went to look and, sure enough, there was blood around the top edge of the scabbard. At that point, we restrained Beck."

"Restrained?"

"Yes, he resisted, but I felt it was necessary to make sure he was available for questioning when the Officer of the Day arrived," said Shields.

"And what did the Officer of the Day do when he got there?" Merrill asked.

"He asked me to contact NIS, which I did."

"What did you do while waiting for them to arrive?"

"I left Beck with two men and took a look around. I found tracks in the frosty grass leading up the side of the building and around to the front. When I went back inside, I realized how wet my shoes were, so I had a look at the shoes under Beck's bunk. They were wet and had bits of grass stuck on them."

"How did you know they were his shoes?"

"I asked him, and he confirmed they were his. They were under his bed."

"What happened next?"

"NIS showed up and I went back to my duty station."

"Thank you, Petty Officer Shields."

Commander Wells looked at Carmichael as if expecting him and not Sydney to cross-examine the witness. Sydney turned toward Carmichael and raised her eyebrows in question. He nodded for her to go ahead. That was what they had agreed upon.

"Mr. Shields," she began. Too late Carmichael remembered he needed to straighten her out on how to address military personnel. Oh well, nothing else about her was standard navy-issue either. "Mr. Shields, do you have any training in police work, either in the service or in civilian life?"

"No, ma'am."

"Did you by any chance mention to Mr. Beck that he had a right to a lawyer if he wanted one?"

"No, ma'am."

"Did you tell Mr. Beck that he had a right to remain silent or that statements he might make could be held against him in a court of law?"

"No, ma'am."

"Did you mention that the Navy would provide a free lawyer for his defense if he made that request?"

Shields looked at Carmichael as if to ask what the hell was going on. "No, ma'am."

"Can you tell us again how you knew that the wet shoes you found were his?" Sydney asked.

"Well, like I said, they were by his bed. I asked him if they were his, and he said they were."

Sydney then turned to Commander Wells. "I'd like to note, for the record, that the defense will object to this statement by the defendant being admitted at trial." The yeoman court reporter duly repeated it into his muffled mic.

Sydney moved to the large demonstration tablet mounted on a movable stand that she and Carmichael had set up at one side of the conference table. She took a marker pen and began sketching a rough outline of the barracks. When she had finished, she turned to face the witness with her next question.

"Now, Mr. Shields, is this an accurate rough diagram of the lower floor of Barracks One?" She had very quickly done an excellent sketch. It included the separate front lounge-lobby area and the duty office that opened onto the lobby in front and back into the bunkroom behind.

"Yes, ma'am, pretty much."

"May we please mark this for identification?" Sydney addressed her question to the court reporter. After repeating the question into his mouthpiece, the reporter wrote down "Defense Exhibit A" on a small yellow tag and handed it to Sydney to stick on the drawing.

She turned and addressed Shields. "The drawing you just referred to is now marked 'Defense Exhibit A', is that correct?"

"Yes, ma'am." Shields seemed bored by all the repetition.

"Now will you show us by marking on 'Exhibit A' where the tracks that you found in the frost were located."

Shields stood up and took the marker from her. He drew a series of arrows down the side of the building. "Right along here," he said.

"Please indicate your duty station on this drawing." Shields put an "x" on the drawing, and at Sydney's suggestion, wrote out "Duty Office" with the pen. "Thank you, Mr. Shields. Please be seated." When Shields was back in his chair she continued. "When you were in the process of getting the situation sorted out, putting Mr. Beck under restraint and checking on his knife and shoes, were there other men in the vicinity of the first floor in addition to the men who bunked there?"

"Yes, some of the men came down from above, from upstairs, to see what all the fuss was about."

"How many would you say came down?"

"Oh, quite a few, twelve, fifteen. I'm not really sure," he said.

"Who told you about the blood on the knife?"

"I'm not sure who was first to notice. Several guys saw it. As soon as they said something to me, I went over to have a look. There it was, drooling down the scabbard."

"Did you check anyone else's shoes for moisture, any shoes other than Beck's?" she asked. "Downstairs or upstairs."

"Well no, ma'am. I didn't see any need. By that time we already knew . . .," He stopped in mid-sentence, obviously aware he had said the wrong thing. The reporter was echoing his mistake for the record. But Sydney didn't bother with an objection that was pointless at this stage.

"You say there was blood on the knife. Was there any blood found on Mr. Beck's person? On his hands or clothes, for example."

"Nope. Not that I know of."

Sydney started to sit down, then just before doing so, turned and asked, "When you first went to the back of the building to investigate the disturbance, you left the front door unlocked?"

"Yes, ma'am." Defensively, he added, "The front door is always unlocked."

"Thank you, Mr. Shields. That is all I have." She sat down.

Carmichael leaned over and said, "Well done." He was thinking that she might have gained them a slight edge by potentially eliminating Beck's admission that they were his shoes. And with her questions about the absence of blood on Beck's person. The response, however, was a cold prickly stare and a silent shake of the head as if to say: what had he expected?

The hearing continued through Thursday afternoon and was picked up again on Friday morning when Jerome's good friend, Petty Officer Ross Gordon, testified. He described in detail the bar fight between Beck and Jerome on the Friday night before the murder. It didn't do Beck any good. The only witness who testified the least bit favorably to Beck was his friend, Seaman Billy Ogden, known as "Oggie." Oggie, a large, menacing looking man, had been present the night Beck fought with Jerome. He insisted that Beck's actions had been purely defensive, but it was evident that friendship weighed heavily in his assessment of the situation.

As the hearing drew to a close, Carmichael felt that Beck's case stood about where they had figured. The one bright spot was that there was a slim chance they might be able to suppress Beck's admission that the wet shoes were his. But it wouldn't be much help in the long run, since they were the only shoes found under his bunk, they were his size, and if they were somebody else's shoes, where were his, and what had he been wearing the day before? Their defense would still need to be that someone else had purloined and worn them.

Sydney also made what Carmichael believed was an unlikely constitutional argument against the jurisdiction of the military in a case involving a murder that is unrelated to the maintenance of military discipline. Everyone listened politely; no one seemed particularly interested or concerned. But that didn't matter. The comments had been made for the record—maybe they would help later on appeal, if necessary. In Carmichael's view, how could the on base murder of a fellow sailor not be related to military discipline? Still, he had to admit she'd written a sound brief. And she'd presented her argument with confidence.

All in all, the case for Beck's innocence did not look good. But not hopeless either. Then, just before the close of the hearing, Frank Merrill handed out a few last-minute documents from Beck's service record, and Commander Wells read them into evidence. Neither Carmichael nor Sydney had seen the documents before. They were entered as "Investigation Exhibit 10." The documents included a notation on Beck's application for service that read: "13a Prior Convictions: On March 9, 1977, the applicant was convicted in Washington State's Stevens County Superior Court of assault with a knife with intent to do great bodily harm. Sentence suspended on condition of entry into the U.S. Naval Service."

There it was in black and white. Beck had a prior civilian conviction involving the use of a knife, something he'd failed to tell them. Carmichael turned to their client who gave him his usual "I don't give a shit" stare back. Then he caught sight of Sydney's face with its look of shock and disappointment. Well, she couldn't say he hadn't warned her.

This prior conviction nudged Carmichael past that line of believing Beck was *probably* guilty to being fairly certain of his guilt. It made no real difference. Carmichael's job would be exactly the same in any event.

Chapter 6

Thursday, February 23, 1978
Sand Point Naval Station, Seattle
Law Center, 13th Naval District

On the Thursday morning of the week following the pretrial investigation, Sydney met with Carmichael to plan their next moves. She hadn't been looking forward to it, but the warm, genuine smile he gave her as she entered his office tempered her latent hostility. He did take his job seriously, after all, even if for all the wrong reasons. It seemed to her that it probably didn't matter to Carmichael if Beck was convicted or not, as long as he, Carmichael, played the game well. She knew their client wasn't particularly likable; in fact, it was downright hard to like much of anything about him. But who knew what forces were responsible for making him what he was? And if he was innocent as he claimed, which was absolutely possible, he did not deserve to be sent to a federal prison like Leavenworth. She'd never been there, but she was sure it was probably a medieval hellhole.

"I've been thinking about this case," Carmichael said. "Given Beck's claim that he was framed, I've got a suggestion for how we might approach it."

"Okay."

"As defense lawyers it's our job to act as though Beck is telling us the truth. So at least for purpose of defending him, let's assume that he is innocent. That means we need to focus on who else might have done it."

That blew her away. "Aren't you the guy who thinks they always lie?"

He smiled, perhaps with a trace of indulgence. "Oh, they do. Or at least a good part of the time. Even so, I believe it's my job to at least *take* what a client says at face value. Investigate what he tells me. Treat it as true, even if I'm convinced that it may very well turn out to be false."

Sydney thought about that. Even if he didn't believe his clients were telling the truth, maybe his approach more or less amounted to the same thing.

"I agree completely," she said simply. There was no need to challenge him. This officer was anything but stupid. Maybe this was his indirect way of admitting he'd been wrong, or that he could relate to her position. She put her leather handbag on the floor beside her chair and crossed her legs, suddenly self-conscious about the way the soft blue material of her dress clung to her body. Out of the corner of her eye she saw Carmichael glance over as she smoothed her skirt over her knees. She felt herself blush. Dammit, he might *look* like a Boy Scout . . .

Carmichael reached for a legal pad and carefully squared it in front of him. Next, he pulled out a black Navy-issue pen from a coffee mug with a U.S. Navy JAGC emblem on it and held the pen poised over the pad. "All right, then. Where are we?"

"If Beck was framed, then someone else is guilty," Sydney said. "Just as he claims."

"Let's take this a step at a time, shall we?"

Watching Carmichael get ready to make his list, Sydney wondered if he was one of those compulsive types who had to write everything down to give it reality. She had a sudden vision of him drawing miniature charts of attack plans and using a pointer to refer to the progress of some battle on a map. "Absolutely!" She stifled a smile.

"The first thing we need to consider is who, besides Beck, had reason to kill Jerome." Carmichael wrote a one and circled it, then made a notation.

"I doubt NIS spent much time on that line of thinking." It was hard keeping the sarcasm out of her voice. Of course they hadn't. Everyone had Beck tried and convicted within minutes of discovering the body.

"Probably didn't think it was necessary."

"Obviously."

He blinked a few times, gave her a look, then turned back to his notes. "So, what do we know about Jerome?" He handed her a manila folder. "I copied a few pages from his service record as a start. If we need to see the whole thing, I can arrange it."

Sydney skimmed the pages. "Nothing much here but praise."

"His record *is* exemplary."

"Are these 'exemplary' evaluations common?"

"Can be. But even when there is no actual criticism you can often tell by what's written down if someone is doing a good job or not. I'd say the officers who wrote these do seem to think Jerome was okay."

Sydney looked through the pages again. "Even if they're accurate, this doesn't really tell us much."

"That may be true." Carmichael grinned. "But requesting the copies made Merrill wonder what we're up to."

That made her smile. "So, you're trying to needle the opposition?"

"It doesn't hurt to keep the other side guessing. Merrill's a capable guy."

"How well do you know him?" She still suspected it might be a little too well.

"We've served together here at the Thirteenth Naval District for about a year and a half."

"Is he a guy who likes to hide the ball?" Prosecutors were ethically and legally required to disclose *all* of the evidence to the defense, even if it was unfavorable to the prosecution. Some took that duty a good deal less seriously than others.

"I'd never take anything for granted," he said. "But you should know that Frank's actually a remarkable guy. Something of a war hero."

"Really?"

"He was in Saigon when it fell in 1975. A Navy legal attaché at the

Embassy until the last couple of days. A lieutenant at the time. And a mere JAGC officer to boot. Even so, he managed to somehow commandeer a small civilian ship and help several hundred U.S. loyalist Vietnamese escape. It's quite a story. I gather they got out with only a few hours to spare. Those people would all have died or suffered miserably if they'd been left behind."

She couldn't help but feel impressed.

"He got some kind of medal for it. You should ask him about it sometime."

"I will," she said. "But that's sort of beside the point, right?"

Carmichael nodded. "You're right." He looked down at his legal pad, and she saw him write an "a" under the "one" and next to it, "Complete Service Record." He underlined "complete."

"Make a little 'b' and write down 'girlfriend,'" Sydney suggested, pointing at the pad.

Their eyes met briefly as he obviously tried to sort out whether she was making fun of him. Then he wrote down a "b" and after it, "Girlfriend."

"We also need to consider the frame," she added. He wrote a "2," leaving space to add more under number one if necessary. "And we should list what the killer had to do to frame Beck."

"There's the obvious stuff. Like the knife," Carmichael said.

"And the shoes."

"And knowing where Beck's bunk was."

"And knowing he was a heavy sleeper," Sydney added.

"And knowing about the fight between Jerome and Beck."

"And possibly knowing about the relationship between Beck and Jerome's girlfriend," Sydney said.

"*If* there was a relationship."

"Yes, *if.*"

She waited while Carmichael finished noting down what they'd said. He did seem like a decent guy, she thought. If only he didn't look so . . . so military, like a recruiting poster. She thought his starched shirt collar might cut his neck if he turned his head too quickly.

"Whoever did it was willing to take a big risk," she said. "They could have been seen returning the knife and shoes."

"Uh-huh. Maybe they counted on everyone's attention being elsewhere. But they also couldn't count for sure on anyone noticing the bloody knife or the wet shoes."

"True, although everybody was probably aware of the fight at the tavern." She paused. "And who knows, it could have been the killer who called attention to them."

"Yeah. None of this narrows the field much," Carmichael said. "But it had to be someone familiar with both men and who was there in the barracks when Jerome went into the bathroom area."

Every time he used the word "barracks" she thought of summer camp with its beach campfires and marshmallows. It made her want a s'more. "The shoes were a nice touch," she said.

"Yes, running across frosty grass at zero two hundred, that's either some extraordinary planning or a remarkable extra bonus," Carmichael said.

Couldn't he just say two o'clock like a normal person?

Carmichael continued thoughtfully. "I guess the killer could simply have used someone else's shoes so as to avoid having his own shoes get wet or bloody."

"But when it's both the shoes *and* the knife?" she asked.

"No, you're right. It would have to be directed at Beck."

"And his feet would have to be the same size or smaller than Beck's," she added. "Or he could have taken Beck's shoes with him and scuffed them in the wet grass."

"The killer didn't have much time for that. And nobody mentioned anything about there being unusual markings in the grass near the footprints," Carmichael said.

"Not sure they would have noticed. Any way you look it, this *doesn't* narrow the field much."

"No." Carmichael wrote something on his list. "What about motive? Beck's is clear enough. But what other possible motives could there be?"

Carmichael's note taking was beginning to get on Sydney's nerves. She felt cheated when she said something he didn't write down. And although she had a very retentive memory and could later jot down anything she wanted to remember, it made it seem as though he was in charge.

"There's one thing that really bothers me," she said.

"Just one?"

"One in particular."

He smiled. "What's that?"

"Why scream and wake everyone up? Why not simply go back to your bunk and wait for someone to discover the body?"

"Actually, it's fairly obvious. The killer had to get back to his bunk in the barracks past dozens of other sailors who may or may not be sleeping. He wouldn't want to have someone see him returning from the heads and mention it after the body was found."

"So, he goes out the rear entrance and at the last instant screams to draw their attention to the back of the barracks," she said. "That lures the duty guy, Shields, away from his office up front. The killer slips in the front door, returns the knife and shoes, and simply joins the crowd milling around the body, with nobody the wiser."

"Works for me. Or," Carmichael added, ". . . he returns to his own bunk, takes off his own shoes, replaces his own knife on his own bedpost, and pretends to just be waking up."

"You're not going to cut this guy any slack, are you?"

He wrote something down.

"What are you writing now?" she asked.

"What you said."

"What did I say?"

"About drawing the duty officer away from the front of the barracks," he said.

"Oh."

"Well, I'd say we have enough to get started," he said.

"Really?" It didn't seem to her that they had come up with anything.

"Let's take it from the top," he said.

"The top?"

"Of the list."

"Of course." Why hadn't she thought of that?

After going over the list and speculating about the facts in the case, they decided they needed to ask Petty Officer Ross Gordon a few more questions. Carmichael called Gordon's leading chief and arranged to have him sent over to the Law Center for a further interview. Sydney found it remarkable how an officer's voice on the phone could win immediate cooperation in things like this. She couldn't count the number of times she'd been forced to inveigle and cajole merely for the opportunity to question a witness in a civilian defense. But on the base, everyone seemed to assume cooperation was mandatory. Even with a defending counsel. It was a point in favor of the military system. A small one.

Soon after Carmichael's call, the three of them were seated together in a drab, institutional conference room down the hall from Carmichael's office. It crossed Sydney's mind that the room was yet another metaphor for military life. She suspected that the plain, unremarkable surroundings where these men lived and worked had a dehumanizing effect on their outlook, encouraging, what seemed to her, an unnatural dependence on discipline and the command structure.

Since these Navy men seemed to have a hard time accepting her as an authority figure, she resolved to stay in the background during the interview with Gordon. Let Carmichael talk to him man-to-man. If only she hadn't worn that damned clingy dress today.

"I've already told you everything I know," Gordon said as the three sat down at the table with weak coffee in paper cups from a battered machine down the hall.

"We just have a few more questions, a couple of things we hope you might be able to clarify."

"Sure. Glad to help if I can, sir."

The salute in Gordon's voice as he said "sir" made Sydney wonder if he would try to tell them what he thought they wanted to hear. Was Carmichael so accustomed to that tone that he simply accepted it as a natural part of the order of things?

"We're trying to get a better idea about what Jerome was like," Carmichael began. "Could you tell us how he spent his spare time, maybe give us a list of his friends, that sort of thing?"

"Yes, sir."

"Okay, let's start with how he spent his spare time. What did he like to do?"

"The usual."

"For example?"

Gordon glanced uneasily in Sydney's direction. "You know—drank, played pool, chased women."

Of course, the *usual*.

"He chased women?" Carmichael asked. "What about his girlfriend?"

"He hung around with her enough."

"Did they ever fight about his eye for the ladies?"

"No, not that I know," said Gordon. "Fact is, I think she played around a little too."

"I see. What's her name?"

"Lea. Lea Sackett." Gordon leaned toward Carmichael and said in a low, conspiratorial voice, "Sackett to me." Carmichael seemed to be assiduously avoiding eye contact with her while she concentrated on keeping her face expressionless.

"I take it everyone knew she wasn't a one-man woman."

"Pretty much general knowledge," Gordon said.

"So why did Jerome get so upset when he heard Beck was seeing her?"

"Well, she was *his* girl. Maybe he didn't see things quite like everybody else. Beck only did it to irritate Stevie."

"Why would he do that?"

"Well, look, you've talked with Beck," Gordon said. "He isn't big on mixing with blacks. I can take 'em or leave 'em. Don't see as it makes any difference one way or the other. But Beck, man, he hates 'em. You talk about a racist, he's it."

"You said Jerome played pool."

"Right."

"Did he ever gamble that you knew of?" Carmichael asked.

"No, not really."

"What about money trouble?"

"No, Stevie was always flush."

"He had plenty of money?"

"Always seemed to."

"Wealthy family?"

"You kidding? An enlisted guy in the U.S. Navy?" Gordon laughed. "Not likely."

"What about trouble with the police?"

"Not that I ever heard of."

Carmichael took a deep breath. "Is there anyone you think might have wished Jerome harm? Not necessarily someone you think killed him, but someone who didn't like him much, someone who bore a grudge perhaps. Particularly, someone who resided in Barracks One."

"No, I've thought about it, and I can't think of anyone. We all liked Stevie."

Before Gordon was dismissed, they got a few names of buddies from him and a list of places Jerome had hung out. Then they decided to split their efforts. Carmichael would talk to Jerome's male friends, and Sydney would search out Lea. It wasn't much, but it was a start.

From the top of the list.

CHAPTER 7

Saturday, February 25, 1978
Residential neighborhood, North Seattle
Lea Sackett's apartment

Sydney located Lea easily enough; she was listed in the white pages of the Seattle telephone directory. Lea didn't answer her telephone until evening, but she was more than willing to talk to Sydney. Sydney wanted to meet in person, and Lea agreed to the following morning, a Saturday.

At nine o'clock Saturday morning Sydney was climbing the interior stairway of an apartment complex on a back street a few blocks from the Sand Point Navy Base. It was an older, standard-looking building, the kind with a tiny patio or deck for each unit, worn carpeting, not enough visitor parking, and no elevator. She had to climb to the third floor. When she knocked on the door of unit 337, she could hear someone moving around inside. The tiny peephole in the door turned dark, then the door opened.

Lea's hair was cut short, emphasizing the shape of her head and giving her an exotic African look. She was light skinned with delicate features and large luminous eyes. Wrapped in an embroidered tunic that

Sydney guessed to be Peruvian, Lea was quite striking. She gestured Sydney in, waving one hand in the air.

"Just doing my nails," she explained.

The apartment reminded Sydney of her early college days. There was a couch with an Indian bedspread thrown over it, a few colorful prints on the walls, and a haphazard collection of inexpensive furniture. Lea's eclectic choices had managed to turn a very standard room into a pleasant and interesting place.

"Coffee?" Lea motioned Sydney toward a wicker chair covered with colorful pillows.

"Yes, thank you."

"You take anything in it?"

"No, nothing."

Lea disappeared into another room for a minute and returned carrying an enameled tray with two pottery mugs on it. She handed one to Sydney and sat down across from her on the couch.

"I don't know if I mentioned that I represent Arnie Beck or not." Actually, she knew damn well she hadn't mentioned it. Lea frowned and leaned forward. "Everyone's entitled to a lawyer," Sydney added by way of explanation.

"So they say." Lea leaned back, took a sip of coffee, and openly appraised Sydney. "What's it like to be a lawyer?"

"I like it."

"Good pay?"

"Yes, good enough." Why were they talking about her? "What I wanted to ask was about the fight Jerome and Beck had."

"Jerome and Beck? You sound like one of the boys," Lea said.

"I guess I've been hanging around the base too much of late."

"That can get you in trouble."

"Oh?"

"All those good-looking hunks."

"Of course."

Lea laughed. "You are an uptight one, aren't you?"

"I suppose it may seem that way."

"It does." In spite of the criticism, she gave Sydney a warm smile of encouragement.

"Ah, about Steven . . .," Sydney began.

Lea interrupted. "Everyone called him Stevie."

"Stevie. Did he have any disagreements lately with anyone besides Arnie?"

"Not that I know of," said Lea.

"Any hassles over money?"

"Stevie never worried about money. He was always very generous."

"Had a lot?"

"Seemed fairly flush."

"Do you know where he got it?" Sydney asked.

Lea stood up. "Want a refill?"

"Okay." She didn't need it, but Lea seemed to want to get one for her.

Sydney waited for Lea to return, wondering if her question had prompted the abrupt departure. This time Lea didn't settle back on the couch but sat upright on a nearby chair.

"Look, I didn't know where he got his money, and I didn't really want to know. Stevie got around. He grew up poor, real poor. The only thing he didn't want was to go on being poor." She crossed her arms. That part of the discussion was closed.

"Well, I'd like to talk with some of his friends," Sydney said. "Can you give me any names? Especially anyone that you know bunked in Barracks One." They already had a list, but she wanted to see if they could add to it.

"Sure. Ross was about his best friend. Ross Gordon. I think he and Stevie were in the same barracks. There were some other guys he drank with, but Ross is your best bet."

"What about Arnie? Was he a drinking buddy?"

"Are you kidding? Not likely."

"Had they ever fought before?"

"No, I don't think so," Lea said. "Arnie was just around. People like him are a part of the universe we occupy, know what I mean? Same barracks. Same base. Same places we go, not *with* us, but just *there*, that's all. Can't avoid them."

"But they really got into it that one evening?" Sydney asked

"Why don't you just come out and ask if I was sleeping with the dude?"

"Were you?"

"Hell no! I wouldn't sleep with him if he was the last man on earth. He's an ignorant brute. An animal. Just the thought of him laying a hand on me makes my skin crawl. You've seen him. Would you want to go to bed with that creep?"

Sydney shook her head. "No, but, well, everyone seems to think you were sleeping with him."

"And guess who gave them that idea? Couple of times he fell all over himself trying to score with me. I cooled him off. Went easy at first cuz I didn't know anything about him. Later on, I found out he's a hard-core racist. What did he want with me anyway? Frankly, I think he's twisted, scary."

"But Stevie believed him?"

She suddenly grew subdued. "Yeah, I guess he did. He called me up and was real angry. I couldn't understand why. Stevie falling for that crap—it hurt. Really hurt." She took a sip of coffee. "Look, I admit I wasn't always faithful to Stevie, but I liked him. I sort of hoped that someday . . ." She shrugged. "Well, now that isn't going to happen." She blinked rapidly and drew a Kleenex from her pocket. "Shit. I'm going to cry. I thought I was through crying."

Sydney wanted to reach out and console her, but she didn't think Lea would welcome the gesture. "I'm sorry to upset you like this. But I know you want to help us find Stevie's killer."

Lea looked startled. "What do you mean? They already have the bastard. I just hope they hang him."

"Arnie claims he was framed."

Lea frowned. "My ass he was framed. He's guilty as hell."

"I'm not saying that my client is a good guy," said Sydney. "Not even a little bit, actually. But there is some reason for doubt." If there was no relationship between Beck and Lea, the prosecution's proof of motive would be considerably weakened. "And if he didn't kill Stevie, we need to figure out who did."

Lea's look of disbelief was turning hostile. Sydney hurried on, afraid the interview was soon going to be over. "Look, the one thing that bothers me still is the money. If Stevie was involved in something shady, he might have made a few enemies."

"I didn't say he was involved in anything illegal," Lea said.

"But that's what you think. I'm not asking you to get involved, just give me an idea who I could talk to about it. That's all."

"I don't know where he got the money, but I know where he spent some of it," Lea said.

"Oh?"

"Yeah, he always had a little coke, some weed, or a few pills to pass around to his friends. As I said before, he was generous."

"Do you know where he got the stuff?"

At that, Lea finally closed up. "I already said as much as I'm going to say." She put her coffee aside and stood up. "I appreciate what you're trying to do, but I don't think I can be of further help. If you have any more questions, try talking to Ross."

"Thanks," Sydney said, as she got to her feet. "It was good of you to talk with me." She paused at the door and reached into her wallet. "If you think of anything more . . ." She handed Lea her professional business card with her contact information at the law firm, Steiner, Bentley and Waterhouse.

Lea smiled as she ran her fingers across the face of the card. "Raised letters. Classy."

The following Tuesday was exhausting. Sydney was behind at the office, feeling overwhelmed by what she was supposed to be getting done. When she'd joined the firm, the partners had agreed that she could take on occasional pro-bono or ACLU defense work. And they'd agreed to provide release time. But the reality was somewhat different. She was still in direct competition with other associates when it came to her billable hours. And the partners certainly didn't seem to lighten up on her regular workload just because she'd taken on a pro bono case.

By the time she walked into Carmichael's office in the early afternoon, she was beat. She was also hungry because she'd skipped lunch.

"Hi," she said, collapsing into a chair. He was at his desk looking fresh and well-groomed, like he'd just stepped out of a shower into a clean uniform. God, didn't that uniform ever wrinkle? Then she noticed his hair was damp.

"Is it raining and I was too tired to notice?"

"Huh?"

"Your hair is wet."

"Shower. I run. And work out in the gym on my lunch break."

Of course.

"You look like you could use a cup of coffee," he said.

"Several cups."

He left and returned a few minutes later with two white mugs and a silver coffee carafe on an enameled tray.

"What's this?" she asked. "Not machine fare?"

He made a show of pouring them each a cup. "The CO's secretary has a Mr. Coffee in her office. She sometimes lets the rest of us take advantage. On special occasions."

"So, I'm a 'special occasion' today?"

He gave her a bright smile. "She seems to think so." He sat down and asked, "Learn anything interesting?"

She savored the thick, potent strength of the coffee, breathing deeply of the aromatic steam. It reminded her of the law school cafeteria coffee that used to seep through the pores in their cheap Styrofoam cups.

"I've learned a little. What about you?"

"Not much. I've been working mainly on trying to figure out where Jerome's money came from. There's something there, but I can't get a handle on it."

"Drugs," she announced simply.

"Drugs?" He frowned.

She was pleased with herself for coming up with something that might be useful. "Lea let it out of the bag. She wouldn't give me any names, but she said we should talk to Ross Gordon if we had more questions. What do you think?"

Carmichael's habitual frown deepened. "This time I'm going to talk with him alone."

She wondered what he might have in mind but decided not to ask. "Sounds fine to me."

"Anything else?"

"One more thing . . ." She took another long swallow of coffee, ignoring the look of impatience on Carmichael's face. "Lea claims she never slept with Beck. And I believe her. She hates Beck's guts. Called him a hard-core racist."

"Hmmm." He dropped another sugar cube into his coffee and stirred it with a wooden stick. "What makes you so sure she was telling the truth?"

"Women's intuition."

"You're joking . . ." He obviously wasn't sure.

"Yeah, I'm joking. But I am fairly certain. She's an attractive, intelligent, independent woman. And she really doesn't like him one tiny bit."

"So why did Beck lie to us?"

"Seriously?" She paused for effect. "Some men like to boast about their exploits. Especially if they don't have any to boast about. And my guess is that Lea is popular with the men."

"But under the circumstances . . ."

"Aren't you the one who lectured me on clients lying to their lawyers?"

"We should talk to him again, I suppose."

"You going to ask him to tell you the truth?"

He flashed a quick smile. "Touché." Then he picked up the phone. "It could take over an hour to get him here from the brig."

"Great. That gives me time to get something to eat. I'm starved."

They drove together to a deli in a collection of shops just up the road from the base. She had a tuna salad sandwich while he kept her company with more coffee. They split a piece of carrot cake for dessert. While they ate, they avoided talking about the case, instead they discussed food they liked and other safe topics such as the weather and how the local baseball team was doing. He seemed surprised that she followed sports. It was a pleasant, comfortable meal. And somewhere between the coffee and the cake, he became Duncan instead of Carmichael.

Chapter 8

Tuesday, February 28, 1978
Sand Point Naval Station, Seattle, WA
Law Center, 13th Naval District

They only had to wait a few minutes back at his office before the guards arrived with their client. Under Duncan's watchful eye, the guard carefully removed Beck's handcuffs. Beck shuffled back and forth during the process, complaining and making the guard's task more difficult. When he was free, he made a show of vigorously rubbing his wrists and dismissed his escort with a smirk: "Hang around, Jeeves, I won't be long." Then he gave Duncan a jaunty salute and took his usual place in the chair against the wall. Duncan wasn't impressed.

"We've been talking to a few people, Beck . . .," said Duncan.

"That's nice."

". . . and we'd like a few straight answers from you."

"Shoot."

"That's 'shoot, *sir*.'"

"Shoot, *sir*," Beck mimicked with a smirk.

"Lea claims she never slept with you."

"So?"

"We believe her," Duncan said

"Why her and not me?" He sounded peeved.

"You tell us."

"She wouldn't want to broadcast she's a *whore*."

"I talked to her," Sydney interjected. "She isn't ashamed of her liberal views on sex."

"My, my, ain't we so-fis-ti-ca-ted."

Duncan shook his head in disgust. "Don't you realize that the more you lie the worse things get for you?"

"If you think things look so goddam bad now, what the fuck difference a few lies goin' to make?" Beck looked from Duncan to Sydney and back again. "Why don't you two jus' back off. I ain't gettin' convicted. I didn't do nothin'." He seemed to enjoy sounding like a redneck, taunting them with his attitude.

"Arnie, remember how I told you that you would have to help us if we were going to help you?" Sydney asked. Beck did not respond. "Well, if there is any more you're holding back, now is the time to tell us." Duncan gave her a warning look, but she ignored him.

When Beck didn't say anything, she pushed ahead and asked: "What about drugs, Arnie. Were you and Stevie involved in some sort of drug dealing?"

"Drugs?" Beck looked genuinely surprised. "Is that what this is all about? I should have known. You and those damn NIS cops." He threw up his hands. "Keyrist! I should have known."

Duncan felt his own surprise echoed in Sydney's voice. "NIS?" she said. "You mean the Naval Investigations Service office? Arnie, is there something that happened with them that you haven't told us about?"

"Christ! All anybody in the U.S. Navy gives a shit about is freaking drugs. Who cares if I'm being framed for murder?" Beck crossed his arms and slouched down even further.

"Listen, Arnie," Duncan said. "We need to know exactly what NIS asked you, whether you think it pertains to the murder investigation or not. Do you understand?"

Grudgingly, Beck nodded and pushed himself back up a few inches in his chair. "They asked me about drugs."

"What specifically did they want to know about drugs?"

"Do you use drugs? Did Stevie use drugs? Who was buying and selling drugs?" Beck said it in a mocking tone. "The whole nine yards."

"Did you say anything to indicate that drugs were somehow mixed up in your case?" asked Duncan.

"Nope. That was all their idea. Right from the start—drugs, drugs, drugs."

"This is important, Arnie. There had to be some reason why NIS got the idea that you might know something about drugs. We need to know that reason," Duncan said.

"No damned reason I can think of." Beck sounded certain, like he'd given it some thought.

Duncan leaned forward. "What about Jerome? Do you know if he used drugs?"

"I hardly knew the guy. Don't know nothing about it. I don't do that shit. Don't believe in it. Got nothing to do with it."

Sydney looked him in the eyes. "It's my understanding, Arnie, that Stevie often had a few free samples for his friends."

"I wouldn't know."

"Did you ever receive any of these free samples?"

"I just told you. And I wasn't no friend of his. I don't hang around with niggers and their drugs."

Sydney took a deep breath. "We're just trying to establish whether Stevie was involved in any drug trafficking. It could make a difference to your case if he was."

"Then why ask me if *I* use drugs?"

"Don't you understand, Arnie, if you didn't kill Stevie, then someone else did. Maybe his death had something to do with his drug dealing."

Duncan jumped in. "Now, Beck, I want you to think back carefully. Try to remember exactly what the NIS agents asked you."

"Well, just like I said, did I use drugs, did I sell drugs, or what about Stevie using or selling. Same old thing, over and over. And I just kept trying to get it through their heads that I was framed."

Duncan found himself believing that Beck was probably telling the truth for once. So, why had NIS badgered him about drugs?

After sending Beck off with the same two guards, Duncan took out a fresh legal pad and turned to Sydney. "Well, what do you think?"

"I think NIS was working some angle that they didn't reveal in their report or at the pretrial hearing."

"Yeah, me too." It bothered him. Why would NIS be so secretive about that line of questioning? If they suspected Beck of drug use, you'd think they'd be quite happy to paint him with it—discredit him some more. He reached out and rotated his desk-top Rolodex and then picked up the phone. After only a moment's delay, he had NIS Agent, Lawrence Wyman, on the line.

"Larry," he said, "this is Duncan Carmichael over at the Law Center. When would it be convenient for me and my co-counsel to come over there and have a chat with you and Bob about this Beck case?" He motioned Sydney over to look at the calendar with him and come close enough that she could hear the other end of his conversation as he held the receiver away from his ear.

"So, you're finally getting around to us, eh, Duncan?"

"It's nothing special, just a few things we didn't cover in the pretrial. Whenever you've got time, Larry."

"How about today? Can you make it before 1600?"

Carmichael wrote "right now?" on his pad for Sydney and raised his eyebrows in a question. Sydney nodded.

"How about right now?"

"Sure, that works fine. We're both here. We'll be looking forward to seeing your lovely co-counsel . . . and you too, of course."

"Just like that?" Sydney asked after Duncan hung up. "We go have a talk with the investigating detectives." She was shaking her head in amazement.

He realized that this was not something she'd have typically seen in her civilian practice. "Yep. Simple as that," he said. "We just go ask our questions and see what they have to say. The U.S. Navy. It's all in the family."

CHAPTER 9

Tuesday, February 28, 1978
Sand Point Naval Station, Seattle
Law Center, 13th Naval District

The NIS office was only a short walk from the Law Center. Wyman met the two lawyers in the entry and escorted them to his office, calling for his partner to join them as they passed what Duncan knew was Bob Hansen's open door. Wyman's office was a cubby-hole filled to capacity with bulging filing cabinets, boxes of seized exhibits, and books. With piles of papers littering his desk surrounding his beat-up old Underwood manual typewriter. Duncan knew that somewhere in all those cabinets were files on everybody who'd ever even thought about committing a crime on the Sand Point Naval Base. A battered metal goose-necked lamp rose from the clutter on the desk. The joke at the Law Center was that Wyman used it to shine in the faces of interrogation subjects.

It was probably a one-hundred-fifty-watt bulb.

Wyman was, however, all smiles as he settled the four of them into his small office and took his seat behind the desk. With his 1950's crew cut and locker room bonhomie, Duncan guessed he wouldn't appeal much to Sydney. But he'd known and worked with both Wyman and Hansen for nearly two years, both on prosecutions and defenses. He'd always maintained a friendly working relationship with them, and he didn't want to mess that up . . . unless he absolutely had to.

Bob Hansen, a bulky man who seemed too large for the chair he'd commandeered, got right to the point. "I thought you asked everything you wanted to ask at the hearing."

"Well, there have actually been a few things that have come to light." He paused to let them wonder a little about what those might be.

"For instance?" It was Wyman asking. His fingers tapped a tattoo on a pile of papers on his desk. Beneath it, Duncan could see that his foot was bouncing slightly on the floor.

"For instance, we think there were a few things about Jerome you didn't mention in your report or testimony."

The two agents exchanged glances. Again, it was Wyman who responded. "For instance?" he repeated. The bonhomie was beginning to fade.

"You probably thought it didn't pertain to the murder investigation."

"I'm not seeing what you're getting at."

"We know you already had Jerome under investigation." They didn't know any such thing, but Duncan considered it a damn good guess.

"And just why would you believe that?"

"More to the point, is it true?"

Wyman moved some of the papers on his desk while Hansen tried to find a more comfortable position in his chair. Finally, Wyman answered, "Yes, we are looking into a little matter that concerned Jerome. But you're right, it has nothing to do with the murder."

"Jerome is dead, but it sounds like that hasn't ended your inquiry."

Wyman looked across the cluttered desk directly into Duncan's eyes as if to read his thoughts. "I'm sorry, Duncan, but I'm not at liberty to discuss the details of that investigation with you."

"Not even with Jerome dead?"

"Not even with Jerome dead."

So, there *was* some kind of ongoing investigation. Maybe Jerome was just a small part of it, but that wasn't going to stop Duncan from pressing for what they needed. "Look, Larry, I'm going to give it to you straight. This killing may have been done by someone on the base, involved in selling drugs, maybe someone in the same barracks."

The agents were perfectly still, expressionless. Duncan knew he'd scored a point, but he wasn't sure where to go with it.

Sydney leaned forward and spoke for the first time. "You guys must have known our client would tell us about all the questions you asked him regarding Stevie's involvement with drugs."

"Standard questions. Whenever there's an act of violence, we consider the possibility of drugs being involved. Drugs cause a lot of problems on a military base."

"I see," Sydney said. "Standard questions about what kind of problems?"

But Wyman wasn't going there. "What you might imagine."

"Standard questions that you repeat over and over to the point where you're badgering the person you're interviewing. Even when there's no evidence that he's in any way mixed up in the sale or use of drugs. That's what you mean by standard?"

"Does Beck claim we badgered him?" Wyman smiled broadly, revealing the gold caps at the back of his mouth.

"Mr. Wyman . . ."

"Please, call me Larry."

"Larry . . ." Sydney gave the investigator a sweet smile that Duncan read as a danger sign. Before he could decide whether to try and slow her down, she was already airborne. "You should know that we're going to be looking for a good deal more discovery in this case. What you've just said makes it crystal clear you're not coming clean. One has to ask: why? One of the most likely answers is institutional bias. We're seriously considering a motion to remove Beck's case to a civilian court. If that happens, the rules of your 'game' are changed. Don't you think it might be better for us to have this little matter settled right here today, between ourselves, without involving courts, federal marshals, court reporters, possibly the civilian press, and without a lot of unpleasantness and inconvenience?"

The two agents looked at one another.

"You know I call my own shots here," she continued. "And I'm not limited to practicing in a military court. I wonder how a Federal District Court Judge would view federal law enforcement officers, such as yourselves, secreting evidence essential to a proper federal criminal defense. Keep in mind that Lieutenant Carmichael has neither any responsibility for, nor any control over, my actions. I do what I alone decide is appropriate."

She paused briefly, before delivering her punch line. "How would you and your partner here like to spend three or four days answering questions and going over documents in a discovery deposition related to *all* your cases—not just Beck's? Assembling everything in your files on your current 'investigations,' and I mean *everything*, so it can all be presented to a Federal Judge, *in camera*, for *his* assessment of what is pertinent to Beck's defense and what may not be? Would that appeal to you . . ., Larry?"

Both Wyman and Hansen looked stunned by her aggressiveness. In spite of his reservations about the wisdom of a direct threat, especially something with so little chance of success, Duncan was impressed. Wyman and Hansen had been around for many years, but an off-base civilian lawyer was a new twist. They'd have no real way to know that her threats were basically empty. But they would understand what might be involved if they were suddenly facing a claim of institutional bias.

While it probably wasn't a compliment to Duncan that she'd left him out of her equation, even implied he might be less robust in his defense that she, he was glad she had.

"Well, uh . . ." Wyman said. ". . . I'm not sure I know what to say to that."

Duncan decided to step in. "Look, I'm going to bet there are some things you can tell us without compromising any ongoing investigations. We aren't looking forward to a lot of extra work. Discovery motions, appeals to the Court of Military Appeals or maybe to Federal District Court—they all take time." Good guy, bad guy. Worth a try.

"Well, okay. I'll tell you what. Give me a few minutes to make a call, and I'll see what I can give you."

Wyman went down the hall to make his call from Hansen's office.

As soon as he was out the door, Hansen offered them some coffee, easing the tension a little. All three of them were a bit more relaxed when Wyman finally returned.

"Okay," he said. "Here's what I can tell you. But this is it." He motioned for Hansen to close the door he had left open. "About three weeks ago, we seized a substantial shipment of illegal drugs based on information we received through civilian authorities."

"The Philippines stuff?" Duncan had heard rumors of the seizure of a shipment of marijuana that had come in with a bunch of surplus Vietnam War military equipment bound for storage with the Logistical Support Activity housed at the Sand Point Naval Base. No cases had been filed as far as he knew.

"Uh-huh. We left the shipment in place in Building 17 and put it under surveillance for several days, but no one moved on it. We think we were 'made' by the local help. Finally, we had to seize and secure the stuff properly. And, yes, we did think there might be some reprisals resulting from the seizure. So yeah there could, in theory, have been a connection to your murder. But we've ruled that out."

"How?" Sydney asked.

"I'm afraid I can't tell you that?"

"Of course you can't." Her voice dripped with sarcasm. "Okay, then, why? Why did you feel the need to 'rule him out' as you describe it? You must have had something on Jerome to make you think he might be involved."

"Yes, but it isn't much. We have statements from a couple of sailors who admit buying from Jerome or from someone fitting Jerome's description. That's it. And honestly, the evidence is patently clear that Beck killed Jerome. And it wasn't over drugs. So, it isn't worth considering."

"Was Jerome a plant?" Sydney asked.

"No, he was not."

"Do you or did you have someone else undercover?"

"I'm sorry Miss Warren, but I can't tell you that."

"It's *Ms.* Warren. Or Sydney . . .," she said, smiling.

Wyman did not smile back. He was finally beginning to get the picture. "Sydney."

"So, I guess the answer to that would seem to be a yes," said Duncan thoughtfully. "You do or did have an undercover informant. Are there any prosecutions anticipated arising out of this seizure? I haven't heard of anything coming in over at the Law Center."

Wyman shook his head. "Not unless we learn something new. At this point, we may end up with a pile of Southeast Asian grass and with no local tie-ins, or at least not enough to build a case."

"But you *do* have *something*?" Sydney asked. And then, she continued without pausing for an answer: "And you're *still* investigating? With an informant undercover?"

Wyman shook his head again, this time more decisively. "I'm sorry, but all I can do is assure you that we have nothing that has *anything* to do with your client or with this murder. Really, you are just wasting your time here."

"Maybe so. But unfortunately, Larry, that's not *your* decision to make. You know full well that Jerome could have been killed by someone involved in smuggling that shipment of drugs—maybe someone angry with their loss. You said so yourself. Do any of your suspects bunk in Barracks One?"

Wyman didn't answer. Instead, he studied the two of them, absent-mindedly running his fingers back and forth across an adjacent pile of papers. "Honestly, I can't believe the two of you have fallen for your client's horseshit story that he was framed."

"It is a very real possibility," Duncan said. "And it's potential reasonable doubt. You both know that."

"Come on, Duncan. I could see you guys claiming some kind of self-defense, or maybe even diminished responsibility. Your client is a nut case. But you're never going to prove that kid is entirely innocent."

"We don't tell our clients how to testify," Duncan said, not looking at Sydney. "And we take the facts of the case as they come to us. If the Navy has an undercover drug investigation it doesn't want to risk, it could have avoided the problem by not bringing these charges. It was a command decision. Maybe you'll end up regretting it. But now that this is in court, Beck deserves to have all those facts presented in his defense. If you don't like that, maybe you should ask Frank Merrill to dismiss the case."

Wyman was shaking his head in disgust.

Hansen chimed in. "This is a simple case of racial hatred combined with some jealousy and serious sociopathy. Nothing more."

"You think Beck is a sociopath?" Sydney asked.

"It has crossed my mind. That's just my non-expert personal opinion, off the record."

Wyman stepped in. "Look, we've already said as much as we can. But I am telling you straight when I say that, as far as I'm concerned, you're headed up a blind alley."

Duncan made a move to rise as the two agents got to their feet. But Sydney stayed put.

"Where did you get your information that led you to stake out the warehouse in the first place?" she asked.

Wyman sat back down, looking annoyed. "I can't see how that will help you, but I guess there's no reason you can't know. It's already public information. About three months ago, the Seattle Police arrested a local dealer named Frenchy Paquette down in the University District. He had nearly ten kilos of Southeast Asian marijuana in his apartment.

"The grass was packed in a couple of cardboard cartons, one of which had never been opened. They were brand new cartons made with a slightly unusual cardboard, which alerted the Seattle Detectives and allowed us to identify the boxes as ones provided under contract with the U.S. Navy by a firm in Manila. They're commonly used, among other things, for Navy materiel packed, stored, and shipped at our Logistical Support Center at Subic Bay. As you know, many of the old World War II hangars and warehouses here at Sand Point are currently in use for storage of Navy and Marine Corps supplies that were recovered when we pulled out of Viet Nam in '75. They came here from Subic. Some also went to other Navy sites on the West Coast."

Duncan knew Jerome, along with some other men in Barracks One, had been with the Logistical Support Activity. It followed that they would be potential suspects as a conduit for the drugs. It was another useful Jerome connection.

Wyman pushed his chair away from his desk. "Now that is absolutely all I'm going to tell you."

"We'd like to see your file on this investigation," said Sydney, still staying put.

"I'm sorry, we can't do that."

"Who are the sailors at this Logistical Activity and elsewhere on this base that you have identified as being likely involved with drugs over this time period?"

"I can't tell you that either. Surely you can understand why?"

"I assume you do not believe Jerome was in this on his own," Sydney said. "Do you have information concerning the identities of his potential co-conspirators?"

"There *really* is nothing further I can tell you, uh, Sydney," said Wyman.

"I assume you know these people won't be using this logistical materiel conduit for further drug shipments, at least not any time soon. You must have some additional leads if you have made no arrests but are continuing to investigate. We need to know what those leads are."

"You're wasting your time and ours," Hansen suddenly blurted. "Give it up. We've got nothing further for you."

Sydney leaned down, picked up her thin leather briefcase, and stood. "Time will tell whether *we* are wasting our time, Mr. Hansen. It's certainly clear to me, however, that *you* are." With that, she swept out the door, leaving Duncan in her wake to say his uncomfortable good-byes to the two agents.

"I guess you'll be hearing from us," he said, smiling as pleasantly as he could muster and leaving it at that. He'd be damned if he was going to make apologies for Sydney. Beneath his professional military exterior, he too was peeved.

They walked back to the Law Center in silence. Duncan could feel the indignation emanating off Sydney like a live electrical field. He could understand how the NIS agents might feel they were dealing with a broader problem than one individual's defense. And they undoubtedly had a good deal of time and effort invested in their drug investigation. But he knew better than to defend them with Sydney. The government had chosen to charge Beck. Now that they'd made that decision, they needed to live with the consequences.

"I have to get back to the office," Sydney said as they neared the lot where she had parked her car.

He was a little surprised. He'd anticipated them going back to strategize about future steps. "Yeah, sure," he said. "Why don't I have another go at Gordon—if that's okay with you.

"Sure. That sounds good."

"I'll let you know if I come up with anything."

"Okay, Duncan. I'll give you a call sometime tomorrow."

"Great." As he watched her get in her car, he wished he could have told her what a great job he thought she'd done in pressing Wyman. But he still remembered how she'd responded the last time he'd paid her a compliment.

While they hadn't won the gold, they had learned a lot more than they would have without her incredible tenacity. Wyman and Hansen were probably hacked off. But, what the hell, they deserved it.

Chapter 10

Tuesday, February 28, 1978
Sand Point Naval Station, Seattle
Law Center, 13ᵗʰ Naval District

PN3 Ross Gordon was still at his duty station. Duncan called his leading chief and had him sent to the Law Center. He arrived just before quitting time. He was courteous, as always, but seemed slightly uneasy.

"All right, Gordon, I'm not going to beat around the bush," Duncan said. "You're withholding some things about Jerome. I think it's about time you were straight with me."

Gordon nervously ran a finger back and forth across the knee of his dungarees. "I haven't lied to you."

"Well, you haven't been exactly forthcoming with the truth, either."

"I'm not sure what you mean, sir."

"Do you understand what a JAGC officer is?" Duncan asked.

"Uh, I think I do, sir."

"Obviously, I'm an officer in the U.S. Navy, but I am also a lawyer. And as a lawyer, when I take on the defense of a case, I give my promise to both the court and my client that I will do *everything* ethically possible to defend him. To me, that is a very solemn promise."

Gordon looked puzzled.

"I know you believe," Duncan continued, "that Beck killed your friend. But it is very important to Beck, and to the rest of us, you included, that we be sure of that. Think how you'd feel if someone had framed you for a crime and nobody was willing to seriously search for the person who *actually* did it. Or if the people involved wouldn't tell the full truth about what they knew."

He paused meaningfully. "Suppose I told you that I know you use drugs . . ."

Suddenly Gordon's eyes opened wide.

"Suppose I told you that I thought your buddy, Jerome, a decent guy by all accounts, was actually killed by people he was doing business with?"

"You can't be serious?"

"Deadly serious."

Gordon hesitated. "I don't know what you expect me to say, sir."

"I expect you to tell me the truth about what Jerome was up to."

Gordon gripped his knees. "I don't know that much about it."

"Look, I'm not necessarily asking you to come forward and testify to anything." Duncan pointed a finger at him. "For now, I just want to know everything you can tell me about Jerome's drug dealings. At the moment, there's no reason I have to say a thing to anyone else about what you tell me, or about what I know of your own drug use. Especially if what you tell me leads me somewhere constructive. I'm not a cop. I'm just a lawyer trying to find out who killed your friend."

"Well . . . he wasn't into hard stuff, just pot, some uppers, and like that."

"Do you know any of the people he got it from?" Duncan asked.

"No sir, I don't. All I know is that if someone wanted to buy a little, they could get it from him. We were buddies, sure. But there are some things you don't ask. He knew how I felt about selling that stuff."

"But buying is different?"

"Hey, what's a little occasional recreational use? Everybody does it."

"Is that why Jerome was so popular with the other men?"

"I don't know," Gordon said. "That was maybe a part of it. But Jerome was a good guy."

"Even though he was a drug dealer?"

"Okay, so he probably made a few bucks off it. But he wasn't some kind of big-time pusher."

"When he was killed, didn't it cross your mind that his murder might have been drug-related?"

"Using Beck's knife?"

"Beck says he was framed. He was fast asleep. Would have been easy to borrow his knife."

"Listen, man," Gordon said. "Beck is one mean dude. He likes flashing that knife around. And he's downright crazy when it comes to race. I wouldn't put anything past him."

"So, you didn't even consider the possibility that Jerome might have been killed by one of his drug-selling friends, maybe by someone he got crosswise with?"

Gordon shook his head. "Not really. No, sir."

"But you can give me a name or two, right? In confidence, of course."

"Sorry sir. But I honestly didn't talk with Stevie about it."

Duncan looked down at the blank yellow pad on his desk. There certainly wasn't going to be much to report to Sydney from *this* interview.

"All right, Gordon. I do appreciate you coming in." Duncan got up and extended his hand, an unusual gesture for a military officer to make, but he thought he might need this man's help yet. "There's no need for you to mention this conversation to anyone. If *you* don't, I see no reason anyone is likely to ask you about it. If I need you to testify to something, we can talk about it when the time comes, but it's my guess it's never going to come to that. Okay?" Technically, a military officers' obligations to report knowledge of a criminal offense was less than perfectly clear. A failure to do so would, at a minimum, be frowned upon. In this instance, however, Duncan intended to abide by his promise.

Gordon hesitantly took the offered hand, and the two men shook on their bargain. "Yes, sir. Thank you, sir," he said.

When Gordon was gone, Duncan tried to draw a diagram

suggesting their various avenues of approach. Lines stretched from Jerome's stick figure body in a half-dozen directions, but they all looked like dead ends. The main thing that was becoming clear was that everyone sincerely believed their client was guilty.

Everyone, including so far, at least one of his two lawyers.

Following dinner that evening, Duncan was reading in his room at the Base Officers Quarters when he got a long-distance phone call. The raspy-voiced caller identified himself as Truman Beck, Arnie Beck's father. How had the man found the number for his residential quarters? Carmichael could have told him to call back tomorrow during office hours, but this was his client's *father*.

"Yes, that's right, Mr. Beck. I'm the Navy attorney that's representing your son. What can I do for you?"

"Well, for one thing, you can tell me how it's goin'. I'd like to know what you think my boy's chances are. An' what you been doin' to get him off this thing."

"Well, I've been doing everything I can, but as you probably know, it's a difficult case. I assume you've talked with your son about it."

"Well, um, fact is, him and me, we don't talk much."

"You *do* know this is a murder charge and that he's accused of killing another sailor?"

"Yeah, I heard some black boy got hisself killed."

"The victim was a young man by the name of Steven Jerome." Duncan tried to keep his tone neutral. It seemed clear where Arnie Beck's racial prejudice came from.

"So, what you doin' to keep my kid out of jail, Mister Carmichael?"

"Well, we've had a pretrial investigation. It looks like the charges will be referred to a general court-martial. My co-counsel and I have been interviewing all of the possible witnesses, but our own investigation is just getting started." He paused. There was confidentiality to consider. "You really need to get further information directly from Arnie, Mr. Beck. Do you have the phone number at the Correctional Center where he is being held?"

"Yeah, yeah. I got the number. You goin' to get him off?"

"Well, it's too early to tell. As I said, it is a difficult case. But you do understand that Arnie has two lawyers. Besides myself, there is also a civilian lawyer working for no charge, trying to make sure all of Arnie's rights are protected and that he gets a strong defense."

"Well, yeah, I know that. I'm the one called the ACLU. They claim to care about people bein' discriminated against. What with all this new official BS about the Navy looking out for black people and the like, seemed like that's what's happenin' to my boy, right?"

For someone with Truman Beck's obvious racial bias to have called the liberal ACLU for help suggested he was either desperate or was perhaps looking for some politically ironic justice.

"Look, Mr. Beck, I certainly understand how you must feel about this. But there really isn't much I can tell you about the case without your son's express permission. Unless you have a general legal question, it would be best if you called him direct."

"Yeah. Arnie and me, we don't always get along that good. But I'd hate like hell to see him sent to jail. Look, you need help from me, you let me know. Let me give you my phone here." Duncan wrote down the number. He recognized the prefix for somewhere in the northeastern corner of Washington State near the Canadian border.

He ended the conversation by saying, "I want you to know that everything that can be done for your son will be done, Mr. Beck. My colleague and I will do our best."

The next day Sydney called at about eleven hundred. He filled her in on the unproductive interview with Gordon and on his call from Beck senior. "I guess that leaves us back where we started," he concluded.

"Well, not quite."

"What do you mean?"

"There's still Frenchy Paquette."

CHAPTER 11

Wednesday, March 1, 1978
Seafirst Bank Building, Seattle
Law Offices of Steiner, Bentley and Waterhouse

Wednesday morning Sydney got a call from Jeff, her ACLU contact. "It's about the Beck case you're working on," he said.

"Yes?"

"Look Sydney, I know you took this on because I pressured you into it. It felt like it was something we should do to show we believe in our principles, not just liberal causes. And as I told you, there was no one else available that I thought could handle it. I hope you don't regret it at this point."

"No regrets, Jeff. It's a complex case, and our client definitely needs outside counsel."

"Well, I hope you don't change your mind when I tell you why I called." He paused a moment before continuing. "I got an anonymous call. Someone thinks you are poking your nose in where you're not wanted."

Sydney gripped the receiver and fought to keep her voice calm. "Male or female?"

"Male."

"What did you say?"

"I asked if they had any information relevant to the case."

"And?"

"They said I should tell the bitch to watch her back."

"Wow—you don't believe in sugarcoating, I guess."

"Sorry to be so blunt, but you need to know that you've made someone very unhappy."

"You're not suggesting that I step down, are you?"

"No, for now just take their advice and watch your back. We get threats all the time, and we've learned to take them seriously. Although it's seldom anyone follows through with violence, you never know. So, call me immediately if anything happens that makes you feel unsafe, okay?"

"Will do." She replaced the receiver and flexed her tense fingers. They were obviously stepping on someone's toes, but if they thought she was going to back off because of a phone call . . . She wondered whether she should mention this to Duncan. She didn't want him to pull any protective macho stuff on her. But, on the other hand, perhaps he, too, should be watching his back.

Sydney pulled into a narrow driveway alongside a small, older stucco home. A little girl peeked out the front window, eyes wide in anticipation. Sydney waved, and the little girl shyly waved back before disappearing.

The front door opened slowly as Sydney approached, and the little girl's head peeked around the corner. "Hello, Lindy," Sydney said. Lindy grinned and stuck a finger in her mouth. A black rag doll with yarn pony-tails tied with pink ribbons hung from her other hand, its limp legs dragging on the floor. "Is your mother home?"

"Lindy, who is it?" a voice called from the other room. Lindy immediately ran off in the direction of her mother.

"It's me, Celia. Sydney."

Celia appeared in the doorway to the kitchen, a large wooden spoon in her hand. "Syd," come on in. I'm just making a cake."

She followed Celia into the homey, brightly painted kitchen and sat down at a small table near the window. Lindy climbed into the chair next to her, attention divided between their visitor and the cake batter.

"Help yourself to some coffee," Celia said pointing to a clear Pyrex pot on the counter. "Lindy, get a cup for Syd, will you, honey?"

Lindy quickly scrambled onto the counter from her chair, the rag doll in tow. As her small hand reached into the cupboard, Sydney held her breath, but Celia seemed calm. "Lindy's becoming quite the little helper," she said.

Lindy held up a mug with flowers on it. "This cup, mama?"

"That one's fine, Lindy." Celia motioned toward the doll. "They're inseparable."

"That's a pretty doll you have there, Lindy," Sydney said as the girl solemnly handed her the cup. She nodded in agreement and went back to her chair.

As Sydney poured herself some coffee, Celia started spreading batter into a large pan. "It's good to see you, Syd. It's been a while."

"Well, to be honest, this is only partially a social visit."

"Oh?"

"I need a favor." She didn't want to mislead Celia about the main purpose of her visit. Sydney had defended Celia's husband on a drug charge a few years before. She'd managed to get him off with probation and community service. Celia and she had hit it off and stayed in touch.

Celia scraped the mixing bowl with her spoon and then handed both the spoon and the bowl to Lindy. "Sweetie, take this into the other room please." Still hanging onto her doll, Lindy climbed down from her chair, managed to take hold of the treasure, and quickly hurried into the dining room.

"A favor, huh?" Celia said as she grabbed a cup from the cupboard, poured herself some coffee, and sat down across from Sydney.

"I'm working on an ACLU case," Sydney explained. "A white man accused of murdering a black man on the navy base. Both are military. The question of possible drug involvement has come up."

Celia frowned. "We're straight now. You know that."

"Yes, I know. But I'm hoping Flynn can give me an introduction. I want to talk to a man called Frenchy. Frenchy Paquette. Know him?" She was asking Celia because she was pretty sure Celia could influence her husband, and she wasn't sure Flynn would be as open to the idea on his own.

"Know him?! He's what you might call a highly visible part of the drug scene around here. Bad news." She shook her head.

"What I need is for Flynn to tell Frenchy that he can talk with me and trust that I will keep what he tells me confidential."

"What's in it for Frenchy? That's what he'll want to know."

"Would a little money help?"

"It might. I'll ask Flynn." She paused and took a sip of coffee. "It hasn't been easy. All of our friends, well, you know how it is. Just because we stopped dealing didn't mean our friends stopped using. But Flynn has tried real hard to stay away from that scene, for me and for Lindy."

"But he still has contacts?"

"Yeah, he knows a few people. I'm sure he'll help you out on this. Although I think you're crazy to have anything to do with Frenchy Paquette."

They continued to drink coffee and catch up on what had been going on in their lives since they last saw each other. Sydney was glad Flynn was staying clean and felt guilty for asking him to become involved in her case in even this limited way.

As Sydney left and walked down the uneven sidewalk toward her car, Lindy, her face smudged with chocolate, waved goodbye from the front window.

When Sydney called Duncan and told him that it looked like she would be talking to Frenchy, his response was predictable. "I don't like it, Sydney. You shouldn't be chasing down some drug dealer. That's too dangerous."

"Duncan, I've worked drug cases before. Remember, I spent several years with the public defender's office. I can handle this."

"I still think it's a bad idea."

She struggled to keep her voice steady and neutral. "Duncan, I'm *not* asking for your permission. I'm advising you of what I plan to do."

There was silence or a few seconds on the other end of the line. Then: "If you're determined to do this, I'm coming along."

"Sorry, Duncan, but no. This guy is a drug dealer. The only reason he may agree to talk is that my friend will vouch for me. And I'm a woman, less threatening than a man." What she didn't say out loud was that Duncan looked like the military man he was. Or worse, like a cop. No way Frenchy would talk freely around him. Before he could push back more, she added, "One more thing. You need to know that we've made someone angry." She filled him in on the threat made to the ACLU that Jeff had told her about.

"Damn, Sydney" Duncan's voice vibrated with frustration. "And you think this is a good time to meet on your own with some kind of drug kingpin?"

"I've been crossing the street by myself for some time now."

"Not funny," he said, reluctantly agreeing to *let* her do what he very obviously couldn't stop her from doing in the first place.

~

When Flynn called that evening, he had disappointing news. Frenchy had been arrested again, and although he was out on bail, no one on the street seemed to know where he was. Flynn guessed he was laying low on advice from his lawyer, Leroy something or other. If and when he found out anything, he would let her know.

Sydney put the receiver down and swore out loud, "Damn, damn, damn." She hadn't anticipated having trouble locating Frenchy. And after she'd been so smug with Duncan about her contacts. Damn.

She stood up and began pacing back and forth, trying to decide what to do next. Unfortunately, there was only one thing she could do, but she didn't want to do it. As soon as Flynn had said the name "Leroy," she knew who Frenchy's lawyer was. Leroy Bloom, a local defense lawyer who had been at the public defender's office when she was there. After leaving the public defender's office, Leroy continued to defend criminal clients, working on the fringes of the practice, not always adhering to strict ethical standards. His criminal clients loved him. They assumed he knew every trick in the book and would not hesitate to use them on their behalf. Which was probably true, unless there was something else in it for Bloom. In any event, he was someone she usually went out of her way to avoid. And now she had to seek him out.

~

Thursday morning Sydney asked her secretary to see if she could find out Bloom's schedule from his secretary without letting Bloom know about the inquiry. She explained that she wanted to stage a casual chance meeting at the courthouse rather than set up an appointment.

"I feel like cupid," her secretary said with a wink.

Sydney made a face. "You wouldn't if you'd met Leroy."

Five minutes later her secretary reported that Leroy Bloom would be in court on a motion at 10:30. She could catch up with him when it was completed.

~

It didn't take long to spot Leroy. He was wearing a flashy sports coat and carrying a large black briefcase bulging with papers. Nobody was really sure if Leroy had an actual office. It was said that all he had was a secretarial service and that he conducted his entire practice out of his briefcase, the equivalent of a country doctor's black bag.

From the back of the courtroom, Sydney watched while Bloom argued his motion. Afterward, he jammed a few papers in his briefcase and hurried toward the exit. She jumped up and managed to waylay him just outside the door.

"Hi, Leroy," she said, trying to look happy to see him.

He didn't seem to notice that their roles had been reversed. Usually, he was the one making the approach. "Sydney," he said, stopping immediately. "It's good to see you." His smile was half leer, and his eyes were already wandering south.

She swallowed her dislike of the man. "What have you been up to lately?" she asked.

"The usual." He gave her a too familiar nudge with his elbow for emphasis.

She glanced at her watch. "Oh, can you believe it—for once I'm ahead of schedule. You don't happen to have time for a cup of coffee, do you?" She felt obvious as hell, but Leroy's surprise was quickly replaced by a confident grin. After all, he was a hotshot defense lawyer. Surely all women found him irresistible.

They went down to the tiny coffee bar on the first floor. Leroy insisted on paying for the coffee and led her to a conspicuous table near the entrance. She would have preferred a dark corner near the back, but that also had its disadvantages.

Making conversation with Leroy was easy; all she had to do was listen. Without much effort she was able to ask a few questions that manipulated him into talking about his big-time client, Frenchy Paquette. "He sounds like quite a character," Sydney said.

"Oh, he is. That he is. Why . . ."

Sydney interrupted before he could ask. "You know, it occurs to me that he might have some useful information on a case of mine."

"Oh, I don't know about that. He's keeping his head down while awaiting trial." For the first time, Leroy sounded wary.

Sydney reached across the table and put her hand over his. "It's so thoughtful of you to suggest it."

"Suggest what?" Now he was really suspicious, but he didn't withdraw his hand.

"Meeting with your client."

"I don't remember saying anything about you meeting with my client."

Sydney withdrew her hand. "Oh, I'm sorry. I thought that was what you meant. You see, I'm working on a case where drugs may be involved, and well, I don't know a lot about how dealers work in our area. I'm just looking for background information, nothing specific." She paused. "I don't want to put you on the spot . . ."

Leroy was silent for once, struggling with his infinitesimal conscience.

"I'd owe you one, Leroy." She knew it was true, but she hated saying it.

Leroy suddenly gave her a toothy, lecherous grin, reached across the table, and patted her arm. "And don't you forget it, babe."

Babe? She bit her tongue and watched while Leroy dug in his brief-case. "I can give you a phone number," he said.

She leaned far enough forward to check out the contents of his famous briefcase. No change of underwear as some lawyers claimed. No shaving kit that she could see. No comic books or *Playboy* magazines. Just bent file folders crammed with papers. She was amazed when he was able to secure the right folder and quickly find the number. She wrote it down on the back of her pocket calendar and thanked him profusely.

Although she felt guilty leaving as soon as she had what she wanted, she couldn't resist the impulse to escape. The last words she heard as she rushed off to her alleged appointment were, "Remember, you owe me."

As soon as she was back at the office, Sydney called Flynn and gave him the number. She could tell he wasn't thrilled about contacting Frenchy, but he agreed to do it right away. Less than a half hour later he called back to let her know that he had persuaded Frenchy to meet with her, even though Frenchy had said that his lawyer had warned him not to talk to Sydney.

"That rat," she mumbled as she wrote down the time and place. That worthless piece of crap would betray his own mother. At least she didn't have to worry about owing Leroy Bloom a damn thing.

The small downtown bar Frenchy had chosen for their meeting catered to office employees seeking comfort between the time they got off work and when they headed home. It was packed when she arrived. Flynn had described Frenchy to her, but he spotted her first. He moved toward her slowly, like a big cat approaching its prey. It was only as he got closer that she realized how his eyes and hands were nervously moving back and forth as if they had a life of their own. A short man in his early forties, wearing a beige turtleneck jersey and dark slacks. The only thing French about him was the thin, perfectly straight mustache dividing a wide upper lip. Sydney could picture him checking in the mirror each morning to make certain it was just right.

She didn't offer to shake hands. He didn't look like the type to shake hands with anyone.

"Hi, Syd," he said smoothly as he took her by the elbow and steered her to a dimly lit table at the back of the bar where he'd left his coat on a chair. As they took their seats a waiter appeared with two drinks on a tray, a Scotch on the rocks for him and a glass of white wine for her. He'd apparently made arrangements in advance. "You sounded like the white wine type," he said, raising his glass in salute.

"Thanks, I guess." She didn't know quite how to take the comment.

"Flynn says you're okay."

"I can be trusted to keep my mouth shut if that's what you mean."

"He said he's known you for a long time."

"That's right." Of course, she'd known Leroy for even longer, but that apparently hadn't meant much.

"What I don't understand is why you want to talk with me. What Leroy said didn't make much sense."

"I didn't want to tell Leroy the real reason I wanted to meet with you," she admitted.

"Oh?" He stared, then shrugged. "You've got my attention."

"It *does* have to do with a case I'm working on. My client's name is Arnie Beck." She peered through the gloom at him to gauge his response to her client's name, but if he recognized the name, he didn't show it.

"Never heard of him."

"What about Stevie Jerome. Heard of him?" She thought she saw a glimmer of surprise in Frenchy's eyes, but he didn't miss a beat.

"Jerome? Jerome? No, I don't think so."

"Try a little harder. It's important. And it doesn't involve you."

He pretended to think. "The name *may* sound familiar."

"Look, all I want is confirmation of what I already think I know. My client, Beck, claims he isn't involved in the local drug scene. And I want to believe him. It would be helpful to know if you're telling me the truth when you say you haven't heard of him."

"I've never heard any of my acquaintances talk about him, if that's what you are asking. I am, however, aware that he is accused of killing Jerome."

"Then you *do* know Jerome."

"Small potatoes. But any time a steady customer of mine gets offed, I'm interested."

"So, here's where I'm going with this," Sydney said. "Do you have any reason to suspect someone involved in the, ah, business might have wanted him dead?"

"Sorry, but I haven't heard any rumors to that effect. Everyone assumes your client did it. Don't know why. Except he's supposedly a piece of work."

Sydney thought for a moment while Frenchy rolled his glass back and forth between the palms of his hands, ice clinking softly. "Look, you recently took a fall for possession of some stuff that came in from the Far East. My understanding is that source of supply is now closed up tight. So, what if you gave me a name. Someone who might know something about what was going on at the base. I can assure you they'd never know where I got their name. And unless they have something to do with Jerome's murder, there'd be no reason for *anyone* to ever hear any more about it."

He finished off his drink and leaned toward her. "You sure your client's worth this much trouble?"

"I believe he deserves the best defense I can give him." To do so, she was going far out on a shaky limb making promises of confidentiality to a drug dealer.

Frenchy looked her in the eyes, then said, "Hal." He paused. "You got a good memory? I'll give you his address, but I never write anything down."

She was repeating the address over and over to herself as he rose to leave. "Flynn said you were okay," he repeated.

She nodded to let him know she understood what that meant. And then he was gone.

As soon as he was out of sight, she took out a piece of paper and wrote down the address, spreading the numbers out to disguise what they were. She felt silly doing that, but on the other hand, she felt guilty writing anything down at all. Then she felt stupid for even questioning the need to write down something that she didn't want to forget. Frenchy Paquette had obviously made an impression.

On the way home, she decided to drive past the address he'd given her. It turned out to be a run-down house in a low-rent district with a scraggly lawn and a half-dead tree near the sidewalk. Uneven curtains hung in the windows facing the street. There were no lights on inside. She felt very conspicuous driving by in her polished BMW. All in all, it wasn't the kind of house where you expected the Avon lady to go calling.

CHAPTER 12

Friday, March 3, 1978
Seafirst Bank Building, Seattle
Law Offices of Steiner, Bentley and Waterhouse

Sydney spent most of her lunch hour on Friday researching the address Frenchy had given her. A quick walk over to the county assessor's office got her the name of the owner, the person who paid taxes on the property. His first name wasn't "Hal," but he was listed in the telephone directory. She called him that evening and explained that she was a lawyer and had been given that address for Hal, a renter perhaps? She explained that what she needed was a last name and a telephone number. "I'm hoping you can help me out," she said.

"He in trouble?"

Aha, she had scored. "No, it's a simple request for information that I think can be handled over the telephone."

"You sure you aren't some kind of a salesman?" She could hear a television blaring in the background. She had visions of him standing there in a dirty t-shirt with a can of beer waiting for him on a wobbly table next to his favorite chair in front of the TV.

"As I said, I'm a lawyer. And if I need to, I can drop by the house. But I thought it would be easier for everyone if I just called."

Perhaps wanting to get back to his television program, he coughed up the name. "Halbert Willis," he said. "He's listed."

"Thank . . ."

He interrupted before she could complete her sentence. "If you're really a lawyer, you tell him to get his rent paid on time this month or I'm going to kick his ass out of there." Then he hung up.

Monday morning, she called Duncan and gave him the name of Halbert Willis. It seemed to her that if Willis knew about what was going on at the base, it was likely he was in some way connected with it.

Later that morning Duncan called her back to tell her she'd guessed right. Willis was a second-class petty officer who lived off base at the address she got from Frenchy. Duncan had gone ahead and set up an appointment with Willis for 1500 on Wednesday—three p.m. to anybody else. With luck, Willis just might be the break they'd been hoping for.

With the frequent rearranging of calendars, afternoons at the Navy base, and all of the research time she'd spent on the Beck case, Sydney was way behind on her regular workload. She spent the rest of Monday, all day Tuesday, and Wednesday morning dealing with a long series of depositions in a complicated class action case on which she was second chair. It was a defense involving tens of millions of dollars with complex legal and factual issues and with a client that never balked at paying the firm's high hourly rate. Sydney knew it was reasonable for the firm to expect her to give the case priority over her ACLU work, but each hour she spent on it felt as though she was just biding time until Wednesday came around.

She arrived at Duncan's office promptly at 3:00 on Wednesday afternoon. He greeted her somewhat stiffly she thought. Perhaps he was still bent out of shape about her meeting with Frenchy. And for not telling him right away about the anonymous call to the ACLU. Well, he would just have to remember that she worked *with* him, not *for* him.

Halbert Willis was fifteen minutes late. When he arrived, his face was an expressionless mask. He was polite but distant. Sydney wondered if his tardiness had been an intentional message to let them know that no one was going to pull his strings and make him jump, not even someone of rank.

Sydney watched while Duncan conducted the interview. "As I mentioned on the phone, Willis, we are the lawyers for Arnie Beck, the man accused of the murder of Steven Jerome."

"Yes, sir."

He locked eyes with Willis. "I understand that you were pretty good friends with Jerome."

"I wouldn't say that, no."

"You weren't a drinking buddy?" Duncan asked.

"Upon occasion."

"So, you did know him."

"Yes, I knew him."

"But you didn't consider him a good friend."

"A friend, yes. Not especially a good friend."

Duncan held his gaze. "Mind telling me where you were on Sunday morning, February 5th at about zero two hundred?"

"I suppose I was at home, in bed."

"You suppose or you know you were home that night?" Duncan said firmly.

"I *know.*"

"Home for you is off base, isn't it, Willis?"

"That's right, sir." Willis' deadpan was drooping a bit.

"You live alone?"

"Most of the time." Willis paused. "I've had the occasional woman staying with me."

Carmichael was silent a moment before asking, "I assume you get along well enough on your Navy salary?"

"It's sufficient." Willis was starting to fidget.

"Ever pick up a little extra on the side?"

Willis' chin came up slightly as he asked, "Doing what, sir?"

"That's what I'm asking you."

"My salary's sufficient for my needs, sir." His chin came up another fraction of an inch.

"Would it help your memory, Willis, if I told you that you've been observed selling illegal substances on base?"

Suddenly Willis laughed. "Observed, huh? What are you going to do, turn me in?"

"Do you deny it?"

"Yes, I do, sir. As you must already know."

"How would I know that?" Duncan asked.

"I assume you've been talking to NIS. Why else am I here?"

"NIS?" It was Duncan's turn to look uncomfortable.

"Hey, man, how stupid do you think I am?"

"I'm not understanding you, Willis."

"Come on, you must know that they're running me out of the Navy. My administrative discharge board is scheduled for next Tuesday. Lt. Frost is representing me."

Sydney remembered seeing Frost's name on an office door down the hall from Duncan's.

"Not a court-martial?" Duncan sounded surprised.

Willis made a huffing sound denoting his disdain for the suggestion. "They haven't got any evidence. Some asshole puts the finger on me to get himself a better deal, and as far as they're concerned, I'm guilty. So, they're kicking me out of the Navy despite seven years of good service. Retirement, veteran benefits, all gone. The command wants an admin board, so they get it. Even if there's not anything like enough evidence to convict me in a proper court."

Sydney remembered Duncan telling her that administrative discharge was often used as a second-best alternative to a court-martial.

Duncan sat up even straighter. "Look, Willis, I'm not interested in the sale of drugs on the base. I'm trying to defend my client."

"So why ask me about drugs?"

"Because if Beck didn't kill Jerome, then someone else did. Someone who had a falling out with him. Perhaps over a drug deal."

"I didn't have any falling out with Jerome," Willis shot back.

"Maybe you know of someone who did."

Willis was adamant. "No, as I told you, I didn't hang with him that much."

Duncan let a long silence build between them. Finally, when Willis showed no sign of weakening, he said, "Think it over. You help me with this, and we find out who killed Jerome, you might look a little better to that admin discharge board."

Willis laughed again. "That's pretty goddamn unlikely, wouldn't you say?"

Reluctantly, Duncan agreed. "Maybe."

"Anyway, at this point I couldn't care less. Sooner I get out of this place the better." He stood up. "Will that be all . . ., sir?"

"That will be all, Willis."

After he was gone, Duncan turned to Sydney with a look of exasperation. "NIS again."

"Yeah. And he *was* a friend of Jerome's," Sydney said. "Possibly Frenchy's direct client and Jerome's source."

"Sounded that way to me. But apparently, he'd rather no one knew how good a friend."

"So, where does that leave us?" Duncan seemed to know that her question was rhetorical; she'd already decided what she wanted to do next.

"Nowhere," he said.

"Well, maybe not. There is one other possibility we haven't discussed."

"What's that?"

"We can take NIS to court."

CHAPTER 13

Tuesday, March 14, 1978
Sand Point Naval Station, Seattle
Law Center, 13th Naval District, Main Upstairs Courtroom

"The defense calls Agent Lawrence Wyman."

They were back on the top floor of the old brick Law Center building. But this time, they were in the main courtroom. The room took up most of the west end of the building, but with its sloping ceilings and tiny gabled windows, it still felt confined. There was an impressive fully enclosed dais for the military judge and small tables for the court reporter and the judge's clerk. Another larger table to the right for a court-martial panel. And tables on each side of a central podium for the defense and the prosecution. About a dozen chairs at the back were there for spectators.

There were seldom spectators in military courts. In a downtown civilian courtroom, the gallery always included a scattering of friends and relatives of the accused, maybe a few members of the general public, sometimes other lawyers awaiting their turn before the bench, and quite often the usual "court watch" people taking notes and keeping an eye out for who knows what. But observers were rare in a court-martial.

Today, however, there were several people seated in the back of the room. The air was warm and close. Some of the other lawyers in the Law Center had taken time off to observe. It wasn't every day someone tried to pry added pretrial discovery out of NIS in a criminal defense. If NIS and Frank Merrill were holding something back, it was because that was how the Commanding Officer wanted it. Like it or not, the Navy's civilian employees, and its lawyers, prosecution and defense, paid attention to the wishes of the Command. There were also a couple of civilians there, two men Duncan didn't know. It made him wonder if there could be press interest in the case. But the two men in question didn't much look like reporters. Instead, they seemed out of place—muscular guys in cheap suits. One of them had an ugly burn mark on the left side of his forehead. There wasn't much time to give them careful thought, however.

"State your name and address for the record, please." Duncan made his request in a sharp, official tone. He, too, needed to show some authority here.

"Lawrence R. Wyman. Naval Investigative Service Office, Thirteenth Naval District Headquarters, Room 230, Building Seven, U.S. Naval Support Activity, Sand Point Naval Station, Seattle, Washington." As was typical for police officers of all kinds, Wyman did not state his home address, even though he was a civilian and did not reside on the Navy base. Wyman settled back in his chair, looking confident, as Duncan took him through the preliminaries.

Then he asked, "Are you the agent responsible for the apprehension of Seaman Apprentice Arnie Beck in connection with the killing of one Logistics Specialist Third Class Steven David Jerome on February 5th of this year?"

"Yes. Agent Hansen and I made the arrest jointly."

"And at the time, was there an investigation underway by your office in which the victim of this killing, LS3 Jerome, was suspected of involvement in the smuggling or sale of illegal drugs?"

All eyes in the room moved to where Frank Merrill was seated. It was a broad question; Duncan and Sydney wanted to force Merrill into an early objection, perhaps one that rested the prosecution's argument on relevancy. This would be a weaker argument for the prosecution. A clear initial ruling on relevancy would better position them to overcome a later possible argument based on privilege—based on the claim that NIS needed to keep its investigations confidential.

Wyman hesitated, also glancing over at Merrill. Finally, even the Judge looked his way.

"Objection, your honor," Merrill finally said. "The information sought by that question is irrelevant."

Good. The issue was drawn.

Navy Captain Nicholas Clayton made a striking figure as military judge. He was a small man, but he had an especially impressive head and shoulders, out of proportion to his body. Most people were surprised to discover that he was a scant five foot five inches tall when he stood and walked from behind the judge's bench. Seated, he looked like he could have been a foot taller and a former professional linebacker.

There were two facts about Captain Clayton that were general currency around the Law Center. First, he was said to be very sensitive to the opinions of his military superiors. And second, it was rumored he had an inordinate fear of being reversed on appeal. It was therefore important that they suppress any inkling of special command interest in the case. And they needed to unsettle the Captain's confidence in Merrill's legal position. The judge might just lean their way on the theory that, by giving every advantage to the accused, he was unlikely to be reversed.

"Well, Mr. Carmichael, let's have it. Why is this evidence relevant?" Clayton's deep voice matched his imposing waist-up appearance.

Duncan moved to the center of the podium as a signal that he was taking over the floor and Merrill might just as well sit down. "Your Honor, the point of this motion is to obtain the files of the Naval Investigative Service Office pertaining to the drug ring enterprise of which the victim, Steven Jerome, was a member. We believe the actual motive for this murder will turn out to be quite different from what the prosecution will claim at trial. Through this witness, we would offer to prove that the deceased, Steven Jerome, was believed to be an active member of this ring, that there was a substantial, highly valuable seizure of illegal drugs belonging to the ring, and that because of this seizure there were unmet promises and the potential for reprisals by people who had lost significant investments in this criminal enterprise. Moreover, members of the ring had every reason to believe there might be an informant in their midst, quite possibly Steven Jerome."

"Your offer is noted, Mr. Carmichael. But of what importance would that be to your client?"

Frank Merrill's chair squeaked as he rose behind Duncan, presumably to agree and provide moral support for the Judge's question. But Duncan remained firmly positioned behind the podium and quickly replied, pre-empting Merrill's opportunity to speak.

"Our defense is simple, Your Honor. Seaman Apprentice Beck is innocent of this crime. It was committed by another person who created false evidence to incriminate him. To prove that, we need to know everything the government knows about other persons who had a substantial motive to kill the decedent.

"We understand that a sizable shipment of drugs was intercepted recently due to information NIS received from an unnamed informant. Jerome worked in Logistics where the shipment was discovered. Co-conspirators might easily have suspected Jerome of being the leak and would therefore have had a strong motive to eliminate him. We need the names of suspected members of this drug ring and of any government informants they have or had in place at the time of Jerome's murder or shortly before then.

"It isn't fair to SA Beck that the government be allowed to come to court and present all the evidence they have collected that suggests the defendant's guilt while refusing to disclose evidence they have readily at hand, which suggests that other persons may have had motive and opportunity to commit this crime. To allow this is to perpetuate an insidious lie before the court-martial panel—implying that everything of relevance to this crime has been presented, when it has decidedly not."

Duncan locked eyes with the judge. "None of us here, your honor, wants to spend the next several weeks preparing for and completing a trial only to have the whole exercise turn out to be pointless."

It wasn't subtle, perhaps. But everyone needed a reminder that what they were doing today could be later reversed on appeal. He lifted their legal memorandum briefly above the podium for everyone to see. He and Sydney had worked on it for several long, painstaking days.

"The copious legal authorities on this matter are set forth in our brief." Then he slapped the substantial document back down and, at a nod from Captain Clayton, gathered his notes and papers and stood aside for Frank Merrill to take the podium. As he did so, Duncan glanced toward the back of the courtroom and noticed that one of the two civilian men who had been seated there, the man with the burn, was gone. The other man was taking notes. It made Duncan wonder again who they might be.

Duncan chose to remain standing during Merrill's presentation, out of the way, at the far end of the defense table, but still within visual range of both the judge and the prosecutor. He wanted to remain a presence in the courtroom. Thus, when Merrill made an argument, it was not left hanging unanswered in the air; rather, it was a point which that other lawyer over there stood ready to answer when the opportunity arose.

As he'd once pointed out to Sydney, "It's all a game."

Merrill argued his legal position at length. And he moved seamlessly into an implicit privilege objection as well, making a strong point about the importance of protecting the identity of their confidential informant, arguing that to reveal the name would do grave damage to the ongoing NIS investigation. As he was approaching the end of his presentation, he paused a moment to capture the judge's full attention before going in for the kill.

"Your Honor, suppose for a moment that we accept the defense premise for this motion. Suppose, despite all the evidence to the contrary, we assume SA Beck is correct in his claim that revenge for, or suspicion of, informing on fellow conspirators is a theoretically possible motive in this instance."

He paused. "The flaw in the defense argument is that in demonstrating an alternative motive for the murder of Petty Officer Jerome, the defense will have proven nothing about the innocence of their client. It ignores the fact that *he* may well be, himself, a member of the same ring of smugglers NIS is trying to uncover. If so, it should come as no surprise that SA Beck wants to know what NIS has learned so far about these smuggling activities and the names of their informants. We feel it is not only unwarranted to reveal that information, but it may also be dangerous to the individuals involved."

Merrill turned and looked down at Beck seated nearby at the defense table. The rest of the courtroom did as well. Not for the first time, Duncan had to face the fact that the surly-looking Beck was not their best exhibit.

Returning to the podium, Duncan tried to look confident. "If Your Honor will permit," he said. "I do have a question I'd like to address to the prosecution."

"Mr. Merrill?" the judge said.

Merrill rose. "I don't know where counsel is heading, but I suppose there is no objection."

"Ask your question, Mr. Carmichael."

This would be a moment of truth. He and Sydney had agreed to act on the assumption that their client was not lying. They might be about to find out if that was justified.

"My question for Mr. Merrill is this: Does the prosecution in this case have *any evidence*, any at all, which suggests, *even indirectly*, that Seaman Apprentice Arnie Beck has now or in the past, *ever* been involved in any way whatsoever in the use, possession, smuggling, or sale of illicit drugs?" He made the question incredulous, a cold, direct challenge to the prosecutor's implicit *ad hominem* attack on the accused.

He knew immediately from Merrill's hesitation, that they had scored. It was all he could do to keep a straight face while he waited for Merrill's response.

"Well . . ., no, Your Honor. We don't have any *specific* evidence to that effect, but the investigation is ongoing."

"With all due respect, Your Honor, I didn't ask counsel about *specific* evidence. I simply asked if there was *any* evidence, even the tiniest *shred* of evidence, specific or otherwise, to suggest such a thing."

There was an almost imperceptible smile lurking at the corners of Captain Clayton's mouth. Like most judges, Clayton seemed to enjoy a good combative exchange between opposing counsel—as long as their clash passed respectfully through him.

Merrill responded quickly and forcefully. "My point was, Your Honor, that it would be *entirely possible* that Beck could have committed this crime for reasons in addition to or beyond those of which we are as yet aware. It may well be to the defense's benefit that we are prepared to proceed to trial with the motive we have."

"I believe I understand your position, Mr. Merrill." The judge turned to Duncan. "Counsel, do you have a reply?"

"Yes, I do, Your Honor. You see, as Mr. Merrill has just demonstrated, the prosecution is in an excellent position to *imply* the existence of secret truths about this case because they have the enviable position of being in charge of the investigative facts. The facts—*the truth*—is all we seek here. All we ask is that we, too, be allowed access to any facts that identify other members of this acknowledged drug ring who might have had reason to commit this crime.

"Mr. Merrill has just demonstrated that SA Beck is clean as a hound's tooth as far as drugs are concerned. We'd like to know the names of the victim's associates who are *not*." Then, with the air of getting on with the inevitable, he asked, "May I proceed with my witness, your honor?"

"Well, I'm not sure that's going to be necessary, Mr. Carmichael. I think I understand both positions on the issues. I'll take your comments as an offer of proof. I will need to read these briefs and perhaps give the matter a little thought." He looked at the wall clock. "Will you gentlemen, and . . . ladies be available at nine tomorrow morning?"

Duncan glanced over and got a nod from Sydney. "Yes, Your Honor," he said.

"Yes, Your Honor," Merrill echoed.

"Very well. This court is in recess until 0900 tomorrow."

Frank Merrill cornered them outside Duncan's office on the second floor. He looked and sounded irritated. "You're laying it on a bit thick in this case, aren't you, Duncan?"

"Just defending my client. You know that, Frank."

"Well, I hate to see some of these drug pushers slip through our fingers just to give you a red herring to use at trial. You're not going to convince anyone with your 'bushy-headed man' defense."

Duncan could sense Sydney tensing up beside him, about to protest. Merrill was referring to a controversial case in the 50s in which the defense argued that the crime might have been committed by a "bushy-headed man" the defendant claimed to have seen but who was never actually identified.

"That's the point," he added quickly. "If you won't give us names, then we have to rely on vague witness testimony, what someone *thinks* they saw or may have seen. We aren't looking for red herrings here, Frank. We're looking for *evidence*. Evidence that will be relevant and admissible at trial.

"If you, Wyman, and Hansen wanted to keep your drug suspects and your informants under wraps, you could have damn well held off on this prosecution until the drug investigation was complete. Or dropped this case entirely, since our client is innocent. You can't have it both ways. You chose to charge Beck. Now you need to live with that."

"Come on. You can't believe Beck's 'I was framed' story. It's ludicrous and you both know it. We should be talking about a deal."

This was obviously Merrill's way of providing an opening to negotiate. It was a good thing that was not what they'd wanted because Sydney had used up her patience.

"I take it that someone with a criminal record isn't capable of innocence in your view, Mr. Merrill?"

Merrill looked at her and apparently decided that his irritation extended to her as well. "There's more at stake here than making sure some cheap hood with a chip on his shoulder gets every benefit of the doubt."

"That chip, as you call it, was put there by society, Mr. Merrill. It isn't proof of guilt. And the presumption of innocence and discovery rules are there for all of us, not just for Arnie Beck."

Duncan moved forward as if preparing to step between the two of them. "Uh, Sydney, maybe we should all get back to work." Sydney and Merrill continued to glare at one another. Duncan turned to Merrill. "We'll talk more about all this tomorrow. Okay, Frank?" Then he grasped Sydney's arm, ever so gently, and eased her down the hall toward his open office door. She obviously had a few more choice things to say. But she thankfully allowed herself to be led away.

Merrill turned on his heels and stiffly strode off in the other direction.

∼

When Duncan and Sydney parted company and he returned to his office, he found a stray pen on the floor. He always kept his pens and pencils in a mug on his desk, so it seemed unusual. Like most everyone in the Law Center, he never locked his office door—no one other than his Law Center colleagues ever haunted these halls. But that misplaced pen did cause him to take a close look at his files and at the contents of his desk. Everything seemed in place and as he'd left it. He shrugged the matter off, but not before also wondering about those two unfamiliar men who had been seated in the back of their courtroom, and recalling that both were gone by the time the hearing was adjourned.

∼

The following morning, the lawyers were back before Captain Clayton. To Merrill's chagrin and Sydney's obvious delight, they won their motion, at least on the matter of relevancy. A further session was called for that afternoon in chambers to lay out the parameters of the decision when it came to protecting the government's informants.

Meanwhile, Sydney and Duncan returned to Duncan's office with their client to discuss Merrill's opening for plea bargaining discussions mentioned on the previous day.

Beck was unimpressed. "What you're saying is that they want me to give up without a fight and go to jail for maybe 15 or 20 years?"

"That's right, Arnie," said Sydney. "But keep in mind, if you fight and lose, that 15 or 20 years could become a great deal more; maybe life."

"I didn't do it. Those bastards framed me. That's got to count for something."

"I hope by now you know we will do everything we can to prove your innocence. But this could be the point at which we have to make a hard choice. There is a possibility that no matter what we do, you could lose. And right now, that looks like a very real possibility."

"More than a possibility," Duncan interjected. "At this point, it's a *probability*. Let's be realistic. We've got some sound arguments. But I owe you my honest opinion. And the way things stand, your chances for acquittal are very slim."

"But you guys are still working on it, right? You might come up with something."

"It's possible," Duncan said. "But they're willing to deal at the moment. If things begin to fall their way, they may change their mind."

"What about this file, this NIS file? We could get the names of a bunch of druggies who thought Stevie had ratted them out. Any of them could have killed him and set me up. Even if we can't prove it for sure, isn't that reasonable doubt?" Clearly Beck was tracking their defense perfectly.

"If we're lucky," Sydney replied. "But we don't know what's in that file. I'm guessing there won't be anything very specific. If there was, they'd probably already be acting on it. We expect to get some ammunition for sure. But without something decisive, your court-martial panel is likely to shrug the whole argument off as the desperate claim of a guilty man. The bloody knife, the tracks in the frost, the wet shoes, and your fight the previous Friday night—those are cold hard facts. We're going to need something very convincing to make this frame seem genuinely plausible."

Beck sat up straighter in his chair, looked at the two lawyers, and shook his head. "I'm not quitting," he said firmly. He looked almost smug. "No goddammed way."

"All right then, Beck," Duncan said. "As long as you know the options. If we learn anything more that might affect your decision, we'll discuss it with you. We can always talk about it later if you want to reconsider."

Beck focused an ill-natured glare on Duncan. "I'm not going to re . . . con . . . sider. I was framed. So you can both just get used to the idea that there ain't gonna be no deal."

CHAPTER 14

Tuesday, March 14, 1978
Sand Point Naval Station, Seattle
Law Center, 13th Naval District

While they waited in the hall for Captain Clayton's ruling, Sydney stepped into Duncan's office to use his phone to check in with her secretary.

Duncan could hear snatches of their conversation. "Tell me exactly what he said, please." Then, ". . . no name or number." Then her voice grew softer. A few moments later, she hung up and came back out into the hall, her forehead wrinkled and face flushed.

"Something wrong?" Duncan asked.

"Yes. I got a message at work from a man who wouldn't leave his name or his number and insisted my secretary write down his message word for word."

"What did he say?"

Sydney glanced down at a small notebook. "He said, 'My advice is that you back off on the Beck case and let things take their course.'"

Duncan felt like he'd taken a punch to the gut. "You think it's the same person who called the ACLU?"

"Either that or I've acquired another harasser. He obviously wants me to know that he can track me to my place of work . . . or . . ."

"Dammit, Sydney," Duncan interrupted before she could finish. "We need to report this."

Sydney's eyes turned steely. "We don't have a name or even any idea who is behind the calls. What can the police do?"

Duncan paused, struggling with the competing feelings of helplessness and anger. "They want you to 'back off' but not get off the case. What does that even mean?"

"I don't know." Sydney took a deep breath, color slowly returning to her cheeks. "But unless we can figure out what's behind these calls, I think we have to keep moving forward as planned. Don't you?" Her question sounded like one that demanded a "yes" response.

Duncan desperately wanted to come up with another, safer option. Finally, he nodded. "I guess we take it one step at a time."

It took Captain Clayton some time to personally sort through the files NIS had provided him. But early that afternoon, in a special closed session of the court, he spelled out exactly what the defense would and wouldn't be allowed to see. There were a couple of items they could only read and take notes on. For everything else they were allowed to make copies and take the copies with them. However, the Captain stopped short at making known the identity of the NIS informant who had implicated Steven Jerome in drug use and dealing. Everything related to that person's identity had been redacted on the Captain's orders. But they were allowed to take a look at the rest. It was agreed that it could happen right there in the courtroom. It was a significant win.

In the tense atmosphere of the courtroom, it was difficult to assess what they were seeing—what was important in the new materials provided by the prosecution. They made the permitted copies and took notes. Then they asked if they might question agents Wyman and Hansen informally, out of court, concerning the file documents they were seeing for the first time. Ruling against concerns expressed by

Frank Merrill, the Judge agreed to delay reconvening the hearing until after those informal interviews had also been completed.

Back in Duncan's office Sydney and Duncan fortified themselves with coffee and went through their notes and copies. The only sounds in the room were from the turning of pages and the occasional slurp.

Sydney was the first to interrupt the silent concentration. "Well, well," she said. "Did you notice this?" She handed over a two-page form that had been filled in by hand. She pointed to a place in the hand-written material on the second page. "Small world."

The document was the signed confession of the sailor who seemed likely to have been the one to originally implicate Jerome in the use and sale of marijuana. The informant's identity had been redacted. But there, on page two of the sailor-informant's statement was mention of the familiar name of Petty Officer Second Class Halbert Willis. This unidentified sailor informant had apparently implicated *both* Willis *and* Jerome in the same NIS statement.

Duncan glanced over the two pages and then handed them back to Sydney. "This guy, whoever he is, has to be their secret informant. Too bad we don't have a handwriting sample to compare with this."

"No such luck."

"Hey, wait a minute. When did they take that statement? What's the date there next to his signature?"

She looked. "Redacted, along with the name."

"Okay, so take a look at the first page, at the top. The NIS guys frequently write it in there too."

She flipped the page. "Yeah, here it is. 12/19/77."

"Yeah, that sounds about right. Usually takes them a couple of months to get their act together. It may be easy enough to get this joker's name, after all."

"I don't understand."

"I'll just ask Frost."

"The lawyer representing Willis?" she asked.

"In administrative discharge boards almost anything goes. No rules of evidence. Sometimes no witnesses or cross-examination. The subject can testify and call witnesses, but there's no authority to compel atten-dance. A written statement like that one right there is admissible and plenty good to do the job. The Navy gets rid of its problem, and the sailor ends up with an undesirable discharge and no benefits. Maybe no jail, but at least it's something."

"So, they'll have given him this statement to be used against his client?" she asked.

"Yep."

"Why would they make this guy known to Frost when they won't tell us?"

"Look at the date," said Duncan. "Those drugs that precipitated this whole investigation didn't show up here until, what, the 23rd of January. I bet they didn't get the tipoff on that shipment until just a few days before then. They'll have created Willis's discharge file, launched his admin board, assigned Frost, and given him this statement long before that. I'll bet when those drugs came in and they set this guy up as an informant, they forgot all about it."

Duncan went to see if Frost was in his office and returned immediately. "Frost wasn't there," he said.

"I've been thinking," Sydney said. "Why didn't they just administratively discharge Jerome as well? Seems like Jerome and Willis were in the same situation."

"Hmm, damn good question. They usually act pretty quickly, at least in getting things started. I don't know. Once they were looking at the big drug shipment, they might have been thinking they could find more on him, especially since he worked in Logistical Support. But you would think they'd have both been lined up for admin boards at about the same time."

It was getting late. And Duncan was hungry. It crossed his mind that he could offer to buy her dinner. Not really a date, but close. She was an attractive, eligible woman. And he was growing almost fond of her, in a strange sort of way. Still, they'd managed to develop a fair working relationship, and it would be a shame to risk damaging that.

"It's getting late," Sydney said, finally closing the file and checking her watch. "I need to do some work at my office before I go home. Let's talk tomorrow."

"Okay," he said. And the moment for suggesting dinner together passed.

∼

When he came in to work the following morning, Duncan had a pink message slip on his desk advising him that he should see Captain Wallace immediately. As Commanding Officer of the Law Center, Wallace was Duncan's immediate superior. He had over 25 years of service in the U.S. Navy JAGC Corps. Even though Wallace was Duncan's boss, they seldom interacted in person. Duncan wondered briefly about the purpose of the meeting. But he didn't have time to dwell on it.

"You wanted to see me, sir?" Duncan came to an alert pose in front of Wallace's desk.

"Yes, Mr. Carmichael. I have some great news."

The Captain produced a set of photocopied documents with a signed original on top and handed them across the desk. "You've got orders. You're being transferred to the position of Staff Judge Advocate for the Commander of the Fleet Air Wing at Naval Air Station Whidbey Island at Oak Harbor, here in Washington. You're to report there no later than 0800 Monday. Effective Friday at 1600 your responsibilities here at the Law Center will cease. Lt. Harrington will take over your duties here. It would be good if you'd take some time to fill him in on your current caseload before you leave on Friday.

"Congratulations, Mr. Carmichael. This is a good position for a young career Judge Advocate. I'm proud of you. You're going to do well there."

CHAPTER 15

Wednesday, March 15, 1978
Mindanao, Republic of the Philippines
An old wharf along Sarangani Bay near the town of General
Santos

The elderly couple paused in their daily walk along the shore and looked with surprise at the old ship that had been a fixed part of the scenery for close to three years. There was a deep "clanging" sound coming from somewhere inside the hull. The ship had been pulled up tight against the pier and a gangway had been lowered down to the dock. Two men stood on a log float in the water at the stern, working at the top of the rudder where the rudder shaft entered the hull. Two more men were huddled in conversation on the main deck. A boom had been swung out from the ship's rigging, and a cable dangled down to the dock out of sight behind the warehouse.

"Ready away," called one of the men from the deck. Slowly a piece of equipment rose into sight above the warehouse building. It was swung onto the deck and carefully lowered into place.

The name of the ship had been freshly repainted onto its stern. "Isabela," it said. Its home port was also there: "Colón."

The elderly man had been to sea many times in his youth and recognized that it was a Panamanian registered vessel. "I'll be damned," he said to his companion. "After all these years, this ship is going back into service. You just never know."

CHAPTER 16

Wednesday, March 15, 1978
Queen Anne Hill, Seattle
Private apartment

Sydney got Duncan's call at home on Wednesday evening. She sensed immediately that something was wrong. Always controlled, his tone was unusually bland. Completely flat, like he was *trying* to sound neutral. He made his announcement with no preliminaries: He had orders for a new duty station at Whidbey Island. It wasn't far, only about a two-hour drive upstate and still within the 13th Naval District. But it was far enough from Seattle to make continued representation of Beck impossible. And they weren't wasting any time. He was moving to his new station over the weekend. Unless something official could be done to return him to Sand Point, she was going to have to handle the Beck case on her own or with a newly assigned military defense counsel.

Her first response was disbelief. But anger quickly followed. Hot and fluid, it flooded her body. There was no question about it—the Navy had dealt Beck a low blow that made a mockery of military pretensions about justice. The decision was intolerable. It could not be allowed to stand.

"I don't have any choice in this," Duncan said.

"They're doing this to get you off the Beck case," Sydney said, stating what she considered obvious.

"That's possible. But why on earth should they go to all this trouble . . .?" He ended in mid-sentence.

She was sure this must all be deeply disturbing for him given his belief in the Navy's system of justice. "We'll fight this thing, Duncan. We have to fight it."

Duncan sighed. "We both know Captain Clayton isn't going to step in. We'll have to appeal it. And I don't think the Court of Military Appeals will act on it either. It's a command decision. Almost impossible to change."

"We'll figure something out. I'll be at your office first thing Friday morning."

The minute she entered Duncan's office on Friday morning and saw their client in his usual chair, she could tell Duncan had already told him the news. Beck was even more detached than normal, but he also looked angry. Duncan didn't get up to greet her. He too looked mad at the world.

"Don't interrupt the fun and games just for me," Sydney said as she took a seat amidst their scowls.

Beck managed a guttural "Harrumph," and Duncan said, "It's 'time' on this one, I'm afraid."

She looked from one man to the other and gritted her teeth. "Now listen to me. We have some alternatives." Beck shrugged. Duncan just looked blank.

"The first thing to decide, Arnie, is whether you want to keep Mr. Carmichael on your case."

Beck looked past her as if studying something on the far wall.

"I would advise you to do so," she added.

He continued to stare at the wall.

"Arnie, look at me." Being ordered to do something by her seemed to startle him out of his reverie. His eyes obediently turned toward her.

"We need a commitment from you before we can pursue keeping Mr. Carmichael on the case."

"What difference does it make?" he asked. "This whole thing is bullshit."

"You've got two lawyers who believe in you. It could make a hell of a lot of difference to the outcome of your case."

Beck shifted in his chair, leaning forward with his arms resting on his knees. "Say I *do* want to keep him. What do I do?"

Duncan too leaned forward, as if considering the possibility. "Well, we *could* start with a request up the chain of command for the orders to be rescinded." Then he leaned back. "Not that it would do any good. They've already told me I won't be re-assigned to the case as individual counsel or otherwise. A request up the chain will just piss some people off."

"We'll have to do that anyway in order to exhaust the normal remedies before the court would hear us," Sydney said.

"If it's denied we *could* convene a session of the court-martial. Make a motion on it." Duncan paused and looked directly at Sydney. "Not that they'd listen to you. And as of tomorrow, I'm not even supposed to be working on his case." His shoulders slumped, a very unmilitary look for the career officer she'd come to know.

"Come on," Sydney said with determination. "I did some thinking about this last night. If they turn us down, we'll do an interlocutory appeal. If they turn down the appeal, we'll go to federal court. This decision is wrong, and they're not going to get away with it. Not if I can help it."

"You'd need to take it to the Court of Military Appeals," Duncan agreed. "That could take a lot of time though. But maybe as an expedited matter you might get them to look at it pre-trial."

"You think they'd be sympathetic?"

"I don't know if they'd even hear the case. But if you don't do that first, you'll never get a federal district court to interest itself in this. The federal courts try to stay scrupulously out of military administrative decisions."

"As far as I'm concerned, it's a criminal justice matter, not an administrative one. And it's a constitutional issue. Couldn't be clearer—right to counsel under the Sixth Amendment."

Duncan handed her a book—the Uniform Code of Military Justice. He had it open to a particular passage. "It's not just the Sixth Amendment. It's also in the UCMJ." He pointed at the relevant passage. "Take a look. What they're going to say is that I'm needed up at NAS Whidbey. Military exigency."

Then he paused. "There is one other thought," he said. "If they deny your request to rescind the orders, it's possible you could ride the issue through a trial and then take it up as an appeal issue if you lose. Maybe get a reversal post-conviction. At that point, there's a chance it could be reversed with prejudice. You'd claim Beck's denial of counsel was too egregious to be corrected with a retrial."

"No retrial?"

"Right."

Beck suddenly showed some interest in the exchange, responding no doubt to the word *conviction*. "Whoa," he said. "Are you saying I might be convicted? I wouldn't have to go to Leavenworth, would I? I sure as hell don't want to end up in no federal prison."

"Well," Duncan said slowly, "you would have to await the results of your appeal. You might be sent to Leavenworth in the interim."

"Uh-uh. Not me. You want to work on my case, you do it now. Not after I been sent to prison."

"Then I take it, Arnie, that I have your go-ahead to fight this thing?" Sydney asked.

"You want to fight, be my guest."

"Good," said Sydney.

"Fine," said Duncan. And then, as Sydney was about to terminate the interview so they could get to work, he added, "And by the way, Beck. I got another call from your father last night. Has he called you at the Correctional Center?"

Arnie scowled. "Nope."

"Have you called him?"

"Nope." The scowl deepened.

"Look, why don't you call him? He's obviously worried, and I can't tell him anything without getting your permission first."

"I don't want to call him."

The look on Duncan's face suggested he was losing patience with Beck, but he kept his tone even. "So, what do you want me to tell him about your case?"

"I don't give a shit what you tell him. But I'm not going to call him. I've got nothing to say to him."

Sydney and Duncan spent the rest of the morning in Duncan's office composing a petition up the chain of command requesting rescission of the transfer orders. Sydney wrote and Duncan contributed his thoughts while cleaning out his office and packing his things. He was helpful but not encouraging.

"Once the Navy gets an idea in its collective head on something like this, it's damned near impossible to get it out. I doubt there is anything we could put in that petition that would affect the Admiral. And the folks in D.C. will knee-jerk back him up." He paused and looked at her. "We should write it with the Federal District Court in mind. Assume they may later read it. Make them the intended audience."

Duncan piled another packing box on top of the growing stack of boxes near the door. He turned toward her and said, "I hate leaving you to face this alone." Sydney understood the underlying message, his fear for her safety.

"I'll be fine," she assured him. She realized suddenly that part of what she was feeling was empathy for him. She'd always been mistrustful of the military, but this was his whole life, and he seemed to have been very happy with that life. As a lawyer, he must be finding this transfer disillusioning as well as unwelcome. Then another possibility hit her. "Duncan, could this petition have a further effect on you, on your career?"

He gave her a halfhearted smile. "Probably. They do *not* like being bucked like this. But that doesn't make any difference; I can weather it. It'll blow over eventually."

He didn't sound all that convinced. She didn't know what to say. "I'm sorry," she began. "I came charging in here all agitated about your transfer and didn't even consider what you personally might want to do. You do want to go ahead with this, don't you? Because if you don't . . ."

"It's not my decision. It's our client's. He made it, and I absolutely think he made the right one."

Not for Duncan though, that seemed evident now.

He turned back to his packing. His uniform jacket was on a hanger on the back of his door. The sleeves of his white shirt were rolled up, and there was a smudge of dirt on one arm. Sydney felt a surge of warmth for the man. She had slowly come to respect him as a lawyer. But she also liked him as a person. It was the uniform that she didn't like and the idea that *it* was everything and the man inside nothing.

The petition was hand-delivered that afternoon and, as a safety measure, a "respectfully requested" deadline was stipulated for the following Monday given that their client was in jail awaiting trial. Captain Clayton had agreed to keep his schedule open Tuesday and Wednesday on the assumption that, if the petition was denied, they wouldn't suffer further delay and could arrange a hearing at the last minute.

In an effort not to waste time, Sydney set up an appointment with Larry Wyman on Monday at NIS headquarters on the Navy base. There were still questions that she and Duncan had after reviewing the Jerome drug investigation file.

Even without Duncan, even in the face of anonymous threats and vexing command decisions, work on the case had to proceed.

CHAPTER 17

Monday, March 20, 1978
Seafirst Bank Building, Seattle
Law Offices of Steiner, Bentley and Waterhouse

By Monday morning Duncan was gone, and apparently already settling in at NAS Whidbey. Sydney called him from her office to discuss the conversation he'd had late Friday afternoon with Lieutenant Frost, Willis's attorney. Frost had given him the name of the man who informed on Jerome and Willis. Unfortunately, the man was another dead end. He'd been administratively discharged a month and a half earlier and was now living somewhere in Wisconsin.

Duncan told her he had interviewed the informant on the phone, but the man hadn't added anything new to his statement. He'd told Duncan that he had made small purchases of drugs from both Jerome and Willis at different times late the previous year. End of story. That left the question of why NIS had been so determined to protect the identity of someone who had long since left the Navy and who now lived as a civilian half a continent away.

They had no answer. But with that name, Frost had also given Duncan something else, something that could possibly prove useful.

Apparently, a few days before Jerome's murder, Frost's client Willis had received an anonymous letter in the mail containing what looked like the first page from a confession supposedly written by Jerome. Willis had given it to Frost who, after asking his client's approval, had happily handed it off to Duncan. Sydney's office had one of the new FAX machines, as did the Admin office at the 13th Naval District Law Center, so before he'd left on Friday, Duncan had faxed the one-page document over to her.

It was on the same standard form that they'd seen earlier in use by NIS. This one read:

12/28/77

VOLUNTARY STATEMENT

I, _LS3 Steven David Jerome_, have been advised that I am under suspicion for the crime of:

    transportation, possession, and sale of dangerous drugs

I have been advised of and fully understand my legal rights as follows:

I have the right to remain silent.

Anything I say can be used against me in a court of law.

I have the right to an attorney and to have my attorney present with me during questioning.

If I cannot afford an attorney, one will be appointed to represent me at government expense and at no cost to me.

I fully understand the above warning of rights and make this statement of my own free will. I have been subjected to no threats or promises of any kind in making the following statement and it is true to the best of my belief:

I have become involved in the sale and smuggling of dangerous drugs into the United States by including them in shipments of U.S. Navy logistical supplies shipped to the Logistical Support Activity, Sand Point from

Naval Station Subic Bay, Philippines. I regret these actions and wish to make a clean breast of my activities in hope of leniency in any disciplinary proceeding which may ensue.

I am willing to assist U.S. Navy authorities in the prosecution of those who participated in these illegal deeds. To this end, I state that a large quantity of Marijuana is scheduled to arrive at the Logistical Support Activity Warehouse 17 sometime within the next few weeks. These drugs will come to the U.S. from the Philippines aboard a Navy ship.

There are several other people who are responsible for this shipment and who are involved in smuggling operations with me. The names of these co-conspirators are

Dated: <u>*December 28 1977*</u>

    Initials: ____SJ____

    Page: __*1*__ of __*3*__

That was it. All they had was that single page of what appeared to have been a three-page document. Willis hadn't been sure why someone would have sent the document to him, and he hadn't taken it seriously. According to Frost, as far as Willis knew, Jerome wasn't involved in any drug smuggling. Willis figured it was either some kind of prank or an effort by someone to get Jerome in trouble. He didn't want any part of it, but he'd decided to hedge his bets and show it to Frost.

This signed, typewritten form had not been among any of the materials they'd so far seen in discovery. And there was no way to prove it wasn't a forgery of some kind, as Willis had suspected. But it looked genuine. The hand-written date at the top was absolutely consistent with what Duncan had told her about Wyman's typical practice. Steven Jerome's supposed handwritten initials at the bottom wouldn't be much to go on in making a comparison. But if either Wyman or Hanson admitted to creating it, it could be admitted as evidence. Another possibility was to go through Willis and get him to testify as to how he'd received it. Whether genuine or not, it was potentially proof of their alternative theory. Whether it was the real thing or was faked, it helped Beck.

Given everything that was happening, they agreed not to mention the form to NIS or the prosecution quite yet. Maybe Wyman or Hansen would own up. If not, they could always point to it later as an artful forgery written by someone with a possible motive for killing or perhaps causing others to kill Jerome. Someone other than Beck.

When Sydney showed up for her appointment at 11:00 a.m. Monday, Wyman did not seem particularly happy to see her. Gone was his usual bonhomie. He was, however, civil enough to offer her a cup of coffee, which she politely refused before getting directly to the point.

"I have a few questions after looking over the documents you gave us at the hearing last week, Larry."

"Have at it."

"For instance, it appears as though your investigations of Jerome and Willis dead-ended with the seizure down at pier 17. That happened on January 23rd, correct?"

"Yeah, that's accurate."

"And you convened, or directed, an administrative discharge board for Willis in January to take place in mid-February. Correct?"

"Correct."

"But no action was taken against Jerome?"

Wyman shifted in his chair. It was clear he knew where the questions were going. "That's right," he said, "but . . ."

Sydney interrupted.

"If both men were named by the same informant at the same time, then why not treat both men the same?"

"We were still investigating at the time of Jerome's death."

To Sydney, it sounded like something they decided to say if she brought up the issue, but it didn't really explain anything to her satisfaction. "There's nothing in the file to indicate that you were pursuing other avenues of inquiry. Would you care to expand on that?"

"We were still hopeful that something would show up." He looked directly at Sydney. "I don't understand what this has to do with Beck."

The fact was, Sydney wasn't sure herself. All she knew was that Duncan found the discrepancy curious. That was good enough for her.

"One last thing," she said, ignoring his comment. "Was it just coincidence that the man who informed on Jerome and Willis left the Navy and is now living somewhere in Wisconsin?"

Wyman seemed surprised that she knew about the informant. "What else would it be?" he asked, sounding sincerely puzzled.

She ignored his question. "So, you're saying that your informant was not able to provide sufficient incriminating evidence to convene an administrative discharge board on Jerome, but he was for Willis?"

The NIS agent let out a lengthy, long-suffering sigh. "Sydney, I appreciate what you're trying to do here. I do. And I don't begrudge your client his day in court. He's entitled to a good defense, to the best kind of defense that you can possibly give him. But you know, there's still such a thing as carrying matters too far. I've seen lawyers come and go over the years, good ones and bad ones. And to be honest, you and Carmichael are two of the best. But I have to tell you, you two are wasting your time on this. There isn't one damn thing in this whole file that has a damn thing to do with your client or with the murder of Steven Jerome. Not one damn thing."

Sydney asked, "Are you telling me to back off? To let things take their course?" She studied Wyman's reaction to her deliberate choice of words.

He simply shook his head. Then he lowered his voice and said, "I'll tell you what. Why don't you have that kid Beck checked out by a shrink. Now there's something constructive you could do. See if he's sailing with a full duffel. You're sure as hell more likely to come up with something to defend his ass in court with that than you are by digging around in old drug files or by trying to muscle tired old NIS agents." He gave her a weak smile as a peace offering.

Sydney stood up and extended her hand. "Thanks for the advice, Larry. I'll keep it in mind."

As she left, she found that she wasn't angry with him for his advice or for his suggestion about the shrink. Nor did she think he was the anonymous caller. Despite their differences and whatever he might be holding back, she believed that he had been mostly truthful with her. One day soon, however, she might have to ask him to admit to the authenticity of that first page of Jerome's "confession." That's when they'd find out just how truthful a man he really was.

Sydney eagerly awaited word from the Admiral on their petition. Monday ran out with no response. There was no response Tuesday either, until late afternoon. When it came, the answer was "no." She called Duncan at his new office to let him know it was a go on the special session of the court-martial. Could he be there at nine o'clock the following morning?

"I'm sure they'll give me liberty," he said. "I'll be there."

CHAPTER 18

Wednesday, March 22, 1978
Sand Point Naval Station, Seattle
Law Center, 13th Naval District

The moment Captain Clayton walked into the courtroom Sydney feared the worst. His eyes had flicked over those present, briefly resting with thinly veiled hostility on Beck and Sydney. Just as he was about to call the court to order she saw him spot Duncan seated at the back of the room. Clayton immediately asked him to explain his presence. Duncan stood and responded that his superiors at the Fleet Air Whidbey had given him liberty to attend as an observer. The judge's voice said, "Very well," but the look on his face was one of disapproval.

Lieutenant Dick Harrington, Duncan's official replacement as Beck's appointed counsel, was with Sydney at the defense table. He and Sydney had only talked briefly. Herrington had been in JAGC and out of law school for less than a year. Beck wanted nothing to do with him but hadn't explicitly demanded that he be removed. With no real role to play at the hearing, Herrington sat rigidly at the counsel table, presumably ready to do whatever he was told.

When Beck was called upon to testify on the limited issue of his lawyer-client relationship, he managed to do remarkably well. He clearly and forcefully testified that yes, he had established a confidential relationship with Mr. Carmichael, yes, he had confidence in Mr. Carmichael's abilities, and yes, he wanted to retain Mr. Carmichael as his assigned military lawyer or to have him as his special designated counsel.

Throughout the testimony, Captain Clayton would occasionally look over and survey Beck coolly, causing Beck to straighten his shoulders slightly. It was the sailor's rights against the wishes of the command. From Sydney's point of view, this decision would be an acid test of the military justice system. None of it seemed driven by reverse discrimination. It all felt to her more like jealously guarded institutional power and inertia.

The prosecution called Captain Wallace who testified briefly that the legal officer at NAS Whidbey had been transferred elsewhere. That had left a critically important vacancy that required an immediate replacement. The only appropriate, quickly available candidate was Lieutenant Duncan Carmichael. Sydney launched into her cross-examination but was left helpless when Captain Clayton prevented her from delving into the specifics. Clayton ruled that the exact exigencies requiring Carmichael's transfer were "military judgments" which were "beyond the scope" of the hearing.

There wasn't much of an answer to that.

She felt her argument went well, but Frank Merrill was also effective, and Captain Clayton came to a quick decision, one as reflexive as a salute. In Clayton's opinion, the removal of Carmichael at this stage of the proceedings was not a disparagement of the rights of the accused which had, of military necessity, to be balanced against the needs of the service. Beck had a "very effective" civilian lawyer as well as access to a perfectly capable military lawyer. Trial was still well over a month away, so there would be plenty of time for Beck to prepare his defense without Carmichael. It was not a case of command influence but rather of military necessity.

"Motion denied."

Military justice *did* resemble military music, Sydney thought bitterly when she heard Clayton's decision. But then, why should the

Navy care if one insignificant man was denied his personal choice of an attorney? The Navy "needed" Duncan elsewhere, and the Navy inevitably came first.

Sydney had a brief off to the U.S. Court of Military Appeals by late Wednesday afternoon. She argued the right to counsel was too fundamental to allow an attorney-client relationship, once formed, to be broken so capriciously. The Fourth Amendment guaranteed a Constitutional right to counsel. The Navy was denying that right by transferring Duncan well after a working relationship had been established between him and his client. Furthermore, there was no showing of any compelling military need for Duncan's new assignment at Fleet Air Whidbey. Instead, the transfer was transparent retaliation for what had become a vigorous legal defense of the charges brought against SA Beck. This final claim had a weak foundation in the evidence, but Sydney argued that the criminal justice system, even in the military services, needed to present the "appearance" of fundamental fairness as well as its reality. This command decision had failed that test.

The brief was short, to the point, and impassioned. She felt strongly about the issue, and her feelings were reflected in her writing. Afterward, all she could do was wait and see if the military music from Washington D.C. would be more pleasant to their ears than the local tune.

It wasn't.

The expedited reply came the following Monday. It was not an actual denial of the claim. Rather, it was a refusal to hear the matter at all. According to the Court of Military Appeals, Beck's rights would be adequately protected if this issue was presented on appeal after a trial. In other words, let him be convicted first, spend months more in prison, give the prosecution the benefit of learning everything they could about his defense, let the evidence supporting his defense go cold—and then they would think about whether he should have been accorded his right to the attorney of his choice.

She was livid. But it had ended exactly as Duncan predicted.

Even before they had received the reply from the Court of Military Appeals, she had written a rough draft of her petition to the Federal District Court for the Western District of Washington. If the military wouldn't listen, maybe a civilian judge would. When she told Duncan about her next move, he had agreed, but with obvious unease. She knew he understood that going to federal court meant a lawsuit against the U.S. Navy—a direct challenge to Navy authority. Among the defendants would be the Secretary of the Navy, the Chief of the Bureau of Naval Personnel, Thirteenth Naval District Commandant Admiral Clifford van Damme, the Commanding Officer Naval Station Sand Point, and Captain Wallace—Duncan's former JAGC Commanding Officer, as well as his current commanding officer up at Fleet Air Whidbey. It would become a public matter. And given current post-Vietnam public attitudes toward the U.S. military, the matter might even attract some significant press.

That was a lot of important people to make unhappy. Maybe she was pushing the issue too far, certainly she wasn't backing off. But dammit, she wasn't going down without a fight.

By the end of the following day, Sydney had seen to service of process and an expedited hearing had been scheduled for one week later. Her papers called upon the civilian court to oversee its military brother and to require by federal court order that the Navy return to Arnie Beck the unencumbered services of his original military attorney. The court had agreed to hear the case quickly since, with Beck incarcerated, more delay could affect his right to a speedy trial.

She had also been granted an oral argument. So, the following Tuesday she found herself mounting the steps of the massive, neoclassical Federal Courthouse for the Western District of Washington on 5th Avenue in Seattle. Since an oral argument was unusual on federal motions of this kind, she believed it was a good sign. But she still entered the building with trepidation.

Argument before a federal district court was more formal and more intimidating than before a state court. The judges were in office for life and tended to be bold in wielding their considerable authority, more so than most elected state judges. They were also known to be unsympathetic with attorneys who hadn't done their homework.

Not that Sydney wasn't prepared. Duncan had driven down to join her at the King County Law Library over the weekend, and they had thoroughly researched the issues together. But the brief itself was hers. She had practiced her presentation and was confident there would be no question the judge could ask that she would not be able to answer. And according to the other lawyers in her office, the assigned judge, Judge Taylor Symons, was conservative but fair. He apparently believed in going by the rules and allowed no time to be wasted. She had been advised to get to the point, to be brief, and to stay away from emotional appeals.

The big courtroom was imposing and austere. It was also remarkably quiet in the stillness of the morning before the day's business began. A few people, early for motions, stood around talking in respectful undertones. Their voices faintly echoed off the bare walls and impressively high ceiling.

Duncan was standing near the front of the gallery, looking his usual starched military self. He waved to Sydney as she came in. When she joined him, he said, "Frank Merrill told me the U.S. Attorney is going to let him make the argument."

"That's fine, isn't it?" The arguments would be the same no matter who presented them.

"Yeah, I guess so." He smiled with encouragement. "All set?"

"I hope so." They took their seats. The room was starting to fill with people.

"No matter what happens, at least Beck can't claim we haven't tried," Duncan said. He reached over and took her hand in his and gave it a squeeze, an unusual gesture for him—for them. Their eyes met briefly. Then they both turned toward the front of the room as the judge took the bench and the case of "Beck versus the Secretary of the Navy" was called.

Feeling as nervous as if it was her first trial, Sydney went forward to make her opening statement. She was wearing a dark blue suit with a stark white blouse and a gold pin, Navy colors she had mused when getting dressed that morning. It had taken her three different tries to decide what to wear. Now, as she looked up into the elderly judge's deeply focused eyes, she realized that her concern over what to wear had been pointless; the only thing that was going to influence this judge would be the merits of their case.

She made her argument succinctly and dispassionately, repeating the key points from her brief and arguing the legal authorities. The only response she got from Judge Symons was his unwavering attention. When she finished and returned to her seat, what she'd said was already a blur. But she knew from the look on Duncan's face that she must have done all right. She smiled inwardly: he'd never dare tell her that, of course.

Merrill's presentation was as polished as his shoes. He forcefully repeated all the arguments used by Captain Clayton in making his decision against their motion in the military court, adding some original twists of his own. She had to admit, when Merrill wanted to, he could lay it on. The only difference here was that now he was talking to someone who put the law first rather than the Navy.

When Merrill sat down and Sydney returned for her closing argument, she could tell immediately that the judge had made up his mind. He interrupted her with a question before she had said ten words.

"You feel Lieutenant Carmichael is necessary to Mr. Beck's defense?"

"Yes, Your Honor, I do. He's absolutely critical. Our client believes so as well."

"Very well, Miss Warren, I've read the briefs, and I believe I understand your position." He was dismissing her. As she backed uncertainly away from the lectern, Judge Symons began delivering his decision.

"It is always with great hesitation that a federal court involves itself in a military matter, particularly when the matter involves an administrative consideration like the transfer of a serviceman to a new duty station. In my judgment, however . . ." He cast a brief look at Frank Merrill before continuing. ". . . the constitutional and federal statutory issues are too fundamental to be ignored. Denial of Beck's initially delegated counsel is a clear violation of his rights both under the U.S. Constitution and under the Uniform Code of Military Justice. If Beck wants Lieutenant Carmichael as his counsel, and Carmichael is able to defend Beck, only the very strongest showing of military necessity could possibly support the refusal to allow this—especially after the initial attorney-client relationship has been formed.

"To deny those rights and expect the defendant to proceed to trial without his proper attorney, to start anew, is a fundamental abridgment of his rights. Such a wrong could never be corrected on a retrial, months, perhaps years later. Evidence, investigation, witnesses, all will have been affected by the previous trial and by the passage of time. Moreover, the defendant is now and will apparently continue to be under restraint. Presumably, this restraint would continue through an appeal and through a second trial, but even if that was not the case, my decision would be the same.

"As I've indicated, only the strongest of showings would justify the denial of requested military counsel." He paused and leaned forward to make his final statement. "The showing by the government in this case is barely even colorable in this regard. Not nearly sufficient to justify the denial of Arnie Beck's right to counsel. The motion is granted. The order requested by petitioner will issue."

Sydney was so elated by the decision it was all she could do to maintain her courtroom decorum as she and the others left to the sounds of the next motion being called for hearing. Once they were out in the hall, Frank Merrill came over to offer his congratulations. "I guess the drinks are on me," he said with a wan smile.

"More than a few drinks, I'd say," Duncan replied as he shook Merrill's hand.

"I had to try." Merrill turned to shake hands with Sydney. "Although I don't see that I had a chance against such a good-looking lady lawyer."

Sydney's spirits were too high to register irritation at the remark. "Beck will be pleased," she said.

"The truth is," Merrill said with an air of confidentiality, "I'm just as glad you won. I would hate to have had this thing hanging over our heads at trial. Once I get a conviction, I want it to stick. I don't want a reversal on appeal over something like this."

"Yes," Sydney quickly agreed. "It's best to have it settled now."

Later, Sydney was to remember Merrill's comment about being glad she'd won. Unless it was just bravado, why had he fought so hard against Carmichael staying on the case?

CHAPTER 19

Thursday, April 6, 1978
Sand Point Naval Station, Seattle
Law Center, 13ᵗʰ Naval District

By Thursday morning, April 6th, the Navy had rescinded Duncan's earlier assignment to Fleet Air Whidbey and reassigned him back to the Thirteenth Naval District Law Center. No one had moved into his original office, so he ended up back there as well. The desk, the chair, even the posters on the walls were still there. It was as if nothing had happened.

He could imagine the intake of breath by the Bureau of Naval Personnel in Arlington when they realized that their closely protected military preserve had been invaded by a civilian federal court. He was nervous about the reception he would get, both from Captain Wallace and from Wallace's superior, Admiral van Damme. But it was gratifying to know that, in the final analysis, even the military authorities had to bend to the requirements of federal law and the U.S. Constitution.

Beck had probably been smart not to chance saving the matter as a possible appeal issue after trial. Even if they'd won later on appeal, it was possible he could have been retried. In the meantime, he could have been languishing in prison.

There were some advantages to working a case with a civilian lawyer, Duncan thought. He could at least pretend to be innocent of complicity in taking the matter to the Federal District Court. Let Sydney take the heat on this one. Although, whoever had been behind his untimely transfer was not going to be pleased with the push-back, even if their motives had been pure, which Duncan doubted. He only hoped their win didn't put Sydney in jeopardy.

The whole thing had thrown him off stride. Until now, he'd always managed to convince himself that, despite its flaws, the U.S. Navy usually ended up doing the right thing. But it didn't feel that way this time. First, there was the surprisingly stiff opposition they'd faced in securing proper discovery from the prosecution. Then the unexplained resistance from NIS. And finally, his transfer to Whidbey.

Even if the transfer had been somehow necessary—which Duncan doubted—when it became apparent that following through might prej-udice Beck's defense, allowances should have been made. And if they'd truly needed him there, they could easily have left him on station at Whidbey Island but given him a temporary or part-time assignment to Seattle to complete Beck's defense. That they hadn't was a clear give-away that the transfer itself had been a mere device.

He couldn't help but wonder why this case had suddenly become so important to someone up the chain of command. It had shaken his confidence in Navy justice, caused him to reconsider whether the ACLU's reverse discrimination rationale for getting involved might have some merit, and made him all the more determined to give Beck a vigorous defense.

"Okay, what now?" he said to Sydney when she came in at eleven hundred. "What haven't we done?"

Sydney smiled and took a seat. "You seem raring to go."

"Absolutely."

"Good. Actually, there is one thing in particular I think we might follow up on. Remember this?" She handed him a two-page list. "It was with the materials we got in the first packet of discovery from Merrill before the pretrial. It's the inventory of Jerome's personal effects. Stuff they recovered from his lockers at work and in the barracks."

Carmichael looked at the list. "Yeah, I remember thinking that it didn't look interesting. Has NIS still got all this stuff?"

"According to Frank Merrill they do. And while you were gone last week, I decided I might as well check it out. On the off chance I'd find something, anything. So I called him and asked if I could take a look. Surprise, surprise—he turned me down."

"What the hell. They should let us see these things if we want."

"Merrill says none of it is evidence in the case and they're just preserving it to send to Jerome's family."

"Then why not let us see it?" Carmichael studied the list more closely. "I've got to admit, none of this looks like it amounts to anything." The list contained personal items like toiletries, clothing, keys, a wristwatch, money, paperback books, and a ghetto-blaster radio/tape player. Nothing unusual. The second page listed items taken from Jerome's desk at his duty station: a paperweight, pens and pencils, miscellaneous papers and documents relating to his work at the Logistical Support Activity, and a coffee mug. Nothing stood out.

"Merrill turned you down, huh?"

"I thought he was going to say yes at first. But then he said he'd have to call me back. When he did, he was all charm and personality, but his answer was *no*.

"I don't like the sound of that."

"Neither do I. Like everything else in this case, it makes you wonder."

"All right then, let's make this our first order of business. Let's see what Captain Clayton has to say about this one. Agreed?"

"Agreed."

The following day they were back in court arguing again. Duncan thought the decision would be perfunctory, but it turned out otherwise.

"Just what is it you hope to find among these belongings, Mr. Carmichael?" the Captain asked, looking up from the list and pushing his reading glasses from his nose to the top of his largely bald head. "Which items on this list are the ones that interest you?"

"We'd like to see them all, Your Honor. This is discovery. We can't know what will be important until we see it. Please keep in mind that these are items that belonged to the murdered man and were in his possession at the time of his death. It certainly seems appropriate that we be allowed to examine them. Clearly, the prosecution has done so. It's a simple matter for us to take a look. If there's nothing of interest there, then why not just say yes?"

"So, you feel you need to look at this, ah . . ." He lowered his glasses back to his nose. "One Ban roll-on deodorant . . . or . . . fourteen pair miscellaneous socks. Or perhaps you want to see one carved monkeypod elephant. You seriously think this might be relevant evidence that could help your defense of this case?" Clayton sounded incredulous. "I must tell you, Mr. Carmichael, that these repeated motions of yours and your co-counsel are beginning to try this court's patience." Clayton clearly had not appreciated being overruled by a federal court.

"There would have been no motion, Your Honor," Duncan argued, "if the prosecution hadn't denied our request to see these items—it is not *we* who are responsible for taking up the court's time. As you so appropriately point out, we can't tell anything about an item from a list. There is simply no way to know what might be relevant until it has been physically examined. Also, remember that the prosecution *has* looked at these things. If they are so completely inconsequential, why have they denied the same advantage to the defense? If they had let us take a look, this would all have been over in a few minutes without this court ever having been involved."

"Perhaps they, too, are growing weary of the continuous casting about you people seem to be engaged in on this matter." Clayton held up his hand. "No, I don't want to hear more argument on this, from either side. As far as I can tell, this is just another fishing expedition by the defense. Still . . . I can't see how I can deny the request. Aside from the obvious inconvenience, there's nothing to show that it will prejudice the government's case. And I suppose there is some *ever so slight* possibility that something could come of it." He shook his head to suggest that he doubted his own words. "I'm going to grant the motion," he said, sounding quite thoroughly disgusted.

~

That weekend Carmichael had to deal with another phone call at the BOQ from Beck's father. He told Sydney about it on Monday morning as they walked together from the Law Center over to the NIS offices for their look at Jerome's belongings.

"I don't know what to tell the man. He keeps calling me, usually at the BOQ in the evening. He shouldn't even have the number. And, strangely, he doesn't ask about how Arnie is doing, how he's being treated, anything like that. It's more like he's interested in the details of the case itself. The law. The evidence. That kind of thing. I keep telling him he needs to talk to his son about it, but he just blows off that suggestion."

"Even though they don't get along, he's probably still concerned about his son," Sydney said. Then, "Is Arnie's mother alive?"

"I don't know. Beck never mentions her. I guess we could look at his service record for his next-of-kin. I think the father's some kind of farmer. Lives in Eastern Washington, up near Colville somewhere. Doesn't sound like he's got much education."

"What *have* you told him?"

"Not much. Father or not, I can't pass along information without his son's permission. Even though Arnie said he didn't care what I told him, it puts me in an awkward position."

"Well, do your best. And try not to worry about it."

CHAPTER 20

Monday, April 10, 1978
Sand Point Naval Station, Seattle
NIS Headquarters, 13th Naval District

Larry Wyman greeted them with a poorly concealed smirk as he escorted them into the glass-enclosed conference room where a carton with Jerome's belongings rested on the table. "Have fun!" he said.

Victory on the motion had been theirs. But once they were actually going through Jerome's used toothbrushes and underwear, it was hard not to feel that they'd made fools of themselves.

Sydney was looking at the stuff NIS had collected from Jerome's duty desk one last time, hoping to find something to justify their effort. There were hand-written notes, old duty rosters, some beat-up shipping documents, leave requests, a few phone messages—the kind of thing anyone with Jerome's job might have had in his desk.

"This isn't getting us anywhere," she reluctantly admitted.

"You ready to give it up?"

"I've had enough. You?"

"I sure as hell hate to walk out of here with nothing," he said.

"Me too," she said. "Especially with your buddy Larry sitting out there with that obnoxious grin on his face."

Duncan glanced through the big windows enclosing the conference room. Sure enough, there was Wyman standing by the copy machine looking their way. When he caught Duncan's eye, he gave them a bright two-fingered salute.

"Right you are," said Duncan. He got up and went to the door. "Hey, Larry. Could we see you in here for a minute?" Wyman came in, still smiling. Duncan led him over to the table, reached into the carton, and removed a pair of black Navy standard uniform Oxford shoes. They were substantially identical to those allegedly worn by Beck on the night of the murder.

"Could we get you to mark these shoes as an exhibit and bring them to court when we go to trial?"

"These shoes? These are Jerome's." Wyman seemed surprised.

"Yeah. This pair. There's another pair still in the box there, but it's *this* pair we need. Maybe we could mark them so they don't get mixed up." Duncan reached over and grabbed a piece of chalk from the small chalkboard mounted to the back wall. He turned each shoe over and initialed the bottoms of their soles. "This specific pair, not the other. Make sure they don't get mixed up, okay?"

"Well . . . yeah. Sure. I can do that." Wyman looked at the shoes and at Duncan with open curiosity. Then he took the shoes into the other room, pulled a clear plastic trash bag out of a cupboard, deposited the shoes in the bag, and sealed it with a wire twist fastener. Next, he tied a tag on the bag and initialed it with the date. Standing in the doorway he said, "There you go. You have these on your exhibit list, and I'll bring them along personally. How's that sound?"

"Great, Larry. That'll be great."

Sydney and Duncan managed to make it all the way out of the building, down the steps, and partway down the sidewalk toward the Law Center parking lot before they both broke into uncontrollable laughter.

"You . . . think he'll call Merrill?" said Sydney between gasps.

"What's it been, three minutes? I guarantee he already has." Duncan wiped the corners of his eyes with the back of his hand. "Merrill will be over there five minutes from now. They'll both spend the next hour studying those shoes. And then they'll lay awake all night trying to figure out why the hell we want them." They both burst into laughter once again.

It was nearly noon. Carmichael and Sydney decided to drive off base to a nearby Mexican restaurant for a bite to eat. Over their taco salads, Sydney complained that she'd been getting increasing pressure from her employers to spend more time working on paying cases.

"I spent twenty minutes in Steiner's office before I came over here this morning answering questions about the status of my workload. He was pretty clear that when this Beck thing is over, it's back to working for paying clients. Corporate mergers. Anti-trust. Class actions. Cases that bring in *money*."

"I can't really see how you can blame him."

"Oh, I know. I shouldn't be talking like this. Steiner's been very reasonable. It's a good firm, one of the best in town. I actually do enjoy some of the business work. And the class-action cases are what I wanted to do when I took the job. Still, they did agree to my pro bono work when I signed up. I was supposed to be allowed up to 5% of my time on it. I bet I'm not over that if you take my average over the past year."

"Been pretty heavy lately, though."

"I suppose. And I've got to admit, my perspective has changed somewhat over the past couple of years. The other day I was sitting up on the 48th floor of the Columbia Center in a deposition. In one of those huge conference rooms with big windows and a view of Puget Sound.

"It's this big lawsuit over the collapse of one of those huge warehouse-type retail store buildings in last winter's snow. There are more than a dozen parties. Twenty lawyers in all, given the insurance companies, plaintiffs, contractors, and private corporate counsel involved.

"Thing was, within a few minutes it was obvious that the first witness they'd brought in didn't know anything about the accident. He was just a real estate broker who'd had a listing on the building when it sold recently. Still, if you're the lawyer who set the deposition and subpoenaed this poor schmuck, you've got to ask him something, right? You'd look pretty silly to let the guy go after five minutes.

We spent maybe half an hour on his credentials as a broker. More time on how he went about valuing the building, even though he's not an appraiser. Then he was asked, one by one, about all the papers in his file, and they all got marked as exhibits. At best there's one or two that might be vaguely relevant to the damage claims.

"By the time this lawyer's done, we've spent well over an hour on this poor guy. But that's just the start. There are 19 other lawyers there who have to earn their fees. Over that first hour, they've thought of some questions too. So, we go around the table and each lawyer takes his turn. And when they do, the rest of them think of even more questions to ask on a second time around. We spent six and a half hours in there, nearly a whole damn day. An entire day on a five-minute witness. Do you know what that cost?"

"No."

She laughed. "Well, I do. In between looking at the view and waiting for something to happen that wasn't bullshit, I figured it out: $17,600. You can add it up. Say eight billable hours per lawyer, counting a little prep time, travel time, and follow-up. And you can damn well be sure they billed every minute. Those guys, mostly associates, will bill $100 to $120 an hour, say $110 on average, times eight hours is $880 per lawyer. Times twenty lawyers, that's $17,600. More if you count in any travel or miscellaneous expenses."

"It's a lot of money."

"Even in this day and age, we're talking a year's income for some people. It's disgusting. And we're all paying for that—in our taxes, in insurance premiums, in the cost of the stuff we buy. And all for an essentially worthless five-minute witness who'll be ignored if the case ever goes to trial, which it won't. It will end up being settled."

"I won't disagree with you Sydney. Still, it's our legal system. Everybody needs representation. Lawyers cost money. I don't see how you get around it."

"Yeah, I know you're right. But it bothers me." She laughed. "I guess that's obvious, huh?"

"I would say so."

She laughed again. "I just kept looking around that conference room, which, given its 48th floor view, could maybe rent for $5,000 a month. And I was thinking about Arnie Beck sitting over there in the brig without enough money to hire a lawyer. And it hit me that my share of that $17,600 is paying my part of Arnie Beck's attorney fees. If, that is, I manage to convince Steiner to continue letting me work the case. Seems like a screwy system to me, when you think about it."

"Well, that's your problem right there."

"What? *Thinking* about it? Maybe you're right."

Hearing her cut loose like that made Duncan feel guilty. He hadn't given much thought to how her time on Beck's case might be placing her future with her firm in jeopardy. He'd selfishly been focused on how their battles over discovery, their motions with Captain Clayton, their appeals to the Court of Military Appeals, and the trip to Federal District Court might damage his own career.

Knowing that she was under pressure as well strengthened his respect for her.

After lunch she drove him back to the base. As she was about to pull up and let him out, he thought of one more thing he could do that afternoon before setting the Beck case aside for other work.

"I think I'm going to take a run down to Building 17 and talk with Jerome's superiors," he said. "I'd like to see if Jerome really did deserve those high marks we saw in his performance reviews."

"Want company?"

"Don't you need to get back?"

Sydney gave him a broad smile. "I've already blown half the day." Instead of stopping, she made a U-turn back out into the street and headed in the direction of Building 17. "I'll make up for it tonight. Just have to skip Johnny Carson."

CHAPTER 21

Monday, April 10, 1978
Sand Point Naval Station, Seattle
Building 17, 13th Naval District

Jerome's immediate superior was thoroughly positive about the dead man's work performance. He claimed Jerome had been the best cargo handler and lift truck operator he'd had. Given his praise for the man, Duncan started worrying the prosecution might find some way to use him as a witness and slip in some of his testimony about their victim's fine character.

"Just what were his duties here?" Sydney asked the Leading Chief as they were led back from their tour through the big warehouse.

"Mostly loading, organizing, and sorting cargo so it can be correctly stored or directed to its proper destination. He handled a lift truck when shippers came in. As a petty officer third class, he did some supervision when we had additional men, but we're almost always short-handed here. Jerome spent most of his time working the floor."

"Did he do any filing? Handle any of the paperwork on shipments that came through?"

"Nah, he had plenty to do right out here. There are three good-sized warehouses on this base plus some old aircraft hangars from the WWII days when this was an active airbase. The place was mostly empty until about three years ago.

"When Viet Nam ended, some of the Navy's low-security, non-armament surplus came here. We're now a logistical storage and trans-shipment point for the Pacific Northwest. This one warehouse may look empty right now, but that can change in a hurry.

"When a shipment comes in for storage, we offload it here, sort it, and then ferry the contents to longer-term storage elsewhere on the base. And we assemble shipments here that are headed out. So, we try to keep this space freed up as much as possible. All we keep in here are the occasional household goods. They're seldom around for more than a few days. Everything else gets put away as soon as possible. I take care of the paperwork myself. My boys do the heavy lifting, I like to say."

"He did have a desk though?"

"Yeah, sure. This one right here." The chief laughed. "But it was mainly a place to set his coffee. Maybe sign off on a shipping receipt. He also studied for his third class exams here. While some other guys out on the floor did his job."

"So, if he had shipping invoices in his desk, it would be unusual?" Sydney asked.

"Why do you ask that, ma'am?"

"There were some among his personal effects. We understand they were taken from his desk."

"Dang, I can't imagine why he'd have had any shipping invoices."

"I don't know either, Chief," said Duncan. "But there were a couple of them in with his personal effects. The stuff NIS collected from Jerome's desk after he was killed."

"Well, hell, I'd like to see what those were. Did they look something like this?" He reached inside his office door and took a clipboard off the wall. On it was a pile of light pink and light green-colored invoices printed on the flimsy, pressure-sensitive paper typically used for typing multiple copies of a single standard form.

"Yes, that's it," said Sydney, looking at the top invoice. "Except white."

"White paper? Hell, that wasn't an invoice. Least not one of ours."

He pointed to the clipboard. "There's also blue ones, but those stay with the shipper, so we never keep them here."

"Could it have been a photocopy?"

The Chief smiled. "You see a copy machine anywhere? We've been trying to get one down here for two years. Every time we need a copy, I have to send a guy up to the Admin Office. Damn nuisance. As a result, you don't see many copies lying around. Nah, you must have seen something else. Besides, I'd sure as hell know it if I had an invoice missing."

"And you can't think of any reason Jerome would have had one?

"No reason I know of."

Within minutes after leaving Building 17, the two lawyers were back in the NIS office asking to take another look at Jerome's personal effects. Pursuant to their agreement on the walk over, Duncan engaged Wyman in conversation in the other room while Sydney took another look for the shipping invoices she'd seen earlier. They'd decided not to ask for copies since that would bring them to the attention of the prosecution. Instead, she was to surreptitiously take notes. If they needed copies later, they could come back for them. As long as the original documents remained secure.

When they left NIS for the second time that day, Larry Wyman looked even more puzzled.

"So, what did you find?" Duncan asked the moment they were outside the building.

"I was wrong about how many. There was only one invoice, mixed in with some other miscellaneous papers. But it *is* a shipping invoice, a photocopy. It was labeled "household goods" and was shipped out of Navy Base Subic Bay in December of last year. There's a 'received' stamp on it from Navy Logistics Support Activity, Sand Point dated December 29."

"So, it wasn't from the shipment of drugs they seized?"

"No. There were eight separate cartons listed on the invoice labeled 'household goods' and numbered 1-8. You think these could have been more drugs?"

"I don't know," Duncan said. "Kind of seems unlikely that close to the shipment they caught in late January. Probably has nothing to do with anything. Was there a recipient's name on the invoice?"

"Yeah, it's right here . . . It's Brier. Commander Walter Mathew Brier. It originated at Naval Station Subic. Under 'destination' it said 'LSA Sand Point, Seattle'. Would that mean this was the *final* destination? Or could it have been headed somewhere else?"

"Sounds to me like Brier or his local shipper must have picked the stuff up right here. Could be he was transferred to the Seattle area. Or maybe he retired here. If he's located within the 13th Naval District, I can find that out in a hurry."

Once they were back at his office, Duncan picked up his phone and called his friend, Lt. George Denton, at 13th Naval District Personnel. Commander Brier had indeed retired and been recently transferred to inactive, U.S. Naval Reserve status, so it was fortunate that they still had his service record. He was currently residing at an address in Mountlake Terrace, a suburban community just north of Seattle. Duncan copied down the contact information.

Sydney suggested that Duncan make the call. Keep it "between officers and Navy men." She sounded amused at her own suggestion, and he knew she was teasing him. But she was right. He picked up the phone again and dialed.

Most of the call was unremarkable. Yes, Brier had recently retired. Yes, he'd had his household goods shipped from his former station at Subic Bay to his new home, Seattle. He'd had his whole family with him in Subic for two years. Their belongings had arrived in early January. Nothing had been lost, everything accounted for, "same as when it went in the boxes in Subic."

When Duncan asked Brier if he knew anything about drugs being smuggled in through household goods, Brier seemed sincerely shocked. "Drugs," he said. "I sure don't know anything about any drugs. I hope you don't think I'd be involved in something like that."

"We found your invoice among the belongings of a man murdered on the base," Duncan said.

"Murdered!" Brier repeated. "What does all this have to do with me?"

"Did you have any dealings with a Petty Officer Steven Jerome here at Sand Point?"

"No. None at all. A private mover picked the stuff up at Sand Point and delivered it all right to my doorstep. I didn't deal with anyone at Sand Point. Maybe he had the invoices because of his job. Sorry, I'm afraid I can't help you."

"Right. Well, thanks for the information." Duncan hung up the phone and turned to Sydney.

"So, what did he say?" she asked.

"He said he never came to Sand Point or had any interaction with anyone at Sand Point. Everything was delivered to his home in Mountlake Terrace. Knows nothing about drugs or Jerome." Duncan paused thoughtfully. "Kind of anxious sounding though . . . and he made a point of saying that everything had arrived 'just like it had gone into the boxes in Subic.'"

"What are you thinking?"

"I'm not sure—there *was* one other thing. He said Jerome may have had the invoices because of his job."

She thought for a moment. "You didn't say anything about Jerome's job."

"No. I didn't, did I?"

CHAPTER 22

Tuesday, April 11, 1978
Seafirst Bank Building, Seattle
Law Offices of Steiner, Bentley and Waterhouse

Commander Walter Briar had been reluctant to meet Sydney face-to-face.

"Let me put it to you this way," she'd said when she phoned him on Tuesday morning. "I think you're going to want to hear what I have to tell you. And *you* should want to talk to *me*. It's in *your* best interest." When he didn't respond right away, she felt certain their hunch about him had been right. There was something fishy about that invoice. He agreed to meet her the next afternoon at a cafe near his home in Mountlake Terrace.

To make up for the time she was going to miss at the office the following day, Sydney worked late on Tuesday night. It was after eight when Steiner came in and sat down across from her. He was in his early sixties, a formal man whose idea of relaxing was to loosen his tie. Sydney felt comfortable enough with him, although she was well aware of the fact that his firm was his life's work and his number one priority.

"One of your colleagues tells me you're going to be out of the office tomorrow afternoon." She had declined a partner's request that she stand in for him on a 1:30 motion. Had he complained?

"That's right. I have a meeting in Mountlake Terrace tomorrow afternoon."

"For that Navy case?"

"Yes. I need to speak to a potential witness."

"Dammit, Sydney. You're not making it easy for me. Your billable hours have fallen off substantially in the last couple of months. I assume you know that."

"Yes, sir. I have spent a fair amount of time on the Navy case of late. The trial is scheduled for the end of April." She was feeling defensive but also annoyed. Although the case had become more complicated and time-consuming than she'd originally expected, she didn't think she'd overstepped the bounds of their understanding.

"All right," Steiner said, standing up. "But when the trial's over, that's it. You're going to have to call a halt to pro bono work. At least for a while. You understand?"

"I'm sorry if I've inconvenienced anyone, Mr. Steiner. I won't take on anything new without talking to you." She hoped she didn't sound insubordinate. If she did, Steiner chose not to react. Since she was working until nine or ten o'clock each night to make sure she didn't get too far behind, it seemed unfair of him to criticize her. Although she had to admit that her fellow associate attorneys also put in some very long hours. And on firm business. They were who she was competing with. So maybe he had a point.

At 3:00 p.m. Wednesday afternoon, Sydney was entering a small café near Mountlake Terrace. She and Duncan had decided to have her meet with Brier instead of him on the assumption that she might seem less threatening than a uniformed JAGC officer. The cafe had heavy wooden tables and uncomfortable wood chairs. But it was nearly vacant—the perfect place for a private conversation.

Walter Brier arrived minutes later. From his military ID, she had expected someone thin and stern looking. But the man who walked over and introduced himself reminded her of a teddy bear with glasses. She took an almost immediate and involuntary liking to him.

"Sydney Warren?" he asked, putting out his hand. "Hi, I'm Walt Brier." He looked down at her coffee cup. "Do you want a cookie to go with that?" She assured him she was fine. "I'll be just a minute," he said as he turned toward the counter.

When he came back and sat down across from her, she sensed an underlying uneasiness. Maybe it was his usual demeanor, or maybe, as they suspected, he had something to hide.

"These are good," he said, holding up a very large chocolate chip cookie. "Sure you won't change your mind? I bought an extra one to take home for Myrna. You can have it and I'll get another for her."

"No thanks. Is Myrna your wife?"

"Yes, she wanted to come with me, but I told her this was a Navy thing and wouldn't take long."

"Do the two of you miss the Philippines?" she asked. It was posed as a social inquiry, but she intended it as the first step in steering the conversation in the right direction.

"Myrna does. She loved the shopping. And having help around the house. I think she misses her friends in base housing."

"And you?"

He thought for a moment. "Retirement is hard in some ways. But it's good to be home."

"More rain here I bet."

He laughed. "I'm from Seattle. I know what to expect." Then Brier took a deep breath, and said, "Look, Ms. Warren. I know you didn't drive up here to discuss the weather. I don't mean to be rude, but it's probably best if you just get to the point."

"All right, fair enough." She looked at him without blinking. "You understand who I am and what my position is?"

"Yes, I believe so. You're defending a sailor in a court-martial, right? A murder case."

"That's right. Lieutenant Carmichael and I are co-counsel. The young man we're defending is accused of killing Steven Jerome."

"That's what Carmichael said. What I don't understand is how I have anything to do with it." Brier had begun tearing up the small paper napkin that he had used for his cookie into long thin strips.

"Well, Jerome worked in logistics and handled the shipments that came in from Subic Bay." She paused for effect. "He was also suspected of being involved with drug smuggling."

Brier interrupted. "As I told Mr. Carmichael, I know nothing about Jerome or drugs."

Sydney gave him what she considered her probing look. "So why do you think he had a photocopy of your household goods shipping invoice?"

"I have no idea." He shook his head. "I don't understand. Why wouldn't he?"

She cocked her head to one side as if puzzled, a trick she had learned that was supposed to throw someone off guard. "You're sure that everything in your containers was exactly like it had been when they left Subic Bay?" When he hesitated, she added, "The boxes were numbered, I understand."

"We packed up our things in crates, but someone at the base shipped them."

"So, if something was added to your household goods, you wouldn't know . . . until you received the boxes at this end. Is that correct? You didn't supervise the loading?"

"Well, I did make sure that everything was there." He looked down at the shredded napkin as if surprised at what he had done and hastily pushed it aside.

Sydney sighed a deliberate sound of exasperation and shook her head. "Look, Mr. Brier, I've been sitting here trying to figure out how a nice person like you could have gotten mixed up in a drug smuggling operation. And to be honest, it seems unlikely. Although . . ." She paused to let him feel the full weight of the implicit accusation. "Although," she began again. ". . . *not* impossible. A little extra retirement money. No direct contact with the smugglers. All you had to do was let someone use your household goods delivery to hide the drugs. That's what happened, isn't it?"

"No, that's NOT what happened," he responded quickly. "How

could you possibly think . . ." He stopped abruptly, as if he'd lost his train of thought.

Sydney decided to let him have it. "Let me explain something you might not know about conspiracy law. Something you might not be aware of. A little free legal advice, okay?"

He nodded and stretched his neck as if trying to relieve tension.

"To be guilty of a crime like murder or smuggling as a conspirator or accessory, it isn't necessary that you actually commit the crime yourself. You don't even necessarily have to *know* about it. All that *is* necessary is that you form an understanding and come to some sort of agreement with another participant to perform some illegal act. Once you've done that, and steps are taken in furtherance of the scheme, you're in *all the way*, even to the extent of becoming responsible for other related crimes you may never have originally intended.

"Any participation in a scheme to violate the law, which facilitates or results from the crime you know about, even to a small extent, is sufficient to make you just as guilty as any other participant on all other crimes. It doesn't matter whether you're aware of the specific crime or of the full extent of the conspiracy. Do you understand what I'm telling you?"

"Yes, I think so," he said solemnly.

"But you're in luck. Lieutenant Carmichael and I are *not* the police. We have no obligation to report to the police. No obligation to tell anyone at all if we should happen to learn of the commission of a crime. Is that clear?"

He nodded. Looking only slightly less frightened.

"Our only obligation is to see to it that our client receives a fair trial. In fulfilling that obligation, Mr. Brier, we need to find out what your dealings were with Steven Jerome. We're going to find that out whether you tell me today, or whether we discover it in some other way. You need to understand that we *will* find out. I guarantee that. What I'd like is for you to tell me about it right now, voluntarily."

"Nothing I've done has anything to do with your case. I'm sure of it."

Sydney moved in with her strongest argument. "Look, I don't see why you can't be kept out of this. You and your wife. Depending on what you tell me. I honestly don't think you're someone who would knowingly be involved in a murder. If I'm right, you'll be a lot better off dealing with me than you would be answering to NIS. Or maybe the FBI. I can promise you I'll do my very best to keep this whole conversation just between us. What do you say?"

Brier studied her for a moment, obviously trying to decide what to do. "I'm absolutely sure that what I did had nothing to do with your case."

"Well, if it doesn't, then you're off the hook. Legal or illegal, you'll never hear from me again. I give you my word."

He tossed the shredded napkin into the empty glass ashtray. "It was just a favor for a friend. That's all it was. And I sure as hell never expected it would end up getting me involved in a murder investigation."

"I'm sure you didn't." She tried to look sympathetic. Actually, she *did* feel sorry for him. She believed him when he said he wasn't knowingly involved.

"And it had nothing whatever to do with drugs. Your friend Carmichael mentioned drugs too. But it had nothing to do with that. I just agreed to help a friend get some souvenir rifles into the country in our household goods. Three of them he'd collected when he was in Nam. Viet Cong weapons. He has an in-law who's a gun buff. That's all it was. Three rifles. Just three old rifles, no drugs."

"Rifles?" Sydney was thrown by Brier's confession.

"AK-47s. A lot of soldiers bring a couple home."

"Aren't those illegal to have, I mean outside the military?"

"I don't know. I guess they are, at least to bring into the country like that. It's a common practice. And I've never known of anyone who's been prosecuted for it."

"What did you do?" she asked.

"I just put the extra package in with my stuff. It was to be removed when the containers arrived at Sand Point. I wasn't supposed to ever see that package again. And everything went as planned until . . ."

"Until . . . ?"

"Okay, so yeah, I know Jerome. At least I've spoken with him. He was the one who was supposed to remove the package and pass it along.

Only he got greedy. He called me and wanted another $200. Said he smelled Cosmoline and knew that there were guns in that package. I tried, but I couldn't get him to back off."

"What did you do?" Sydney asked.

"I told my friend about it and he said he'd take care of it."

"And you never heard from Jerome again?"

"Nope. Just that one phone call. And I know what you're thinking, but this friend is someone I've known for years. Someone I'd trust with my life. In fact, I have. He wouldn't have murdered Jerome."

"Would he have paid Jerome off?"

"That's what I assumed. But I never asked. I knew he felt bad about me getting that call, so I just let it go."

"Someone you'd trust with your life, huh?"

"Some years back he was my Commanding Officer for ten months in Vietnam. He absolutely didn't do drugs. There's no way he'd risk his naval career by smuggling them into the states. And he definitely wouldn't get involved in a murder over a couple of souvenir rifles."

Sydney thought about it a moment. "I meant it when I said that I'll keep your secret if it is at all possible. But it does seem to me you *are* involved here. In whatever *it* is."

"Oh God, conspiracy." Brier looked panicked. "Maybe I need to go right now to NIS and tell them all of this. Explain everything to them. Maybe I wouldn't come out too badly."

"Maybe, I can't say."

"Damn. I knew better. I only did it out of friendship."

Sydney was torn. She needed leverage, but she didn't want to press too hard and have him go running to NIS and tip them off to their trial strategy. Nor did she want him running to another lawyer. What she needed was a cooperative witness. In the end, her favorable impression of the man made her decide to be honest with him.

"Look, Mr. Brier. I'm going to tell you something that you need to know. You've been straight with me. Now I'm going to trust you. But first, I want you to promise me that if we need you as a witness in Beck's case, you'll testify. Will you do that?"

"I don't lie under oath, Ms. Warren. I may not have shown very good judgment in this instance, but if I'm called to testify, I'll tell the truth."

"I hope you mean that. If you back out on me, I can guarantee we would find a way to make life very difficult for you. The fact is, however, you're not in all that much risk here."

"But I thought you said . . ."

"That package is long gone. And Jerome is dead. All we have is a shipping number and your name and address on the invoice. That proves nothing in a court of law."

He sighed. "And what I've just told you?"

"Well, it's an admission against interest. Perfectly admissible evidence, if I were to report it, which I have no intention of doing . . . unless you force me to."

Brier looked stunned. "I can't believe it. You've walked me right into this. How stupid could I be?" He shook his head. "Stupid. Stupid."

"I think 'decent,' would be the more accurate description. Of course, you could deny it. They might believe you instead of me. But I meant what I said about not reporting it. I'm not trying to tell you what to do, but if I were you, I'd hang tough on this. I don't think it's certain, or even very likely, that you're going to get involved. Not if you tell me one more thing. The one thing you've been avoiding telling me for the past fifteen minutes."

"What's that?"

"The name of your friend."

"My friend . . ."

"The person who gave you the package to bring back."

"I'd rather not say."

"Of course you wouldn't. But you've already given me some clues. I should be able to figure it out on my own."

"I don't really have any choice, do I?"

"Not the way I see it."

"I don't actually know who physically delivered the package—it was left at the back door of my home one afternoon shortly before we left. But I know who made the arrangements. You have to understand how I feel about this. He is an old friend. Someone I served with in Vietnam. My former CO. We went through hell together and made it out the other side. When I said I trusted him with my life, I meant that literally. I haven't seen much of him lately, but those are experiences you don't forget. You can understand that, can't you?"

"I do understand. But the only way you can stay out of the courtroom, Mr. Brier, is if you tell me that name. It's likely I can follow up without involving you. And I can promise, sincerely, that I will make every effort to do just that."

He hesitated. "You aren't going to believe it when I tell you. But at least you'll understand why it's impossible for him to have had anything to do with that sailor's murder. I'd bet my life on it."

"Who is it, Mr. Brier?"

"It's Clifford van Damme. Rear Admiral Clifford van Damme."

CHAPTER 23

Thursday, April 13, 1978
Sand Point Naval Station, Seattle
Law Center, 13th Naval District

Duncan was in his office when Sydney called the next day to tell him about her conversation with Walter Brier.

"Bullshit," he said in response to her big revelation.

"I'm serious, Duncan. Completely serious. That's it. That's what he told me."

"Bullshit," Duncan said again.

"And I believe him. I'd swear this guy is telling the truth."

"AK-47 rifles?"

"That's what he said."

"I'll be damned."

"Of course, he never opened up the package. He did say it was the right size and felt heavy enough to be guns. But he just made sure it went into the crate with their living room couch. It could have been anything."

"Admiral van Damme, huh?" Duncan considered. "I will say, the rifles seem a lot more likely than drugs. Brier is right, this is something people do. Bring a few 'war trophies' home with them in their household goods. Happens all the time. But van Damme?"

"I'll admit, I'm still a bit skeptical. Think about it. The rifle story would be a pretty good cover if you wanted to convince a friend to ship a package for you without him knowing what was actually in it."

"Was van Damme supposed to pick up the package from Brier?" Duncan asked.

"No, Brier didn't want it in his stuff when they opened the crates at his home because of his wife. Van Damme promised he'd never see the package again after it left Subic. Jerome was apparently his inside guy in logistics, the person who was supposed to pull it from the shipment. I bet he made up that 'smelling Cosmoline' stuff as an excuse to put the squeeze on Brier and turn a few extra bucks. I'd bet all those household goods people know exactly what goes on with those shipments."

"Be pretty stupid, wouldn't it? Jerome puts the squeeze on Brier. Brier runs to van Damme. Bingo, Jerome is in a lot of trouble with the man." Duncan shook his head.

"I don't know. Jerome's knowledge put him in a position of power. He might have decided to take advantage. And he may not have known Brier's connection to van Damme."

"Maybe. But I still can't see it being drugs. There's everything wrong with that. To start with, the U.S. Navy has drug dogs climbing all over its household goods shipments these days. In Subic, and here. That's one of the ways they identified that shipment in January. If something was incredibly well-packaged, I guess it might get through. But it's hard to believe that van Damme would subject a good friend to that kind of risk. Besides, it's the last thing I'd expect of the Admiral. He hates drugs. He's a real hard-ass on all of our drug cases. It doesn't add up."

"He could be under some kind of pressure."

"Nah, the rifles make more sense. Jerome said he smelled Cosmoline." Duncan paused again. "But, either way, I don't think Jerome ended up dead over a lousy $200. Or over a few souvenir rifles."

"Me neither."

They both were silent for a moment. Their simple case was becoming very complicated.

Finally, Sydney said, "Listen, Duncan, I've been thinking about this ever since I spoke with Brier. We need to broaden our investigation. If van Damme isn't as squeaky clean as you seem to think, we've got to start asking ourselves about his role in Beck's prosecution. Think about all the grief we've had getting information out of NIS. You've said yourself that isn't how it usually happens."

"No, not common at all."

"And your transfer. Just think about your transfer and the battle we had getting it reversed."

"I know, but . . ."

"And you were transferred to somewhere within the Thirteenth Naval District. To someplace also under van Damme's jurisdiction, right?" Sydney asked.

"That's true."

"Who was in a better position to warn me to 'back off'?"

"Anonymous threats? It doesn't seem like his style," Duncan said.

"It wouldn't have necessarily been van Damme who initiated them. Maybe somebody he was working with. Someone who didn't mind getting his hands dirty."

"Now you're making him sound like some sort of crime boss."

"Well, remember when we won our motion in Federal District Court? Hell, Frank Merrill as much as admitted to me after court that he was ordered to do it. And I'd swear that Larry Wyman was initially ready to let me have a look at Jerome's personal effects. Until he called back and said 'no'. Who'd he talk to? What changed his mind?"

"He'd have called Frank. Merrill probably stopped him. But still, the question is *why*?"

"The whole thing goes back to our battle to get their drug investigation files. It was like they were keeping some huge secret. At the same time, their informant was long gone—out of the Navy by then. The investigation was at a dead end. And we now believe Jerome was under investigation for using or selling drugs; we even have what we think is part of his confession. So what on earth could have been in that file that's so damaging to the prosecution?

"Even if there's something there that would help us argue that Willis, or maybe some other unknown person, might . . . *might* have had reason to kill Jerome, what's the big deal? We both know it's still a very thin argument. And I'm entirely convinced that if Captain Clayton had denied our motion, we might have had a reversible error. Frank Merrill must have advised them of that risk as well. Why are they pushing back so damn hard?"

"You think they want Beck convicted? Admiral van Damme wants Beck convicted? No matter what?"

"Yeah, I guess I do." She hesitated. Duncan could hear her tapping the phone. "But I don't really believe this is about systemic reverse discrimination, and surely it's not over some war souvenirs. Hypothetically, isn't it possible that van Damme's a part of some drug smuggling ring? If members of the ring killed Jerome, that would put van Damme under a lot of pressure to get a conviction."

"I see it, Sydney. But I still don't believe it. Although, even if there's nothing to all this drug smuggling, or even without the guns for that matter, we may have a case for some kind of command influence here."

"Command influence?"

"Under Article 37 of the Uniform Code of Military Justice, a commanding officer is prohibited from exercising undue influence on the court process, including on the prosecutor, defense counsel, or the judge hearing the case."

"All right then, I've got another question."

"Okay."

"We still don't know why Willis was sent before an admin discharge board while they left Jerome alone."

Duncan sat back in his chair and thought about it while Sydney continued her line of thought.

"Both were implicated by the same person at the same time, and for that matter, in the same statement. Willis gets an admin board. Jerome gets nothing. Why?"

"They were looking for more evidence to take him to a court-martial?"

"They had his confession—assuming that thing we got from Willis and Frost is the real thing. What more did they need?" she asked.

"You're right. It all fits. Maybe they were protecting Jerome because he knew something the Admiral didn't want revealed." Duncan paused.

"Unfortunately, if we claim command influence at this point, all they'd do is move the case to another command. Remedy their problem, and we're back to square one."

"But we think there's a lot more to this, right? So, let's find out."

"How?"

"We won't make any motion. But you simply ask Frank Merrill who was pushing such a hard line on your transfer. Ask him if he told Wyman not to let us see Jerome's personal effects. Ask him why he didn't want us to see the drug investigation file. Ask him, and maybe Wyman too, who stopped Wyman from letting us see Jerome's stuff."

"We may not get straight answers to those questions."

"We may get something, though. And we'll shake them up a bit. Isn't it worth a try?"

Duncan started with Wyman, catching him off guard by stopping by NIS unannounced. When asked about the Jerome drug investigation file, Wyman waffled but, when asked directly, finally acknowledged that it was the Commandant's office that had insisted, even before their discovery request, that the investigation be considered privileged.

"They wanted NIS to keep that investigation open, to continue working all possible leads, and to keep the informant who had implicated Jerome confidential. I didn't see the logic, but, hey, I work for the U.S. Navy. If they want to keep working on a dead-end investigation, it's up to them. As for Jerome's personal belongings, it was Merrill who held things up. And, when a case is headed for trial, NIS investigators do what the prosecution asks them to do."

After talking with Wyman, Duncan decided to skip his noon workout and arranged to get together with Frank Merrill over lunch at the Officer's Mess. They exchanged comfortable, normal chitchat until the Filipino Steward had delivered their Cobb salads. Then Duncan made what he hoped sounded like a casual, friendly inquiry about why Merrill had made such a big deal over their request to see Jerome's personal belongings since there was obviously nothing there.

Merrill grinned. "*Obviously*, there was. You found that other pair of shoes. And some worthless paperwork." He looked at Duncan across his ham sandwich and turned mock serious. "Anyway, what makes you think there's nothing there?" He wiggled his eyebrows up and down. "We still haven't listed our exhibits for trial." He took a bite of sandwich.

Duncan got serious. "Look Frank, we need to be square with one another. We both know resisting our motion to view those belongings was a bullshit call. And I for one have too much respect for you as a lawyer to believe you'd waste everybody's time, including the court's, just to make points in some silly game. You did that for a reason. And I don't think it has a damn thing to do with the merits of the case."

Merrill suddenly seemed uncomfortable, a bit angry even. His response was firm. "Look, I am not going to discuss my communications with my client any more than I'd expect you to discuss your communications with yours."

"I see."

Merrill glared at him. "See what?"

"You communicated with your client about this. It's exactly as I thought. It wasn't your idea to obstruct our investigation. It came from the Commandant's office."

"I did *not* say that."

"Oookay. So how about another one? Who was it that was so determined to get me transferred to Fleet Air Whidbey and take me off the case? I know damn well you would *never* have readily agreed to that. I suspect you recommended very strongly against it. Regardless of your well-presented arguments in court, you and I both know full well that to have taken me off the case would have resulted in reversible error."

"Maybe."

"*Maybe?* I don't think so; more like a sure thing. And if so, it would have been a huge waste of everybody's time, including yours."

This time Merrill said nothing. He just shrugged.

"Look Frank, you and I are both Navy lawyers. We're professional colleagues. Personally, I get damned angry when some line CO starts interfering with my independence as an attorney and officer of the court. And I'd bet you do too. You may not *have* to tell me who it was that made my transfer happen. But if you *want* to, there is nothing in the ethics or otherwise to prevent that."

Duncan gave Merrill a moment to consider what he was saying before adding, "Moreover, I believe you take your special obligations as a prosecutor seriously as well. As you know better than most, unlike a defense counsel, you have an obligation as trial counsel to see justice done, to assure that the system functions as the law requires. And as a fellow lawyer who cares about doing the right thing, I think you *want* to tell me. Here's your chance: It was Captain Wallace who directed you to fight for that transfer, wasn't it?"

Frank Merrill sat silent over his cooling coffee and his half-eaten sandwich. He leaned back and crossed his arms. For a moment, he just stared at Duncan. Then he made a slight, but unmistakable nod. Finally, he took the napkin from his lap, crushed it, dropped it on the table, and stood. "Well, I'd better get back to work. Got a lot to do if I'm going to make sure that nutcase client of yours pays for his crimes."

CHAPTER 24

Thursday, April 13, 1978
Sand Point Naval Station, Seattle
Law Center, 13th Naval District

After mulling over his conversation with Merrill while finishing his lunch, Duncan headed back to the Law Center. At the top of the stairs, rather than turning left toward his own office, he turned right toward the office of the Law Center commanding officer. Captain Wallace's door was ajar, but his civil service secretary announced Duncan over the intercom anyway.

"Yes, Carmichael. Come in."

"I hope I'm not interrupting, sir. I have something I believe is important…"

"No, no. Come on in. What can I do for you?"

Duncan drew a questioning glance from the Captain when, unbidden, he gently closed the office door behind him. Then, at a wave from Wallace, he took a seat in the indicated chair. "It's about this Beck case, Captain. I'd like to ask your opinion on something. If you don't mind."

Wallace smiled. "You can always ask."

"Yes, sir." With his prepared introduction delivered, Duncan got to the point: "It has to do with my transfer to Whidbey. Were you surprised at the outcome we got from the Federal District Court, Captain?"

"Well . . .," Wallace smiled again. "Yes and no. I was surprised they took jurisdiction. But not really surprised at the outcome. Why do you ask?"

"So, it must be your opinion that removing me from Beck's case would have violated his rights to Navy counsel?"

"I did think there might be some doubt. But that young woman you're working with made a sound point. I think the outcome was probably the right one." Wallace raised his eyebrows. "But of what possible interest can my opinion be to you at this stage?"

"Well, sir, if you'll bear with me . . ." Duncan felt the tension in his shoulders as he continued. "Am I correct in assuming that you advised Admiral van Damme of your view of this matter?" When Captain Wallace didn't immediately respond, Duncan tried another approach. "As you'll recall, before going to Federal District Court, Ms. Warren sent Beck's petition to set the transfer aside up the chain of command. When the Admiral made his decision on that petition, did he have the benefit of your opinion on this matter?"

Captain Wallace settled into his high-backed chair and smiled thoughtfully across his large desk. "I sometimes forget this side of you, Lieutenant. You're the picture of a competent and respectful Navy officer. But underneath you're all lawyer. And you never let up, do you?" He sighed. "Well, you've got your job to do. But I guess you know I have mine. As you are aware, I can't answer that question. In a matter of this type, my relationship with the Commandant is one of attorney and client. Our discussions concerning that petition are confidential."

To the taboos Duncan had already broken in this case, he could now add tricking his own JAGC Commanding Officer into an indiscretion. Wallace was fair-minded. But he would remember this exchange.

"I understand, sir. I hope you didn't mind my asking."

He began to rise in anticipation of leaving. But the Captain remained seated, still leaning back in his chair but with more to say: "Don't tell me you're seriously intending to claim command influence by the convening authority on this one?"

"Oh, no. No, sir." Duncan realized that the last thing he and Sydney needed, at this point, was to have Captain Wallace report *that* to Admiral van Damme. There might be a claim of command influence, but they certainly didn't want the Command getting prepared for it ahead of time, let alone being warned in time to maybe even change the convening authority. "No, I was coming back from lunch, and, well, I've been curious. I've never had a situation like the one with the transfer before. It seemed to me that it ended up getting resolved correctly. I just wanted to understand a bit more about how it happened." His explanation sounded feeble, even to him.

But Wallace's smile was back. Perhaps he'd dodged the bullet. "Well, you keep up the good work, Carmichael. It's a shame we couldn't put you in that Fleet Air Whidbey job. But we'll keep our eye out for something just as good for your next berth."

Duncan walked back to his own office wondering whether the Captain's kindly parting words had been a promise . . . or a threat.

When he called Sydney back after he met with Captain Wallace, she seemed to think the evidence was clear. But Duncan was not as convinced. He still found it hard to believe that there was even a small chance that Admiral van Damme could be involved in drug smuggling. But neither could he see how the much smaller matter of smuggling in some war souvenirs was enough to explain what they had learned. And now, in addition to everything else, they could add the fact that the Admiral was apparently willing to buck the advice of his own lawyers and to risk a likely reversal of the case on appeal just to assure a conviction of SA Arnie Beck. Why the hell would Beck's conviction or acquittal make the least difference to a U.S. Navy Rear Admiral?

"You say Captain Wallace wouldn't actually admit to advising the Admiral of this?" Sydney persisted.

"No, but it's clear to me that he must have. And Frank Merrill admitted it too, with Captain Wallace. It's fairly obvious that the Admiral chose to ignore their advice."

"Duncan, we essentially know van Damme is involved in an illegal shipment of some kind—maybe guns, but also quite possibly drugs. In either case, Jerome was a confederate in the matter and was paid money to keep silent after he threatened to reveal the transaction. We also think it's likely that Jerome was protected from an administrative discharge, maybe even prosecution, perhaps because of his involvement and his knowledge. And we're pretty sure your boss, van Damme, has been torpedoing our case in hopes of assuring our client's conviction. The only question left is, what are we going to do about it?"

"Well, to start with, we need to lay this out for our client. If we act on this 'information' it's going to create a firestorm. And he's the one who'll be at its very center. Maybe the one who'll face the worst of the consequences."

CHAPTER 25

Thursday, April 13, 1978
Sand Point Naval Station, Seattle
Law Center, 13th Naval District

Sydney walked into Duncan's office just before 1500 that same afternoon. And soon afterward, Seaman Apprentice Beck arrived. He had clearly lost some weight and was looking unkempt. He needed a haircut and had some stubble on his chin.

"How are you, Arnie?" Sydney asked. She sounded concerned, but to Duncan it seemed a gratuitous question. What did it matter if he'd lost a few pounds and hadn't cleaned up for them?

Beck didn't answer.

"Are they feeding you properly?" she persisted.

He shrugged. "Whatever."

"If you're not getting proper food and treatment, you'll let us know, right?" Duncan asked to make Sydney happy.

"Screw that," Beck said, with force. "I don't give a damn about the food. You just concentrate on getting me the hell out of there, okay?"

Duncan motioned to Sydney that she should proceed. After all, she was the one on a first-name basis with their client.

"Arnie, we've discovered some unusual things about your case that we thought you should know. It looks like you may have been caught up in something more complicated than we expected. And you will have to decide what you want us to do next."

Beck at least looked interested.

"You need to understand, right off, that we're not 100% sure about what we're about to tell you. But we are beginning to suspect that the flag officer who is officially responsible for bringing this murder charge against you may actually be connected to people that have been smuggling drugs into the U.S. through the Logistics Support Activity here at Sand Point."

Beck blinked, as though not fully comprehending what she'd said.

Sydney continued. "We've been trying to trace this drugs angle, and . . ."

"NIS? You're saying NIS is smuggling drugs?"

"No, not NIS, Arnie. We're talking about the Commandant here at the 13th Naval District, Admiral van Damme."

"Admiral van Damme?" Beck stared at them with his mouth open. "No way."

"I know it's hard to believe but, if we're right about this, it's going to be *a very big deal*. And if we bring it up, a lot of powerful people are going to be upset. There's some risk involved, for you and your case."

"Admiral van Damme." Beck was shaking his head.

"Here's the deal, Arnie," Sydney said. "If Admiral van Damme is involved, he has a strong personal reason to want to see you convicted. You understand what I'm saying?"

"You mean he had something to do with framing me?" Beck seemed to be having an even harder time than Duncan had believing the Admiral was involved.

"We can't be sure yet. I suppose it *is* possible. But what we've discovered is that it is Admiral van Damme who has been giving us such a hard time defending your case."

"Huh?"

"You know how the prosecution has fought us every step of the way, right? We wanted the drug investigation file—they denied it. Mr. Carmichael was doing a good job defending you—they tried to remove him. We needed to see Jerome's personal belongings—they refused. It's happened again and again. We're convinced all that was a concerted effort by Admiral van Damme to make absolutely sure you get convicted. The way it looks to us, the Admiral has been trying to torpedo your defense from the very start."

Beck seemed flabbergasted, eyes wide in disbelief. After what felt like a long silence, he asked, "Can't you make some kind of motion or something? Like you did before? Make him stop?"

"It isn't really that simple, Arnie. We need to have evidence, good evidence, if we're going to prove it. At this point, we don't have enough. It will be very risky to bring it up without the serious ammunition to prove it. But just as important, if we bring a motion like that, and even if we win, they will simply hand your case over to another command and use another officer to convene your court. And we'll end up starting from scratch. We might have a case for appeal, but you'd almost certainly spend many more months while we waited to get a decision. And we could lose on that appeal as well."

Beck was looking at the floor as she talked, shaking his head. Suddenly, he exploded. "Fucking A!" he said, taking a deep, exasperated breath. "I should of fucking known!" One look at Sydney's face told Duncan that she was as startled by the outburst as he was.

Sydney leaned forward. "A couple of days ago I talked with a man who may have unwittingly helped Admiral van Damme bring some of these drugs into the country. He may be willing to testify, but he could also fold on us if he's pushed. One of the things we need to decide, Arnie, is whether to go to NIS with this. Or perhaps to the FBI."

"No!"

"No?" Sydney said. "You don't want us to report this?"

"No! Oh shit! I should've known."

Sydney looked puzzled. "What should you have known, Arnie?"

"Shit!" Beck crossed his arms and sank into what looked like a very bitter and determined silence.

"If there's something you haven't told us, Arnie, start coming clean right now," Sydney said. "We're doing our very best to help you, at some personal risk to ourselves and our careers. But as I told you the first day we met, we can't succeed if you tie our hands by keeping secrets from us."

Oh great, thought Duncan. Here it comes. At this point, they had scratched up the makings of a halfway reasonable defense. Whatever this guy was hiding, Duncan had serious doubts about whether he really wanted to hear it.

Beck seemed to have suddenly shrunk in stature as he slouched in his chair and silently glared around the room from beneath Duncan's anti-drug "Keep off the Grass" poster on the wall behind him. He sighed heavily, avoiding their eyes, finally looking at the floor and withdrawing further into himself.

"We need to know what you're thinking, Arnie." Sydney coaxed. "You must trust us. Honestly, I don't see how you have any other choice. It's you that's looking at a possible life in prison. Please let us help you avoid that."

Finally, after a lengthy and uncomfortable gap in their conversation, Beck looked up at her. "Whatever we talk about is just between us, right?"

"That's right, Arnie. It's confidential. Both the law and our ethical rules as lawyers prohibit us from ever revealing anything you tell us without your clear permission."

"You gotta promise me. You gotta swear if I tell you this, you won't say anything to anybody. I mean it. Not *anything*. Ever."

"We do swear that, Arnie. It will be our secret."

Beck looked uncertainly at Duncan. Sydney looked too. Duncan hesitated, then nodded in agreement. Nowhere to go but forward. "Whatever you tell us will be absolutely confidential," he said.

Beck sighed again. He looked around the room as if checking to make sure they were alone. "All right, look, it's like this. See, my dad's in this group. A bunch of people who don't like what's happening in this country. I mean with the Negroes and the immigrants and with the war against religion and like all that. My dad's group wants to have their own country. Someplace where they can make their own laws and be left alone. They already have this big place where I come from, over in Eastern Washington. There's this church, and a meeting hall, and a place to practice fighting and that sort of thing. They have friends in other groups all over the U.S. In Canada too."

Duncan had originally picked up his pen to start taking notes, but the reference to "their own country" left him frozen. Where the hell was their client going with this!?

Sydney seemed just as astonished, but that didn't prevent her from encouraging Beck to continue. "All right," she said. "I see."

The rest of the story came out in a rush: "Well, they've made this deal, my dad and your Admiral. There's a bunch of M-16 rifles that were grabbed up at the end of the Viet Nam war. They're on their way here from the Philippines. It's Admiral van Damme that has them. He's got a whole shipload he's selling. He gave my dad some samples. I saw 'em myself. Back in January. And now they're trying to nail me for a murder I didn't commit."

"I don't understand, Arnie," Sydney said. "Why would they do that?"

"I don't know. Shit, man! They'll do anything for the cause. They've prob'ly decided I'd rat 'em out or something. Van Damme was supposed to protect me. Now you're telling me that he's screwing me over. Sure as hell, nobody's gonna believe a convicted murderer about nothin'."

"The Admiral was supposed to protect you?" Duncan asked. "How?"

"Keep me out of jail. Hah, look how that worked out. My dad said the Admiral would make sure they got me off. Said he was going to get me the best lawyer on the base. Hell . . ." He looked at Duncan. "It was *you* he was talking about. He's the reason I got you in the first place. Maybe you're in on it. How the hell do I know?"

Duncan shook his head. The story was incredible. Van Damme could easily have asked Captain Wallace to have him assigned to this defense. Wallace would never have thought twice about it. They would have expected him to make a solid defense, but probably a predictable one. Instead, he and Sydney picked up every rock and looked under it.

"Then someone told my dad he should contact the ACLU. We figured the more lawyers the better. But I've been sittin' in that damn cell for months and nothin's happening. Now you tell me about all these roadblocks you been runnin' into. Seems to me they've changed their minds. Decided to sell me out." Beck shook his head. "Maybe they're the ones that set me up in the first place. Oh, Christ . . ."

"Have you talked with your father about all this?" Sydney asked.

"No, I don't . . ." Then Beck suddenly looked at Duncan. "But *you've* talked with my dad, right? What've you told him? Does he know you caught on to what this Admiral is doin'? Have you told him you know I'm bein' screwed?"

"No. I've told him I can't discuss your case without your permission. It's all right, Beck. I'm sure he doesn't know we suspect anything."

Beck seemed satisfied. Sounding even more bitter, he said, "My dad doesn't give a shit about me. Never has. All he cares about is his goddamned Independence League. I figured they were helping me in order to keep me quiet. But I didn't care why. Long as I got out of that goddamned brig. Now this . . ."

Duncan's first impulse was to discount Beck's story. But there was too much corroborating evidence. He realized now that Brier's package must have contained arms after all, just as Brier claimed. But not some old, captured AK-47s as Brier had been told. Instead, they were probably three brand new U.S. M-16s, the most advanced light infantry weapons in history, the best the U.S. military had in its arsenal. They'd be the "samples" Beck senior had been shown. And now, there was supposedly a whole shipload of them coming, whatever the hell that meant.

As he studied Beck, Duncan felt that for perhaps the first time this client was actually telling them the truth. In a moment of weakness, he found himself feeling sympathetic toward this sailor who believed his own father might allow him to be unjustly convicted of murder if it meant protecting the interests of a group of right-wing crazies. Having spoken to Beck senior several times on the phone, Duncan was forced to reluctantly agree that the son's assessment of his father might be correct.

Sydney seemed to find Beck's confession intriguing rather than overwhelming. "And this shipment . . . the rest of these guns . . . when is that supposed to happen?"

"Any time now. It's coming into Canada. Mid to late April is what my dad said."

It was already April 13th. If Beck was right, there was precious little time to do anything about it.

"Arnie, if we're going to do you any good," said Sydney, "if we're going to prove that the Admiral has prejudiced your case or that he and others may have been involved in fabricating evidence against you, we're going to need help from the authorities. Maybe the FBI. You need to let us report this."

Beck snapped to attention. "No way!" he said loudly. "No goddamned way! You promised that this would be our secret. You say anything, you're going to get me killed."

Sydney held up a hand, palm down. "Don't worry, Arnie. We're not going to tell anyone unless you give us the go-ahead. But if you don't let us report this arms shipment, you're likely to end up convicted of murder. You do understand that, right?"

"I only told you so's you can get this Admiral van Damme off my case. That stuff you said about 'command influence.' You got to stop him from screwing me over. But if you make trouble for Dad or the Leader, they'll kill me. I'm serious. They'd kill all of us, sure as we're sittin' here. This is heavy shit for them. They're goin' to keep what they need of those M-16s for our own guys and sell the rest to groups all over the country. They stand to make a whole lot of money. This is the leverage they need to get national support for the cause, to become its leaders. You've got to keep this a secret. You've got to." He sounded truly terrified.

"We will, Arnie," Sydney reassured him as Beck turned to Duncan.

"Don't worry," said Duncan. "We'll keep your secret."

It was at this point that they were interrupted by a buzz from Duncan's office intercom. The civilian receptionist apologized for interrupting, but there was an important call for Sydney. She stood to take the call at the phone on Duncan's desk.

". . . uh-huh," she said. "Uh-huh. Have you looked on my desk? Right on the outside corner next to the Dictaphone there are some papers on this case. Uh-huh . . ., I see. All right then, I'm about through here. I'll be there within half an hour. Just copy everything and get it ready. . . No problem . . . I'm sure it's there somewhere. Don't worry, I'll find it."

She looked harried and frustrated as she put down the receiver and turned to Beck. "I have a problem to take care of at my office, Arnie. Mr. Carmichael and I are going to have to talk with you again in a day or two when we've thought this through. But you did the right thing to tell us about it. It's going to help—I'm sure of it. In the meantime, don't worry about your secret. It's safe with us."

With this final assurance, Beck was sent back to the brig. As soon as he was gone, Sydney picked up her jacket and her briefcase. "I'll call you later," she said. "We need to talk. Damn, I wish this hadn't come up right now."

"What is it?" asked Duncan.

"An exhibit for a brief that has to go out in tonight's mail. I'd swear I had it with the rest of the materials I gave my secretary this morning, but apparently not. I've got to get back to the office before the evening mail goes out so I can find the damn thing and my secretary can get it attached to the brief. I've had too much on my mind lately; I'm feeling scattered."

"Look, I'm really blown away by what's happening here. We need to discuss it."

"I know. I agree."

"Why don't I follow you downtown in my own car. We can talk at your office as easily as we can here. After you find your exhibit, we can sit down and try to figure out what the hell to do next."

She hesitated only for a moment. "Sure," she said as she headed toward the door. "Sounds good. Park in the garage and come up. We'll comp your parking. I'll see you there."

CHAPTER 26

Thursday, April 13, 1978
Seafirst Bank Building, Seattle
Law Offices of Steiner, Bentley and Waterhouse

"A Lieutenant Carmichael is here to see you."

"I'll be right out."

Sydney dropped off the missing exhibit with her secretary, gave her some last-minute instructions, made an apology for being so rushed, and headed for the lobby. Duncan was standing in the plush Steiner, Bentley and Waterhouse reception area examining the artwork as if he was in a museum. She suppressed a smile, thinking about how difficult it was for her to feel comfortable in his utilitarian environment, and now here he was getting a taste of the legal profession from her perspective.

"My office is down the hall," she said as she stepped alongside him. He turned toward her and blinked as though seeing her for the first time. She found herself wondering what he thought of her workplace . . . and of her. Was she attractive to this man?

The secretaries watched furtively as she led Duncan down the hall. She was acutely aware of the stir her visitor was creating. He *was* impressive in his dark uniform with its polished brass buttons and gold insignia. No doubt the staff grapevine would conclude that *he* was the reason she was spending so much time on the case. Oh well, let them gossip.

Once inside her office, she relaxed, but she could tell that Duncan was still feeling uncomfortable. He turned his hat round and round in his hands while checking out her office. "This suits you," he said finally.

What did that mean? "I like it," she said a bit defensively.

Their eyes met and held for a moment.

She sat down behind her desk and took out two legal pads. Duncan laid his hat on the couch, pulled his chair in front of her desk, and carefully centered one of the legal pads as was his inevitably irritating habit.

"So, what do you think?" she asked.

"I honestly don't know what to think. I sure as hell didn't see *this* coming."

"I assume we can proceed as if it *is* a matter of arms and not drugs."

"Well, if that's the situation, we're starting from scratch. We've got some serious work to do on our defense. And we have to decide what to do about that shipment of arms."

"It's not as if Arnie has made up some story to get himself off the hook for the murder charge. This doesn't necessarily do him any good. Hard to see how it suggests other suspects."

"Maybe. But unexplained complications are never a good thing for the prosecution." She saw Duncan put a number one on his legal pad and write "arms shipment" next to it. "Damn," he said. Then he wrote down "report to authorities?" as a subpoint.

Sydney read it upside down and protested. "You know we can't do that." She leaned forward, reached out, and put her finger on the subpoint. "Are you saying, 'The hell with client confidentiality'?"

"No, I'm just not sure where the line is. Aren't we required to report knowledge of crimes that are planned but not yet committed?"

"Yes. That's my understanding. But this isn't a crime *our client* is going to commit. What we have is knowledge of a potential future crime, which may be committed by third parties. And in order to report that, we would have to reveal the confidences of our client."

"These are *weapons*, Sydney. Freaking M-16s. A lot of them. Headed into the hands of what sounds like a bunch of dangerous radicals who are connected to other radicals. Who knows where these guns may end up? Or how they may be used."

"Don't you think I'm aware of the possibilities?" She shook her head angrily. "But Arnie was very specific about not wanting the information leaked. He's terrified."

"Maybe an anonymous tip . . .?"

"Sure. I can hear it now. You call up the Royal Canadian Mounted Police, disguise your voice, and say, 'Hi, I'm an American. Your friendly citizen informer. I can't give you my name. Or any real proof. But I happen to believe that a respected U.S. Navy Admiral is smuggling a shipload of surplus military arms into your county in the next couple of weeks and will be selling them to some neo-Nazis. I don't know where they will be unloaded . . . or when. But it should be stopped.'"

"Okay, okay. You've made your point," Duncan said.

"And if we report it, it *will* get back to Beck's father and ultimately implicate Arnie. And then us. If we plan to ever practice law again, we can't do that."

"Okay, I agree it's a bad idea." He wrote down a number two. "How about the fact that the arms are coming into Canada?"

"Do you think that affects our legal obligation to him?" she asked.

"Not really. But we should consider whether it makes a difference if the crime to be committed violates the laws of a foreign country."

Sydney rolled her uncapped ballpoint pen back and forth across the top of her blank legal pad. "Even if there is some exception to the rule, I don't think we have a choice. I think we have to keep our promise to our client. It's something he told us under the bond of confidentiality with the understanding it would be kept secret."

"I understand the ethics involved. But think about this in human terms. How are you going to feel when those guns are used against innocent people? All across the country."

They sat in silence for a few minutes. Finally, Duncan said, "We need to do some research."

"Okay, let's do it. You can leave your jacket here." Without his jacket he might be less conspicuous. She stood up.

"You mean we can do the research here?"

She smiled and motioned for him to follow.

The firm's impressive law library was just down the hall. She left him there working with the Washington Annotated Court Rules while she went to get them both coffees. When she returned, he'd already found the rule involved.

"Here," he said. "It's Rule for Professional Conduct—1.6. It's pretty specific. Been awhile since I actually read it. Take a look for yourself." He slid the book in her direction.

"CONFIDENTIALITY

1. A lawyer shall not reveal confidences or secrets relating to representation of a client unless the client consents after consultation . . . etc. . . . . except as stated in paragraph (b)
2. A lawyer may reveal such confidences or secrets to the extent the lawyer reasonably believes necessary:
3. To prevent the client from committing a crime . . ."

"That settles it then. Arnie is *not* the one who might be committing a crime with this shipment of guns."

Duncan looked defeated. "Even the American Bar Association agrees it has to be a crime committed by the client, not third parties."

"Then we keep our mouths shut, right?"

He closed the volume and put it back on the shelf. "Yes," he agreed. "The law is clear, but I don't have to like it." He sat down at the table and took a sip of coffee. "There's a moral issue here that I'm struggling with. I'm not sure I can live with myself knowing that I could have stopped those arms from entering the country."

Did he think *she* didn't care about the human consequences of remaining silent? "Well, if we continue to investigate, we might find something we can use to help our client and at the same time come up with a way to prevent those guns from getting into the wrong hands. You don't know until you've tried."

"What good will it do Beck to prove the shipment of guns exists? It just confirms that Jerome's demand for more money might have made the Admiral very nervous."

"It shows there were others involved who might have had motive to kill Jerome, including, strange as it may seem, perhaps the admiral who convened his court-martial. It certainly demonstrates why van Damme is not qualified to convene the case."

"Again, if we push that, they'll just have someone else convene it."

"Even so, I think we need to investigate van Damme." She looked at her watch. It was nearly six. "You hungry?"

"Now there's something we can definitely agree on."

"I wouldn't mind finding some place to talk where I wouldn't have to stare at a pile of work files. Let's go out to get something."

They went back to her office to grab their jackets, and she buzzed the night receptionist to tell her she was going out for a few hours. "If I get any calls, you can tell them I should be back in again later." Given the hours she was working lately, it was a good thing she didn't have a family to answer to. Or a boyfriend. Or any hobbies. Or a social life for that matter.

They headed for an unmarked back door that opened into the opposite end of the elevator bank hallway. Most of the offices were quiet. Only a few secretaries were still around, but quite a few of the lawyers were in their offices cramming in critical billable hours during the only part of the day when their phones finally stopped ringing. Several sets of curious eyes followed them as they passed by open office doors and glass-fronted conference rooms. Being seen with Duncan wasn't going to help her keep a low profile on her pro bono work. It would have been better if he had remained an anonymous military figure instead of a good-looking flesh and blood male in an imposing uniform.

"Your car or mine?" she asked as the elevator doors closed.

"Mine. As long as we're going somewhere, I'd just as soon get my car out of that high-priced concrete prison."

She laughed. "I picked up a parking comp card. But you obviously made the mistake of reading the rate schedule at the entrance."

"Fancy prices for fancy downtown lawyers. That I can understand. Other folks like the secretaries, clerks, and the like, I guess they take the bus, huh?"

His reference to fancy downtown lawyers rubbed her the wrong way, but she tried not to let it show. "Actually, the lawyers in the building get a monthly rate. And we comp visits by the firm's clients even though most of them can afford it. But the garage *is* pricey for a lot of people. That's what happens when there's a shortage of parking spaces."

"Good city planning."

"They're trying to 'encourage' people to ride the bus."

"It all probably works out fine for those who can afford not to."

She couldn't help smiling when she saw his car. His Plymouth four-door sedan was a dark, nondescript color and so lacking in personality that she would have pegged it a government motor pool vehicle if it hadn't been so old and worn out looking. He had parked on the fourth level from the street where the car was wedged into a space clearly labeled for a compact. She barely got the door open wide enough on the passenger side to get in.

"I know a fish-and-chips place out at Shilshole. Sound good?" she said.

"Sounds great."

She gave him directions, smiling to herself as they drove out of downtown toward Ballard. If he wanted inexpensive, she would give him inexpensive. There was a tiny take-out stand at the marina. They had good food, but there were no amenities. They'd have to eat outside at a wood picnic table or a bench along the waterfront. It was a reasonably nice evening for April. What did it matter that she wasn't dressed for it? A soiled skirt would be a small price to pay for taking that smug look off his face.

As they pulled into the parking lot near the north end of Shilshole Bay Marina, Duncan asked, "That it?" If he was surprised by the small square wooden structure surrounded by parking spaces, he didn't show it.

"Yes. We can either sit at one of those picnic tables or find a bench along the water."

"Sounds good." He exchanged his uniform jacket for a windbreaker, carefully laid out his jacket on the back seat, and placed his hat on top.

Pointing at the uniform jacket, she said: "That looks like it would be too warm in the summertime."

"In the summer they make khakis the uniform of the day. They're a lot cooler."

"Umm," she said, withholding comment concerning the whole alien notion of a "uniform of the day."

They went over and placed their orders. Then, while they waited, they sat at a table near the boat launch. A man and a young boy were attempting to get a small sailboat into the water, but the boat didn't want to slide off the trailer. The man in the pick-up truck kept backing further and further down the ramp until the truck's back wheels were partly submerged. The boy jumped up and down on the trailer hitch, trying to dislodge the boat. When it finally came free and the man then tried to drive the pick-up back up the ramp, the rear wheels spun out on the underwater slime. The event was accompanied by anxious shouts and curses.

After their orders were called, they went back to the same table. The pick-up truck was still there, its rear end even deeper in the water, with a rising tide. Another car had backed down in front of the truck, and they were stringing a rope between the vehicles.

They ate in silence while they watched the pick-up being towed to dry land. The boy was waiting impatiently by the sailboat at an adjacent float. Sydney started to relax, remembering other evenings like this when she and her family had taken their sailboat out for an evening run. Those were happy times.

It was getting dark, and with the darkness came a chilly breeze. Still, she was reluctant to leave. It was so peaceful sitting there, looking at the boats and the water.

"This is nice," Duncan said, interrupting her reverie.

"I've always liked the water."

"Didn't you mention that you used to go boating with your parents when you were young?"

Had she told him that? "Yes, Dad still keeps his boat here."

"Is it nearby?"

"At the other end of the marina."

"Do you have access to it? Is it big enough for us to get some work done there? Is there a table or something in it?"

"Yes, I have a key. And, yes, there's a table. It's plenty big enough for a yellow pad so you can make your lists." She was trying to be funny, but from the look on his face, she wasn't sure that was how he took it. "Sorry, I didn't mean that like it sounded."

"You didn't mean to imply that you think I'm anal retentive?"

"No, you're just . . . linear, that's all."

"Linear?"

"Yeah, you know . . ."

Simultaneously they said, "anal retentive." Then they both laughed.

They decided to drive the half mile plus to the other end of the marina, past row after row of boats stretching out from the shore toward the breakwater, masts, and rigging, all moored in nearly straight lines, all a bit different, like a parade of soldiers slightly out of step. Near the middle of the marina, they drove past the building complex that housed two restaurants, a number of offices, and a few shops. The parking lot was nearly full in that area, but further south they easily found another place to park.

"Does it cost much to moor here?" Duncan asked as they got out of the car.

"It's getting more expensive all the time. Even though it's saltwater and there's no covered moorage, you pay for the first-class facilities and for convenient access to Puget Sound. In-city waterfront property is a limited resource."

"A bit like downtown parking," Duncan said with a smile.

Sydney unlocked the high chain-link gate at the head of the long cement dock and led him past a series of finger floats and a long row of expensive looking yachts. The *Spindrift* was moored at a slip near the outer end of the dock. It was impressive looking, especially from the bow which was high, sharply pointed, and heavily reinforced with fiberglass. Oiled ironbark guards ran down both sides, protecting the fiberglass hull from damage by the anchor. A big heavy bronze casting with an anchor roller capped the entire point of the bow, and a thick bronze half-round ran down the front of the stem, disappearing beneath the water.

"Impressive," he said as he stood admiring the *Spindrift*. "I've never been around big pleasure boats."

"We've always had boats," Sydney said, not without a trace of pride.

"Mainly sailboats when I was younger. Dad bought the *Spindrift* for speed. Said he didn't have as much time to waste anymore. Sadly, he seldom uses it now. My brother and his family use it from time to time during the summer. And I occasionally take it out. We all kinda treat it as our own."

"How big is it?"

"Forty-six feet. It sleeps eight comfortably."

"We had a tent once that slept four. Not all that comfortably."

She glanced at him to make sure he was teasing. "I never had a tent," she said.

"Must have been tough."

She climbed a set of steps mounted to the dock and leading to the deck level, then stepped aboard. He followed, pausing on the deck to take a look around while she unlocked the door.

There was a single light on in the main cabin. She switched on a few more lights to brighten the atmosphere. Duncan gave the main salon a thorough once-over. "I didn't realize they had furniture in boats," he said. Everything in the main cabin was plush and expensive looking. It was basically a custom-built living room. Sydney never gave it much thought, but suddenly she was seeing it through Duncan's eyes.

"All the comforts of home. Except everything is fastened down," she said. She took off her jacket and headed toward the compact teak bar. "Want a drink?"

"You mean it literally, huh? All the comforts of home."

"I don't know about you, but I could use one."

"What do you have?"

"Gin, scotch, whiskey—whatever."

"Is there ice?"

"Yes, no lime though." She was pouring herself a gin and tonic.

"No lime. What a shame. Any soft drinks?"

"Sure. Coke. Ginger Ale. Root beer.

"Make mine Coke. On the rocks."

What a shame. Was he being sarcastic? She took a sip of her drink and coughed when it went down the wrong way.

"It just isn't the same without the lime, I guess?"

She regained her composure but couldn't think of a comeback. She had grown up in a wealthy family. So what? It wasn't something to be ashamed of. If he was proud of his ascetic lifestyle and humble beginnings, that was his choice.

Changing the subject, he said, "I didn't bring any paper."

She went over to a row of built-in polished wood drawers and found two legal pads and pens. "I sometimes work here," she explained a tad defensively as she handed him his writing tools. She sat down, and they squared off with their writing pads.

"Sorry," he said. "That was uncalled for. Truce?"

She hesitated.

"I won't make fun of your wealthy upbringing if you don't make fun of the chip on my shoulder," he added.

His overture seemed sincere. "Agreed. Truce."

"Good." He smiled and picked up a pen. She found herself smiling back. He could be very charming when he made an effort. "Now then," he said. "Should we take it from the top?" His expressive coffee-colored eyes danced with amusement.

"How else?" Maybe he did have a sense of humor, after all. "Your Admiral is at the top of my list." She wrote down 'Admiral van Damme'.

"*My* Admiral?"

"Well, he sure isn't mine."

He also wrote "Admiral van Damme" at the top of his page. "What do we need to know about *our* Admiral?"

"Like what makes him tick. Maybe do a credit check? Look at his service record. Question his neighbors. You know, *investigate* him. See if he's the kind of man who might be involved in selling arms to neo-Nazis. And if so, why."

"Hmmm. I think I might be able to get a look at his service record. I've got a friend in personnel." He wrote that down, and so did she. "Not sure we have time for a credit check. We need answers right away. Credit checks usually take time."

"Well, I might be able to expedite the process. I know a guy." She smiled across the table at him: "I can get exceptionally fast service if I call it in for the firm."

"Of course you can," he said with exaggerated emphasis. "But I bet you still have to wait in line at Starbucks . . ."

"Not if the order is called in from the office."

He laughed. "You win." They wrote down "credit check."

Then they stared at their legal pads for almost a minute before addressing the issue both of them were thinking about. "So," Sydney began, "what happens when your Admiral friend gets wind of what we're up to? For example, how will he react if Captain Wallace tips him off that we're maybe considering the issue of convening authority interference?"

"It's unlikely Wallace will bring it up unless we make a motion. I'm guessing he won't want to upset the Admiral unnecessarily. Still, something might happen to cause him to mention it. We can't be sure. Even if he does, it's unlikely van Damme would guess we're aware of how far it all goes."

"And there's Brier. We can't be 100 percent certain that he won't tell the Admiral about my little talk with him. They're long-time friends, after all."

"We're sort of walking on eggshells here, aren't we? I guess the question is what van Damme might do if he thinks we're becoming too suspicious. Or what his buddies in the Independence League might do."

Sydney took a long drink and tried to focus on the source of her sudden case of nerves. "You think we're in danger? If the Admiral is involved in an illegal smuggling operation, and if he is responsible, even indirectly, for one man's death . . ."

"If we're on the right track, and even if van Damme isn't connected to Jerome's death, we are dealing with violent extremists here."

"But we're defending the son of one of their members."

"Our client didn't seem to think that counted for much."

"No, he didn't." She took another sip of her drink. "Maybe we should have paid more attention to those threatening phone calls. We haven't been too clever, have we?"

"In our defense, I would have to say that there was no reason to suspect things would get this complicated."

"But they have, and we've exposed ourselves badly."

"All for an undesirable client."

"We can't look at it that way."

"Hey, I may agree that our obligation to our client comes first, but that doesn't mean I have to like the guy."

"Do you think he's a member of this neo-Nazi group?"

"Who knows. He certainly seems to share their racist views."

She thought for a moment. "To be honest, we both knew from the start that Beck was a racist. But if I'd known this thing involved some kind of neo-Nazi group, ACLU or not, I wouldn't have gone anywhere near this case. Sure, everyone is entitled to a good defense. But it wouldn't have been the kind of thing I'd have chosen to become involved with."

"And yet here you are."

"Here *we* are."

"Maybe I should put in for hazardous duty pay."

She knew he was trying to lighten up the discussion, but she was beginning to feel the full weight of what they were facing. "Maybe you're right about that other thing. About finding some anonymous way to alert the authorities to that arms deal."

"Maybe." He looked down at what he had written. "It looks as though we are long on problems and short on options."

"And there's one other complication you should put on your list."

"Which is . . .?"

"Beck's father. Why is he always calling you and not his son? That bothers me."

"Arnie may be right. He may be concerned his son will talk about the arms deal."

"He may not realize we can't legally reveal any information we get from Arnie. You've told him that. But it may not have really sunk in. I rather doubt he's a man who's used to worrying much about ethical conflicts." She paused. "You don't think Beck will get in touch with his father to tell him we know about the arms deal, do you?"

"Christ. I sure as hell hope not. It sounded like that was the *last* thing he'd want to do. He may or may not hate his father, but one thing I'm sure of, he's damned afraid of him."

She suddenly noticed that Duncan had doodled in the margin of his legal pad, large flamboyant swirls and intricate designs. It seemed so uncharacteristic of her image of him that she laughed.

"What? What's so funny?"

"You." She pointed at the doodles. "That isn't exactly linear."

"Give me a chance and I might surprise you with how non-linear I can be."

Their eyes met and she felt a tingle of excitement. Dammit, she told herself, don't you dare fall for a line like that.

"A penny for your thoughts," he said. "Or does it cost more on your side of the tracks?"

She felt herself flush with embarrassment and renewed anger. "I was thinking what an obnoxious SOB you can be."

"And here I was thinking about how attractive you are."

She knew he was teasing her again, but it threw her off balance. "Why can't you think of me as just another lawyer and forget all the game playing crap?"

"Because you aren't 'just another lawyer.'" He paused. Then: "Sorry. You seem to bring out the worst in me."

"And I'm not even trying."

"Back to the drawing board, okay?"

"Okay."

Her eyes fell on the words, "Beck's father." "What *have* you told him?" she asked, pointing.

"Not much. He thinks we're looking for a drug connection. I promised to let him know if we made any breakthroughs."

"Why did you promise him anything?" she asked.

"To get him off my back."

"How do we know that Arnie's father isn't involved in Jerome's death?"

"Even knowing what we know, I can't think of a single good reason why van Damme or the neo-Nazis would have wanted to kill Jerome. Jerome got his extra $200. They got their samples. A deal was made. And the shipment is on its way."

"Maybe Jerome tried more blackmail. Or maybe they stopped trusting him after he demanded more money," she said.

"I'd use it at trial if we get the chance. But it still seems pretty far-fetched that they'd kill Jerome and pin it on Beck's son. Doesn't track." Duncan looked at his list. "So, what *do* we have?"

"A major confidentiality problem, a number of complications, considerable risk, and few if any alternatives."

"In other words, a non-productive session."

"Oh, I wouldn't say that," she countered.

"Why?"

"We have a truce, don't we?"

A boat coming into the marina around the end of breakwater drew their attention, its running lights bright against the darkening night sky. As it went by it startled several seagulls into flight. Suddenly the intimacy of the small cabin, the darkness outside, the casual repartee, and the sense of shared danger all became heavy with significance.

"Maybe it wouldn't hurt to knock this off for tonight," Sydney said. "We can come back when we're fresh."

He smiled a gentle smile that said he felt the same internal conflict. "You've got to go back to the office and that pile of unfinished work, huh?"

She struggled against the urge to let herself relax and enjoy his company. They might be from two different worlds, but it was a lovely night. And he was an attractive man. "I could leave it until tomorrow," she conceded. "I'd need to call in and let them know I won't be back."

"Good." He seemed surprised but genuinely pleased. "Nothing more for us to do on the case tonight. I'll tell you what. Why don't we celebrate our truce by having another couple of drinks and maybe turning on some music? I bet you have music on this boat, right?"

"What kind do you like?"

CHAPTER 27

Friday, April 14, 1978
Sand Point Naval Station, Seattle
Headquarters, 13th Naval District

After dropping Sydney off downtown the following morning, Duncan headed back to Sand Point. Despite the difficulties they faced in the days ahead, he found himself humming. He had very much enjoyed his evening with Sydney Warren, and he looked forward to seeing her again later in the day to compare notes on the tasks they'd mapped out for themselves.

His first order of business was to take a close look at van Damme's service record. That would not be a simple matter, since Navy personnel records were confidential. A legal officer could get access to records of his own clients, of course. And he might also be provided access to other relevant records if he had a cooperative prosecutor or if he could get the court to compel it. He could not, however, just wander in and ask to see anything he liked.

Still, the Navy's strict technical rules were sometimes bent. One of the facts of navy life was that an officer could often get a good deal more done through gladhanding and intimidation than by filing bureaucratic requests. Duncan would have been willing to bet that, if he chose his moment with care, and if he made sure the more senior people were out of the office, he could walk into the Personnel Office, take the no-nonsense tone of an officer in no mood to be deterred, demand to see a particular service record, and walk out with that record in his hands a few minutes later.

But not the record of a flag officer who happened to be the Commandant of the 13th Naval District. Getting his hands on *that* service record was going to be a good deal more challenging.

In the end, Duncan decided to call in some chits he had due from Lieutenant George Denton. Denton was an occasional running companion and deeply grateful former client. He did not look forward to asking his friend to violate Navy protocols. But that seemed to him to be the only real option.

"Duncan? How're things with the legal eagles this morning?" Denton said, sounding happy to hear from him.

"Fine, thanks. Ah, George, I have another favor to ask." Maybe a little chitchat had been in order, but Duncan was feeling uneasy about the call and wanted to get it over with.

"Sure. How can I help?"

"Maybe you'd better hear what it is first."

"Uh, oh. Sounds serious," Denton said.

"It is, George. But I wouldn't ask if it wasn't important."

"Okay, let's hear it."

"I need to look at a service record."

Denton hesitated. "I take it you don't have authorization?"

"You might say that."

"Uh-huh. And I guess you know the sixteen kinds of shit I could get into if I do this. Can you tell me what this is all about?"

"I think you'd actually rather not know," Duncan said. "But as I said, it's important."

"It better be."

"You know I'd never reveal what you did."

"Not even under oath? No, don't answer that." Denton paused and sighed. "What the hell, why not? Whose file do you need to see?"

Keeping his voice level, Duncan said, "Clifford van Damme's."

"Jesus! You sure can pick them." The line went silent. Duncan could almost feel the turmoil his request had caused. Finally, Denton said, "Shit, I guess if I'd do it with an E-2, I can do it with an admiral."

"Thanks, George. I can't tell you how much I appreciate this." He became aware he had been holding his breath, and his stomach was in a knot. Flagrantly violating Navy Regulations in this manner was as big a deal for him as it was for George Denton. Ordinarily, he'd never take this kind of risk, but nothing about this case seemed normal.

"Don't thank me yet. When shall we do this?"

"Mind skipping your workout today?" Duncan asked.

"Lunch is probably as good a time as any. Nobody here."

"See you around noon."

Shortly after twelve hundred, Duncan climbed the back steps into the Administration Building—it was the same building that housed the Admiral's office up on the second floor. He knocked quietly on Denton's office door. It was at the end of the hall, just inside the back entrance, so it had the advantage of privacy. Denton greeted him cordially, but he was obviously nervous. He sat Duncan down in his office at his own desk. The Admiral's thick service jacket peeked from under a stack of papers.

"Make it quick, will you?" Denton said. "I only have a quarter of a pack." He was a smoker and intended to stand guard on the porch, just outside the back door, having a smoke like he often did when taking a break.

"Puff slowly and don't inhale deeply," Duncan said with a half-smile.

Denton rolled his eyes to let Duncan know his joke wasn't funny. Then he took up his post, leaving the doors ajar so they could see each other in case it was necessary for him to signal that someone was coming.

Duncan flipped through the large file to get a feel for what it contained. He needed to work quickly, covering as much of van

Damme's twenty-eight years of service as possible. He wouldn't know what was important until he came across it.

The file detailed Admiral Clifford van Damme's impressive career, starting with graduation from the Naval Academy with distinction. Initially, he had served as a junior officer aboard a destroyer, followed by several tours at sea and a dangerous year of service as a Mekong River patrol boat skipper in Viet Nam early in the war.

By pure chance, van Damme had been ashore on a training assignment in Da Nang during the Tet Offensive in early 1968. A letter in the file described how, on the morning of the initial assault, he had experienced some extended close combat when the VC had nearly taken the small apartment building in which he and several U.S. civilians were temporarily housed. Equipped with only small arms and very little ammunition, he and three Navy yeomen had distinguished themselves by successfully holding off the VC for nearly two hours until reinforcements arrived, saving themselves and a number of civilians.

After another sea tour as an Executive Officer, he'd returned to Viet Nam late in 1974 where he was promoted to Captain and became a Naval Attaché to the U.S. Embassy in Saigon. He was one of the last Americans to be evacuated just before the fall of the South Vietnamese government. Following Vietnam, he'd been stationed at Subic Bay. And then Seattle. It wasn't clear why he had been moved from operational commands to an administrative post, but there could have been many reasons, including his own preference.

Van Damme's advancement to Rear Admiral had shortly predated his assignment as Commandant, 13th Naval District. It was rumored that Naval District Commandant was often a last command of choice for flag officers approaching retirement. Perhaps van Damme was thinking about leaving the Navy.

Duncan hadn't expected to find anything really incriminating, but van Damme's file did not so much as hint at a single irregularity in his lengthy career, other than the sudden move into administration after the end of Viet Nam. He appeared to be an exemplary Navy officer, capable and dedicated. The kind of man Duncan himself tried to be. He certainly did not seem like someone likely to become an arms merchant or someone who would have dealings with a domestic extremist group.

Duncan turned to the applications van Damme had completed back in 1950 when he'd first entered the U.S. Navy. Maybe there were answers in the man's civilian life.

According to his application form, he had grown up in the Seattle area and worked as a youth in the commercial fishing industry. This also suggested possible retirement plans and explained his choice of late career duty at the 13th Naval District. Since he'd attended Annapolis, it was likely his family had some kind of political pull. His pay record indicated that he'd married a woman from the town of Everett, WA following his return from his first tour in Viet Nam in 1968. They had a ten-year-old daughter who'd resided with her mother since the couple's divorce four years ago.

Duncan wasn't completely satisfied but felt like he had taken as much time as he should with the file. He closed it and signaled Denton that he was through. Denton's shoulders slumped with relief as he quickly put out a half-smoked cigarette, came back into the office, scooped up the file, and slipped it into his top desk drawer. "My stomach couldn't have taken much more of that," he said. "I think I need a Tums. Or maybe a stiff drink."

"I'm really sorry to put you through this, George."

"Was it worth it?" Denton asked.

"I'm not sure."

Denton ran long fingers across the top of his head, a nervous habit that was also his well-known poker tell. "Just keep quiet about this, okay?"

"I will if you will."

It took a second for Denton to realize his friend was kidding. "Bet on it," he said.

"I owe you one," Duncan said as he stepped out the door. "Big time."

On his way out of the building, Duncan happened to glance over his shoulder as he headed up the walk past the Admin Building's front entrance. He caught a quick glance of a civilian man just entering the building. For a moment he was sure it was the same man he'd seen that day several weeks earlier in the upstairs courtroom at the law center the day of Beck's pretrial hearing—the man with the burn on his face. But the man disappeared inside before he could get a good look.

Back in his office, Duncan studied his calendar. He had some free time, if he was willing to let a few things slide. On impulse, he grabbed his hat and headed out, stopping at the front office to tell the receptionist that he'd be gone for a few hours.

As he drove up the freeway headed for Everett, Duncan found himself studying his rear-view mirror and wondering if there could be some danger associated with continuing to investigate van Damme. It was both troubling and embarrassing to find himself feeling unsettled by the possibility of personal risk. And there was also Sydney to consider. He needed to find a tactful way to remind her to be careful.

On the other hand, the sense of danger was also exhilarating. Everything about the Beck case was turning out to be a new experience for him. There were the strange lines of inquiry, the struggles over discovery, the Federal District Court, and Sydney with her edgy appeal, family money, and prestigious downtown law firm. And now he was breaking rules, doing things he never would have considered before. The case was slowly drawing him out of the ascetic, self-disciplined life he'd settled into over the past several years. This was a new and different world.

He loved being a trial lawyer. And he'd spent a good deal more time in court as a JAGC officer than he ever would have in nearly any normal civilian practice. Unfortunately, he was approaching the point in his career when advancement would move him into administration and away from trial advocacy. He'd be doing work more like the job he'd been briefly assigned at Fleet Air Whidbey. Between stints of pushing papers, he might occasionally serve as a military judge. But that wasn't the same as actual trial advocacy. In truth, he wasn't looking forward to the next phase of his career with the U.S. Navy.

After a 40-minute drive, he pulled into the parking garage at the Snohomish County Courthouse. It stood on a rise near the center of town. A pretty, young assistant in the Superior Court Clerk's Office seemed happy to help, smiling warmly at him as she took notes on what he wanted. Within a few minutes of his arrival, Duncan was reviewing the public court records on the domestic relations case of June Alice van

Damme versus Clifford Jan van Damme, which had ended four years earlier in the dissolution of their marriage.

A glance at the thickness of the file suggested it had been a lengthy fight. There were numerous affidavits and counter-affidavits submitted by their lawyers in support of motions for discovery regarding marital community assets, temporary support, and custody of the couple's daughter. There was also a court-approved property settlement with inventories of assets claimed and awarded to each of the parties in the final decree.

At the time, their daughter had been six years old. The various affidavits submitted in their custody dispute contained bitterly pointed claims and arguments from each side. Van Damme had, at the time, been stationed mostly overseas. His ex-wife had argued that his Navy career always came first and that his frequent travel would make it impossible for him to provide consistent parental care for their daughter. Van Damme's local Everett attorney had tried valiantly to counter the claims, but predictably, temporary custody had been awarded to the mother. And by the time of the final settlement agreement, van Damme had clearly given up on custody, settling for visitation.

Duncan's main discovery was that van Damme owned a fish packing business inherited intact from his parents 12 years earlier. The inventory showed an appraised equity in the business at the time of the divorce of approximately $5 million. North Ocean Fisheries' home office address was on Seattle's Duwamish River. Since then, Van Damme had been operating the business as an absentee owner.

Unfortunately for van Damme, he'd also involved his wife in the management of the business—she'd handled matters that were impossible for him to deal with from his various Navy duty stations, often thousands of miles away. And he had invested his own time in the business without accounting for it and without being paid a separate salary by the North Ocean Fisheries Corporation. Under Washington community property law, those actions had led to "co-mingling" of community assets—his and his wife's labors comingled with his inherited asset. Instead of the fish business being his separate property, his wife had ended up owning half.

Both during and since the divorce, van Damme had been making substantial payments for spousal and child support. His wife was apparently also entitled to a share of his anticipated U.S. Navy pension. And he was on the hook for his daughter's future support expenses as well. These outcomes were to be expected. But it was obvious from the final property settlement agreement that he had also paid dearly to buy out his wife's community interest in North Ocean Fisheries. Not only had he signed over his entire share of their equity in the couple's pricey Mercer Island home, but he'd agreed to pay substantial ongoing spousal support payments until such time as his ex-wife remarried—if ever.

Overall, it looked like van Damme had ended up with very little, aside from clear ownership of North Ocean Fisheries. If he was considering retirement from the Navy, his fish packing company would have to feature prominently in his plans for the future.

It was after closing hours at the Law Center by the time Duncan made it back to Sand Point. Sydney's secretary said she was "in conference" when he called, but she got back to him almost immediately.

"He owns a fish-packing company," she told him when he answered.

He laughed. "I know." He was vaguely disappointed that she'd beat him to the punch.

"You know? How do you know that? Surely that wasn't in his service record?"

"His divorce. I spent the afternoon in Everett looking at the court file. How did you find out about the fish business?" And then he remembered. "Of course, your buddy at the collections agency."

"Yep. Mel's been on the phone all day. A real whiz. Wait until you hear what he's come up with."

"Mel, huh? You're on a first name basis with a collection agent?"

"After today I am. Mel Marshall owns the company. First Class Credit and Collections. And you'd be amazed at what the prospect of a little added work from the Steiner firm can do for a researcher's motivation. First of all, did you know that van Damme is in financial trouble?"

"Really?"

"He is unless he's got some hidden assets. His fish business, North Ocean Fisheries, has been on a 'cash-only' basis with several of its main suppliers for almost a year. They haven't filed for bankruptcy, but a few months ago they worked out an 'accommodation of creditors' under which they are making agreed-upon reduced payments on back debts while still continuing to do business. Among the people good ol' Mel spoke to is the attorney for one of the creditors who signed the deal. He represents a company that has a continuing service contract to maintain North Ocean's extensive refrigeration equipment. Basically, they keep it all running 24-7. The attorney says North Ocean is just barely surviving. It used to be one of the principal suppliers of seafood in the Northwest. But it has gone steadily downhill since van Damme's father died some years ago. What do you think about that?"

"I think you're right. Sounds like Van Damme needs money."

"Unless there are other assets, other than his Navy salary."

"There aren't. At least not according to his divorce file. Except for North Ocean, his ex-wife cleaned him out. On top of everything, he's paying child support *and* spousal support. And she'll get a big chunk of his anticipated pension. I think that fish company is *it* for him."

"I wonder why he's hung onto it all these years if it isn't making a profit."

"According to the divorce file, his father built up that company from scratch. Clifford worked there as a kid. He gave up a lot in his divorce to keep it. At a guess, I'd say he has a strong emotional attachment."

"Oh, by the way," she interjected. "He has a brother. A thoracic surgeon here in Seattle. Mel says he's some kind of big deal."

"There you go," said Duncan. "He's also living up to a high standard—sibling competition and all that. Any indication that the brother also inherited an interest in this business?"

"Nope. Mel says it belongs solely to van Damme."

"So, van Damme either bought the brother out, or he worked out a deal to receive the company as his share of their father's estate. Either way, it's obvious he wanted it badly."

"Want to know what I think?" Sydney said. "I think we've got our motive for this gun deal."

"And there's one other thing. Van Damme was in Saigon in April of '75. He was there at the time it fell."

"Okay . . . ?"

"So, Arnie Beck's story holds up," said Duncan. "Van Damme might well have had the opportunity to get his hands on some stray military ordinance. When Saigon collapsed, I guess you know it was a complete mess. Total upheaval."

"So, if he's hoping to run this business following his retirement, he badly needs some serious cash to make that happen. These M-16s may be the only way he's going to get that cash."

"Yep," he said.

"Unless," she said, her tone playful. "He *could* sell his . . . yacht."

"Yacht?" She was obviously delighted to surprise him with that bit of information.

"It's in van Damme's name, personally. He bought it recently, soon after his posting to Seattle. Mel says the attorney he talked to was peeved about it. He and some of the other creditors think it should be sold to cover debt. But since it isn't an asset of the corporation, the creditors can't do much without giving up on their existing 'accommodation' and filing to compel bankruptcy. And there isn't much equity in the boat anyway. So, there's not a lot for them to get out of it even if they pushed the issue."

"Is it documented?"

"Yes, it is. And I'm way ahead of you. It's called the *Sea Leave*. Over lunch I went down to the Coast Guard Documentation Office and had a look. It's mortgaged with Rainier Bank for $78,000—which looks to be most of its value. It's a classic fifty-six-footer, built in 1971. Wood. It's at Shilshole. Probably a nice boat. Your Admiral certainly likes living on the financial edge."

"You *have* been busy."

"All compliments of First Class Credit and Collections. Mel was happy to help. He loves Steiner Law. And I will make sure he continues to get our business."

"Now you're just trying to get a rise out of me," Duncan said. "Get me to call you out on trading in influence."

"Wouldn't dream of it," she said with a notable trace of humor.

"So, anything else to report?"

"Actually, there is." His question hadn't really been serious. It already seemed like she'd had an incredibly productive day. "I spent some time at the Seattle Public Library, doing a little reading."

"About . . . ?"

"Neo-Nazi groups in the area. In the Pacific Northwest."

"Groups? Plural?"

"Yes, it looks like there are several. There has been at least one shoot-out with the police and a couple of robberies attributed to them."

"That's encouraging," he said. "Why *here*, do you suppose?"

"Who knows? Maybe it's all the rural areas and cheap land. They can keep a low profile in the countryside, stay out of sight. Keep all those bleeding-heart liberals west of the mountains at arms-length."

They both paused. It was a lot to take in and to determine what it might all mean for their case. The guy with the burn scar came to mind, but Duncan was hesitant to bring him up. His attendance at their evidentiary hearing several weeks earlier was curious, and seeing him again earlier this day was a bit troubling. Still, he hesitated to worry Sydney until he had more than a vague feeling of unease.

Duncan hesitated, then dove in. "Um, is there any chance we could get together tonight, later?"

"Sorry, I don't see how, Duncan. I've got masses of work to do. I'm probably going to be here most of the weekend as it is."

His disappointment surprised him. "Well, I'll talk to you Monday after we've both thought through some of these new developments. Keep your doors locked, okay?"

She took the warning in stride. "Sure. You too," she replied.

After he hung up, Duncan looked around at the unrelieved bleakness of his tiny institutional office with its grey metal desk and its threadbare carpet. Despite himself, he couldn't help making the comparison with Sydney's tasteful, luxurious workspace at her downtown Steiner law firm. And although he knew he shouldn't consider Sydney's response a rejection, he felt decidedly let down. With a forced sigh, he rose, put on and buttoned his jacket, took his hat from its hook behind the door, and left the Law Center for his Friday evening dinner at the Officers' Mess. Perhaps after dinner he might read for a few hours in his room at the BOQ.

Or maybe go to a movie.

CHAPTER 28

Monday, April 17, 1978
West Seattle
Industrial port area along the Duwamish River

Sydney had gone home to change into casual clothes before heading for North Ocean Fisheries on the Duwamish River. The Duwamish ran through an industrial section of the waterfront before emptying into Elliot Bay south of town. It was just a short drive from downtown, but it was a far different landscape from the skyscrapers and busy city streets. The water-related industries that bordered the river were not picturesque; they didn't try to be. Some of the buildings looked as though they had been there nearly as long as the river. There were no shops, no corner delis, no works of public art, and no green spaces with park benches where neatly dressed office workers could sit during breaks.

Just functional faded wood-framed industrial buildings served by gravel parking lots behind chain-linked fences.

The entrance to North Ocean Fisheries was through an open gate in a tall board fence that badly needed a coat of paint and was heavily over-grown with the Northwest's ubiquitous invasive blackberries. She drove into a dusty, crushed-rock lot and parked in a row of equally dusty cars facing the plant. The collection of weathered green buildings huddled along the edge of the narrow murky river had seen better days. There were long strips of peeling paint curling away from the siding on the sunny side of the main building. The entire structure was bleached by sun and weather, its roof dotted with mossy patches. What looked like a small tree was growing out of a gutter.

Still, based on the number of cars in the lot and the sounds coming from within, it was an active enterprise. Sydney could hear the low, smooth hum of heavy refrigeration and workers moving around inside. She knew from experience that most of Seattle's fish processing plants had been in existence for quite a long time, so she wasn't surprised at North Ocean Fisheries' rundown appearance. The question would be what it looked like inside where business was conducted and whether the functional portions of the plant were clean, modern, and operational.

There was no one in sight as she made her way toward a paved, covered passage that ran between the two main buildings. To her right, a forklift emerged from a warehouse bearing a load of metal trays filled with fish. It slowly swung away from her and disappeared around the corner of the building. She waited until it was out of sight before heading for the open doors.

A blast of cold air washed over her from above as she stepped inside. She glanced up at the noisy blower. Did the rush of air keep out bugs, she wondered? Did it help maintain the cool air inside? Or was it simply intended to mess up the appearance of anyone who came in uninvited? She smoothed her hair back in place and looked around.

The concrete floor was puddled with water. To her right, a young man was cleaning the floor with a hose. Everything seemed cool and damp, with the faint aroma of fish lingering at the edge of consciousness. Before leaving her office, she'd called one of North Ocean's competitors to find out what kind of fish were coming in and whether this was a busy time of year. She was told there had recently been a brief halibut opening in Alaska. All of the processors were scurrying to get the halibut either frozen and packed away or out to the fresh market as quickly as possible.

Straight ahead there were two rows of workers standing across from each other at a long metal table. They all wore rubber boots, aprons, and gloves. Bright yellow and orange aprons were splattered with dark spots. The drab olive aprons were less noticeably stained, faint splotches barely visible against the darker material. Some of the workers wore black boots, others smudged yellow ones. The gloves were also an array of colors. The blur of movement as they worked was an oddly colorful dance in orange, yellow, dark green, and black.

A pipe above the worktable contained a series of outlets attached to several short lengths of hose that provided running water for each work-station. In the middle of the table lay a pile of large, brown-skinned fish she recognized as halibut. The big inert shapes were pushed around the table with amazing ease by the busy workers.

There were several large plastic tubs with wheels lined up against the far wall. They were overflowing with fish. One by one fish were taken from the tubs by a tall man in a very dirty yellow apron and held beneath a machine that cut off their heads before he passed them along to the rows of workers. A huge pile of heads lay on the floor at his feet. Everyone at the table was intent on cutting, washing, and filleting. No one looked up as Sydney moved closer. At the far end of the table the fish fillets were placed in small, consumer-sized plastic bags and then loaded onto trays like the ones she had seen on the forklift. The trays were filling up fast.

Sydney watched for a while before deciding there was no way she was going to get a chance to talk to any of these employees. She went back out through the blast of cold air into what, in contrast, felt like almost balmy weather and continued along the walkway between the buildings. There was an outside stairway leading up the side of the next building with a sign that said "Office" and an arrow pointing up. If she didn't find out the information she wanted from plant employees, she would come back and tackle whoever was available in that office. However, she preferred to talk to someone with a less personal link to the owners of this establishment.

The pier beyond the buildings was covered with heavy looking, well-worn planking turned gray from the weather. In places, large sheets of rusting steel plate had been laid down, presumably for the benefit of the occasional forklift truck. The dock was supported by black creosote covered pilings which ran along the front of the pier and around the corner of the building to the north.

There were two boats tied to the outside of the pilings along the river. Quite a few people were bustling around the smaller of the two vessels. Fish were being hoisted out of its hold with a large square aluminum bucket. Once up at pier level, the bucket was then swung in and fish were dumped onto a long aluminum table with high sides. Several people in boots and aprons were sorting the fish and putting them into the large, wheeled plastic containers she'd seen inside. Everyone seemed incredibly busy. Sydney was beginning to wonder if she would ever find someone who had enough time to talk to her.

The second boat, beyond, was larger, maybe a hundred twenty to a hundred thirty feet long. As she looked down at the vessel from the pier, she could see several men working on the aft deck, leaning over an open hold from time to time to talk to someone below. She was trying to decide if it was feasible for her to climb down the ladder to the deck, when a young man in overalls came alongside her.

"Need help finding something?" he asked. He had friendly blue eyes the same color as the blue handkerchief sweatband wrapped around his forehead.

"No, I'm just looking around." She smiled. "It's an interesting place."

"Personally, I'd rather be out to sea," he said. He motioned toward the vessel just below. "We just came in. Pretty good haul."

"Halibut?"

"No, cod. Frozen fillets. Processed aboard. Best white fish around."

"Even after working on a fishing boat, you still eat fish?" She had always felt like it was better not to see or think much about anything "animal" before it appeared on her dinner plate.

He laughed. "I didn't say that. That's just the sales pitch."

She was warming to his good-humored openness and his blue eyes. "Have you been doing this long?"

"A few years. Sure as hell beats a nine-to-five."

"It's hard work though?"

He shrugged. "Work is work."

"Do you always bring your fish here?" It was a question intended to move the conversation away from the young man's opinions and maybe learn something about the business.

"Mostly."

"This place has been here for a long time, hasn't it?" she asked.

"I think almost forever."

"That *is* a long time." They both laughed. "Looks like they're doing okay."

He paused and seemed to reassess her. "You some kind of fish cop?"

"No, not any kind of fish cop," she assured him with a smile. "My brother's coming down from Alaska with a load of halibut. It's his first season, and he's looking for a good place to sell. I told him I'd check North Ocean out."

"Well, I'm just crew, but my boss seems to like these folks. I think this place is as good as any. They're fast and efficient, I can say that. And their checks must be good cuz I just got paid."

She was about to follow up when one of the men on the aft deck of the vessel below looked up at them and yelled, "Hey, Lyle, get your butt down here and give us a hand."

"You must be Lyle," Sydney said.

He winked at her and nodded as he climbed over the edge of the pier and down the rusty steel ladder to the ship's deck.

She watched the activity below for a few more moments before continuing around to the far end of the building. There she found a large workshop that looked as though it had been added to the main structure as an afterthought. It jutted from the side with large rolling doors open at its front facing downriver. Two men holding stained coffee mugs were standing just inside the opening. One was tall with dark unkempt hair; the other shorter with thinning blond wisps of hair at either side of his head, poking from under a greasy General Motors Diesel cap.

"Hello," Sydney said. "This is quite a shop you've got here." The comment sounded contrived to her own ears even though the large workspace was filled with all sorts of impressive-looking power tools and equipment and wood benches piled high with cans, mechanical parts, and hand tools.

"You looking for someone?" The question from the dark-haired man was not unfriendly, but she sensed visitors weren't particularly common or welcome.

"Just looking around. My brother is thinking of selling some fish here. I told him that I'd check it out."

"Where's he been fishing?" the second man asked.

"Southeast Alaska. For halibut. He did okay for his first time out." She gestured toward a shelf of paint cans that she recognized as bottom paint. "You do boat work here?"

"Just some upkeep and minor repairs. The company has a couple of packers of their own."

Sydney looked back toward the pier. "The one unloading over there belongs to the company?"

Both men nodded.

"Does upkeep on their boats keep you fairly busy?"

The dark-haired man gave her a closer look. Then he shrugged as if deciding she was nothing more than a nosy woman trying to make conversation. "The company's been chartering some additional boats to keep up with demand," he said. "But they're getting another of their own in a couple of weeks."

"A new packer?"

"No," the man with the General Motors Diesel cap said. "A small freighter, an older ship. We're staffing up to convert her to a factory processor. Then they'll be able to buy fish on the grounds, process and freeze them right on board. Great for the company." He smiled. "Should keep *us* busy for a while."

"An older ship? One that was still in use?" She hoped the questions seemed both appropriate and casual.

"I don't know for sure. I heard it's been carrying cargo somewhere in the Far East. There's always a few like that around. Must have been built in the U.S. though."

"Or *mostly* assembled here," the dark-haired man said. "There are ways to get around the law."

They were interrupted by another employee who needed help. The two men put down their coffee mugs and went off with him without so much as an "it was nice talking with you." Sydney didn't care; she had what she needed. Now the question was whether she followed up with a visit to the office or left before calling any more attention to herself. If the ship these two men were expecting was "the" ship, she had already learned more than she and Duncan had hoped from this visit to van Damme's fish company. But could it possibly be the same ship Beck had told them about? Would van Damme use it to transport arms and then attach it to his fishing business? And if so, why didn't the ship's ownership show up on van Damme's credit record?

The more she thought about it, the more she felt the need to talk to Duncan before she did anything that might jeopardize their position. Together they could decide whether or not to pursue the lead, and if so, what was the best way to go about it.

She called Duncan from a pay telephone at a nearby gas station, but he was out. Feeling irritated because he wasn't there when she wanted to reach him, she left a message saying she had called and would try again later. She was on the Highway 99 viaduct headed back to return to her office when the thought crossed her mind that it would be interesting to see van Damme's yacht, the *Sea Leave*. It was well ahead of the evening rush hour, so it wouldn't involve too much traffic angst for her to make a quick side trip to Shilshole to have a look.

All the way to the marina she kept thinking about the ship the two workers had mentioned. She was likely jumping to an unwarranted conclusion. The Admiral could have picked up a ship in an entirely different transaction. But the timing . . . a coincidence?

When she arrived at the marina, she tried Duncan again, but he still wasn't answering. She left another message saying she would call back in about half an hour, adding that it was important she talk to him soon.

She stopped at the marina office to find out where the *Sea Leave* was moored. Each of the docks had their own entry code, so getting past the locked gate was a hurdle. She counted on the fact that a well-dressed woman alone wasn't particularly threatening, so a story about wanting to check to see if a friend was aboard his boat might convince someone heading for their boat or coming back to the parking area to let her in. If she'd had more time, she could have grabbed the dinghy off her father's boat and rowed over. But subterfuge was hopefully faster.

She noted the name on the stern of a boat she could see moored about halfway out the dock in case someone asked her which boat her friend owned. She didn't want to mention the *Sea Leave* in case they knew the Admiral. Hopefully the person she approached wouldn't turn out to be the owner of the boat she claimed belonged to her friend.

The first person to come along was an older woman with a small, mean-looking dog. When Sydney asked to be let in the woman informed her, quite officiously, that the purpose of a locked gate was to keep out anyone who wasn't specifically authorized. The woman's obnoxious little dog growled deep in his throat to emphasize the message. Sydney backed off.

She was starting to feel uncomfortable hanging about near the gate when a young man in his early thirties appeared. He had no qualms about letting Sydney in. She barely had time to make her appeal before the two of them were on the other side, walking down the dock together. Two slips down the man stopped and said, "This is me, here." He pointed to a small sleek sailboat that looked fast and comfortable.

"She's a beauty," Sydney acknowledged.

"You like to sail?"

"Love it." She couldn't help gazing longingly at the young man's sailboat. It had been far too long since she'd been sailing.

"Where's your friend's boat?"

For a moment she had almost forgotten the purpose of her visit. "Ah, further out," she said.

"Well, my name's Paul." He offered his hand. "If your friend isn't there, stop by for a cup of coffee on your way back, okay?"

"Sure." She thanked him and moved off down the dock, flattered by the invitation. How long had it been since she had done anything but work? Maybe it was time she started thinking about a social life. The guy hadn't been bad looking, quite nice looking, in fact. And he was a boater. Then she remembered that she needed to talk to Duncan. She didn't have time to take Paul up on his offer.

She hurried past the other boats, barely seeing them. The Admiral's yacht was in one of the slips near the end. As she approached, she was instantly taken with it. It was a lovely older vessel with a varnished mahogany cabin and gleaming white hull. Everywhere she looked she could see signs of care. It was in perfect shape.

Sydney walked back and forth, seeing a little more to appreciate each time she passed. The carved eagle on the front of the flying bridge, bronze cleats and chocks, the large spotlight mounted to the right of the eagle, modern radar, all the antennas. It looked not only like a well-kept yacht but a well-equipped one too. Still, she wasn't sure its value much exceeded its $78,000 mortgage. It was, after all, an older wooden boat.

There seemed to be no one about. But if someone saw her step aboard and challenged her right to be there, what would she say? Oh, the hell with it. She could always claim she had the wrong boat. Besides, she didn't look like a criminal, did she?

She stepped onto the bronze step-plate with its rubber center pad and quickly climbed aboard. The aft windows offered a good view of the interior. There was a rich looking couch along the right-hand wall opposite a large settee. The galley started at the back of the settee and ran around the corner. To the right of the galley was a doorway, then a pilot seat. Between the pilot seat and the couch was a chart table.

Her eyes flicked over the interior a second time. She noticed that there were a couple of magazines on the small table next to the couch, a jar of peanut butter on the galley counter next to a box of crackers. One cupboard stood ajar. Through the opening she could see that the shelves looked full. There was a new roll of paper towels on the towel rack and a tin of coffee next to the stove. Was the Admiral provisioned for a trip? Or, like her, did he like to come down on weekends and stay on board?

Then, peering in the window on the other side of the back door, she saw the clincher—there were several full grocery bags lined up on the floor of the galley beside the stove. She continued on around the rest of the boat. Were the water and fuel tanks filled, she wondered. She glanced over the side and noticed the boat was settled into the water very close to its waterline. It looked to her like the Admiral might be able to step aboard and take her out at a moment's notice.

A glance at her watch told her it had been more than half an hour since she had left the last message for Duncan. If he wasn't there this time, she wasn't sure what she would do. She was dying to talk to him about what she had discovered at North Ocean Fisheries, and now about what she had seen at the marina. If she could bounce her ideas off him, maybe together they could make sense out of everything.

Fortunately, Paul wasn't outside when she passed by his sailboat. Nor did she see anyone else on the dock as she made her way up the ramp, through the gate, and back into the parking lot. There her luck ran out. There was someone in the telephone booth near the entrance and another person waiting. Frustrated, she set off in search of another phone.

By the time she finally found a free phone and dialed his number she was so irritated it took her a minute to register the fact that she actually had Duncan on the line. "You're there," she said in an accusatory tone.

"Yes, I'm here," he said evenly.

"It's about time." She knew she was being unreasonable, but she couldn't seem to control her frustration.

"Ah, I do work for a living."

"And you think I don't?"

"Sydney, take a deep breath and tell me what this is all about."

She started to tell him that she didn't need to take a deep breath but caught herself in time to realize that she probably did. "Sorry, it's just that I have some new information."

"Shoot."

At that instant someone came up and stood there, right next to the open phone kiosk, tapping his foot impatiently. How could the fates be so unkind? She felt like yelling at him to go away.

"Duncan, it's a little awkward talking about this over the telephone." Hint, hint. "I'm calling from the marina, a pay telephone. It's public."

"What do you suggest?"

"I could come there . . ." She didn't really relish the drive to the base, but that might be the easiest thing to do. "Or, if I knew where you were going to be, I could call you from home."

"How about a compromise? I know of a good little café in the Fremont district, just down from the library."

"You mean the one on the corner?"

"That's the place. I can leave right away."

"Me too. Twenty minutes. See you there."

. . .

Their timing was perfect. They met at the door of the restaurant. He looked as fresh and starched as usual. She, on the other hand, was in her jeans.

"You look good in those," he said with an approving smile.

"You like a woman who dresses for dinner, huh?"

"Oh, you think I'm going to buy you dinner?" he joked.

"Perhaps I'll buy yours."

He hesitated briefly, then grinned and said, "I'd be delighted."

They were seated right away; it was still a bit early for the dinner crowd, even on a Friday evening. As soon as the waiter was out of earshot, Sydney said, "North Ocean Fisheries is acquiring a ship that they plan on converting into a factory processor."

"Really?" Duncan sounded genuinely impressed with her announcement.

"It's an old freighter, one that's on its way from Asia. It should arrive in the next couple of weeks. They are going to do the conversion at their plant on the Duwamish."

Duncan shook his head in admiration.

"You thinking what I'm thinking?"

"It fits," he said. "But would he do that? It seems risky—bring in a shipment of arms and then keep and register the ship in the U.S. I don't know. Maybe."

"I guess if he gets away with the smuggling, then there'd be no reason not to. Is it legal to bring a foreign ship like that into the country?"

"I'm not sure. But unless the hull was originally built in the U.S., I believe the Jones Act keeps it from being registered to participate in U.S. fisheries. With an old ship like that though, who knows?"

"Won't there be records of ownership?"

"If it's documented in the U.S., certainly. I'd guess, yes, even if it is documented elsewhere. If that's his plan, he probably has that figured out."

"I guess we know where the money's coming from for the conversion. Anyway, there's more."

"Okay."

"I checked out his yacht at Shilshole. It looks like it may be all provisioned up and ready to go."

The waiter arrived with two glasses of water while he digested that. "We aren't ready to order yet," Duncan said. "But bring us two glasses of your house red." Then" They have a good house wine," he said to Sydney as the waiter left.

"That's fine." Somehow, she didn't mind the fact that he had ordered wine without consulting her. In some ways it was nice to have someone anticipate her needs. At the same time, she was starting to feel let down. "I was so excited when I found out about the ship," she said. "But now that I think about it, what good does the information do us?"

"Well, if it's *the* ship . . ."

"Even if we're right about that, it doesn't put us any closer to solving our confidentiality problems or stopping the arms sale."

"No, but it puts us closer to a good dinner." He handed her a menu. "I'm hungry. We can talk while we eat."

She browsed the menu without really seeing it. "Whatever you recommend," she said.

He seemed surprised. "Hey," he said. "You're finally succumbing to my masculine charm?"

She rolled her eyes but pushed the menu to the end of the table. "Me Jane," she said.

"Did you know that Tarzan slept outside of Jane's tent with a knife between his teeth in order to protect her?" He grinned. "Seriously. It's in the book."

"I didn't know anyone actually read the book."

"I read it as a kid. It wasn't bad," he said.

"And he's been your role model ever since."

"Except for the chimp. Don't like chimps. Scary, nasty little critters."

She smiled to herself. For some reason she liked the fact that he'd read books as a kid. And that he admitted to disliking chimps.

They ordered dinner and continued exploring their options. "Whatever we do, it can't wait much longer," Duncan said. "Once the ship arrives and the crime has been committed it will be a moot point—for us at least. Probably impossible to find evidence for use in court to support our alternative motives theory."

They went round and round regarding what they should do but couldn't decide on anything that seemed both reasonable and safe. After dinner he walked her to her car. As she looked at him beneath the pale glow of a nearby mercury-vapor streetlamp, she felt strangely drawn to this man who she didn't really know.

"We do need to keep trying to figure this out," Duncan said as he looked down at her.

Without thinking about it she said, "You looking forward to spending tonight in your quarters at the base?"

He looked somewhat surprised, but he was ready with an answer. "I was afraid you'd never ask."

CHAPTER 29

Sydney's apartment had been something of a surprise, though on reflection, Duncan knew it shouldn't have been. Somehow, he'd pictured her living in an expensive, coldly modern high-rise condominium protected by a uniformed guard, with contemporary art in the lobby, underground parking, an indoor pool, and big windows with a sweeping view of Elliot Bay.

He'd been right about the view. But not about any of the rest.

She rented the upper floor of a large, older white wood frame house high on the southwest side of Queen Anne Hill. It was on a winding dead-end street with grass growing up through cracks in the pavement. There were no sidewalks, and the street was so narrow that, in order to allow other cars to pass, you had to park so the passenger side of your car was pressed tight up against a laurel hedge that bordered the downhill edge of the road. Across, on the uphill side of the road, a brick stairway climbed to a walkway that meandered through a cultivated if slightly overgrown front yard to the side of the house. There, a steep outside wooden stairway led up to Sydney's private second floor entrance.

Inside, the most striking features were the strategically placed large green plants and the array of eclectic art objects on display around the room. Best of all was that view. Directly ahead was Elliot Bay with its ships and piers and the Seattle waterfront. To the right, green and white ferries crossed the Sound. To the left was Seattle Center and the Space Needle with downtown Seattle beyond. On clear days, he was certain she must be able to see Mount Rainier in the distance beyond.

He followed her into the kitchen where she asked what he wanted to drink. Duncan particularly liked the copper pans, utensils, and garlic and pepper bouquets hanging from an iron rack attached to the ceiling. It looked like the apartment of someone who appreciated good food.

It was a decided contrast with his institutional quarters at the BOQ. And with the always reliably ordinary officers' mess.

While she fixed their drinks, he wandered around her apartment, trying to get a feel for her life, looking for clues as to what was important to her. He peeked in a back bedroom that she used as a study and saw an entire wall covered by bookshelves filled with paperback and hardbound books. In her remodeled bathroom with its artistic tile design, there was a basket full of magazines with *Bon Appetit* and the *Bar News* visible on top. There were more magazines on the end table in the living room— *The New Yorker* and *Time Magazine* side by side. There was also an impressive collection of LP records and cassette tapes and what looked like a great sound system. Tucked away on a cabinet in a corner of her kitchen was an older, tiny, portable twelve-inch TV, the only one he'd seen in the apartment.

It was a secluded, civilized oasis in the midst of a densely populated city. It made her seem much more real and approachable.

Tuesday morning, Duncan launched energetically into his work at the Law Center. At about nine, he walked down the hall to beg for a cup of real coffee. The Captain's admin wasn't around but her Mr. Coffee was just getting started on a fresh pot. As he waited for it to stop burbling and for her to return, he glanced in through the Captain's open office door. Captain Wallace was gone. Duncan took a moment to appreciate the view through the Captain's office window. Even from where he stood, he could see a slice of the familiar Sand Point Navy Base landscape with its carefully trimmed lawns and shrubberies. The view looked past the Headquarters Building, between the old hangars down near the airfield, and out toward the lake and the distant Cascade Mountains beyond.

Perks of the office.

Standing there, Duncan reflected on the conclusions about the Beck case that he and Sydney had drawn the evening before.

First, they were both convinced that a shipment of illegal arms was about to come into Canada, assuming it hadn't already happened. Second, they believed Beck about Admiral van Damme's involvement with this shipment. That meant the ship destined for conversion at North Ocean Fisheries might very well be the same one being used to transport the arms. And third, due to their understanding of legal ethics and confidentiality, anything they did with this information had to be done without violating Beck's wishes. If they were to stop or document that transaction, they had to do it quietly, independently, and anonymously. And without breaching confidentiality.

It was a tall order and, in the final analysis, probably not a very realistic one. If they couldn't contact the police, they were essentially helpless. They could still argue the drugs angle at trial, but it was paper-thin as a defense. Realistically, Beck was likely looking at life in prison.

Sydney would be at the base around 1100. They planned to make one more try at convincing their client to let them report the arms shipment, although they didn't really expect him to change his mind. At the very least they would pump him for every scrap of information they could get. You never knew what might turn out to be useful.

Before then, she was going to contact her friend Mel at First Class Credit and Collections again to see if she could arrange an appointment with the attorney for the North Ocean creditor he'd spoken to previously. They wanted to know if the ship or the funds that had purchased it had been among the assets inventoried by the creditors at the time of the accommodation agreement. If not, one way to discourage the shipment might be to nudge the creditor into notifying North Ocean that they would be slapping a federal lien on the ship once it entered U.S. waters. *If* that could be done in time. They'd also need to decide if even that would be possible to do without violating Beck's confidences.

The Mr. Coffee burped its final dribble of fresh brew into the pot. He was just turning away from the view to pour his cup when it hit him. There was something different. He turned back and looked out toward the Headquarters Building.

The Admiral's flag was gone!

He stared at the vacant pole for a moment as the significance of this fact sank in. On the next pole over, the tallest one, the American Flag flapped proudly in the breeze as usual. But the Admiral's starred flag was nowhere to be seen.

Admiral van Damme was not on station.

Forgetting about his coffee, Duncan raced down the hall. Back at his desk, he fumbled for the phone. The first place he called was the Personnel Office. He waited impatiently as George Denton's Yeoman 3rd Class assistant first tried Lieutenant Denton's office and then paged him on the office intercom.

Come on! Come on, George. Duncan tapped a loud tattoo on the corner of his desk as he waited. Just as he was about to give up and walk over there instead, Denton picked up the phone. Duncan heard what he thought was someone chewing. Then Denton said, "Lieutenant Denton speaking."

"George, where's the Admiral?"

"That you Duncan? Hey, why such an early call?"

"Just wondering about the Admiral, George. His flag's gone. Where'd he go?"

"Where? Hell, I don't know. He took leave. That's all."

"Listen, George. Will you check it out for me? See where he went and how long he'll be gone? It's important."

"Sure thing, Duncan. I'll give you a call back later, okay?"

"No. No, look right now, will you George? I need to know right away. It's urgent. An emergency."

". . . okay. Sure. I can do that. Just relax. Hang tight, I'll be right back." There was the sound of the phone being placed on hold. Then silence and a seemingly interminable wait. Finally, Denton's voice came back on the line. "Looks like he took two weeks leave. Was here first thing this morning and put in his papers. Was in kind of a big hurry. Insisted that they process everything immediately so he could be on his way. Pain in the butt. His leave commences at 0800 today. Two weeks, with a leave address . . . uh . . . he left his home as his contact address. Just says: 'Commanding Officer's Residence,' And his residence phone. That's strange."

"Thanks, George. Appreciate it." Duncan slammed down the receiver and was almost immediately thumbing through the base phone directory for the number of the Commanding Officer's Residence. He dialed quickly, frustrated by the sluggish movement of the old dial phone, wishing for the umpteenth time that the Navy would catch up with the rest of the world and switch to touch-tone telephones.

Finally, the phone started to ring. If there was an answer, he could make up a story. Or hang up. But all he heard was the empty sound of the phone as it rang, and rang, and rang. He was sure that a Rear Admiral and Naval District Commandant would have at least one Filipino steward in residence. Maybe the steward had been given time off.

His third call was to Sydney. Anxious seconds passed as the phone at the Steiner firm also rang and rang. Then, after the receptionist finally picked up, he was forced to listen to classical violin while she tried Sydney's office. The receptionist came back on and informed him he could either leave a message or, if it was urgent, they could page her on the firm's intercom. He said it was very urgent and waited impatiently while they tried to find Sydney.

As soon as he heard her voice on the other end of the line, he quickly filled her in. "Van Damme is gone. Two weeks' leave. Left shortly after 0800 this morning. Was in a big hurry. He left his residence as a leave address, but there's no one there." He paused long enough to take a breath, then concluded, "He's gone to meet that shipment. I'd bet anything on it."

There was silence on the other end of the line.

"Did you hear me?" Duncan asked. "Van Damme is gone."

"I heard you. I'm thinking."

Duncan realized he was sounding more frantic than professional, but he was upset. "Better think fast," he said. "Whatever he's up to, it's happening *now.*"

"I bet he took his boat," she said. "Remember me saying that it was all provisioned up?"

"I remember."

"I'll call Shilshole and see if I can find someone to tell me if his boat is gone. In the meantime, put in a leave request. Starting *now.*"

"A leave request? Me? Why?" Then he understood. "Wait a minute. I hope you're not thinking what I think you're thinking."

"I'm not thinking anything until I find out if his boat is gone. But if it is, we'll have to act fast. Get going on that leave request. I'll call you back."

"Sydney . . ." he said. But she had hung up.

It was crazy. When he'd called her the idea of following the Admiral had been only a half-formed thought, not a real possibility. But she was apparently considering taking off on some impulsive chase. He paced back and forth, trying to decide what was the practical thing for them to do while he waited for her return call. It came within minutes.

"It's gone, Duncan," she said. "I talked to the moorage attendant who went down and unplugged van Damme's electricity. They read the meter when you're gone for any length of time; sometimes they moor transient boats in the vacant slips. Anyway, the attendant says the *Sea Leave* pulled out less than half an hour ago. He didn't ask where it was headed."

"What are you thinking, Sydney?"

She sighed. "I think this is it. Our one chance to get out of the hole we're in. We've either got to follow him or just forget about the whole thing. Unless you've changed your mind about anonymously contacting the police. I haven't. And I hope you haven't."

"No, I guess not." It was all coming too fast for Duncan. "What do you want to do, follow with your dad's boat? Can you do that?"

"No problem. Look, the *Spindrift* has a powerful radar, thirty-six miles. And it'll do twenty-two knots. The *Sea Leave* is a displacement boat. An old one. I bet it does eight or nine at best. We can catch him. Once we get visual contact, we can just back off and follow. He'll never know we're there. When he gets where he's going, we'll wait and see what he does. Meanwhile, we're wasting time."

"But he's gone. Who knows where he's headed?"

"He will have headed north. That's all we need to know. We'll be traveling at over twice his speed. Even with a two or three-hour lead, we'll be on him by the time he passes Port Townsend."

"I don't know, Sydney . . ." It sounded crazy. And possibly dangerous.

"We're not going to catch him if we keep talking about it," she pressed. "Can you get the leave?"

"This fast? Hell, I don't know. I guess I can try."

"Well, find out. I'm going to rearrange my calendar here and start getting organized. I'll call you before I go. If you can't get the leave, I'll have to go without you."

Jesus! At this point he knew her well enough to know she wasn't bluffing. If he didn't go with her, she would absolutely go on her own. "All right," he reluctantly agreed. "I'll get started on it right now. Don't go without me. I'm coming with you no matter what happens, okay?"

"Okay, Duncan. I'll call you back."

He hung up and immediately called Denton. "George, how long would it take to get a leave request for a couple of weeks processed for me if I hand carry the paperwork over?"

"It wouldn't take long, I suppose. Why? What's going on? No, don't tell me. As long as Captain Wallace signs it, I'll put it through. When do you want it to start?

"Now. As of right now."

He hurried from his office and down the hall to the front desk. The yeoman/receptionist pulled the forms from his cabinet and handed them over. Duncan filled them out standing at the reception counter. Then, instructing the receptionist to come find him if Sydney Warren called, he headed to Captain Wallace's office. He was in luck. The Captain was in.

"Captain, I've got a leave request here," he said. And then, improvising on the spot: "It's an emergency. My father's ill. I just heard. I'm flying back to Indiana later this morning." The lie escaped his lips so smoothly he almost believed it himself. He had left that portion of the form blank. Now, newly resolved, he held the leave request against the plaster wall and wrote in his parent's home as his leave address. "I'm awfully sorry about this, but is there a chance we can do this right away? I've got a plane I'm hoping to catch."

Captain Wallace readily accepted Duncan's lie; there were some advantages to being considered an "officer and a gentleman" whether you deserved it or not. The Captain wanted to know about workload and appointments, and Duncan assured him there would be no problem. He'd give some quick instructions to his yeoman and then he'd be as free as a bird. His next actual court appearance was not until the Beck case itself went to trial in about two weeks. He'd be back long before then.

After personally delivering the signed and completed forms to Personnel and collecting his approved leave form, he returned to his office to find a phone message on his desk from Sydney. He returned the call immediately.

"Where've you been?" she said. "I'm ready to get out of here."

"So am I, Sydney. I'll stop by my room for some clothes and head to the marina."

"Forget the clothes. Just get down to the boat. We haven't got time."

"Hell, I'm in uniform."

"Yeah, well, I'm not exactly dressed for sea either. There'll be something on the boat that we can wear. Just get there as fast as you can."

"All right, Sydney. I'll see you there."

The morning rush had tapered off, but there was still a string of unsynchronized traffic lights that cared not about schedules, emergencies, or arms smugglers. The good spirits he'd enjoyed less than an hour before had vanished. He had no sympathy for slow drivers, no patience for self-involved pedestrians, and no tolerance for crowding. At one point he drove around a residential block to avoid a large truck that was backing into a loading dock. He ended up two cars behind where he would have been if he had waited.

As he drove, he tried to work through the logic of what they were about to do. To find some flaw in their reasoning. To come up with a way to convince Sydney—or even himself—that the endeavor they were about to launch was not *their* responsibility, that it was an impossible undertaking, that it was foolhardy. It was clearly *all* of those things. But somehow not sufficiently any one of them to prevent their going ahead with it.

In the end he concluded that Sydney's plan to follow the Admiral *was* plausible. And by going with her, he could see to it that she took no unnecessary risks. This was perhaps the first time in his life that he wished he owned a handgun. Navy lawyers weren't issued guns. The only times he carried one was on Officer-of-the-Day duty. Also, possession of an unlicensed firearm was a serious crime in Canada so taking a gun on this venture wasn't really an option. Fortunately, their plan was to maintain a safe distance and simply observe. Not call attention to themselves. Just see what happened and hope they might learn something they could use.

It wasn't much of a plan, but it was better than doing nothing. At a minimum, what they learned might be something that would convince their client to let them use what they knew.

By the time he arrived at Shilshole, he was resigned to the trip. He parked the car and hurried to the dock where the Warren family yacht was moored. The chain-link gate at the top of the tide ramp was locked, and the *Spindrift* was out of sight toward the outer end of the dock. He was at the point of seriously assessing whether he could climb over the barbed-wire fence when Sydney appeared behind him with her arms full of paper shopping bags.

"What's all this?" he said, peeking into one of the sacks as he took it from her. It seemed to be filled with various kinds of donuts.

"Food." She handed him a second bag, and with her free hand, unlocked the gate.

He hadn't thought about what they were going to eat.

"When I got here," she said, "I realized there isn't much of anything on the boat right now. Decided I'd have just enough time to make a run on the marina restaurant before you got here. Been waiting long?"

"Just arrived."

"Good."

"Donuts? We're going to be eating donuts?"

"Yeah, and apple pie." She laughed. "It's a restaurant, not a grocery store. Don't worry, I also talked them into selling me a couple dozen eggs and three loaves of bread. And a few other things. I overpaid, but it won't be so bad."

She'd left the *Spindrift* running. Her two powerful engines rumbled deeply as they warmed, spitting and spluttering water from two wet exhaust outlets at the base of her transom and, in the absence of a breeze, engulfing the entire area with smelly carbon monoxide. Sydney jumped aboard and set down her load on the back deck. Duncan handed over his two bags as well and was on the point of following her aboard when she stopped him.

"Cast off," she said, then turned to head up the stainless and teak ladder to the flying bridge.

It took him a moment to realize that they were actually leaving—immediately. Of course they were. He quickly untied the line holding the stern from the heavy cleat mounted at the edge of the float and rushed to the bow and removed that line too, tossing it onto the front deck. Then, hurrying because the boat was already beginning to drift away from the float, he climbed the boarding steps mounted to the float and stepped across the widening gap onto the side deck.

He was no sooner aboard than Sydney shifted the engines into reverse, and with a rumble of power, the boat surged backward out of its slip. He would have lost his balance had he not been holding on. The big boat slid into the open water between the docks, stopped, rotated, and began to move forward toward the main channel that ran along behind the breakwater and led to the marina entrance.

Duncan climbed to the flying bridge and stood beside Sydney. "How's the fuel?" he called to her over the sound of the engines.

"Full. We fill up when we come in. Less condensation."

That was all the conversation there was time for. As soon as the bow was pointed away from the other boats and toward clear water, Sydney flagrantly ignored longstanding boater's etiquette, not to mention the multitude of signs that read: SPEED LIMIT 3 KNOTS—WATCH YOUR WAKE. Without hesitation, she pressed the throttles hard forward. The uncertain rumble of the engines was suddenly replaced by a deafening roar.

The bow rose and the hull lifted in the water. The breakwater to their left and the floats and other vessels moored to their right began to rush past with increasing speed. A man working on his boat looked up and waved his arms, palms down, to signal them to slow down. Whatever he yelled at them probably included an oath, but it was drowned out by the penetrating engine noise as the heavy yacht came up onto a full plane, and they blasted through the entrance headed north.

Duncan removed his hat for fear of losing it in the heightening breeze. For a moment he considered pulling down the mostly decorative, brass-inlaid chin strap and using it for its actual intended purpose, to hold the hat on his head. After all, an officer's "cover" was to be worn at all times when out of doors. Then with a soft laugh, he tossed the hat into a safe corner on the deck beneath the bridge console.

The speed was liberating. It was as if ordinary rules of conduct no longer applied. Sitting high on that flying bridge, hurtling toward open water on their possibly absurd adventure, it all suddenly made perfect sense.

The chase was on.

Part Two

Sunset

"Meanwhile the sunsets are mad orange fools
raging in the gloom..."
Jack Kerouac

CHAPTER 30

Tuesday, April 18, 1978
Northern Puget Sound, Washington State
One mile northeast of Point No Point

It was a beautiful April day, bright and clear, warm enough to hint at the summer to come. As they thundered out of the Shilshole Bay Marina, Sydney had felt a surge of power and freedom, like she always did when beginning a boat trip. There was something intoxicating about the unobstructed vistas of sky and water blending into one another, about the thrill of velocity as the boat picked up speed, about the wind rushing past and the spray spreading wide beside the bow. About setting forth on a body of water that could carry you to anywhere on the planet.

There had, no doubt, been a good many yachtsmen back in the marina angered by their flagrant violation of boating etiquette. She knew the *Spindrift* threw one hell of a wake. But if their estimates were correct, they were already two and a half hours behind the Admiral's yacht, maybe more. There wasn't time for niceties; there wasn't even time to worry about getting a ticket, although if she had seen a police boat she would have definitely taken it back a few notches.

As the boat settled in for the long run, she looked over at Duncan. He seemed so solid and reliable seated next to her on the flying bridge. Solid, reliable, and loyal. She suspected he had come primarily because he hadn't wanted her to go on her own. In some ways she felt guilty, but it was the right decision. At least, she hoped to God it was.

Although he had removed his hat, Duncan still wore his uniform. As an actual U.S. Navy officer in full blues, one would think he'd have looked right in place on a boat, but for some reason he didn't. Maybe she was too used to seeing pleasure boaters in their stylish yachting attire. She had a momentary vision of Duncan in white duck trousers, one of those Gore-Tex jackets, and Sperry Top-Sider deck shoes. She couldn't help but smile; the image was so entirely unlike him.

He'd told her that his boating experience was limited to a few runs he had made on Navy shore barges and a couple of brief visits aboard Navy ships. When they'd cast off, he'd seemed a bit uncertain. But he'd managed fine. Even though it wasn't supposed to be a pleasure cruise, she somehow found herself wanting him to like this activity that had always been such an important part of her life.

She scanned the water ahead watching for drift, then turned toward Duncan when she heard him chuckle. "What's so funny?" she asked.

"Us."

"Us?"

"Yep. Here we are headed for freaking Canada, specific destination unknown, hoping to find a way to prevent a group of fanatic neo-Nazis from taking possession of a shipment of smuggled firearms. Does that sound real to you?"

Sydney smiled. "Well, I've got to admit, it isn't exactly something I'd marked down on today's calendar."

"What would *your* friends say?" he said.

"They've all given up on me," she said.

"Because you spend all your time working?"

"Yep."

"Be the same with mine. What would your father say? After all, it's his boat."

"I've gone out on my own before," she said. "But he'd probably say the same as you: 'What in God's name do you think you're doing?'"

He suddenly grew serious. "Well, what *are* we doing? Is this really a better move than the unethical anonymous tip we decided against making?"

"I suppose it's splitting hairs, but if we actually witness a crime being committed, wouldn't we have an independent obligation to report it?"

"It *is* splitting hairs. Look, we're on our way to who knows where based on what Beck told us. We can't exactly make a case for 'happening' across a crime being committed."

"But if we call the Canadian Coast Guard on the VHF radio from some place in Canada, no one has to know it's us."

"Come on," he replied. "The origin of the call would become obvious after the fact. And, if you don't identify yourself, what makes you think they'll take you seriously?"

"Because we'll have specific information."

"So, you've decided you're going to call the Coast Guard if you see something suspicious?"

"I'm not sure, but you have convinced me that we can't stand by and let an arms shipment enter the U.S." She thought about that. "I do have a great camera. With a telephoto lens. We might get a good distance photo or two, if we're careful."

"Depending on what we learn, Beck could still change his mind. This stuff could cut either way at trial. It might give the prosecution more ammunition for a conviction. But if, as he claims, he isn't involved, it could also suggest other powerfully motivated suspects."

"Other suspects that he believes would kill him if they found out he gave them up."

They were flying along, the April sun playing across the smooth water, intensifying reflections. It was pleasant despite the chilly wind buffeting the flying bridge. As it got cooler, and once they were beyond the area where there was a lot of small boat traffic, Sydney switched on the autopilot, and they climbed off the flying bridge and went into the pilothouse. It was quieter there because the cabin helped cut the engine noise from the outside exhaust and from the water. It was good to be out of the wind.

Today, Puget Sound was relatively flat, with occasional wakes from other boats. Sydney generally preferred the ocean, at least in good weather. There you could feel the motion of the waves and look out across a seemingly unending expanse of water. Suddenly it occurred to her that Duncan might not be as excited as she was about being on the open water. "Do you know if you get seasick?" she asked.

"I don't think so." He sounded surprised by the question. "I've been aboard ships a few times before and didn't have a problem."

"Some people react more when on a small boat like this."

"Well, I sure hope I don't. There's enough to think about without that."

She was pleased that he hadn't pulled the "men don't get seasick" routine that she had heard so often. She had never been seasick, but she didn't accept the notion that it was all in someone's head. Her father got seasick from time to time, and he certainly wasn't someone to succumb without a physical cause.

"When will we overtake him?" Duncan asked, looking into the hooded radar unit mounted on the deck beside the wheel, studying the blips on the radar screen.

"If I'm right about him doing about eight or nine knots, we should catch up somewhere off Port Townsend. He might do some night traveling, unless he's alone. It probably depends on where he's headed."

"If he stops, we stop?"

"Well, hopefully it won't be as obvious as all that."

"And you're convinced that it makes sense for a ship coming from the Philippines to Seattle to stop off in Canada?"

"I do. There's the *Ocean Passages of the World* on that shelf there, in the blue cardboard sleeve. Look in there and see what you think." She had been meaning to take a look herself. "Check the charts for power vessels."

"As opposed to 'sailing' vessels, you mean?"

"Yeah, I think there are several charts—one for sailing, one for auxiliary power, and one for power." She waited patiently while Duncan methodically went through the collection of charts and located the right one.

"Look at that," he said, holding up the chart for her to see. "It *does* make sense. At least distance wise."

She glanced over at the green arrows indicating the shipping lane routes. The great circle route from almost anywhere in the Far East went right past the sparsely populated outside coast of Vancouver Island. "There's lots of nice, uninhabited bays up there where one could easily offload in calm water onto smaller local vessels."

"Sure looks that way."

"They'd have no real choice," she said. "Once a vessel of any serious size passes Cape Flattery, it is closely tracked by the U.S. Coast Guard's Vessel Traffic System. After that, there's no way you could count on quietly offloading much of anything without a customs search. It would become obvious. Be a huge risk. If they're going to offload that stuff somewhere, it has to happen up there in Canada."

Duncan continued to peruse the various charts.

"Well, as long as you're in the business," she said, "see how far it is from Port Townsend to possible stopovers tonight." She handed him a pair of dividers and the two Marine Atlases. "It's easier to figure distance on these."

He spread them on the chart table, got out a notepad, and made a list of possible stops. Next to each possibility he drew a small square. Then he made his calculations and entered them in the appropriate squares. When he finished, he said, "If he got underway shortly after nine like we think he did, at nine knots, he'll be off Port Townsend around noon. And if he heads west, as we expect, he'll be off Port Angeles in about four and at Neah Bay about eleven tonight. What do you think?"

"Well, I don't think he will want to go through Canadian customs. So, my guess is he will avoid stopping in Canada. Given that, he might stop off for the night at Neah Bay. Depends on where he's headed tomorrow and when he needs to be there. Most yachtsmen don't like running at night."

"How far can we get without stopping for fuel?"

"Once we slow down, at nine knots we'll use quite a bit less than usual. Say five gallons an hour. We've got 400 gallons, so eighty hours times nine knots, what does that come to?"

"About 720 miles," he said, doing the numbers in his head.

"Make that 500 to be safe. I'm not really sure of the fuel consumption. But we should be fine. We might have to chance stopping in a Canadian port at some point. My guess is that he will need fuel if we do."

The sense of speed had diminished now, both because they were inside the cabin and because on calm water away from land there was nothing to make their speed relative. Neither Duncan nor Sydney spoke for a time, relishing the smooth movement over water.

"This is nice," he said suddenly. "But it's going to be a long day."

"I'll expect you to spell me at the wheel."

"And I'll expect a couple of those donuts," he said.

"I figured you for a guy who might appreciate a donut."

For the next hour, Duncan played tourist as Sydney pointed out various places of interest along the shore. He spent much of the time looking through binoculars, admiring waterfront homes, and talking about how different the area was from where he had grown up in Indiana. It almost felt like they were on vacation.

Then, as they had anticipated, only a short distance beyond Port Townsend and past Point Wilson, they caught sight of the Admiral's yacht. Sydney studied the other boat through binoculars.

"That's him," she finally announced. "He's headed West. Now that we have him in sight, we can back off and follow. We'll let him get well ahead so he's not suspicious and then keep a close eye on the radar so we're sure we're tracking the right boat.

On the Straits of Juan de Fuca, the water had become choppy with the westerly breeze. And the ride worsened as they slowed down and came off a plane so as not to overtake the *Sea Leave.*

"Is it always like this here?"

"Always a bit rough, you mean?"

"Well, not exactly pleasant."

"It should get better after the tide change," Sydney said. "It sometimes feels better when you get offshore. The roll tends to be more gradual on the open water, unless it gets windy, of course." She gave him a big smile. "Not regretting those three glazed donuts, I hope?"

"I didn't know you were counting."

"How about you pilot for a while. That usually helps me orient myself."

He smiled and she smiled back. "You just want to loaf around while I do all the work."

"Sounds like a plan."

They gave the *Sea Leave* plenty of room while keeping careful track of it on their radar screen. After the tide change, the water did settle down. As expected, the *Sea Leave* continued West, out the Juan de Fuca Straits toward the open Pacific.

"He's staying on the south side of the Straits," Duncan noted not long after they passed Port Angeles.

"We may be right about him stopping at Neah Bay."

"Won't he notice us if we come in right behind him?" he asked.

"We won't be right behind him. It's a big bay with a good deal of boat traffic. I don't think we need to worry about him spotting us there in the dark. We'll give him a good long head start in the morning."

Duncan looked down at his white shirt. "You mentioned something about spare clothes?"

"Go below and have a look. See if you can find something to wear. Feel free to go through the drawers and closets. And there's a 12-volt converter and a shaver if you need it in the morning."

"All the comforts of home," he teased.

"Still no lime," she countered.

Duncan went below and came back a little later wearing a pullover and a faded pair of dungaree jeans. "There was quite a selection," he said. "These jeans are a little short." He looked down at his exposed ankles above his brightly polished Navy shoes. "But they'll do."

"I think they belong to my brother."

"Well, I hope he won't mind if I borrow them."

"I'm sure he won't. We always leave clothes on board, just in case we decide to go out on the spur of the moment." She gave him a once-over. "You look good in boating casual," she said.

"I don't *always* wear a uniform." He sounded a bit testy.

"But you're comfortable in the uniform, right?" Did that sound like an accusation?

"I like my uniform, yes. But when you get right down to it, men who wear suits every day to work are wearing a type of uniform."

"But they can choose the color," she said.

"Gray, dark blue, or the not-recommended-by-those-with-fashion-sense dark brown."

"You read dress for success books."

"I like to know about what's going on in the rest of the world," he said. "I've even been known to watch television. And once I actually read a book. In addition to *Tarzan of the Apes*, that is."

"Okay, okay, you've made your point."

There was a beautiful sunset that night. Sydney and Duncan opened a bottle of wine and enjoyed the fading daylight and a three-star dinner of canned chili and toast while exchanging turns at the wheel.

"This is the perfect wine with canned chili," Duncan said. "Fruity and aromatic, with a faint hint of the cask."

"One more remark like that and you can stay on the wheel the rest of the trip."

"Please, don't keelhaul me for insubordination. Oh, and would you hand me another weevilly biscuit, Captain?"

The *Sea Leave* pulled into Neah Bay shortly before ten that night. The yacht disappeared from their radar screen as it entered the harbor. Over an hour later, when they came around the corner, it was difficult to see much in the dark. Several boats were anchored behind the long breakwater. It took them a while to figure out which was the *Sea Leave*. When they did, they made sure to drop their anchor on the opposite side of the harbor, well away, but with a clear view of the entrance. It was a great relief when the anchor went down and their big engines finally went silent.

"We'll have to stand watch," Sydney said.

"I was just figuring that out."

"How about two hours on, two off?" she suggested.

"Sounds miserable but acceptable."

"Do you want me to sleep first, or do you want to?"

"I have too much sugar coursing through my veins to sleep," he said. "Why don't you sleep first?"

"Okay, stay away from the donuts, and wake me in two hours. And don't try to be all gentlemanly about this and let me sleep. We *both* have to be fully alert tomorrow."

CHAPTER 31

Wednesday, April 19, 1978
Neah Bay, WA
Aboard the Spindrift

It was after one o'clock when Duncan shook Sydney awake and led her to a steaming cup of coffee. Beside her cup there was a donut. "Not another donut," she groaned.

"Blame it on the purser," he said with a laugh.

Two hours later she was leading him to a cup of coffee, sans donut. "In a couple of hours, I'm going to fix us a real breakfast," she said.

Just before five, he woke her up. "He's leaving. We have to follow now."

"Thanks." She rolled off the bunk and tried to focus. "You're right. We have to be on his tail so we don't lose him after he leaves the harbor. Once outside we can dog it until he gets a good lead on us."

Sydney started the engines, and they pulled anchor. As they emerged from the harbor, they could still make out the *Sea Leave* in the distance in the early morning light. Van Damme was headed northwest, up the Vancouver Island coast. They idled along slowly until the other boat was at least an hour ahead, well out of sight, before following.

The ocean was surprisingly calm but with a large, oily, southwesterly swell coming up on their beam. It gave the boat a slow, lazy roll that came to be almost comforting as the hours passed. As promised, Sydney made them a big breakfast. Eggs and toast with some canned ham she found in the cupboard. Then they settled into a routine. First Duncan napped while Sydney stood watch, then Sydney took a turn in the bunk while Duncan took over the helm. They continued their on-and-off recuperation plan until midday when both finally felt reasonably rested.

When they passed Ucluelet, the *Sea Leave* stayed a good three or four miles offshore. Van Damme clearly had no plans to check in with Canadian Customs. It was another confirmation that this was no pleasure cruise. Just in case van Damme was paying close attention to his own radar, they pulled in close, just outside the Ucluelet harbor entrance, and hung out for about fifteen minutes. Then, they came back out around the headland and picked up the chase.

"From the chart, that Barkley Sound area sure looks interesting," Duncan commented as they ate lunch.

"It's a boaters' paradise," Sydney said. "We used to spend a lot of time there when I was young."

"Maybe some time when we aren't pressed, you might bring me up here again."

"I just might." She was pleased that he seemed to like being on the boat. Although she told herself, that still didn't change who he was at heart. It was, however, getting more and more difficult to think of him solely as a military officer.

This second day seemed longer than the first. The smell of fried eggs and coffee lingered in the small cabin. The remaining donuts were getting stale. And there was nothing else to snack on except for some dry bread and a sweet, soggy apple pie. In the afternoon a light northwest breeze came up, creating a low chop that jarred the boat and put spray on their windshield. But the weather remained fair and the sea generally tractable. With no end in sight, all they could do was try to enjoy the open ocean and the distant scenery.

While keeping a close eye on the radar reflection of that boat ten miles ahead.

It was getting quite late and growing dark when things changed.

"I think he's going in," Duncan said, leaving the wheel for a moment to stare for the umpteenth time into the hooded screen of the big Decca radar. It was almost ten. There was no moon. Only a few stars and a last distant western glow relieved the blackness of the night and the water.

Sydney got up from the couch and went over to look at the radar. "Hmm," she said. She looked at the chart. "I think he's going into Esperanza Inlet."

Duncan stepped over for a moment and took a glance at the chart. "Doesn't narrow things down much, does it?"

"Well, yes and no. He could be heading up one of the smaller inlets, but I doubt they'd want to take a ship of the size we expect too far inland. There's an anchorage just behind Rosa Island that looks like it would be a great spot for a rendezvous. Probably quite calm. Place to anchor with lots of space."

"What'll we do? Just nose in and keep our eyes open?"

"We should be able to spot a ship. If they're anchored up, or meeting someone, there'll be lights. But let's speed up a little so we don't lose him up the inlet."

Forty minutes later they were leaving the ocean swells behind. As they'd anticipated, the *Sea Leave* had turned in behind Rosa Island. Sydney and Duncan kept the *Spindrift* out toward the center of the broad inlet, but the Rosa Island anchorage was now coming into view off to their right. Sydney caught sight of what looked to be multiple anchored vessels on the radar screen—at about the same time Duncan spotted them visually. There were lights on the ship, and with the binoculars he could make out three smaller vessels tied to it on either side.

"Don't slow down. We need to look like we know where we're going," Sydney said, studying the chart. "There's a small anchorage up this inlet on our left, directly across the channel. Queen's Cove."

Duncan was scanning the open bay and the anchored ship. "There's the *Sea Leave*," he said. He handed her the binoculars. "Here, take a look. You can see its lights against the smaller boat on this side of the ship."

Steadying the glasses against the movement and vibration of the boat, she managed to make out a large ship with three smaller vessels rafted to it. One of the smaller vessels looked like it was van Damme's yacht. "That sews it up, wouldn't you say?"

"It does for me."

As they motored past and across to the far side of the inlet, Sydney suddenly felt apprehensive. It had been one thing to talk about an arms deal that might take place in some remote part of Canada, another to be on their own and within sight of the very event. This was an illegal undertaking by serious criminals with automatic weapons. She found herself lowering her voice as if they could be overheard. She could feel her heart beating and wondered if Duncan was feeling similarly uneasy.

They entered their small bay carefully under radar. She scanned the screen, then checked the bay with binoculars. She turned to Duncan. "So, what do you think now? Plan A?"

"Well, we haven't actually seen a crime being committed. And I sure as hell don't intend to whip back over there and ask what they're up to."

"We've come too far to back down now." In spite of her words, she was feeling both fearful and uncertain. "I sure don't see how we're likely to get any useful pictures in the dark. And I bet they'll be gone by morning."

"Let's anchor up and shut down these damned engines, okay? I don't know about you, but I can't think with all the noise."

With careful use of their radar and the chart, they eased the *Spindrift* into position and dropped the hook in about five fathoms of water. When the engines went silent, the cool, quiet, fir-scented night air washed Sydney with relief.

Then, almost immediately, they both heard the sound of outboard motors in the distance.

Duncan grabbed the binoculars and peered into the darkness in the direction of the sound. "It looks like there are two rubber boats, like your Zodiac, coming our way. From across the inlet. It's them. Shit!"

"Oh my god. You don't think they suspect something, do you?"

"I don't know, but they sure as hell aren't coming over here for a social visit. And it's too late to run." He looked around the cabin. "We need to do something. Let's get you out of sight just in case. Where the hell can you hide?"

Sydney quickly went through possible hiding places in her mind.

None seemed feasible. Then she thought of something. "Help me get into the engine compartment. It's here under these hatches. They might not look there." He didn't question the wisdom of the decision. They couldn't both hide, and she knew he wouldn't let her be the one to stay topside and deal with whatever was about to happen.

The engine compartment access was through two large removable trap doors in the pilothouse floor. Her choice wasn't driven by the secrecy of the space—anyone familiar with boats would know there'd have to be an engine compartment there. Rather, she chose it because it was small and awkward and might seem to be an unlikely place for someone to hide. On the *Spindrift*, it really was the only choice. And while the hatches were ringed with bronze edges that were entirely visible, they were still quite unobtrusive in the otherwise teak-planked pilothouse floor.

She barely had time to squeeze into the space alongside the engine when she heard the distinctive howl of outboard motors winding down. Duncan eased the hatch door closed, and she heard his footsteps as he quickly headed out onto the back deck.

It was dark, hot, and suffocating in the tiny space. Her arm was uncomfortably close to the exhaust manifold on one of the engines, still piping hot from the hard day's run. And there was something sharp pressing against her ankle. She tried to shift her weight to get more comfortable, but there was no room to maneuver. The space was much smaller than she had anticipated, clearly not designed for human occupation once the hatch was closed.

Pouring with perspiration, Sydney remained crouched in her awkward position and tried to be patient, summoning her inner Yogi.

CHAPTER 32

Wednesday, April 19, 1978
West coast of Vancouver Island, B.C.
A small cove on the north shore of Esperanza Inlet

There was nothing further to do but to face the thing head-on. Either the people in the Zodiacs suspected something or they were just being cautious. For a brief moment, Duncan considered the possibility that these were Canadian Coast Guard officers. The *Spindrift* had, after all, entered the country without checking customs. But he dismissed it as extremely unlikely and, as they drew closer, it was obvious these were not government boats.

There were so many ways in which he and Sydney might have been given away—through Commander Brier, through their client, by the Admiral figuring things out on his own. Even so, there was still a chance the men in the Zodiacs wouldn't be sure who he was or why he was here. The only course was to try to brazen it out.

Duncan stepped outside the cabin and stood in open greeting as the two speedboats slowed and pulled along each side of the anchored *Spindrift* and shut down their engines. They bumped gently against the hull in the wash of their own wakes.

"Ahoy there. You plannin' on anchorin' up here long?" said a man in one of the boats. The deep gravelly voice sounded familiar, but it was hard to see faces in the dark.

"Just for the evening, I guess," said Duncan. "Is there a problem?"

"Kind of a long way from home, aren't you?" the man said, indicating *Spindrift's* transom where "Seattle" was clearly written as her hailing port.

"Yeah, a ways, I guess," said Duncan, trying to sound relaxed. "Doing a little fishing. I hear the King salmon get pretty big up in this area in the spring." Perhaps they didn't know what he was doing there, after all. Maybe they were just being careful.

"Well, whadda ya know. Ha! Somehow I doubt that, Mr. Carmichael." There was a pause. "It *is* Carmichael, isn't it?"

The voice . . . now he remembered. From all those phone calls. This had to be Truman Beck, Arnie Beck's father. "Do I know you?" Duncan's question sounded hollow, even to him.

"Don't tell me you don't recognize my voice. I sure as hell recognize yours."

"Is that . . . Mr. Beck?" he said hesitantly.

"Yep, the same." Beck swung over the side onto *Spindrift's* back deck, leaving a second man in the boat. One of the two men from the other boat also swung himself aboard. He had a burn scar on his face that Duncan immediately recognized. "So," Beck said, "I guess we finally meet, huh?"

"I guess so." Duncan could see Truman Beck's vague resemblance to their client in the dim 12-volt overhead light mounted under the cabin overhang. Beck senior was a tall, fit-looking man in his late-forties. His hair was dark and closely cropped, his clothing and bearing also seemed almost military. His clear menace was in no way masked by the man's fake country charm. Duncan tried to ignore it: "So, um, what're you and your friends doing up here?"

Beck laughed. "I guess if *you're* here, *you* must know, huh? Goddammit, I been sayin' you were smarter'n we been giving you credit for. I guess my boy told you all about it, huh?"

Duncan tried one last time. "I don't know what you mean, Mr.

Beck. I'm just here for a little fishing. Needed to use up some accumulated leave time."

"Come off it, Carmichael. Clifford and me have had you on our radar ever since Cape Flattery. Got to admit, we weren't real sure till you tried that little 'fake-out' at Ucluelet. You ain't the only boat with a radar. You've had us worried—wonderin' who you were. But not too many yachts come across there without goin' through customs. Pretty gutsy coming here like this. Maybe also damned foolish." He turned to his companion. "Hey Lars, take a look below, will you? See if there's anyone else aboard."

Duncan wanted to object to Lars going through the boat, but the de-facto threat was clear. While they waited for Lars to complete his search, Beck stared at Duncan, studying his response to what was happening. Meanwhile, Duncan's mind was racing as he tried desperately to come up with some plausible rationale, something that might get Sydney and him out of this spot. He'd already tried the fishing ploy; he couldn't think of anything else.

"Fine lookin' boat," Beck said, glancing around. "Maybe a bit more'n one might expect on a Navy lieutenant's salary."

"Belongs to a friend. I use it from time to time." He was acutely aware of Beck's scrutiny and hoped his poker face would hide how worried he was about what Lars might find. Both he and Sydney had made their beds. But were there other signs of multiple occupants aboard the boat? Would Lars go through drawers and check the registration? How thorough would he be?

When Lars finally came out of the cabin he had a grin on his face. "Sucker came alone," he said.

"Well, that was good of you," Beck said. "That makes it easier for us." He motioned toward one of the Zodiacs. "Okay, Mr. Carmichael. You, me, and Clifford are going to have us a little heart-to-heart. I think you'll find it interesting. Let's go for a ride."

There were no guns in sight, but there were four of them, and in any case, he wanted them off the boat to avoid a more thorough search. If they looked more closely, they might notice the two coffee mugs, there in plain sight on the bridge console, or see some other evidence of Sydney's presence aboard.

Clearly Beck had no interest in listening to excuses, but perhaps van Damme would be more reasonable. Maybe there was still some way he could talk himself out of this mess. His only choice was to play along and hope he could convince them he was harmless to their endeavor.

"You want someone to stick around here, Mr. Beck?" asked Lars. "Keep an eye on things?"

Beck hesitated. Carmichael tried to appear unconcerned. The vision of Sydney crouching in the cramped engine compartment under the floor of the pilothouse made him weak with fear. He could easily picture one of the men reaching down to lift one of those all-too-obvious trap doors over the engine compartment.

"I don't think so," Beck finally replied. "Not much point. We're not going to be here more than a few hours. And we'll need everybody back at the ship if we want to get finished up and on our way."

Duncan climbed into the Zodiac with Beck, seating himself in front, facing backward. Lars jumped into the other one. Almost immediately the man in the rear cast off, started the outboard and, in moments. they were accelerating across the cold, dark, rippled inlet.

As Duncan looked back at the *Spindrift*, it grew smaller with the increasing distance and finally disappeared into the darkness. All he could think about was Sydney. If she acted quickly, and if whoever might be watching the radars on the vessels anchored across the inlet didn't call it out immediately, she might have a chance. The *Spindrift* was fast for her size. Not as fast as one of these Zodiacs, but if she could get the anchor up and get out to sea in a hurry, she just might escape. And, hopefully, bring help.

Sydney had no doubt heard what had been said by Truman Beck and him, but it was hard to know if she'd risk an emergency call to the Coast Guard on VHF channel 16. If she did, these folks would definitely hear that call. She might be better off giving him some time to try to talk his way out of it. Or simply make a run for it and then call the Coast Guard once she was clear.

The men rounded the end of Rosa Island and the ship came into sight. It was clear that the loading operation was well in hand. When they'd passed earlier, the lights and the focus of activity had been on the old wooden fish packer rafted along the shoreward side of the large ship.

Now the lights and booms had moved to a second packer on the opposite side.

The *Sea Leave* was rafted up to this second packer, toward its lower stern. The big wooden packer was at least forty feet longer than the *Sea Leave* with the large black expanse of its forward end and bow clearly visible as they approached. But it was dwarfed by the huge ship. He could see crates being lowered in nets down the side of the ship onto the forward hold of the packer. The ship itself was relatively small for a freighter, perhaps 300 feet long at most. But it towered over all three of the much smaller vessels tied beside it.

The Zodiac in which Duncan rode headed directly for the Admiral's yacht. Duncan allowed himself a moment of hope. Would the Admiral intercede for him? Could he convince van Damme that he wasn't a threat?

CHAPTER 33

Wednesday, April 19, 1978
West coast of Vancouver Island, B.C.
Behind Rosa Island

Van Damme was standing on the after deck of his yacht. When Duncan stuck his head above the transom and swung himself aboard, van Damme's surprise was obvious.

"Look what I got," said Beck.

"Carmichael? Jesus Christ, Carmichael!"

"Admiral," said Duncan, nodding his head.

"Goddammit, what do you mean by coming here?"

Beck said, "I don't guess he's here to fish for salmon, like he told me, huh?"

"Goddammit, Carmichael. Have you got any idea how badly you've screwed up?"

"Only if you think I have, Admiral. I can explain." On the ride over, Duncan had been thinking feverishly about his pitch. Now might be his only chance to make it.

"It better be one hell of an explanation."

"Well, Admiral, this may not be as serious as you think."

"This ought to be good," said Beck, rolling his eyes.

"All right, goddammit," said van Damme. "Get in here and we'll talk."

Van Damme motioned for Duncan to precede him into the close warm cabin of the yacht. "Beck," he said. "Go and see how the loading is coming along. I can deal with this."

Ignoring the Admiral, Beck instead pushed his way inside. "Nuh-uh," he said. "Nope. This I'm keeping my eye on."

Beck sat heavily on the small couch/berth across the central aisle from the settee table. When he sat, his unzipped jacket opened in front and Duncan caught sight of a handgun holstered under his left arm. Duncan sat on the upholstered bench to one side of the table. Van Damme slid in on the other side.

"I can't believe this," said van Damme. "I suppose you're here because your client told you about this?"

"Well, that's actually the point, Admiral," Duncan replied, launching his argument. "I can't tell you that. Or anything else about what my client might have told me. It's all confidential."

"Jesus, where do you stop, Carmichael? How far do you go to get some killer like Beck off?"

Beck senior leaned forward. "That's my boy you're talking about here. And he didn't do it."

"Look," said Duncan, "You don't have anything to worry about with me. I can't repeat any of this if I learned about it from my client. The lawyer's ethics won't permit it. That's why I'm here and not the police."

"Bullshit," said Beck.

"It's true." Duncan turned toward Beck. "I'm not permitted to report this because my presence here and my knowledge about what's happening is based on a confidential communication with a client. That's why I never told you anything in our phone conversations, Mr. Beck. It's protected by law."

"I knew you were holding out on me. Maybe you and Lars here have already run across each other. I had him keeping tabs on you."

"Look, Beck. I couldn't tell you anything. And I can't tell anyone else either. Your son has sworn me to secrecy. I'd be disbarred if I reported it."

"I knew that boy had some good sense."

"I suppose your co-counsel knows where you are?" said van Damme.

"Yes. Yes, sir, she does." For whatever that was worth. "We agreed that I should come up to see if I could learn something that might be helpful for our defense. Something SA Beck would let us use."

"Goddammit, Carmichael, I'd like to believe you, but I'm finding it difficult."

Beck laughed. "Of course you are. 'Cause it's bullshit. Total bullshit!"

"You know what else you've done, don't you?" said van Damme. "You know the unbelievable irony of all this?"

Duncan waited for the Admiral to continue.

"You and that ACLU woman didn't need to do a goddamn thing. You could've sat on your butts in defending that case. I've been trying to get that kid off for the past two months." He shook his head in disgust.

Duncan tried to see where this was going.

"You've just been screwing things up," van Damme said, "with all your motions, federal appeals, and legal crap. You and that woman lawyer have been a pain in the ass from beginning to end."

Truman Beck shook his head. "We gave you two fair warnings to take it down a notch. But you wouldn't take the hint."

Suddenly the light dawned.

The hard time they'd had from the Commandant's Office had not been an effort to get Beck convicted. Quite the contrary. Each step of the way, van Damme had been trying to provide a plausible excuse to reverse the conviction when he reviewed the case after the trial. Each roadblock, the denial of discovery of the drug investigation, withholding examination of Jerome's personal effects, and especially Duncan's transfer to Fleet Air Whidbey, all had been the Admiral's effort to plausibly inject reversible error into the case. Even if he didn't reverse it himself, Captain Clayton might have done so at trial. Or it would have ultimately been reversed on appeal. This is what SA Beck had been talking about when he'd said the Admiral was supposed to get him off.

It was obviously a part of the broader understanding between Truman Beck and the Admiral. This was also why van Damme felt safe out here in the wilds of British Columbia, completing this transaction in person with these armed and desperate men. Truman Beck needed van Damme in place to protect his son.

Duncan was staggered at the realization that each time they'd successfully thwarted one of van Damme's efforts, they had brought their client one step closer to a permanent residence at Leavenworth Federal Penitentiary.

Van Damme was watching him react to this news. He shook his head. "I guess you get it now, huh? But that still doesn't answer the question of what to do with you."

"I haven't reported any of this. If I had, I wouldn't be here, and you'd have the police all over you by now. Once your people have finished here and your boats are on their way, I'm no further threat to you. What am I going to do—make an anonymous and completely unethical call to the Canadian Mounties and tell them that somewhere out there are some boats with guns aboard and would they please go look for them?"

Van Damme's glance wandered in the direction of Beck. "Maybe not." Duncan was starting to appreciate that van Damme wasn't the man in charge here.

"Anyway, I can't even do that," he continued. "I can't do a thing. I can't say a thing. I've got to respect my client's confidence. Follow his instructions. It's that simple."

"I suppose we can keep you prisoner for a while . . ."

"No fucking way," Beck interrupted. "This is all a line of crap. You know it, Clifford. And I know it. There's only one thing to do with this asshole. Save us all a lot of trouble."

"I'm not going to have any unnecessary violence, Beck. These are *my* weapons. It's *my* ship. We'll do this my way."

Beck scoffed. "Not anymore, they're not. Anyway, it doesn't matter whose they are. I can guarantee you I'm not letting this walking time bomb leave here. No way." The rural drawl had disappeared, leaving a hard, practical, no-nonsense authority to his speech.

Duncan began thinking about escape. His eyes wandered about the room, measuring what it would take for him to make a run for it. If he leaped up unexpectedly, could he force his way outside? If he jumped overboard, could he swim to shore in the icy water in the dark? Or hide beneath one of these vessels? Being a Navy lawyer, even one in fairly good physical shape, he wasn't even faintly prepared for this kind of situation. He couldn't imagine how any of those rash actions could succeed.

Lars was half-seated on the high bulwark outside the cabin doorway with his arms resting at his sides. There was the unmistakable blue steel glint of the .38 automatic he held in his right hand. Duncan knew his dreams of escape were just that, dreams. Reality was two trained men with guns, Lars and Beck. Men who weren't about to let him get away. There would be no fancy karate kick. No daring race for the railing. No miraculous leap to safety. No physical courage in the face of danger. His fate lay in the hands of van Damme and Beck, in the interplay between their characters, in whatever uncertain authority Admiral van Damme still retained in this explosive situation. And in his own ability to persuade them.

He also realized that even if Sydney escaped, she and the authorities would clearly be far too late to do him any good. This situation placed a whole new twist on the law of attorney-client privilege. Ironically, with his life in immediate danger, he suspected the rules would change—not that legal niceties would make any difference to her decision. But that was all irrelevant now. By the time she got help, by the time the authorities were notified, convinced, urged on, and brought to the scene of this drama, it would be far too late to save him. By then, these boats and their cargo would be long gone.

And so would he.

Whatever thin hope there might be lay in delay.

"You're making a mistake, Beck," he said, turning his arguments on the man he now knew held the balance of power. "I understand why you think I'm a risk. But I'm not. This is how things work. The reason you couldn't get anything out of me on those phone calls you made. I couldn't talk about the case because it was confidential. Any lawyer will tell you the same thing. Admiral van Damme knows this; he deals with us all the time. He knows what I'm saying is true."

Duncan looked to van Damme for support and received a grudging, tentative nod. Van Damme must be aware that there were limits to the confidentiality rule, but it appeared that outright murder went beyond his comfort zone.

"Think about it, Beck. I've worked my ass off for your son—you know that. I walk out of here, there're no complications. Sydney Warren doesn't start wondering why I didn't come back from this excursion. You get your rifles. The Admiral gets his money. We go back to work on your son's case, keep our mouths shut, van Damme does his thing on the case review, and your son goes free. Just like everybody wants."

Beck was shaking his head, unimpressed.

"For God's sake, man, that's my job. That's what I'm supposed to do, get your son off. Can't you see that? We're almost home. Now that I've got the whole picture here, I can help things along rather than hindering them. Help give the Admiral the excuse he needs to reverse your son's case if he gets convicted."

Duncan took a quick breath. "If I don't come back, you think Sydney Warren's going to help you? Help your son? She knows about this shipment of yours. She's going to guess what happened to me. What do you think she's going to do, give your son a medal?"

Beck sneered. "Cross that bridge when we get to it, is all. She won't know shit. And it'll be way too late for her to do much by then. Anyways, if we have to, we'll deal with her too."

There was a moment of silence. The crackle of a distant vessel's call on channel 16 came over the VHF radio mounted over the pilot seat. The hum of the auxiliary power plants on the freighter above drifted on the night air. Fenders squeaked quietly against the side of the yacht where it was moored to the packer. Water lapped softly against the hull. And the grind of machinery and occasional calls of the crew could be heard outside as the offloading of crates of arms continued.

Van Damme slid to the outside edge of the upholstered settee bench and stood to his full height. He was an impressive man. His short, prematurely greying hair brushed against the overhead. "This is all pointless," he said with a voice matured by years of military command. "Carmichael, get your ass up forward and stay put until we decide what to do with you. Lars, go with this man and keep an eye on him."

It was a play for power. Duncan quickly moved to the end of the bench to comply, but Lars, standing there in the doorway, was not moving. Instead, he was looking to Beck for instructions. Lars was obviously Beck's man, not van Damme's. The deckhands working on the neighboring packer, the men receiving the shipment, all of them would be Beck's men too. The crew of the ship high above might report to van Damme, but they were too far away to be of any help. In any case, they were no more than ordinary sailors who'd sailed this ship across the Pacific. They might not even be armed. It seemed unlikely they'd be primed and ready for this kind of situation in the way that Beck's white supremacist true-believer acolytes clearly were.

Then Beck spoke. "Sit down, Clifford. I said, *sit down*. I'm not having this jaybird walking around loose no matter what you'd like. That's just the way it is."

Van Damme reluctantly sat back down on the end of the settee bench, as ordered. Duncan recognized that van Damme's defeat marked his own demise.

Beck looked over at Duncan and said, "Lars, we're going to need you to perform a good deed for God and country." He turned and looked directly at Lars. "You think you're up to that?"

Lars had moved inside the doorway and had his automatic aimed up at a forty-five-degree angle. His forefinger rested along the side of the trigger guard. Duncan wondered fleetingly if the safety was on or off. But he also realized that it made no difference. Even if there had been no gun, he could never take on both, or maybe all three of these fit and determined men.

Lars nodded. He was ready to serve his Leader, ready to kill to eliminate an enemy of the cause. Duncan was going to end up just another story in the *Navy Times,* a tiny back-page headline: "JAGC Officer Disappears While on Leave."

Duncan launched his plea again in a last desperate effort to save his life. "This isn't necessary, Beck. All you'll be doing is making problems for yourself and making it that much more difficult for your son. Think about it, man, give it some time and think it through."

But it was no good. Beck nodded to Lars and Lars motioned with his gun for Duncan to come outside. For a moment Duncan wondered if he had a better chance staying where he was, but he couldn't see how. As he stood up, he considered grabbing hold of Beck and somehow using him as a shield, but the idea quickly faded. He had no weapon, and Beck's right hand had now moved beneath his jacket and was obviously resting on his own gun. Beck was a big man and clearly a strong one. In any case, Lars would shoot him before he took a second step.

Lars backed out of the door and moved aside so that Duncan could get through. For the first time, the gun was aimed somewhere in the area of Duncan's lower chest. The trigger finger no longer lay along the guard; it now rested lightly on the trigger itself. Duncan was now very sure that the safety was off. And the man's aim was steady as a rock.

As he stood there in the doorway, half in and half out, he looked toward the side of the boat and then back at the gun. He pictured himself in the icy water, his heavy clothing dragging him down, people shooting at him from point-blank range. He looked again. It was too far. He'd never make it.

For one self-insightful moment, the irony of the situation almost made him laugh. All those years perfecting his persuasive skills as a courtroom lawyer, and he'd failed this final, life-in-the-balance test: convincing Beck to let him go. All those runs and lunch-hour workouts, what good were they now as he faced down an automatic? He had the crazy impulse to tell someone about this sudden discovery, this last stinging truth.

In that moment of silence inside the cabin, there was another crackle of a call coming over the VHF radio.

"Turn that fucker up," said Beck suddenly.

Van Damme stood, reached over, and turned up the volume.

CHAPTER 34

Wednesday, April 19, 1978
West coast of Vancouver Island, B.C.
Behind Rosa Island

"Guard back to *Spindrift*. Canadian Coast Guard back to the vessel *Spindrift*. Over."

"*Spindrift* to Coast Guard. This is an emergency. I repeat, this is an emergency. Immediate law enforcement assistance is required as a matter of life or death. Do you copy? Over."

Duncan recognized Sydney's voice as well as the now-familiar noise of marine engines howling in the background. She was free as he had hoped. And she had the anchor up and was under way. From the sound of it, probably at speed. He watched the others closely to see how this call might affect his situation as he stood motionless in the doorway, acutely conscious of the black bottomless hole at the end of Lars' .38 automatic.

"*Spindrift* back. My location is at latitude forty-nine degrees, fifty point five minutes north, longitude one twenty-seven degrees two minutes west. I am at the entrance to Esperanza Inlet, North end of

Nootka Island at an anchorage behind Rosa Island. Do you copy? Over."

The Coast Guard radio operator faithfully repeated the location. Van Damme and Beck were both standing now, motionless, as if struck dumb by the call. Then, Beck suddenly spun around, pushed past Duncan and Lars, and went out onto the back deck.

"Hey, boys," he shouted. "Hey there. Listen up. We got us a problem. We got cops coming. Wind this shit up fast and let's all get out of here. Forget the rest of that. Let's get all three of these tubs the hell out of here while there's still time."

Inside the cabin, the call continued. "*Spindrift* to Coast Guard. Roger. That is correct. The situation here is that a shipload of illegal military arms is at the present moment being loaded off a ship onto two large fish packers. There is human life in immediate danger. Do you copy that? Over."

Van Damme didn't move. He seemed unable to act, unable to decide what to do given the change in circumstances. Then slowly he turned and looked at Duncan. Of the various emotions that crossed his face, the most salient was nothing more than simple, profound disappointment.

Finally, van Damme too came to life. He started the yacht's engines. Then he went out the door past Duncan and Lars. During all this time Lars's gun never once wavered.

"Goddammit Lars, what're you standing there for?" Beck suddenly screamed from the deck of the packer. "Git rid of this fucker. Do it now! Then get over here and give us a hand."

Duncan tensed. He had decided that it would be better to die in a dive for freedom than to let himself be slaughtered. Good or bad, he would take whatever opportunity presented itself.

Lars motioned him to move away from the cabin. But at that moment, at the edge of consciousness, above the din of shouts and the clatter of diesel engines starting, from across the dark water there arose a distant, high-pitched, metallic howl—the sound of heavy marine engines wound up tight at top speed. It was overcast and pitch-black outside. No moon or stars were visible—especially blinded by the ship's floodlights shining from above. Even the nearby shadow of land was hard to distinguish. The howl quickly became a roar and then a scream. Lars was distracted by it. As was Beck. And van Damme. They all paused to peer into the night.

"There! Look there," said Beck. They all turned in the direction he was pointing. Duncan saw the unmistakable glow of running lights. Red *and* Green! Both were visible together only when seen from straight ahead. And coming closer. Fast!

He knew the sound of those engines; he had listened to them for two full days and could not mistake their peculiar deep-throated, animal resonance, their penetrating, syncopated rhythm as they ran on full power together.

It was Sydney. Sydney, heading in their direction. With the *Spindrift* under power, on a plane, and running flat out from the sound of it. Sydney screaming out of the darkness in her massive boat at twenty-two knots. All the while, he could hear her still talking to the Coast Guard, obtaining that last assurance, the final certainty that help was on its way. And soon.

But this was crazy. What could she do? What was even conceivably possible? She had no weapons, nothing to fight with. She would be helpless against these men. Even though the Canadian authorities were alerted, it would take a long time, possibly hours before they could have officers on the scene. Duncan could imagine the cumbersome bureaucracy slowly gearing up. First deciding if the call was credible. Then determining how quickly they could respond. Selecting the agency, the personnel, the equipment, and the level and type of preparedness for the response team. If they took as long to get there as the U.S. Navy would take, he was certain there would be nothing left to find when they finally arrived.

Other than two bodies floating on the outgoing tide.

The other men watched, frozen, as the *Spindrift* approached, not certain what to do, perhaps wondering if this speeding vessel could be the Canadian Coast Guard already on the scene. Only Duncan knew better. And he couldn't think of a single way to use that small advantage.

The entire time, the radio call continued to blare: "I repeat. I repeat again. Rosa Island anchorage. West Coast Vancouver Island.

Esperanza Inlet. There is an entire shipment of military arms being loaded onto two smaller vessels, which appear to be fish packers. There is also a U.S. registry yacht by the name of *Sea Leave* owned by one Clifford van Damme. Van Damme, the yacht, and the ship are all in Canada illegally. These vessels will escape unless immediate assistance is rendered. The smugglers have also taken a hostage. The matter is life and death. I repeat, the matter is life and death. Do you read? Over?"

Out beyond the stern of the ship, Duncan could see the first, now fully-loaded packer, the one that had been rafted up to the other side of the ship. It was now untied and backing away in anticipation of making its escape. A clanking noise could be heard from the opposite direction, from somewhere toward the bow of the ship, the sound of a heavy anchor being raised. But on the *Sea Leave* and behind them on the decks of the second packer, all eyes were turned in the direction of the howling phantom coming at them from the black of night.

Suddenly, Duncan was blinded by two powerful searchlights, one on each side of the *Spindrift's* flying bridge. They illuminated the entire scene: the tall dark ship, the packer with its high wood-planked bow, the smaller yacht rafted up near the packer's stern, and the men standing transfixed.

With the searchlights glaring, it was clear that the *Spindrift* was closer than he'd thought; she was almost on top of them. And still traveling at top speed, the engines at full power, hurtling in their direction like a twelve-ton surface borne guided torpedo.

In that instant, he realized exactly what Sydney was about to do.

She wasn't slowing down. She had no plan to somehow take on this gang of desperate men alone. Her plan was simpler and much more direct.

She was taking aim!

The *Spindrift's* pointed, bronze-capped, heavily reinforced bow was directed unerringly, just ahead of the bow of the *Sea Leave,* aimed at the broadest, tallest, most vulnerable place on the high planked side of the remaining packer.

The others saw that now, as well. Some stood motionless in disbelief. Two men began to scramble away from the obvious point of impact. One man had begun climbing the long boarding ladder hanging down over the side of the ship.

The *Spindrift* wasn't slowing. It wasn't turning.

Sydney was going to ram them.

Duncan almost laughed out loud.

After the build-up and anticipation, the collision itself was almost anti-climactic. There were no screams. There was no explosion. There was only a single, violent, wrenching crash, a powerful lurch as twelve tons of yacht slammed at twenty-two knots directly into the high, wood-planked side of the second packer, and then the futile shriek of the *Spindrift's* engines as they churned up useless foam in the dark still water.

Then, they too fell silent.

CHAPTER 35

AFTERMATH
April, 1978
British Columbia, Canada

Before daylight on the morning following the events in Esperanza Inlet, the cargo vessel Isabela was seized thirty miles off the coast of Vancouver Island. Among those on board the ship were Truman Beck, Lars, and several other members of Beck's white nationalist group. In addition, there were accomplices identified as Canadian neo-Nazis from cross-border groups affiliated with the U.S.-based Independence League. There were also several Philippine nationals and an American skipper employed by North Ocean Fisheries in Seattle, WA, USA.

The ship's cargo hold was empty. In an apparent pact of silence, none of the crew initially admitted knowing anything about the weapons, the balance of which were assumed to have been jettisoned into the ocean overnight. Later, however, after they'd all secured legal representation, their collective silence was ultimately fractured as the individual benefits of cooperation with the government became clear.

Van Damme and his yacht managed to escape entirely. The Canadian and U.S. Coast Guards actively searched for him for several days, but he had disappeared.

What seemed obvious to Sydney and Duncan was that van Damme's long-standing financial problems had undoubtedly been the catalyst for his criminal enterprise. The remaining weapons seized from the hold of the half-loaded, beached, and partly sunken packer left behind at the Rosa Island anchorage were soon identified by the U.S. Army Supply Corps as having come from a much larger inventory of M-16s which had been requisitioned late in the Viet Nam War, intended for use by ARVN forces. They'd been believed abandoned by the retreating U.S. Army, their loss written off as just one more casualty of the fall of Saigon.

In the months that followed, Sydney and Duncan speculated endlessly about how van Damme had ended up in possession of those rifles. As a military liaison officer at the U.S. Embassy in Saigon, he would not have had access to military materiel. But he would have had ready contact with officials of the South Vietnamese government, including ARVN officers who did have such access. At the war's end, there had been a big news story about lost military materiel abandoned upon the fall of Saigon. There'd been mention of an ARVN colonel, a Colonel Du, who was said to have made off with a large quantity of abandoned U.S. military equipment and supplies before disappearing.

Colonel Du or someone like him could easily have taken possession of those weapons and could also have had the kind of black-market connections needed to find a ready buyer. But he'd have needed a way to get them out of the country. Conveniently, there was this U.S. Navy officer who was desperate for money and who owned a ship. It would have been a partnership made in heaven for both of them.

But the rifles had obviously NOT been sold.

Instead, they'd been kept somewhere in storage for three years before van Damme had finally struck a deal with Truman Beck and the Independence League. Keeping the ship and those weapons stored for all that time seemed like a horrible risk for van Damme to have taken, a risk he'd never have taken intentionally.

Given the turmoil at the time, it seemed likely that van Damme's Vietnamese contact had delivered the weapons and then vanished in the chaos of the collapse, leaving van Damme in possession of the rifles without a buyer. When van Damme was elevated to Rear Admiral and reassigned as Commandant at the 13th Naval District back stateside, he would have been left with a big problem and very few options.

By the fall of 1977, his creditors were closing in. Sydney and Duncan had learned from Mel Marshall how van Damme had managed to keep his personal ownership of the Isabela secret from North Ocean Fisheries' creditors. His "accommodation of creditors" agreement had saved him for a time, but now those creditors were beginning to circle, looking for personal assets owned by van Damme himself, intending to "pierce the corporate veil" and hold van Damme personally liable for the debts of his "closely-held" corporation. It wouldn't be long before they found the Isabela. And soon after that, the ship and its contents could end up under the control of a bankruptcy court. The court's first action would be to have it closely examined and appraised by a court-appointed marine surveyor. Time was running out.

Sometime in the fall of the previous year, the Seattle Post-Intelligencer had carried an article about a right-wing neo-Nazi group in Northeastern Washington that had received a substantial bequest from the estate of a wealthy deceased Yakima County hops farmer. Van Damme may well have seen the article or heard about it and approached them about the sale of the M-16s.

Selling those rifles would have been his Hail Mary, his last hope of a way out for his beloved fish company and for a stable retirement.

A few days after the events at Rosa Island anchorage and the seizure of the ship, the second packer, the one that had escaped fully loaded, was discovered empty and abandoned, tied to a transient dock at Port Hardy, B.C. Those rifles, too, were presumably somewhere at the bottom of the sea.

The day before the empty fish packer's discovery three men had taken a chartered flight from Port Hardy to Vancouver, B.C. No one could give a good description of any of the men. And the man who'd arranged the charter had used a false ID.

After landing in Vancouver, they, like the rifles, had vanished.

Chapter 36

Wednesday, May 3, 1978
Sand Point Naval Station, Seattle
Law Center—Upstairs Courtroom, 13th Naval District

"Your Honor and members of the court."

When Sydney Warren squared off for her final summation to the court-martial panel, she knew she had their full attention. This was the first time some of them had sat on a jury—military or otherwise. And it was certainly the first time any of them had seen a Navy case argued by a civilian lawyer, let alone by a woman. They were all in uniform, all in the same employment, all schooled in military discipline, and all men. She couldn't help but mistrust their ability to set aside their military bias when listening to the facts. Still, maybe Duncan was right. Maybe their military dress was more superficial than she believed. Maybe what these people wore wasn't all that different from the civilian clothing worn by most businesspeople. Including downtown attorneys like her.

"The evidence you have heard these past several days has been a powerful demonstration of a fundamental fact about the human mind. A fact we all find it easy to forget, despite life's constant reminders. That fact is . . . that things are not always what they seem. As humans, we all yearn for simple, reliable truths. But the very fact that appears to be most certain may be the very one that requires your most careful scrutiny. In our desire to make sense of things, we sometimes see connections that aren't really there. And miss the ones that are."

Overall, Sydney was not unhappy with the court-martial panel. Pursuant to the ACLU's reasons for asking her to become involved, Sydney had probed carefully for any sign of reverse discrimination by the Navy. She'd found nothing. In fact, the court-martial panel was all white. In a civilian court, if the victim and the person accused were both employees of the same company, or the same agency of government, any prospective juror who was also likewise employed would almost certainly be rejected from the panel. No matter how large that company or agency might be. At best, this group reflected a cross-section of a very tightly-knit Navy hierarchy.

"Arnie Beck was but a pawn in a massive game of blackmail, neo-Nazi plots, and the smuggling of military arms. During the weeks and months preceding Steven Jerome's murder, a complicated series of events was unfolding that had nothing whatever to do with Seaman Apprentice Beck. They were none of his making, yet they sucked him inexorably into a circumstantial role as the scapegoat for the wrongs of others. Some of them were wrongs committed at the highest levels of the Navy hierarchy.

"You have heard evidence that Beck publicly argued with Steven Jerome two days before the murder. Seaman Apprentice Beck doesn't deny that. But ask yourself, how could he have more publicly brought himself to the attention of the real killers who, at that point, already had a plan in play? You have also heard that Beck was believed by his peers to be a racist. Doubtless you disapprove of such views. But if this evidence is true, who better to choose as the fall guy for the killing of a black man?

"You have heard that Beck was also known to carry a knife. And that he left his knife hanging openly beside his bed when he slept. What more obvious weapon could be found for such a crime? You have heard he left his shoes, as all the sailors did, beneath his bed at night. How could it possibly be easier to misdirect the blame than to wear the proxy's shoes while committing the crime, to walk with them in the frosty grass, and to replace them beneath Beck's bunk when he, along with everyone else, predictably went to investigate the disturbance at the back of the barracks?

"Arnie Beck is *not* the killer. Rather, he is a handy scapegoat. A person who, like you or me, like any person in this courtroom, can become an easy target when others will not look beyond appearances. He is alone, and he is fighting for his life."

Arnie had been consistently uncooperative. But his confidence was badly shaken when he came to understand that he no longer had Admiral van Damme in his corner and that his father was under arrest and facing criminal charges in Canada as well as likely extradition for further charges by the U.S. Attorney. Arnie was angry with them. But he was also a realist. With characteristic inconsistency, he kept Sydney and Duncan on as his lawyers. And he agreed that they could use the events in Canada as a part of his defense. Fortunately, this washed away any breach of confidentiality. Thankfully, they'd never need to test their legal theory that an imminent threat to human life would be an exception to the lawyer-client privilege.

This also gave them their strongest argument in his defense. They claimed that several people other than Arnie wanted Jerome out of the picture. For example, the drug ring operating out of the base had reason to be upset with Jerome—*someone* had sent what NIS insisted was a fake partial confession to Hal Willis in an apparent attempt to get Jerome fingered and possibly killed. And now, with the arms trading evidence, they could also show that both van Damme and the Independence League had been deeply concerned about the threat Arnie Beck had posed to their criminal enterprise as well.

"When you look carefully at the circumstances surrounding Jerome's murder, you will see that his death was not the result of an angry outburst by a single man. Rather, it was the product of careful planning by a cunning group of desperate men, men whose motives were far more powerful, immeasurably more compelling than a mere insult or racial bias. Their motive was self-protection, gentlemen. Fear of financial losses. Fear of criminal disclosure. Fear of prison.

"Consider Jerome's likely confederates in the drug smuggling ring.

They knew his part in their operation had been discovered. They were unscrupulous men. They wanted to prevent his testimony.

"Consider Admiral van Damme and the Independence League. They were frightened that Jerome had become unreliable; they feared what he might reveal about their enterprise. There was a lot of money at stake. Van Damme needed his share to save his fish processing company. And the Independence League had big plans for the weapons they were purchasing from him. This deal would put them on the map.

"A lot of people with very strong motives wanted Steven Jerome dead. And Arnie Beck was the perfect scapegoat. Estranged from his father, with no connection whatsoever to drugs, and only a tenuous connection to the Independence League. There was nothing that would lead him back to either group. All that would be needed to put him in the crosshairs of Navy investigators would be to manufacture a couple of 'indisputable' facts. His wet shoes and that bloody knife were not an accident. They were an absolute necessity. They would be decisive evidence against Arnie Beck. And for the real killer, creating them was as simple as it could be."

Sydney had prepared this argument carefully and had performed it again and again for Duncan, assimilating his suggestions, making changes, refining. She was sorry he could not be the one to deliver it. But his role as a witness had required his disqualification from participating as defense counsel at trial. Arnie had accepted this decision easily enough. For her and for Duncan, however, it had been a difficult one. This meant he'd been excluded from the courtroom during the trial, along with the rest of the witnesses. But it also enhanced the credibility of his testimony, an important factor considering how indispensable his testimony was in establishing the key elements of their client's defense.

As a witness on Arnie's behalf, Duncan had been allowed to tell the court-martial panel his theory of events in explaining the motivation for his own conduct. First, there was the Admiral's plan to import the weapons and sell them to the Independence League. He described their pursuit of the Admiral's yacht up the coast to its rendezvous with the illegal shipment. He related van Damme's admission of his part in the enterprise. And he told them about his own brush with death, of Sydney's call for help, and her dramatic arrival on the scene. How he'd managed in the confusion to leap aboard the sinking packer and hide there while the Admiral had cut his yacht loose and made his escape into the night.

And while Truman Beck and the rest of his cohorts had swarmed aboard the *Isabela*, cut the sinking packer free, and made their own escape. He described how he and Sydney had used the significantly damaged but intact and operational *Spindrift* to power the sinking packer into shallow water so its partial cargo of arms could serve as evidence when the Canadian authorities arrived.

"Remember, Arnie Beck had nothing to do with drugs, with arms shipments, or with any of the other illegal activities swirling around him, other than that he'd been told about them. He was an innocent young man surrounded by vipers.

"Please think long and hard about the motive the prosecution has alleged, Beck's dislike of Jerome. They may have fought, but Beck was the victor, not Jerome. Beck had no romantic interest in Jerome's girl-friend, Lea. And no one even knew that she had turned him down. Everyone thought he was sleeping with her, even Jerome. Their alleged relationship might have provided a reason for *Jerome* to want revenge on *Beck*, but not the other way around."

Sydney and Duncan felt that the weakest element of the prosecu-tion's case was proving motive. Beck may have disliked Jerome for his race, but in this situation, that didn't seem like a sufficiently powerful motive for murder. They'd considered and discarded calling Beck as a witness in his own defense. They were convinced he'd be a poor witness and vulnerable on cross-examination. In addition, his testimony would make his prior conviction known to the court-martial panel; they simply could not afford that.

"If Arnie Beck had murder on his mind, he could have killed Jerome that Friday night, immediately after he and Jerome came to blows. But why would he have done that? His manhood was intact. He hadn't lost the fight; it had been stopped by others. He hadn't been forced back on his claim to have slept with Lea; Jerome had believed it. The fact is, after that fight, there was nothing left to fester and explode into violence."

Both the prosecution and the defense had been left with one final uncertainty that could have provided some answers: following the collision at Rosa Island, Admiral Clifford van Damme and the *Sea Leave* had vanished into the night. On balance, van Damme's disappearance had been very good for the defense. It infused the trial with a sense of mystery as well as fostered general doubt about the events surrounding Jerome's murder.

The RCMP and FBI were inclined to believe that van Damme may have been killed by his disillusioned associates and that his yacht, the *Sea Leave*, had been scuttled offshore. To Sydney's surprise, Duncan told her that he preferred to believe the Admiral had perhaps escaped to another country and might now be relaxing in Fiji or some similar place, living under a new identity, ignoring the support payments he owed to his ex-wife. At that very moment, he might be sipping a cool drink on the back deck of a renamed *Sea Leave*, gazing out over clear blue water under a bright sun.

Sydney, however, secretly thought van Damme had killed himself. Here was a man in his late forties, divorced, financially strapped, and prevented from being with a much-loved daughter. His prestigious military career was over. He had failed in a desperate gamble to redeem the dying heritage of his family business. And if caught, he faced financial ruin, prosecution, and total disgrace. In her view, suicide did not seem at all unlikely. Sydney pictured him aiming the *Sea Leave* west, out into the deep, inhospitable reaches of the North Pacific Ocean where he and his vessel either succumbed to the ravages of weather or he opened the seacocks and let his vessel sink. To her, it all seemed consistent with his military legacy.

"In education, in rank, or in any of the other ways life makes us different from one another, it may be hard for you to see Arnie Beck as your equal. Still, in this courtroom, he is a fellow citizen, a peer, and a fellow human being. A part of the diverse society that makes America great. He does *not* ask that you apply a lower standard of behavior to him because of the differences between you. But he does ask that you permit yourselves to empathize, at least somewhat, with the position in which he finds himself."

This was the key to their case. If these men could empathize with Beck's plight, there was the chance they might conclude that there was reasonable doubt to acquit. Like any good lawyer, Sydney believed her own arguments at the moment she made them. But her feelings about this case went deeper. She had come to believe in Beck's innocence. This panel needed to be made to believe in it as well.

"Any one of us could one day find ourselves sitting where Beck is today. Confronted by the force of circumstantial evidence that makes things seem true that are not. We could find ourselves confronted by the limitless resources of government and the overwhelming power of group condemnation. We could suffer the impotence, the hopelessness of standing alone against society—innocent but without clear proof of that innocence—relying upon the compassion, the justice, the perception, and the good sense of people just . . . like . . . you.

"That is why, in the instructions you will be given by the court, you will be told clearly and without equivocation that a man is *presumed innocent* until *proven* guilty by the prosecution. *They* must *prove* to you that the person who killed Petty Officer Steven Jerome was Arnie Beck, and no one else. And, most important of all, they must prove those facts to you beyond *any reasonable doubt.*

"Without that proof, he *must* go free. That is the law, and rightfully so. Your insistence that the government live up to its responsibility to present evidence that eliminates any reasonable doubt in your mind as to his guilt is not just your duty to Arnie Beck or to the law, it is also your duty to yourselves, to all of us. This is your part in preserving the integrity of our society's entire, lumbering, uncertain, always potentially fallible, but absolutely essential criminal justice system."

She thought back to the time Duncan had told her that the practice of law was all a game. Maybe one day she, too, would come to a similar conclusion. But here in this courtroom, in this moment, she was arguing for justice. She was entirely convinced that there was more than a reasonable doubt about Arnie Beck's guilt. There were too many other people with better reasons to have killed Steven Jerome.

"For all of us here in this courtroom, except for Arnie Beck, this trial will be a transitory inconvenience, taken seriously I would hope, but a bother today that will be over tomorrow or the next day. Mr. Merrill— the prosecutor there, the judge, the court reporter, you, the members of this panel, and me—we will go home to our families, will return to our jobs and our daily lives. For every one of us but Arnie Beck, this trial will quickly fade from memory. We may discuss it with friends, family, or co-workers, but in a week we will all but have forgotten the fate of this young man.

"And our role in deciding it.

"Arnie Beck, however, must live with the results of this trial for the rest of his life. Everything he is or could ever become, all his hopes and aspirations, his future and the meaning of his past, anything he might ever contribute to society, all of this hangs upon the decision you make when you enter that conference room next door just a few moments from now.

"Gentlemen, do not be wrong.

"If there is one plea my client can make, it is the one he makes not just on his own behalf, but also on behalf of all people who ever were or ever could one day become falsely accused, who might, on this very day, be languishing in a prison cell, their lives in ruins, their dreams destroyed by crimes they did *not* commit.

"The plea Arnie Beck makes to you is please do not be wrong. Please, listen to the judge when he tells you to acquit unless you are *certain* beyond *any reasonable doubt*. He asks you to please not find him guilty of this crime unless you are very, very sure."

The prosecution's rebuttal, the court's final instructions, the members of the panel filing into the adjoining conference room, and the long wait for the verdict—all of it went by in a blur for Sydney. For most of the wait, she and Duncan sat downstairs in Duncan's office, drinking coffee and trying not to think about what was going on with the jury.

At noon, the panel members were escorted from the building for lunch, so Sydney and Duncan did the same. They went to a coffee shop off base, returning when the panel resumed its deliberations at 1:00 p.m. By 5:00 p.m., Captain Clayton called them out of their deliberations and offered them the option of adjourning for the night. But the panel president asked if they could have some food brought in and continue their discussions through dinner. Captain Clayton agreed to their request.

It was not until well after 8:00 that evening that Frank Merrill knocked on Duncan's office door and told them the panel had reached a verdict. With the testimony concluded, Duncan was free to enter the courtroom and join Sydney and his former client to hear the jury's decision.

Arnie sat tense and sullen beside her. His cold, withdrawn demeanor suggested that he clearly believed he was about to be convicted. Despite all their work. And despite Sydney's belief in her client's innocence, she was nonetheless convinced that this panel of military officers and enlisted men would convict her client. In her gut, she genuinely expected the verdict to be little more than an anticlimactic, foregone conclusion by an inherently biased military judicial system. She knew Duncan, on the other hand, believed that Beck was probably guilty. He felt they'd provided a strong defense. But he, for somewhat different reasons from hers, also expected a guilty verdict.

When the panel returned and took their places behind their table, both she and Duncan were poised to hear an outcome that would confirm their long-standing perspectives on military service and on military law.

So, it was a startling surprise for Arnie Beck, Sydney Warren, and Duncan Carmichael when they heard the final verdict:

"Not guilty."

Part Three

Present Day
Midnight

"I refuse to accept the view that mankind is so tragically bound to the starless midnight of racism and war that the bright daybreak of peace and brotherhood can never become a reality..."
Martin Luther King, Jr.

CHAPTER 37

Early June
North Coast of Vancouver Island, B.C.
A few miles east of Cape Scott

A thirty-four-foot CHB Trawler traveled west, close along the north coast of Vancouver Island, British Columbia, Canada. There was almost no wind. The sea was calm, except for the low westerly swell common on Queen Charlotte Sound in the summer. Suddenly, the vessel slowed and made a decisive turn to the left toward shore.

"This is it," said the younger of the two men in the pilothouse. He pulled back further on the throttle and eased the boat ever closer to shore on course to a waypoint illuminated on the GPS receiver mounted overhead above the wheel. "That's got to be the bay, right in there beyond that rocky point."

"Jesus, I hope so. It all looks the same to me," said the older man. "You better know what the fuck you're doing. I don't like the look of this one bit."

A chart was laid out on the galley table behind them. Various pencil lines had been drawn on the chart. Calculations were written in its margins. An arrow had been drawn in pencil on the chart pointing at a tiny bay further in. The distance to their waypoint was steadily spooling down on the GPS. A small digital depth sounder showed them to be in seven fathoms of water.

As they worked their way closer to shore, the smooth beam swells grew taller and steeper, heaving the boat sharply side to side. "I sure don't see how we're going to drop an anchor in this shit," said the older man.

"It ought to be calmer behind that headland." A small cove with a rocky beach was coming into view. It looked like the headland might offer some limited protection.

Suddenly the younger man pulled all the way back on the throttle. "Fuck, look at that! We're under two fathoms." He slammed the engine into reverse and powered up to stop the boat. "There's something wrong," he said, his voice shaking.

The boat slowed. But then a large steep swell that had built up in the shallower water swept beneath them. It lifted the boat high and carried it to the left. As it passed beneath, the boat rolled sharply to the right and dropped into the deep trough.

There was a violent, shattering crash!

"Fuck!" the younger man shouted.

"Christ Almighty," the older man said under his breath.

The boat lifted on another swell and again came down on the rocks with a second terrifying crunch.

By the time the boat rose again on the next swell, the man at the wheel was finally reversing at full speed. The boat slid backward into deeper water and, when it fell to the bottom of the following trough, to their huge relief, there was no impact. But now the vessel felt sluggish. They were taking on water. Fast.

The older man leaned out the side door of the pilothouse and scanned the shore. When he pulled his head back inside, the younger man had the mic in his hand for the VHF Radio and was talking on channel 16, the emergency frequency. ". . . we're on the rocks at Cape Scott, we're sinking." He screamed: "Mayday, Mayday. . ." The older man snatched the mic out of his hand.

"You stupid shit! What the fuck are you doing?"

"We're sinking," the younger man sobbed, on the verge of hysteria. Both of them could see that the boat's lower cabin area, at the foot of a small gangway just beneath them, was sloshing with water. "This thing is fucking going down!"

The radio crackled with a reply: "This is Coast Guard Canada back to the vessel in distress. What is your position? Over."

The older man reached up and turned off the radio. Then he pushed the younger man aside and took the wheel. He slowed the engine, shifted into forward, and throttled up. "We're running this piece of shit on the beach," he said. Without further comment, he headed the boat at full speed to their left, around the rocky point, and toward a broad, open sandy beach. They somehow managed not to hit any more rocks and, after some moments of agonizing uncertainty, the vessel came to a final slow, churning halt in the surf thirty yards or so off a broad sandy shore. Almost immediately, the engine sputtered and died.

Surrounded by breakers, the small yacht pivoted sideways to the waves, tilted sharply to the left toward the sandy beach, and settled into a steady rhythm of lurching concussions against the bottom.

The younger man immediately climbed out onto the seaward side of the boat, scrambled across the steeply sloping trunk cabin, and made a sudden leap from the rail into the water toward shore. The water turned out to be shallower than he expected, and he landed hard. Limping badly, he continued toward shore. Once on the beach, he collapsed on the damp sand.

After the younger man had fled the pilothouse, the older man just shook his head and went below. Wading through knee-deep water and fighting the constant violent movement of the boat, he gathered up a few papers, money, wallets and ID, a local roadmap, and some heavy clothing, and shoved it all into a small backpack. Then he put a few survival items and some canned food into a canvas bag. Finally, he grabbed a knife from the galley and shoved it in his inside jacket pocket. After a last look around, he shrugged on the pack, slung the bag over his shoulder, and climbed up the gangway and out the door onto the sloping, rocking deck.

Barely able to stay upright, he managed to make his way through the spray to the rear of the boat. There, he cut the lashings on a small inflatable skiff that rested on its edge across the stern on a swim platform. The inflatable fell free into the water and was immediately pushed toward the beach by the surf and the light onshore breeze.

The older man then eased himself carefully over the lee side into the water and waded clumsily to shore, leaving the unlucky yacht to its fate amongst the breakers. Once in shallow water, he splashed over to the small inflatable, grabbed its painter, and dragged it behind him to the top of the beach. Only then did he go back to see how the younger man was doing.

The younger man was sitting upright on the sand, calmer but definitely distraught. "I think I broke something," he complained. The older man pulled him to his feet, and the two of them slowly made their way up the beach toward the skiff and some sun-bleached logs just above the high tide line.

They sat on a log, and the older man pulled out his cell phone. "Figures," he said. "No reception." He opened the roadmap and studied it a few moments before folding it and putting it in his pack. "We need to go inland," he said. "You think you can walk with a stick?"

"I'm not sure. I'll try . . ."

The two of them—the younger man hobbling along with the help of a length of driftwood and the older dragging the rubber skiff behind —made their way along the beach for a bit and then disappeared into the surrounding trees.

CHAPTER 38

Saturday, late June
Downtown Seattle
Columbia Tower Starbucks

"Where the hell did you get this?" Kyle Marshall poked at the tiny plastic object that had been placed in the center of their small table and leaned closer, his short black hair with its fade lines at the back, looked freshly trimmed. "You know it's illegal to possess one of these things."

Loud chanting interrupted their conversation. Just outside the window, people were assembling to protest yet another shooting of an unarmed black youth by a police officer. A few cars caught by the crowd struggled vainly to crawl up Fourth Avenue. Cherry was officially closed and was packed with pedestrians making their way up the hill to Fifth. Fifth was also closed all the way through town.

Duncan Carmichael couldn't help noting how most of their fellow Starbucks coffee shop patrons seemed oblivious to what was happening outside, just a few feet away. They were engaged in business as usual—trading gossip, doing deals, advising, consulting. Some sat alone, staring at computers and cell phone screens—suited professionals drinking their lattes in a safe, familiar space.

On the street, however, people were marching for change. There were thousands of them, all headed for Seattle Police Department headquarters just up the hill on Fifth. Sydney Warren, Duncan's friend and law partner, was one of the protesters. Right now, she'd be up there on the street in front of police headquarters carrying a sign and adding her voice to the cries for police reform.

Just as he was about to tell Kyle the story behind the object on the table, there was a sudden heavy clatter of automatic weapons fire. Duncan recognized it instantly. Its sharp, repetitive thump echoed off the tall surrounding buildings and was clearly audible through the Starbucks' thick windows.

The room went instantly silent. Startled patrons looked up from their conversations, their mobiles, and their lattes.

On the street, the crowd froze in confusion. Then, seconds later, there was chaos as the protesters realized what was happening.

Duncan was on his feet. "Jesus . . . Sydney!"

"She's out there?"

Duncan didn't answer. Completely forgetting about the object he'd brought for his ex-CIA friend to look at, he headed for the door. Moments later he was fighting his way up Cherry Street against the fleeing crowd. By the time he reached the corner at Fifth, the gunfire had ceased. But people were still running, some headed down the hill, some skirting through alleys and side streets, while others still cowered in recessed doorways and behind office building columns.

Duncan saw several people crouched against the decorative cast-iron bases of city streetlights. One woman was kneeling behind a Postal Service mailbox on the sidewalk in front of police headquarters. Other marchers huddled together in tight groups out in the open, perhaps more terrified and dazed than injured. Just across Fifth, a small child cried inconsolably beside his prone, motionless mother.

And there, sprawled awkwardly on the pavement directly at Duncan's feet, was the inert body of another woman surrounded by a spreading pool of blood. Her hand still gripped her protest sign: "I Can't Breathe."

His heart racing, Duncan scanned the area for Sydney. Hopefully she'd already managed to escape. But then he saw her, out in the open in the very center of the street. Her stylishly cut silver-grey hair was easy to identify. Oblivious to the danger, she was kneeling beside an injured man, tying her brightly colored silk scarf around his bleeding leg, using what looked like the broken-off handle of a protest sign to make a tourniquet. A fleeting sense of relief was replaced by concern. What if the shooter was still around? What if there were several?

Without hesitation, he rushed toward her. Sydney Warren had been a huge part of his life for some forty years now, a formidable woman to whom he was hugely indebted and whom he deeply respected and admired.

She stood when she saw him and raised her hand to acknowledge his presence and pushed her hair back from her face before turning toward another injured marcher. Resigned that she was doing what she damn-well intended to do, he also set about rendering aid to those in need—while keeping a close eye out for more shooters. Staying close to Sydney. Ready to hustle her away if the need arose.

Assuming she'd even allow it.

Among those who were later listed as dead was an unidentified man wearing body armor, a covid mask, and a long dark overcoat. He'd apparently been killed by a lucky shot to the neck in return fire from the police. A Chinese-made, automatic-fire assault weapon was found on the pavement beside him.

Several witnesses also reported seeing a second masked man fleeing up James Street. He was also dressed in black and carrying what appeared to be an assault rifle. He was said to have been bleeding from a wound to his left arm and was seen by other witnesses getting into a white van parked in a nearby public lot beneath the freeway. The van had then taken off down 6th toward the nearby I-5 on-ramp.

Three days later, a stolen white van was recovered from a Park-N-Ride lot along I-90 near North Bend. The same van had been caught on a traffic camera entering I-5 just after the shooting. There were blood smears inside, but no fingerprints or other trace evidence. DNA testing matched the blood from the van with samples recovered from the sidewalk on James Street. Samples and a likeness were also taken from the masked man who had died.

There was no match for any of it in the FBI database.

CHAPTER 39

Saturday, late June
Issaquah, WA
District Office of U.S. Congressman Frank Merrill (R)

After waiting to make her statement to the police, Sydney had to battle her way through badly messed up traffic and seriously push the speed limit in order to make it to Issaquah on time. Personal meetings with Congressman Franklin Merrill were hard to arrange. He spent most of his time in D.C., and when he was in-district, his schedule was crammed with endless campaigning and fund-raising events.

She arrived with minutes to spare. Merrill came out to greet her and shook her hand warmly. "Duncan asked me to say 'Hi,'" she said. It was a strategic white lie designed to remind Merrill of her connection to Duncan Carmichael.

Although they'd had occasional contact with one another for many years, ever since working opposite sides on the Arnie Beck case early in her legal career, she'd never had a warm relationship with Frank Merrill. Duncan and Merrill had been colleagues, serving together as JAGC officers in the U.S. Navy and the two men had stayed loosely in touch over the years. When Merrill, a Republican, ran for office, Duncan supported him with occasional modest campaign contributions. Merrill had never received any contributions or support from Sydney though.

"I'm surprised you made it," Merrill said. "Given what's happening in Seattle."

"I was motivated," she said, smiling.

The two of them took their seats in Merrill's office, and Sydney removed a brief position paper from her leather case and slid it across his wide walnut desk. "If this legislation has *any* real hope, Frank, it looks like you're it. There was no way I was going to miss this chance to help you find a way to come on board."

Merrill gave her his toothy politician's smile. "Okay, you've got my attention, Sydney. Give it your best shot."

Sydney was a volunteer board member for a local group affiliated with a national non-profit that represented the operators of battered women's shelters. In addition, she occasionally personally represented battered and fugitive women pro bono in court. She was there to lobby for a federal budget appropriation under consideration in Congress. The appropriation would finally properly fund the modest federal program that assisted local shelters throughout the country. Merrill was on the critical Health and Human Services Subcommittee for House Appropriations. His vote was pivotal.

"You've read the language of the appropriation?"

"I have," he said.

"I'm sure you understand the need; maybe I'd best use our time to answer your questions."

Merrill nodded. "I have a couple. Why the federal government? And why me? These shelters, 'care facilities' as you call them, have been mostly funded through private donations and with state money. Our state already supports them, so we're covered here at home. Why should we suddenly turn this into a big federal responsibility? It's my under-standing that many states don't even want them."

Sydney took a deep breath. This was the crux of the matter. "For exactly that reason, Frank," she replied firmly. "Because there are thou-sands of terrified battered women, *American citizens*, people you're responsible for in those very states, women who desperately need your help. When their lives are threatened, they have no place to turn. It's bad enough here in Washington. Think how awful their situation is in states that refuse to help. And they can't even go to a neighboring state, because the programs there are often only available to local residents. The '*men*' who control those states you're talking about and who are elected from them to Congress and to their local state legislatures won't provide funding. The only option is for the federal government to step in." She pointed across the desk. "That means *you*."

"I understand what you're saying, but I represent the 8th District, and I'm fairly certain my constituents don't want me spending their federal tax money to pay for something in other states that the people in those states don't even want." He tilted his head and telegraphed a concerned *I'm-giving-it-some-thought* pose.

Then, as if drawing a reluctant conclusion, he said, "Here's the thing, Sydney. I'm sympathetic with your cause. I hate seeing women victimized in abusive relationships. But if I do as you ask, I'm not only going to disappoint my own constituents, I'm going to make some of my Congressional colleagues very angry. This is a significant expenditure. The bottom line? I'm not sure it's a great move for me."

Sydney would rather have avoided making her request political but, in the end, everything became political. She didn't feel she had a choice. "So," she said. "I hear a rumor that maybe you're considering a run for the Senate this next time around."

Merrill sat back and smiled blandly. "Nothing's decided. But I do always like to be open to new possibilities." It sounded like a memorized response.

Sydney forced herself to return his smile. "To pull that off, at least in the general election, you're going to need some support from the moderate left. Something like this would help you there, Frank."

Merrill blinked, perhaps in anticipation of where the conversation was headed.

"I could maybe put in a good word with some of the people I know locally that work in this women's shelter arena," she continued. "The folks in our groups care about their *cause* far more than they do about partisanship. I bet I could get you an appearance or two at their events. Maybe get some favorable mention in their newsletters. Who knows, even a contribution or two. That could result in some decent press, show that you have state-wide, cross-aisle appeal. It would help broaden your base if you want to be competitive in a race for the Senate."

"I'd appreciate that."

"And last I heard," she added. "Those folks you're talking about, the ones from those states that don't want this money and might be unhappy with you for supporting it . . .?"

"Yeah . . .?"

"Well, maybe you're right. Maybe they will be unhappy. But here's the thing, Frank—last I heard, those folks don't vote in Washington State's elections . . . *My* people do."

CHAPTER 40

Saturday, late June
Preston-Martin Building, Seattle
Law Offices of Warren and Carmichael

"Was Sydney pleased that you rushed to her rescue?" Kyle Marshall stood at the window of Duncan Carmichael's office looking toward the streets far below, streets still jammed with stalled traffic. He was dressed casually, like an outdoorsman who was careful about his appearance.

"You know Sydney, what do you think?"

Kyle laughed. "Well, I wish her luck with Congressman Merrill. *If* she managed to get through that snarl-up down there."

Duncan knew that Kyle considered marches more symbolic than practical—even a protest in which, as a middle-aged black man, he might have been thought to have a particular interest. But Kyle preferred more direct tools, like providing free security and investigative services for minority candidates for office, or doing pro bono work on Sydney's various civil rights and class action cases. Many years earlier, after a decade with the CIA, he'd taken over the family business from his deceased father, Mel Marshall. Sydney and Duncan had used the small but reliable firm in the early years of their own law practice. When Kyle became CEO, First Class Credit and Collections became Marshall Security and Investigations (MSI). It was soon one of the top private security and investigations firms in the Northwest. Quite an accomplishment for a man who'd grown up in a middle-class neighborhood in Seattle's Central district.

"You forgot this by the way." Kyle reached into a pocket and placed the tiny black object on Duncan's desk—the item the two men had been discussing before the shooting. Then he took a seat in the client chair. "As you know, this is a bug," Kyle said. "And a fairly sophisticated one. In the trade we call these things M&Ms for obvious reasons."

"You were about to tell me why they're illegal. And who uses this kind of equipment."

"Let me tell you first how they work. They're cellular and are typically set to transmit in the middle of the night when nobody's around. Just a brief nightly burst to pass along whatever it has recorded. When they're not transmitting, they can be very hard to find."

"Can you track them to the source?"

"If the perpetrators are taking care, it takes some doing. And honestly, in your case, I think it's pointless. You said you discovered the break-in yesterday morning and called the police. During their investigation they found one of these in your office, right?"

"Under the edge of my desk."

"That's actually pretty amazing. Someone either knew what they were looking for or lucked out. I assume the police took it with them."

"Yes. They didn't say much about it though. That's why I contacted you later, after we found this one on a window frame in the conference room."

Kyle nodded. "My guess is that whoever planted these will have shut things down by now. They might have transmitted from this one here last night, but if so, they know their M&Ms have been found, and they're probably busy covering their tracks."

"Couldn't they be listening to us right now? Through this?"

"It could be recording, but this transmitter is undoubtedly off. Just to be certain, we might want to make sure this one never gets the chance to transmit whatever it may have already recorded. While I'm at it, I'll see if I can find a manufacturer's tracking number. I would also like to have one of my people take a good look around your office in case there are more of these. They can be hard little suckers to spot. Besides, there's a good chance whoever put them in your offices may have come back last night and removed any others. I doubt they're pleased to have lost two of these."

"Where would it transmit to?"

"They're cellular. So, pretty much anywhere."

"Any guesses about who might have bugged us with this kind of equipment?"

"If I didn't know you, I'd say you're under criminal investigation by a government agency." He raised his eyebrows.

"Not that I know of." Duncan picked up the device. "If not the government . . .?" He left the question hanging.

"Hard to know. But definitely not your local burglar or low-budget PI. These are big boy toys. And Washington laws are pretty strict. If it wasn't a law enforcement sanctioned operation, someone took some risk to listen in on you. The question is 'why'? Are you working a case where someone with clout and a lot to lose would have an interest?"

"We've got a fair amount of legal work passing through this place. There's Sydney's civil rights cases, of course, my civil litigation, and some insurance defense. But nothing we're working on seems likely to be a magnet for something like this."

"Well, you've definitely got someone's attention. Talk with your staff to see if anyone has even an inkling as to what might have been targeted. And make sure they keep an eye out for more of these things."

Duncan laughed. "They're all paranoid about this—I've seen them whispering to each other in the halls. Several who weren't in court yesterday took their laptops and worked from home in the afternoon, and some are still at home today. They're sure as hell on the lookout for any more of *these*."

Kyle leaned back in his chair. "They're right to be nervous," he said philosophically, shaking his head. "We're all at risk." He pointed at the bug. "In my opinion, shit like this . . . it represents a serious threat to our privacy—to our whole democratic system of government."

Duncan gave him a questioning look.

"Think about it," Kyle continued. "With this kind of tech, and with cameras and mics on our phones, our computers, even our cable TVs . . . with this stuff and the gargantuan database at NSA, all now accessible by artificial intelligence and all in the hands of whoever might end up running things—I think it puts our very way of life in jeopardy."

"That's pretty pessimistic."

"You may feel I'm a bit paranoid, but we're not far from letting it happen," Kyle said. "Take for example your buddy, Frank Merrill. His eighth district is a perfect microcosm of the State of Washington overall. He has a significant Western Washington, urban/suburban constituency over there in Bellevue and up I-90. But he also represents a sizable chunk of the State's rural, conservative eastside. There are districts like his and states like ours all over the country. Let's say he does run for the Senate and wins. You think he's going to be a moderate? You think he's going to stand up for individual and minority rights? This country is approaching its political midnight, Duncan. His buddies and him are inches from having their hands on all this stuff."

Duncan listened, but he'd heard it all before. Like Sydney, Kyle was concerned that right-wing politicians were going to move the entire country to the far right, destroying the freedoms and constitutional protections essential to democracy.

"He may seem like a moderate now," Kyle continued. "He has to look that way if he's to have any chance at getting elected in our largely blue state—but, Duncan, if he takes one of those Senate seats, and the Senate falls to ultra-conservatives, none of us is going to like where that ends up."

"I get what you're saying, Kyle."

"But you disagree."

"Not entirely . . ."

Kyle leaned back in his chair, picked up the coffee he'd been given when they'd arrived, and studied Duncan across the top of the mug. "Sydney has given you the same lecture, right?"

Duncan laughed. "She's not nearly so polite about it."

"I can only imagine."

"And, meanwhile, she's not above driving up to Issaquah to ask for

Merrill's support on an appropriation for women's shelters." Duncan shook his head. "Politics!"

"She's a realist. But that's what makes it all so scary. If he does what she asks, some of her liberal backers could actually help him get elected."

There was a lull in their conversation; silence washed away any lingering tension.

"I'm curious, Duncan. You've never talked about how you and Sydney met. How two such opposites came together to build this amazing law practice. It's clear you two are close—" He hesitated, obviously conscious of how personal he was getting. "I probably shouldn't ask, but I have to admit, I've always wondered if you were at some point, um, a couple."

It was late on a Saturday afternoon, and it had been a tough day. Duncan could understand why Kyle was curious, but he was right to hesitate. It *was* personal. This wasn't the first time someone had asked Duncan this question, and it was a question he never answered.

Duncan leaned back in his chair and smiled. "Early in our careers we worked together on a very difficult case," he said. "We bonded."

It was all he was ever willing to reveal.

CHAPTER 41

Early July
North Coast of Vancouver Island, B.C.
A few miles east of Cape Scott

It was a rugged but interesting hike with stretches of uneven boardwalks, sandy beaches, steep headlands, and long treks through tall forests on quiet pathways padded with fir needles. There was a wolf advisory and the couple knew they weren't supposed to have their dog along. There were also some steep sections of trail where you had to use ropes to navigate. But they had decided to bring their black lab, Murphy, with them anyway. They had a harness for him that had allowed them to successfully haul him up and over difficult spots and across rushing streams. But he'd been allowed to run free.

They had seen bear scat, but, so far, Murphy had not been in any confrontations with local wildlife.

They left the Laura Creek campsite early to get across Dakota Creek and make it to Nissen Bight before the weather turned wet as predicted for later in the day. One of the creeks ahead had a cable car and another had a narrow swinging bridge with handrails. But the most problematic was Dakota Creek. There they'd have to shimmy across on a large log that all of the guide-books warned was "very slippery."

When they reached Dakota Creek, they put Murphy on a leash so they could keep him under control as he forged the creek below the log while they shimmied across above. Once in the water, Murphy didn't waste any time paddling for the other side. The hardest part turned out to be keeping Murphy from pulling his owners off the log.

They had crossed the last stream for the day and Murphy was off his leash, when he suddenly raced ahead. They both called out to him but he was making a beeline for something off the trail in the dense woods ahead to their right. The woman slipped out of her pack and raced after him. "Don't," her husband yelled as he slipped off his own pack. "It could be a wolf!"

Murphy disappeared behind some thick brush and began barking wildly. The couple had no choice but to follow. "If it's a wolf," the husband said, "remember to make noise and wave your arms in the air."

But it wasn't a wolf.

It was what was left of the hastily buried body of a man.

Chapter 42

Early July
Preston-Martin Building, Seattle
Law offices of Warren and Carmichael

Duncan was at his computer when there was a tentative knock on his open door.

Bradley Mason, one of the associates, stood in the doorway holding a thin file. He raised his eyebrows and pointed at the file. "Have a minute?"

Duncan swiveled away from his computer. "Sure. Now's good."

Bradley slid the file across Duncan's desk. "It's a case that Dwight sent over a week or so back."

Dwight Peters was a lead claims adjuster at United Maritime Insurance, a friend and a significant client of the Warren-Carmichael firm.

"What have you got?" Duncan asked as Bradley took a seat in one of the leather client chairs in front of his desk.

"Well, it's one of their subrogation matters. It involves a charter yacht that was lost off Vancouver Island earlier this summer. Their insured is Northern Yacht Charters out of Port Hardy, BC. We got the case because the charter company's customer, the guy that chartered and then lost the boat, is an American citizen who lives in Eastern Washington. Dwight called this morning to tell us he wants the file back. Says he's settled the case. I'm not sure I understand. I thought I'd better mention it to you."

"Hmm." Duncan perused the papers in the file. The claim United had paid amounted to about $63,000 Canadian on an older fiberglass trawler-yacht that had been in the insured's fleet for several years. It wasn't a total loss, but it was close. The dollar amount seemed about right. When one of the firm's insurance company clients paid a claim on a lost vessel, they'd often hire Warren-Carmichael to sue any third party who was responsible for the loss. The insured owner of the lost vessel, Northern Yacht Charters in this case, would technically be the firm's client. The charter company's customer, the guy who'd lost the boat, would be the defendant. But most of what they recovered in the lawsuit would go back to the insurance company. The insured could get back their deductible, and maybe any miscellaneous damages that hadn't been covered by the policy. But hopefully the insurance company would get their payout money back.

"I just got started on it a few days ago. It looks like their charter customer is an American. Lives in Eastern Washington. He's married, owns a home and a lot of undeveloped rangelands over near Colville. He may have some cash assets as well. Just seems like there's some value there."

"But Dwight says he's settled it?"

"Yeah, and not a word to us before now. No email. Nothing. Isn't that kind of unusual? I mean, once they send us the file, don't we take the lead from that point? If Dwight had something going with this guy, you'd think he'd have let us know."

"Yeah . . . I agree, it's strange." Maybe there was more to it, but probably not anything important.

"He said we should send him a bill," said Bradley. "We're on a contingency, right? Twenty-five percent before trial? I have done a fair amount of work. But what do we bill him for—the full contingency fee? Hourly? Just expenses? Thought I'd better ask."

"Leave the file with me," Duncan said. "I'll give him a call and see what he wants us to do about the fee." It had been a while since he had talked with Dwight. After all these years of working together, he considered Dwight a personal friend. This would be a chance to clear up any issues about the file and see how Dwight was doing at the same time.

"Oh, yeah, and that's another thing," Bradley added as he stood to leave. "He wants the file back. The actual file, not just a copy. I guess, technically, the file belongs to him. Still, it doesn't seem like we'd want to do that. After you've talked with him, should I just go ahead and send him the original? Make a copy for us?"

"Don't worry about it. I'll ask Madeline to make a full copy and we'll return the original to him. Thanks for checking with me on this." Duncan thought maybe he might hand-deliver that original file—use it as an excuse to reconnect with his long-time friend and client.

Duncan watched as Bradley Mason left. After only six months, Bradley was becoming one of those quietly indispensable people who fit in wherever they go. Duncan still loved the practice of law. But he knew he couldn't do it forever. When he did retire, he wanted to leave behind a strong cadre of partners and associates to take over the firm he and Sydney had spent the last forty years building.

He glanced at the file again before placing the call. "Hey, Dwight. It's Duncan. Got a minute?"

"Yeah, Duncan. What can I do you for?" Dwight Peters sounded tentative.

Duncan hoped he'd caught him at a good time. "I've just got a quick question. It's about this Northern Yacht Charters case you sent over. Bradley says you've settled it."

"Yeah. They're going to pay the loss. No need for you guys to be involved."

"Well, that's good news." In fact, it sounded a bit too good to Duncan. "So, our defendant, the charter customer, um . . ." he glanced at his file ". . . Gilbert, Josef Gilbert, he turned out to be insured after all?" According to the file Dwight had initially sent them, there'd been no liability insurance that would cover Gilbert on this loss.

"Uh . . . no, they're, uh, he's paying it himself. Turns out he's good for it personally. Pretty well off, it seems."

"I see. Sure, that sounds fine." Actually, Duncan found it surprising. According to the file, the charter skipper had disappeared following the loss. Dwight's people must have tracked him down. "Did he say what happened?" In a case like this, they had to move carefully on their subrogation claim or they could end up provoking some kind of countersuit for damages. "I guess we're looking good if nothing went wrong with the boat to cause this thing."

"Our insured thinks the boat's operator just got his navigation screwed up. Ran it on the rocks. Gilbert wants to pay it and move on."

Duncan guessed there were people who took full responsibility for their actions. But in his many years of practicing law, he hadn't met a lot of them. He couldn't help feeling that Dwight sounded uneasy. "So, uh, I guess Bradley's only got a few hours into this. We haven't really earned our contingency. How about I just bill you hourly for his time?"

"Sure, that would be great. And it was good talking to you, but I've got to run; I have a meeting."

"Let's have lunch. I'll drop off the original file and we can catch up?"

"Sure. Okay. I'll give you a call. Gotta go. Bye."

Duncan sat for several minutes at his desk studying the thin file and thinking about their conversation. Dwight had sure sounded hurried, though that wasn't all that unusual. Duncan wasn't concerned about losing the small contingency fee. United was a good client. They'd make that up. It was just that the whole exchange had seemed very odd. Finally, still unsatisfied, he set the file aside and moved on to tackle the next of several tasks.

CHAPTER 43

Early July
Preston-Martin Building, Seattle
Law offices of Warren and Carmichael

Sydney was in the lobby when Duncan's wife Kate arrived with their grandchild Lilly. "Auntie Syd," Lilly called out in her high-pitched, little girl voice as she ran toward Sydney. She was wearing a short yellow and blue plaid dress with blue leggings. Her blond hair was tied back with a yellow ribbon. Although technically she wasn't Lilly's aunt, Lilly's mother had long ago called Sydney "Auntie," and the title had stuck. With no children of her own, Sydney enjoyed her role as an honorary member of Duncan and Kate's family.

"Lilly, how good to see you." Sydney bent over and gave her a big hug, pleased to feel the small arms returning the hug with enthusiasm. Not too long ago she had been able to scoop up the little girl and carry her. But Lilly was getting heavier, and Sydney was getting older.

Sydney straightened up and then hunched slightly to hug the petite Kate while Lilly said hello to the receptionist and claimed a piece of candy from the dish on the counter. "Just one," Kate called after her. It was a ritual: the admonition, Lilly's nodded response, and the surreptitious taking of two candies. Lilly was, after all, Kate and Duncan's grandchild.

"So," Sydney began, ". . . are you here to steal Duncan for lunch?"

"Yes, can you join us?"

"I'd love to, but I can't today."

Kate shook her head, her straight greying blonde hair swinging "You two need to work less." It was a statement she often made. Duncan and Sydney would agree, at least in theory, then go right on working as hard as ever. They both loved their jobs. Both were old enough and secure enough to retire. But neither of them was ready to call it quits.

"Let me walk you back," Sydney said. They started down the long hallway to Duncan's office, Lilly running ahead.

Kate pulled a folded newspaper from her handbag. It was the Northwest section of the *Seattle Times* print edition. "Did you see this?" she asked, handing the paper to Sydney and pointing to a small article on an inside page. "I saw it this morning and noticed that the victim in that murder in Canada is somehow connected to a right-wing group in Northeast Washington. Wasn't that Navy kid you two defended years ago associated in some way with the Independence League?"

The trial had happened long before Duncan and Kate had married, but they had all talked about it together many times since. It was the case that had finally convinced Duncan to leave the U.S. Navy. The case that had propelled Duncan and Sydney to form their original private law partnership.

"Apparently some hikers from Seattle found a body on Vancouver Island last week," Kate continued. "It looks like they've linked the dead guy to that same group. Small world, huh?"

Sydney felt her fingers tightening on the newspaper.

A very small world indeed!

When Duncan, Kate, and Lilly headed off to lunch, Sydney took the *Seattle Times* article into her office and reread it. It was obviously a follow-up piece from an earlier report. The firm had a subscription, so she brought the *Times* archives up on her laptop and searched back for stories on the same topic, but there was no story on the original boat grounding in early June. Apparently, a lost charter yacht halfway up the Canadian Coast wasn't considered all that newsworthy in Seattle. But when hikers had recently found a body near the grounding, and it turned out to be an American and a resident of the Colville area of Eastern Washington, the *Times* had picked up both stories.

It didn't take long to find the original article online in the Vancouver BC press. The Canadian reporters had made quite a big deal out of the mystery surrounding the lost boat and the missing men who'd both been present at the time of its charter. Especially since the name on the credit card for the rental was not a match for either of the two missing men. Now that the RCMP had retrieved a body with a knife wound and recovered an inflatable skiff hidden in the nearby woods, the story was attracting a lot of new interest in the Canadian press.

The Mounties were investigating the death as a murder.

In the more recent *Seattle Times* article, the local reporter took credit for "discovering" that the dead man was a known member of the Independence League, a right-wing group from Eastern Washington that had made the news on a number of occasions over the years. He'd probably made the discovery by simply asking the police, but he was the first reporter to write about the connection. What Sydney found fascinating was that this was the same group that had been associated with the father of the client she and Duncan had represented early in their legal careers.

As she read further, Sydney was not surprised to learn that several members of the group had been among those present at the storming of the U.S. Capitol on January 6 of 2021 and that they had now developed a national profile as a domestic terrorist group. It made her wonder if there was any possibility that the group had been involved with the shooting at the protest in June. Their racism would definitely put them at odds with the protesters.

She printed a copy of the older on-line article from the *Vancouver Sun* and clipped it together with a more recent one and with the one Kate had seen in the *Seattle Times*. Then she put them on the credenza beside her desk and tried to move on, to focus on work. But she found it difficult. Her mind kept going back to that old case. It had been both challenging and memorable. Arnie Beck, their reluctant and at times hostile client, had been responsible for bringing Duncan and her together. It had been a long and bitter battle defending him on a U.S. Navy murder charge. There'd been the specter of drug smuggling and other conspiracies. Now, all these years later, here was this man from the Independence League found dead near a grounded yacht in an isolated bay in Canada. Someone mixed up with a whole new generation of haters.

What had happened? Why had it happened there? Was the other missing man a murderer? Or was he a body in the woods somewhere, waiting to be found? And who had paid to charter the yacht? What was their role in all this?

Finally, she picked up the articles and walked down the hall to Duncan's office. Taking a Post-it from the supply he always kept in his top drawer, she wrote, "We need to talk." She left the articles with the Post-it in the center of his otherwise uncluttered desk.

Chapter 44

______

Mid July
Preston-Martin Building, Seattle
Law offices of Carmichael-Warren

"We may have a problem," said Duncan, as Sydney entered his office shortly after lunch. He motioned for her to close the door.

He tapped the newspaper articles she'd left on his desk with his index finger. "Kate mentioned this over lunch, and I'm fairly certain it's the same boat that is the subject of a subrogation case Dwight Peters sent over a couple of weeks ago."

"Really?" she said. Another coincidence—

"I've had Brad working on it. He was chasing things down to file when Dwight pulled the case."

"Pulled the case? He's sending it to someone else?" That would be bad news. United was one of their firm's best clients.

"No, he says he's settled it."

"After turning it over to us? That seems strange."

"I agree. So, I called him back. He says the guy wants to pay the loss. All of it."

"Who? You mean the insured?"

"No, the defendant. The guy who allegedly chartered the boat."

"Uh . . . I'm not sure I understand. Isn't the guy who chartered the boat this dead guy mentioned in the article?"

"Yes and no. Whoever chartered the boat did so under a false identity. He was working for someone else."

"Now I *know* I don't understand. So, who is it that wants to settle this maritime loss claim?"

"According to Dwight, it's a Josef Gilbert, the holder of the credit card used to make the charter. According to news coverage, the dead guy is named James Tyson. They're both from Colville over in Eastern Washington. It appears that Tyson chartered the boat, but he did so using Gilbert's ID and credit card. Apparently with Gilbert's OK. I'm not getting a full story from <u>Dwight, and</u> I don't understand why."

"What did he say, exactly?"

"He said they'd settled the case, and he didn't want us to do any more work on it. And would we please send the file to him. *Our* file. The original."

"Doesn't he already have almost everything in the file anyway?" she asked.

It was Duncan's regular practice to make sure that a copy of every document of any significance that was received or generated by the office was sent along to their client, especially to insurance clients, usually by email. Most everything in the office these days was electronic anyway, so it was an easy thing to do. Even if the client didn't actually read it all, they appreciated being kept up to date. The law practice inevitably generated an impressive amount of paperwork. And when a client saw copies, it made them feel more like they were getting something for their money. They were happier to pay the bill when it came.

"Yeah, he does." Duncan shook his head.

"Who is this Josef Gilbert? And what the hell does Dwight need the original file for?" she asked.

"I can't imagine.

"Is the original signed charter document with it? Something like that could have fingerprints."

"Fingerprints?" Duncan gave that some thought. "One thing that really bothers me is that Dwight told me that this Josef Gilbert wanted to settle because the accident was entirely the operator's fault, a navigation mistake or something. If he wasn't there, how the hell would he know that?"

"Well . . ., he wouldn't. Not unless he's getting messages from the dead . . . or has spoken with the guy who went missing." Sydney frowned. "Or is lying about everything.""

"I would think the RCMP would be all over this."

"We're missing something."

"Dwight sounded really stressed out," Duncan said. "I suggested we send him a bill for our hours, even though it's one of our usual contingency fee subrogation cases."

"How much would it have been worth to us?"

"More, for sure. But not a lot. At 25%, maybe a $15,000 fee at most —that's *if* we won everything. And we could have ended up putting in a lot of hours. I don't care about the money. It's Dwight I'm worried about. This isn't like him."

"What if . . .," she began, then paused to think. "What if he's in some kind of trouble over this case? Maybe with the company? How sure are you that he's squeaky clean?"

"Well, Sydney, I'm as sure as I could be about anyone. What I'm afraid of is that he *is* in trouble, but maybe not over anything illegal that *he's* done. What I'm afraid of is that this may be connected to the Independence League."

CHAPTER 45

Mid July
Columbia Center, Seattle
United Maritime Insurance Company

Duncan arrived unannounced.

He entered the United Maritime Insurance offices on the 25th floor, avoiding their closely attended main reception area on twenty-four. He waited a few minutes outside the glass entrance panel until the overworked 25th floor receptionist was momentarily diverted. Then he casually entered and slipped unnoticed down the hallway to Dwight's Office.

The sign on the door read:

Dwight Peters, Senior Manager
Property Loss and Subrogation Claims Team

"Enter," Dwight responded to Duncan's knock. And Duncan did. The surprise and then look of consternation on Dwight's face was palpable. "Duncan . . . uh, what are you doing here?"

"Wow," Duncan said, looking at his phone. "I hope I've got the right day. We're on for lunch, right?" This was the lead-in he'd planned. His goal was to prevent Dwight from avoiding him or having a prepared response to his questions. "I've brought you that file you wanted." He put a manila envelope down on Dwight's desk.

"Were we . . . I don't remember . . . uh, I guess I must have missed that on my calendar. Jeez, I'm really jammed up at the moment. Can I take a raincheck?"

"Hey, Dwight. I'm here. And you've got to eat." Duncan hated it when other people pushed *him* like this, but he'd decided in advance that he wasn't going to let Dwight off the hook easily. If it turned out his support was truly unwelcome, he'd walk away, but not until he knew what was going on with his friend. "Come on. We can grab something quick at The Grill downstairs. I'll have you back in a half-hour, tops. We haven't done this in months. It's high time. I'm paying."

Dwight had risen, but he still hesitated.

"Come *on*," Duncan insisted. He grabbed Dwight's sports jacket off its hanger behind the office door and all but took his friend by the arm to lead him into the hallway. Once in motion, Dwight acquiesced. Duncan made small talk in the hall, in the elevator, and while they waited in line to order their food. He asked about Dwight's family and the seemingly endless remodel project on their recreational beach cabin on San Juan Island.

After they got their sandwiches, they found a table in the spacious elevator atrium far enough away from other customers to give them some privacy. Dwight had begun to relax slightly and had confidently taken his first bite when Duncan made his move.

"Look Dwight," he said, locking eyes across the small table. "You and I have known each other, both as professionals and as good friends, for what . . ., some twenty-five years now, right? So, I can tell when something's bothering you. What you've told me about that Northern Yacht Charters file doesn't add up—we both know it. If you're in some kind of trouble, I want you to tell me. Maybe I can help."

Dwight put down his sandwich and looked around like a trapped animal. For a moment, Duncan thought he was going to bolt.

"Consider me your personal attorney on this," Duncan suggested. "We'll treat what you tell me as a confidential lawyer-client communication. There is no reason I'd ever need to reveal anything if that's what you want. But whatever this is, I think you should tell me about it."

Dwight took a deep breath, held it a moment, and slowly let it out. "I don't know what to do," he said. He looked around again. "They're threatening my wife and grandkids. They took pictures of the kids at school and left them in my mailbox at home. I can't go to the police. I can't say anything to my daughter and her husband. I don't even know who's behind this. Or what it's about." Dwight's hand was trembling as he pushed his uneaten sandwich away. "I'm not a person that can deal with this kind of thing. Hell, I'm an aging insurance company drone, counting the days until retirement." He slumped down, looking miserable.

"Who's doing this, Dwight. Is it this Josef Gilbert?"

"I don't know for sure how exactly he's involved. As I understand it, the dead guy, Tyson, used Gilbert's ID and credit card to complete the charter. They must be connected because the real Gilbert wants to pay the claim."

"So, not a stolen credit card?"

"No. Dead guy was more like an agent or employee or something."

"And Gilbert definitely isn't the other guy—the one who's still in the wind?"

"No, I don't think so. The RCMP would have checked that out," Dwight said.

"Yeah. Assuming the two governments are fully cooperating."

Dwight straightened his shoulders, obviously struggling to get control of his emotions. "Look, I appreciate your concern, Duncan. But you can't help me. If you try, you're going to be screwed over just like me. These are bad people. Seriously, walk away right now and stay as far away from me as you can until all this is over. I'm going to give them what they want and hope that's the end of it. Gilbert will be paying the claim in full, so nobody comes up short. There won't be anything to investigate. What they want me to do is completely legal—I'd probably have done it without all the threats. Now, I just want to get through this without anyone getting hurt."

"And the file? Why do you need the file?"

"They want it. All the originals. I have no idea why?"

Duncan didn't know what to say. Things sounded way worse than anything he'd imagined. "OK, I get it, Dwight," he said. "I won't make waves unless we talk first. But you need to promise me you'll keep me informed. Anything happens, I want to know about it. You understand?"

"Sure. Sure." Dwight said.

It didn't sound to Duncan like he really meant it. And no matter what, Duncan wasn't about to let Dwight down.

CHAPTER 46

Late July
Preston-Martin Building, Seattle
Law offices of Warren and Carmichael

"He died in prison?"

Sydney had become curious. She'd wondered what had happened to Arnie Beck's father, Truman Beck, following his arrest a few days before his son's Navy court-martial back in the late 70s. She called a friend in the U.S. Attorney's Office and asked her to check the FBI criminal records database. Somehow Sydney had pictured someone as mean and conniving as Truman Beck living forever. Or maybe dying in some Waco-style shootout with the FBI. Not someone who would quietly succumb to cancer in a prison hospital ward.

"How long ago?" she asked. She jotted down the date on a memo pad on her desk and hung up the phone. Truman Beck had died about three months earlier. He'd been in his 80s.

There was a soft "tap, tap, tap" at her office door. Then, after that brief warning, Duncan came in without an invitation. "I've been thinking," he said.

"Me too," she said. Neither of them needed to be more specific.

Over the years, they'd developed a mental connection that was sometimes uncanny. She simply assumed they were thinking about exactly the same thing. "This case with Dwight is both complicated *and* dangerous. But I don't see how we can simply ignore it. I think we need to figure out what's going on."

"I couldn't agree more," Duncan said.

"Do you think we should put Kyle on it?" she asked. "On our dime, of course."

"Count me in. But he'll need to be discreet—keep a low profile."

"Absolutely," she said as he sat down across from her.

"By the way," she continued. "I've just learned that Arnie's father died in prison about three months ago. Cancer."

"I can't say I'm all that sorry."

"No," Sydney agreed, "I can't say that I am either."

She punched in Kyle's number. "Kyle," she said when he answered. "This is Sydney and Duncan. You're on speaker."

"Hi," Duncan said. "How's business?"

"Great. There will always be plenty of wandering spouses, embezzling employees, and identity thieves to keep us busy 24-7." He laughed. "Please tell me you have something other than another jealous spouse. Another bug perhaps?"

"You can relax. It's not a domestic," Duncan said.

"But not a bug either," Sydney added.

"Glad to hear it. It's impressive to have both of you on the phone. These days I usually only hear from your admins and associates."

"Here's the deal, Kyle," Sydney said. "We're calling you directly because this isn't for a client. This one is for us. You're the best in the business, and that's what we need right now, the best."

Kyle laughed. "Flattery won't get you a discount."

"Oh-oh. A little too thick?"

"Just a little. So, this isn't related to that bug, is it?"

"We think it might be," said Duncan. "It has to do with a group we had dealings with some years ago, the Independence League from Northeastern Washington. Heard of them?"

"Oh yeah. If they're the ones checking on you, you'd better step carefully," Kyle said. "What I hear, those folks are something else. If you're at odds with them, being white won't necessarily protect you. They don't play by the rules—any rules."

"We know that. That's why we want you to take extra precautions when poking your nose into their business. We're not sure what we're looking for. Just dig up anything you can about their current status and activities. Their financial situation. How many members. Their current leadership. That sort of thing."

"Sounds interesting. Any ideas on why you may have gotten yourselves crosswise with these folks?"

"It's complicated," Duncan said.

"Always is."

"And we really do need some caution on this one," Sydney emphasized.

"Always careful."

"Um, the thing is," Duncan continued, "we think they're threatening a good friend of ours who works in the claims office of one of our insurer clients. The man's name is Dwight Peters. He's in subrogation claims with United Maritime Insurance in their Seattle downtown office. If you start to get close, please be sure not to tip the Leaguers off. They might get nervous and take it out on Dwight and his family."

"Understood, Duncan. Discretion is my middle name."

"No it isn't," said Sydney, smiling at Duncan. "I happen to know your middle name is Pearlie, after your grandfather from Detroit."

"What the hell, now you're checking up on *me*?" said Kyle, feigning offense. "Oh well, worry not, I'm all over this. You keep that Pearlie business to yourselves, okay?"

CHAPTER 47

Early August
Joseph Vance Building, Seattle
Hallway outside a conference room

Sydney was schmoozing in the hall in advance of an 8:00 a.m. board meeting when she got Kyle Marshall's call.

"You're at it early," she said as she stepped away from the other attendees. "What have you got for us?"

"Not a lot so far, but a few interesting tidbits," Kyle began. "Yesterday afternoon, I talked with a friend at the Stevens County Sheriff's office. Not only is the Independence League considered a domestic terrorist group, but their membership appears to be growing. There has been increased activity at their gated compound a few miles outside Colville. The place is owned by the guy you mentioned, Josef Gilbert, a wealthy rancher. They've been gathering there—meeting, training, and conjuring up plans for years. But things are heating up. It's all pretty unnerving actually.

"Not only has the number of cars coming and going caught the attention of local authorities, but the FBI also has recently asked the Sheriff to keep an eye on the League. Maybe you know this, but several of those who attended the January 6, 2021 storming of the U.S. Capitol are members. They're also 'persons of interest' in the Seattle protest shooting. And, as I'm sure you know, one of those Seattle shooters is still on the loose."

She thanked him for the information, hung up, and gazed thoughtfully at her phone for a moment before rejoining the other board members from the Affordable Housing Coalition as they slowly filtered into their meeting room.

Most of Sydney's fellow board members came from organizations that provided housing or similar services for homeless or low-income families and individuals. But there were also members with more indirect connections or those who, like herself, simply cared about the issue. She had been on the board for several years, and she occasionally contributed pro bono legal services to the organization in the same way she did for fugitive battered women. Her volunteer work contrasted sharply with most of her current legal practice, but it was work she believed in.

As she was about to step into the room, she felt a light touch on her arm. It was the government affairs director and lobbyist with Sydney's battered women's refuge group.

"Hey, Joanie," Sydney said. "I didn't realize you were involved with housing. It's great to see you."

"Yeah, you, too." Joanie waived in the direction of the meeting room. "It's a personal thing," she said. "Do what I can." Then, changing the subject, "Hey, I just wanted to thank you for meeting with Congressman Merrill. Looks like you did some good there."

"Really?

"The Human Services Subcommittee met yesterday. They reported out with a positive recommendation on our appropriation. Merrill voted yes."

Sydney was pleased; she'd been so busy she'd lost track. "I'm really glad to hear it."

"It was a close vote. Merrill made the difference—the only conservative that voted yes. So, thank you. I have no doubt at all that it was *your* doing."

The good news gave Sydney a small boost as she took her seat around the big conference table. As usual, the meeting was slow to start. As attendees entered, they crowded around the refreshments table, drinking coffee and looking over the pastries that were quickly disappearing.

"Hey, Syd." Another board member sat down next to her. He was a reinsurance broker in his professional life. "I hope you won't be offended that I was eavesdropping, but I was in the hall when you were on the phone. I heard you mention the protest shooting. Do you know if they caught that other guy yet?"

"I don't think so," she said.

"I have to tell you, that shootout caused a few tense moments at our office," he said with feeling. "We're in the Columbia Center, right across the intersection from where it happened. It was hard to see what was going on so far below, but we could sure as hell hear the shots and the screams and see people running away."

Another nearby board member joined in. "I'd like to have ten minutes alone with one of those shooters," he said. Then he looked at Sydney, smiled, and added. "Of course, I wouldn't do anything illegal . . ."

Sydney smiled back and said, "Well, just in case, you can be glad you know a good lawyer."

Walking back to her office after the meeting, she thought about the protest rally and the shooting. Thought about what the other board members had said. Thought about all of the things that had been happening of late. The shooters at the rally . . . The break-in/bugging at their office . . . The charter yacht going aground in Canada . . . The dead Independence League member found in the woods a few days later. And the strange situation Duncan had mentioned with Dwight Peters.

These couldn't be random events. Was it possible that the United Maritime file on the yacht was the target of the break-in and the reason for someone placing those bugs in their office? It was serendipitous that their associate had taken that file home to work on that evening. Not that there had been anything of substance in it. But then, the person or persons doing the search wouldn't necessarily have known that. And that would explain why Dwight had gone out of his way to ask for the original file to be returned.

The question was: what in that file could possibly be important enough to go to all that trouble? Was there something included in the original charter contract that someone didn't want them to see? Gilbert's name and connection to that charter was known to the authorities well before the break-in, as well as to Dwight and their associate Bradley Mason. There had to be some other connection, something they hadn't yet considered.

CHAPTER 48

Early August
Preston-Martin Building, Seattle
Law Offices of Warren and Carmichael

"I've been thinking," Sydney said as she sat down in Duncan's client chair.

Oh-oh—something in her voice made him feel like what was coming was something he might not want to hear. "And . . .?"

"Dwight doesn't really know why the Independence League guy who chartered that boat back in June is so set on avoiding litigation and settling that claim, right? Nor why they want the file kept secret. And why they're threatening his family."

"True."

"And for whatever reason, the Canadians either aren't connecting the insurance claim with the murdered man or are taking their time investigating the death."

"True."

"I've looked through the copy, but there's nothing there that looks unusual."

"So have I, Syd."

"One way or the other, I'm guessing you would like to help Dwight if you can . . .?"

"Yes," he said hesitantly, not sure where she was going with her questions.

"I think we ought to go check out that yacht. It's still in Port Hardy."

"Do you know that for sure?" he asked.

She nodded, "After I looked at the file, I made a few calls. We could fly up there in the morning and return the next day. It'll be nice to get away from the office. We're entitled to a pleasant distraction now and then. And it might give us some answers. What do you say?"

The first thing that leaped out for Duncan was that he hadn't told his wife all of the details about Dwight's situation. Dwight was much too frightened to bring in the police, and he'd insisted that no one else know. But it was more than a question of honoring his request—Duncan hadn't wanted to worry Kate unnecessarily or to somehow put her in danger. Still, maybe Sydney was onto something.

"I know what you're thinking. *What could we possibly find out? The trip would have to be on our dime.*" She raised her eyebrows in question. "Anything else?"

"I hate to leave Kate alone. We have some plans . . .," he hedged.

She nodded and started to get up. "Sure, I can understand and appreciate that. No problem. If I find anything, I'll call and we can decide what to do next."

It was deja vu. He should have seen it coming.

"No . . . no. I can't let you go alone," he said, right on script.

"Is that right?" Sydney said. She'd taken that thoroughly familiar tone that told Duncan he was in dangerous territory. And had a look on her face with which he'd had years of experience. She'd used this strategy so many times before she doubtless knew exactly how he'd respond. Then she broke into a broad smile, and he knew he'd been had. Surely, after all these years, he should have known better.

Still, he had to agree that it might be interesting to see that yacht. And he really didn't want her to go alone. So, he diplomatically reversed himself. "Okay, let's do it. I owe it to Dwight to try and help. Two sets of eyes are better than one."

"But if Kate will be upset . . ."

"I'll talk to her. She'll be fine."

"If you're sure." When he nodded, she said, "I'll make the reservations."

Damn. Sydney Warren had always known the right buttons to push to get him where she wanted him. Between Sydney and Kate, he was never entirely sure who was running his life, but he knew for certain that it wasn't him.

CHAPTER 49

Early August
Port Hardy, B.C.
Offices of the RCMP

The next day Sydney and Duncan took a seaplane charter from North Lake Washington to Port Hardy. Only a few clouds dotted the otherwise clear skies. There was a light breeze, but even without much wind, the small plane felt at times like a carnival ride. Still, the view was incredible. Neither of them had to use the airsick bags and, in under an hour and a half, they were touching down on Port Hardy Bay.

The previous afternoon Sydney had called ahead and made an appointment to talk with an officer from the Royal Canadian Mounted Police detachment in Port Hardy. Duncan wasn't clear on how much help a private U.S. citizen could hope for in this kind of a situation, but it sounded like the Mountie was willing to let them take a look inside the boat. He wondered if Sydney had fudged a little about their firm's connection to the insurance case, but he didn't ask. It might be better not to know.

They walked from the seaplane float into town. When they arrived at the one-story brown RCMP building, Sydney turned to Duncan. "Let me handle this." He put his hands in the air in mock surrender.

The Mountie was a young Constable by the name of Eric Brown. He was dressed in a disappointing light blue shirt and navy pants. Somehow Duncan had expected a bright red jacket. And frisky horses tied up out front. After a brief exchange about the weather and their trip, Sydney quickly got down to business.

"What was the condition of the boat? Was everything still intact? What have you learned so far about what happened."

"There wasn't much," said Brown. "The boat had apparently run onto some rocks, suffered quite a bit of damage, and ended up on the beach. The likely rocks are clearly marked on the chart and, as near as we could tell, there was nothing wrong with the steering or the engine. The cause of the accident is puzzling, although events of this kind are not that rare. Skippers fall asleep, get confused in the dark or in bad weather, or think they are someplace else on the chart. There are endless possibilities.

"Since there was no skiff found aboard the boat, we all initially assumed that whoever was on board had managed to get off at some point before it came ashore. The Coast Guard wasted two days unsuccessfully searching the shoreline for the skiff or hoping the operators showed up in town on their own. Now, after having found the skiff in the woods near the body, we suspect that someone from the boat had brought the skiff ashore and hidden it specifically to misdirect the ensuing search so they could safely escape on foot.

"By the time the Coast Guard arrived the tide had receded, and the boat was high and dry. Since it couldn't be left where it was, the charter firm that owned the boat hired a salvage company to recover it. They made a few temporary emergency repairs to seal the hull, pumped the boat out, and on the next high tide pulled it free and towed it back to Port Hardy where it was immediately hauled out of the water and stored in a work yard.

"Initially, there wasn't that much more for us to do. But when someone finds a man's hastily buried body with a broken foot and a mortal knife wound in his abdomen, that gets our attention. We've preserved the damaged vessel as a possible crime scene. It is presently in storage under RCMP seal awaiting further investigation.

"We're basically done with the boat at this point," Constable Brown continued. "I've asked for permission on your behalf—I'll need to accompany you, but you're free to take a look."

"What about the missing man—do you have a name?"

"Unfortunately, no. The dead guy used Josef Gilbert's credit card to charter the boat." The constable raised his eyebrows. "Seems like nobody asked for ID. And all we have for the second man is a vague description— he didn't make much of an impression on the clerk. But the clerk *was* able to verify from a photo that Gilbert is not the missing man. The Stevens County Sheriff's office sent out a deputy to talk with Gilbert, but he claims to know nothing about any other man. Just says Tyson was authorized to use his card." The Constable rolled his eyes. "The deputy from the Sheriff's office told us that Gilbert is connected to some right-wing political group and wasn't particularly eager to talk about the boat rental. But since the guy using the fake ID is dead and Gilbert is okay with paying for the rental, the only thing we can do is continue to look for the other guy."

"Oh." Duncan glanced at Sydney. When she didn't speak up, it was clear to him that she had no intention of telling the constable about Gilbert's willingness to also pay the insurance claim. He went along— they were there to help Dwight, not to complicate his life even more.

Constable Brown drove them to a nearby marina where the boat was cribbed up high and dry in a storage yard. The three of them climbed aboard using a ladder borrowed from the marina office.

The interior of the boat was a mess. The lower trunk cabin had been badly flooded, bringing in mud and sand that still remained in untidy lumps on the floor. The upholstery was splotched with mold and smelled faintly like dirty laundry. Dishes, pans, and other galley equipment were scattered everywhere, along with the remains of whatever food had been stored below. Wet sheets of newspaper had dried in place against what once had been nicely crafted hardwood cabinets. It didn't look like much would be learned from that part of the boat.

Higher up, however, the pilothouse had fared much better. The electronics mounted overhead were completely intact. A popular cruising guide and some charts had slid off a settee table onto one of the bench seats. A parallel rule and some dividers peeked from beneath the charts. A couple of coffee cups had rolled to the side of the bridge and spilled their contents, leaving dark stains behind. Otherwise, things looked somewhat normal. On impulse, Sydney reached up and flipped the switch on an overhead light and was pleased to see the light come on.

"They cleaned up a few things in the engine compartment," Brown explained. "And we've had a charger on the batteries the past couple of weeks. But I'm told the engine itself is a dead loss." He directed their attention to a chart spread out on the table to show them where the boat had been discovered. The rocks the boat had most likely hit were clearly marked.

There was a GPS above the steering station. Sydney asked Constable Brown if they had checked it out. When he said he didn't know if anyone had, she asked permission to turn it on. The GPS came on with a faint humming sound, the screen seemingly fully functional. Sydney brought up the last waypoint that had been used. She picked up the dividers from the settee and sat down to study the chart while her law partner and Constable Brown stood by, watching.

"Look at this," she said after a few minutes. She pointed to a place in the margins of the chart with the dividers. The latitude and longitude for the same waypoint as on the GPS were hand-printed there in pencil. There was another waypoint neatly printed next to it. She stood up and studied the GPS again and punched a button a couple of times. "Would you look at that," she said. The second waypoint penciled on the chart was also programmed into the GPS.

Sydney went back to the local chart and, using the dividers, carefully plotted the two waypoints. "Well, that explains one thing," she said, pointing at the chart again. "If they were using these waypoints to navigate, no wonder they hit the rocks."

The three of them looked back and forth between the chart and the GPS. Duncan was confident the same question he was asking himself was swirling through Sydney's mind as well. He assumed Constable Brown might be having similar thoughts: Where did the men on the yacht get those bad waypoints?

In addition, he knew that Sydney would, like him, also be

wondering why Josef Gilbert had been so eager to cover the losses with the charter company and its insurer. And, how, why, and to what extent was the Independence League involved in everything that had happened?

So far, checking out the boat had produced more questions than answers.

CHAPTER 50

Early August
Port Hardy, B.C.
Marine storage and work yard

They were in the constable's car headed back to the RCMP office when it hit her . . .

She took a deep breath, staring at the backs of the two men seated in front of her.

"Um, I'm so sorry to ask, Constable," she said, leaning forward. "But would you mind if we went back and took another look at those charts aboard the boat? Maybe it's nothing, but I think I may know what put them on that rock."

Back aboard the boat, Sydney sat again at the settee and carefully reexamined the charts on the table. Then she stood, flipped on and momentarily studied the GPS receiver above the wheel. Finally, she sat back with a satisfied smile.

"Okay, so . . .?" Duncan asked.

"I think they made a Loran C conversion mistake. A bad one."

"I don't know what that means," Constable Brown said. "What's Loran C?"

"Loran was a big deal back before satellite navigation. There used to be Loran C transmitting stations all up and down the West Coast—all over the world. But they've been completely decommissioned; all the stations are gone. Today, everybody uses GPS."

"You seem to know a lot about it," Constable Brown commented.

Sydney smiled. "One small advantage of advancing age," she said. "At this point, Loran C is ancient history. But I'd almost guarantee that it's part of the puzzle here." She laid out a large, small-scale chart on the settee table.

"I noticed this chart when we were here earlier," she said. "It's a Loran C chart. Look at the publication date: 1976. There's no reason you'd ever see one of these charts on a modern vessel—especially one being let for charter. So, I asked myself, what's this old Loran C chart doing here when there's also a perfectly good modern navigational chart and a GPS?" She paused and looked from Brown to Duncan with a faint smile on her face.

"It sounds like you're about to answer your own question," Duncan observed.

"First, there's one more bit of information you need to know. Loran C was really accurate. Almost as good as Sat Nav. People loved it. But it had a problem. The signals deformed when they passed over land. So, you couldn't plot a Loran position on a chart if you were anywhere near land. Look here on this Loran chart." The two men leaned forward. "There are no Loran orientation lines printed on it anywhere near shore or on inside waters."

"So," said Constable Brown uncertainly. ". . . I guess it wasn't much use near shore, right? "

"Actually, that's not entirely true," Sydney explained. "You just couldn't use a chart. Even though the signals were deformed by land masses, they were very stable. And very reliable. If you had a Loran C receiver on your boat and you recorded a waypoint on that receiver when you were physically at a known location, that waypoint, wrong as it was, could be relied on to always remain exactly the same. You could use it in the future with your Loran C receiver with complete confidence. And someone else using the same waypoint on their Loran C could do so too."

"Let me see if I've got this," said Constable Brown. "You're saying you think these waypoints were plotted improperly on this Loran C chart?" He pointed at the boat's electronics. "But all they've got here is a GPS."

"No. What I think is that these waypoints were taken many years ago from a Loran C receiver at a time when Loran C was still in use. The old Loran Cs would give you a latitude-longitude readout. Somebody took that lat/long readout and wrote it down—probably right here on this old chart. I think the guys that chartered the boat brought this chart with them. If they'd tried plotting this position on the new chart, they'd have immediately seen the problem. Instead, I think they simply punched those same latitude-longitude coordinates as waypoints into this modern GPS receiver. So, rather than leading them into the harbor, those waypoints put them on the rocks."

Constable Brown looked from Sydney to Carmichael and back again. "I'll be damned," he said. Then he considered: "But where did these waypoints come from? And why were they using them?"

"Yes, well," Sydney said. "I guess we'll have to get back to you on that one."

~

Later, as Sydney and Duncan walked from the RCMP office over to the Inn where they'd reserved rooms for the night, Duncan repeated Constable Brown's parting questions. "What do you think they *were* doing there? And why were they using those outdated waypoints?"

Sydney frowned. "I don't know. But there's some reason they abandoned that boat. Some reason they didn't want to be caught there. Some reason that man was killed. And now, there's some reason they're going out of their way to avoid any extended legal confrontation with the boat's insurer."

Duncan wrinkled his forehead in concentration. "There's one more thing to consider. I'd be willing to bet there's some link between them shutting down the insurance claim and our office being burglarized and bugged. I'd say they wanted to see that file."

They continued in silence for a few steps. Then they both stopped at the same instant and turned toward each other, staring. From the look on his face Sydney knew they were both thinking exactly the same thing—had come to exactly the same conclusion.

"Holy shit!" he said.

She nodded vigorously.

In almost perfect unison, they said: "We need to see Nissen Bight."

CHAPTER 51

Early August
North coast of Vancouver Island, B.C.
Nissen Bight

They woke to a wet fog.

Condensation clung to the underside of Sydney's tent and ran down her neck when she brushed up against it. Her clothes were still damp from the previous day's hike. And it was a major struggle to pull on the stiff new hiking boots she'd bought in Port Hardy the day before they left.

Kyle had a campfire going, coffee perking in a glass bubble-topped aluminum pot on a small grate at the edge of the fire. Sydney and Duncan gratefully sipped the strong coffee with its smattering of stray grounds floating on top and instantly felt their spirits rise. It also helped when the sun finally made a weak but welcome appearance.

"Before my dad died, he warned me about you two," Kyle said, as he slid a nicely-browned flapjack onto Sydney's light aluminum plate.

Duncan rose to the bait. "Warned you? How?"

"He said that whenever he worked for you guys, nothing ever

turned out quite like he expected. Something out of the ordinary always seemed to pop up."

"Your dad was a prince," Sydney offered. "I guess you know he worked on this Independence League matter back in the day. He's the one who discovered Admiral van Damme's involvement in the first place." She and Duncan had filled in most of the final blanks for Kyle on their long hike the day before. "We'd never have made that boat chase up Vancouver Island if it hadn't been for him."

Kyle grinned. "Like I said, he warned me."

Sydney smiled to herself. Kyle was a lot like his father Mel. Quiet but competent. A man to be trusted. One who could be counted on to get the job done, no matter what.

Kyle had flown in the day before, loaded down with backpacks, tents, camping supplies, a GPS, a first aid kit, bear pepper spray, a satellite phone, a metal detector, and a few other necessities. Still in his forties and an enthusiastic backpacker, he'd been excited about the hike.

Yesterday, they made the seemingly endless dusty drive in a well-used dirt-streaked shuttle van over rutted dirt roads all the way from Port Hardy. The hour-plus drive was followed by a muddy five-hour hike in from the Cape Scott trailhead. It had been far too many years since Sydney had carried a backpack. She'd noted that Duncan hadn't fared a great deal better. Only Kyle had kept his good spirits as they slogged their way through the rough terrain, pausing occasionally to scrape the incredibly sticky mud off their boots.

When they'd finally arrived, they'd found an unofficial but nicely protected campsite at the western end of Nissan Bight. Pleased to have survived the hike, Sydney had no complaints about the mundane campers' dinner, her tiny tent with its condensation on the underside, and her damp lumpy sleeping bag. In spite of conditions, she'd had a good night's sleep and was ready to face the next stage in their venture.

The abandoned yacht had been found on the exposed open beach very near their campsite. With its roiling surf, Nissen Bight seemed like a bad place to unload heavy crates of guns. But based on charts of the area, it looked like the adjacent Fisherman Bay was a spot where a sizable shipment of military arms could have been put ashore under the right weather conditions.

That was what she and Duncan had finally concluded and what had brought them here.

Fisherman Bay was right along the route from the Rosa Island anchorage at Esperanza Inlet to Port Hardy where that second packer had been found empty a couple of days after their fateful encounter with the smugglers back in 1978. That packer had been fully-loaded when it left Rosa Island. She and Duncan now suspected that those rifles had not, as they'd always assumed, been tossed overboard. This was the only out-of-the-way place along that route where the arms could conceivably have safely been put ashore.

It was far too big a coincidence. It definitely required a closer look.

After the short walk across the waist of a forested headland from Nissan Bight, and once she'd seen the rocky shoreline inside Fisherman Bay, Sydney wondered whether they had made a serious error. Although Fisherman Bay had very little wave action, at least in decent weather, it was also quite shallow and rocky. Anchoring a heavy 70' packer drawing seven or eight feet in the bay would have been difficult, except perhaps on a high tide in very calm weather. Still, theoretically, she decided they could easily have anchored outside the entrance in six or seven fathoms. From there it would have been possible to ferry their cargo into Fisherman Bay with multiple trips in small boats.

But now that they were standing there on-site, looking at the shoreline in person, it did not look inviting.

Sydney's eyes traveled along the unwelcoming rocky shore to a steep beach of pea gravel tucked into one protected corner behind some rocks on the eastern shore. The craggy point beyond kept it calm there. She felt the tension in her shoulders lessen. That small beach could have been a perfect place to bring a skiff ashore. And everything else fit.

Forty-five years ago, this area had already been designated as a Provincial Park, but it had been completely undeveloped and rarely visited by the public. This would have been the perfect spot, perhaps the only spot, where a fleeing crew of wanted men might have offloaded and hidden those rifles.

If she was right, someone had saved that old Loran chart on which they'd written the waypoints that had originally been taken at Fisherman Bay, not Nissen Bight. The most likely scenario was that the chart and waypoints had ended up in the hands of their leader, Truman Beck. Once incarcerated and out of power, Beck had decided, for reasons known only to him, to keep that information to himself—possibly as future leverage, the secret kind of insurance that can be treasured by a man who is locked away for years in a federal prison. The timing of events made it seem likely that shortly before Truman Beck's impending death, he'd turned the chart and its waypoints over to someone he trusted in the Independence League. If, as seemed likely, using those old waypoints had been the cause of the recent grounding of that chartered yacht, then the men who had chartered it had very likely come there to find those weapons.

Given that scenario, it all added up.

"So, where do we start looking?" Kyle asked as he surveyed the rugged expanse of beach.

Sydney was holding her GPS in one hand and a small hikers' compass in the other. She nodded for them to follow as she walked toward the steep gravel beach. It had been a long time, but she doubted this wild, untouched terrain had changed much. Today, of course, the area was often visited by hikers and campers. But back in the late 1970s, those men would have felt like they were at the ends of the earth when they hauled those rifles ashore and buried them here.

Duncan turned to Kyle. "I assume you know how to use that metal detector you brought."

Kyle laughed. "Second nature. My dad used to take me treasure hunting. That's what *he* called it. Although we never actually found anything valuable. You want to find the aluminum peel-off tab from one of those old beer cans, I'm your guy."

"I vaguely remember your dad mentioning some military buttons," Duncan said.

"Oh, yeah. I was with him that time. He was so thrilled. I'm afraid I didn't think it was much of a big deal. I was hoping for a chest full of gold coins."

Duncan turned to Sydney, "What do you think?"

"Well, I think we have to use some common sense," she said. "There's really only one prime spot where you could easily beach a small boat. That's right here. I'm guessing they would have been in a hurry.

And the boxes would have been heavy. Let's look for places that are both nearby and where it would have been easy to dig and conceal them."

The three of them stood at the top of the small expanse of beach and looked around, studying the surrounding terrain. There was a kind of ruin nearby—the foundational remains of some long-gone structure at the top of the beach. Somebody had actually lived here once. But Sydney dismissed that as a possibility and pointed in the other direction.

"How about that flat area behind the brush over there. It's high and dry, out of the weather, somewhat hidden, and easily accessible from where they would have come ashore. That's where I'd have put them."

Duncan looked around. "Hope we don't get too many hikers asking questions," he said. There had been no other campers with them on the beach at Nissen Bight, and they hadn't seen anyone yet that morning. But it was said to be a popular spot.

"We probably have a few hours before anyone can make it here from another campsite," Kyle said. "If they buried as many guns as you think they did, they should show up on this gizmo pretty decisively."

The area concerned was about 20 yards wide and maybe 40 yards long. It was well above the line of driftwood, and only lightly overgrown with stunted trees and scattered brush. It was a simple matter for Kyle to start at one end and work his way back and forth to the other with the metal detector.

They were prepared for a long search with possible interruptions from hikers, and even failure. So, they were shocked when after only a very few minutes Kyle announced, "There's something here." He was standing just a few feet from where he had started. "Not sure yet how big it is."

While Kyle continued scanning the surroundings, Sydney picked up the shovels they'd brought with them. "Guess we don't have time to lounge around," she said as she handed Duncan a shovel. "Let's get to work."

After a short period of silent digging, Duncan and Sydney simultaneously yelled, "I've got something!" Sydney had secretly hoped to be the first to find the cache, but she was thrilled they *had* actually found something.

"Let's clear out the area around where you're digging," she said, moving over to help Duncan. Working together to cut away the sod, it didn't take long to uncover a heavy black plastic tarp. "Come see what we've found," she called to Kyle. She felt nearly as excited as the day she learned she'd passed the Bar.

Kyle joined them. "I'll be damned."

When they pulled back the dirt-encrusted tarp, they found themselves staring at the rotting remains of a wooden crate with military markings on it. The markings were obscured by dirt and age, and the wood was very soft. Duncan's shovel had easily poked a hole in the end of the crate. Sydney looked from Kyle to Duncan and realized they were all standing there with big silly grins on their faces.

"I feel like Indiana Jones," Duncan said. "Without the hat."

"I'll be damned," Kyle said again, shaking his head.

"Better than buttons, I guess?" Duncan said.

"See if you can get the lid off," Sydney urged. She was holding up her phone, snapping pictures.

The wood lid cracked and started to cave in as Duncan tried to pry open the box with the tip of his shovel. Kyle knelt down and easily pulled some of the wood strips off the top with his hands. Inside they could clearly see what seemed to be several rifles lined up in a row and individually vacuum wrapped in translucent plastic. "Is this how they were packaged by the manufacturer?" Kyle asked as he reached down with a knife and cut the plastic.

"Maybe. I don't know," Duncan said. "Maybe van Damme's partners repackaged this stuff to store it for an extended wait after the war."

Kyle pulled one of the guns out, unwrapped it, and looked it over. Sydney could smell some kind of waxy preservative. The rifle looked to be coated with it. But even after all these years, there were no obvious signs of deterioration or rust.

"Wow," Kyle said holding it up. "Impressive! Whatever they did, it sure worked. I've got to admit, I didn't expect much—stashed out here for all those years." He looked at his hand and rubbed his fingers together. "Greasy though. Really greasy." He sniffed the barrel.

"Cosmoline," Duncan said. "They used to use it all the time." He reached out, took the gun from Kyle, and held it up to look more closely. "This is in amazing shape."

Sydney leaned over the crate. "What's that over there?" she asked. She was still holding her phone, snapping pictures. She pointed at a small red waxy box packed in another deteriorating crate next to the first.

Kyle reached down, brushed aside some soil and wood debris, and picked up what looked to her like a large cube of wax-wrapped cheese. "Ammo," he said. He reached into the opened plastic packaging again and came up with two more items. "And a clip and a field loader. It looks like they've got the magazines packed with each gun."

"I wonder . . ." Duncan said.

Kyle and Duncan exchanged a grin that Sydney immediately interpreted as, "Let's play."

"No," Sydney said. "We've found what we came for. That's it. It's time to bring in the authorities."

Duncan reached for the ammo. "There's no one around," he said. "Wouldn't you like to know if they still work after all these years?"

"What difference could that make?" Sydney challenged.

"None," Duncan and Kyle agreed together, grinning. "Just curious," Duncan added. He took a poncho from his pack, spread it on the ground, and started to disassemble the rifle. As he worked, he turned to Kyle and asked, "You think you could find me a couple of rags. And that first aid kit?"

From the first aid kit, Duncan took out the small plastic bottle of denatured alcohol. He explained to Sydney and Kyle that some of the Cosmoline had become dried and crusty. Using a length of string, he drew a small piece of alcohol-soaked rag through the rifle's barrel several times. Then he meticulously cleaned several of the small parts.

Finally, he carefully reassembled everything. "It's been quite a few years," he said. "But I guess it's like riding a bike." He peeled back the wax coating on a package of ammunition. "Let's have a look at this." He took out several cartridges and studied them. "This stuff looks perfect as far as I can see. What the hell." He loaded a single cartridge into the weapon and checked the safety.

"What if it explodes?" Sydney said. "What do I tell Kate?"

"More likely nothing at all will happen," Duncan said. "Old

ammo." He raised the gun and aimed at a tree in the distance. Both Kyle and Sydney took a few steps back.

The single shot echoed sharply around the empty bay.

"We aren't making a war movie," Sydney complained. But she wondered how it would feel to hold and fire the gun herself. She'd been brought up around guns and had for years gone with her dad to a shooting range. He'd been an avid hunter. She hadn't liked hunting, but she'd enjoyed the precision of firing at an inanimate object. Over time, her views on guns had changed though.

Duncan said, "I think loading a clip is pretty straightforward. If I remember correctly . . ." Using the clip loader, he pushed the cartridges into place and jammed the clip into the gun. Then he hesitated. "If there's anyone in the area, this *will* attract attention." He sounded disappointed. Sydney didn't have to tell him what a bad idea it was to test the clip-on automatic. Duncan wiped his hands on his pants. "Still greasy," he said. Then, without a word, he removed the clip, put a single bullet in the gun, and handed it to Kyle. "Want to give it a try?"

Kyle didn't complain. He aimed at a log well up on the beach and smiled broadly when he hit his target. "We had some training with these in the CIA," he said. Then he turned to Sydney. "How about you?" he said, half-serious.

This was a gun from the past, a relic of the Vietnam War. She was itching to try it out despite how ridiculous it might be. And she was irritated that the two men seemed to assume she'd be unwilling or unable to fire the thing. On impulse, she took it from Kyle, checked the safety, aimed it at the same log, and planted a round within a foot of Kyle's. Both Kyle and Duncan looked impressed.

Then she cleared the breach and handed it back to Duncan. "Time to put away the toys, cover this back up, and hike out of here," she said. "If we hustle, we might still make the one o'clock shuttle."

When these weapons had been put here, they'd been the absolute top-of-the-line, high-tech, light-infantry firearm in the U.S. arsenal. They were a part of America's proud military past.

Now it was up to them to be sure these things would not also become a part of its ugly racist future.

CHAPTER 52

Early August
Port Hardy, B.C.
Offices of the RCMP

When they went in to see Constable Brown first thing the next morning, they had a plan. It involved setting a trap. They wanted to lure whoever had threatened Dwight Peters to the arms cache at Fisherman Bay and to catch them recovering the rifles.

Although Constable Brown agreed that having the RCMP remove the weapons would reduce the chance of catching the people who put them there in the first place, he couldn't approve involving civilians, especially three U.S. citizens. At their insistence, he reluctantly ran the plan past his superiors. But they also considered it too risky. What they wanted was for Brown to take a look at the site and report back. That was it. Furthermore, they were short-handed and couldn't pull their 65' marine patrol boat off of other duties to remove the weapons for three days.

Even after the decision had been made, Duncan refused to let it go. "Those rifles are still workable," he pointed out to Constable Brown.

"We can't let them fall into the hands of dangerous people like the Independence League."

"Look, I have a satellite phone," said Kyle. "What if the three of us go back and stand watch to see if they show up? If they don't, so be it. But if they do, we can call it in. If you guys or the Coast Guard don't arrive in time to catch them in the act, you can still chase them down—but only *if* you know who and what to look for."

"I can't make you stay away from the site," Constable Brown finally said. "But I strongly advise that you limit yourself to surveillance; don't take any action. If anything happens . . . *anything*, I expect you to call me. Immediately."

Sydney was uncomfortable with the idea of the three of them acting as lookouts, but she and Duncan had failed to stop the Independence League forty-five years earlier. This would likely be their only chance to make that right.

In exchange for showing him the site, Constable Brown agreed to let them ride along out to Fisherman Bay on the detachment's 21' outboard-powered aluminum skiff. If they were lucky, they might get a ride back with the RCMP when the cutter finally came to pick up the weapons. If not, they could always make the long hike out to the trailhead and use Kyle's satellite phone to call a shuttle into town. They arranged to meet the constable at the marina two hours later.

Back at their motel, while they packed up their belongings, Duncan, Sydney, and Kyle had an extended discussion about whether they should call Dwight even though Constable Brown had warned them not to.

"If no one shows up before the Canadians confiscate those weapons, then there's no accountability. Not even a slap on the wrist," Kyle complained.

"But at least they won't have the weapons," Sydney argued.

"There's another way to look at this," Duncan said. "From Dwight's point of view."

"What do you mean?"

"If those bozos come here and discover their cache of guns is gone, they could easily think that Dwight was the leak. But if he makes this call, he protects himself and his family by pointing to me as the one who most likely contacted the officials about the rifles."

Sydney gave that some thought. "I hate that Dwight and his family are in the crosshairs because of something we did years ago." After only a brief hesitation, she gave in. "Okay, what the hell? Let's do it. Let's ask him to make the call."

Duncan got on the phone and put Dwight on speaker.

"I'm not at all sure about this," Dwight said after Duncan explained the plan. "Besides, other than Josef Gilbert, I don't even have a name, just a phone number, probably a burner. If I call Gilbert, he's just going to deny having anything to do with it."

"Forget about Gilbert. Call the other number. Leave a message if you have to. If they call you back, here's what you say: tell them that your company attorney, me, Duncan Carmichael contacted you and told you he'd put two and two together and figured out what that chartered cruiser had been up to when it ran aground. Tell them that I suspect it's related to the dead Independence League man found there.

"Then explain that I'm going to take some time off work starting Friday to go up to Fisherman Bay on Vancouver Island to check it out. Say that I told you that I have a pretty good idea where to find some evidence that may be connected to a case I worked on many years ago during my Navy days.

"Emphasize that you are terrified for your family's safety and that you called because you don't want them to run across me at the site and to think that you ratted them out to me."

"If they don't show before Friday," Kyle interjected. "... the RCMP will take possession of the rifles. But at least the League will know it was Duncan and not you they have to blame for that."

"And, Dwight," Sydney added. "Make sure you tell them that you tried to persuade Carmichael not to go there, but that you failed."

In the end, Dwight reluctantly agreed to make the call.

Half an hour later he called back. "I still don't have a name," he said. "But whoever called me back was really excited. He acted like I had done them a favor. He kept saying how much he appreciated that I had called. The whole thing felt like a business transaction rather than me trying to get a scary asshole out of my life."

"You're sure he understands where to look?" Duncan said.

"Oh yeah. He got it right away. It sounded to me like they were already planning to go back out there. I think we definitely lit a fire under them."

"Great. With a little luck, this may all get resolved very soon."

CHAPTER 53

Early August
North coast of Vancouver Island, B.C.
Nissen Bight

Their second boat trip to Nissen Bight was a lot easier than the first. It was a calm day leavened only by a long low ocean swell rolling in from Cape Scott. The light RCMP skiff was fast. In less than two hours they were beaching the skiff at that same calm gravelly beach in Fisherman Bay. Getting their equipment ashore was a piece of cake.

They felt guilty not telling Constable Brown about violating their agreement, but they *were* committed to limiting themselves to surveillance. And they intended to be very vigilant. They'd agreed among themselves that they would call for help the moment anything happened, and then they would make themselves scarce.

Constable Brown scanned the shoreline. "I don't see anything," he said.

They led him up the beach and through the brush to the arms cache and removed the old branches and sod they had used to temporarily rebury it. After seeing the size of the cache and the obvious pristine condition of the weapons, however reluctant he had been to leave them there without police protection initially, he was even more concerned now.

"Damn," he said. "This is impressive."

"You see why we want to be sure they don't get a chance to make off with this stuff?" Duncan said.

"I understand, but I don't like leaving you here alone."

"Don't worry," Duncan said. "We'll stay out of sight. Just make sure you answer your phone if we call."

Brown helped them hide the cache again and then left. They watched as his skiff rose and fell across the oily swells of Queen Charlotte Sound and then finally disappeared beyond the point to the east, back in the direction of Port Hardy.

As the whine of the outboard motor faded in the distance, Sydney's misgivings returned. With no normal cell reception, they would be relying entirely on Kyle's satellite phone as their link to the outside world. He'd also brought a couple of cheap, hand-held Citizens Band "walkie talkie" radios so they could communicate with each other. But Kyle's high-tech sat phone would be their lifeline over the next three days. It suddenly seemed like a very thin and problematic thread.

"I sure hope you charged your phone," she told Kyle, shaking her head.

"It's fully charged," he said. "I won't use it for anything else. Promise."

They were committed; they'd set things in motion; it was too late to back out now. The League might not show before the RCMP 65-footer arrived on Friday, three days away. If they didn't, at that point it would all be over. She took a deep breath, leaned down, and shouldered one of the packs. It was just a short distance across the headland to where they would set up camp again at the western end of Nissen Bight.

They used the same campsite as before. Sydney had read that it rained a good deal along this coast, even in August. But the sky was currently clear with no storms anticipated. Even in summer, though, the weather was often unpredictable on the Sound. They were keeping their fingers crossed. If the weather soured, the Independence League might be less likely to attempt a weapons extraction—the surge in Fisherman Bay could easily make it impossible.

Figuring out what had happened to the weapons in the first place had been an interesting challenge—one she'd found hard to resist. But it was no longer an intellectual puzzle. Now, they'd been personally drawn back into the danger zone. Forty-five years earlier, she and Duncan had been young and invulnerable. Today they were neither. And even then, they'd barely escaped alive. Sydney desperately wanted the whole thing to be over.

As soon as they had their campsite operational, they returned to Fisherman Bay and scouted the area for locations from which to observe the beach and the bay without being seen. They assumed they'd be on the lookout for a boat. Fisherman Bay was much too small to land a seaplane. And further out, even when it was calm, there was a constant, westerly swell. Besides, the cache was much too large—it would take many trips with a small plane. Most likely the Leaguers would come for the weapons by boat, probably approaching from the east, from the direction of Port Hardy.

They found two good lookout spots. One was in the trees along the western shore of the bay some distance from the cache on the headland and well away from the trailhead. It had a good view out of the little bay, across Nissen Bight to the east, and in the direction from which they thought it most likely the Independence Leaguers would come. The second location was on the rocky headland itself, above and behind the ruin on the shore and only a hundred-fifty yards or so from the arms cache. It was also much closer to the trailhead. From there, in the cover of the trees, it should be possible to get some good pictures of anyone who showed up. And they would be able to see if or when the Independence Leaguers actually found the cache of weapons while remaining hidden to make their call.

It rained lightly during the night, but there was no wind to speak of, no wild animals came sniffing around, and the night passed without mishap. In the morning, the rain clouds lingered, but they were able to make breakfast before the clouds thickened and the light misty rain resumed. They filled two thermoses with coffee, grabbed their equipment, pulled up their hoods, and headed for their watching posts. They considered the second day after Dwight's phone call as the most likely time to expect the Leaguers to show up, although that was only a guess, assuming they took the bait. Sydney knew Duncan was hoping they'd show before the Mounties returned so they could be apprehended. Her concern was that Duncan and Kyle might be tempted to intervene if the Mounties couldn't get there in time. If it was in her power to do so, she intended on holding them to their promise to remain out of sight and out of play.

They each had binoculars but, beyond the cameras on their otherwise useless phones, they had only one first-rate digital camera with an optical telephoto lens. The first day, Duncan and Sydney took the post along the west shore, the one furthest away from the trailhead. They had the satellite phone with them, since that was the spot from which they would best be able to see any approaching vessels. Kyle watched from the other site behind some heavy underbrush in the trees, closer to the cache and the trailhead. He was in the best position to document anything that happened at the cache, so he had the camera. But until a boat showed up, all they could do was wait.

A heavy mist kept rolling in from up the valley to the south. It made it difficult to see as far out across the water as they'd hoped. Fortunately, they'd anticipated needing some protection from the rain and had brought two small camo-colored tarps to hang between the trees. Sydney and Duncan stayed under the tarp, taking turns sitting on the small camp stool that provided a better line of sight than the mossy log next to it. They were thankful for their thermos of breakfast coffee. But that was soon gone.

"I know stakeouts are supposedly boring. But this truly sucks," Sydney said.

Duncan laughed. "Not quite the outdoors adventure one envisions. Would you rather we were a couple of cops cooped up in an old sedan parked on the streets of Los Angeles with a bottle to pee in and a bag of stale Cheetos?"

"I don't know," she said. "A nice warm, dry, comfortably cushioned car seat. A hot cup of coffee. Some snacks. A place to relieve oneself. Sounds rather nice, right now."

The rain let up late in the afternoon and visibility improved. Sydney and Duncan took turns stretching their legs with short walks along an animal track that led into the woods. Sydney's pleasant forays into the woods were dampened by Constable Brown's strongly worded recommendation to keep pepper spray handy at all times in case they ran into bears or the occasional pack of wolves. Her extreme boredom had a way of overcoming her perfectly legitimate fears.

When the sun disappeared beyond the tree line, they decided to call it a day. It seemed doubtful anyone who had run onto offshore rocks on a previous trip was going to try for a nighttime landfall here. An arrival early the next day seemed increasingly likely. *If* they came.

The path from the Bay to the Bight was dark, but they were prepared with small LED flashlights. Kyle really had thought of everything.

The rain held off until after dinner. Then it started in again. They retreated into their respective tents. Sydney was glad she had brought along her Kindle. She wasn't sleepy, and she had done all of the thinking and self-reflection she cared to do for the day. She quickly escaped into her beloved world of mystery fiction.

Day two passed even more slowly than the first. She had switched posts with Kyle, and being alone made the monotonous routine of watching and waiting even worse. There was only an occasional shower, but the day remained overcast and gloomy. A pair of hikers appeared around noon and ate lunch sitting on a log on the beach. Other than them, and the occasional eagle flying by, the day was uneventful.

They enjoyed their last evening campfire in spite of their disappointment that no one had come to retrieve the guns. But again, they were driven inside early by the rain.

When Friday, day three arrived, they started early. Sydney was already looking forward to departing late that afternoon when the RCMP Patrol Boat was expected. It seemed unlikely the Leaguers would come on the same day they'd been told Duncan planned on arriving. Nevertheless, Kyle and Duncan headed over the headland to Fisherman Bay to begin their last vigil. Sydney stayed behind and set about packing up their things and breaking camp.

In all honesty, Sydney was glad the Leaguers hadn't shown up. The plan to document their arrival had seemed reasonable at the time, but there were too many things that could have gone wrong. The important thing was that they had found the weapons. And by mid-afternoon, this whole adventure would finally be over.

CHAPTER 54

Early August
North coast of Vancouver Island, B.C.
Fisherman Bay

Duncan scanned the bay and then out to sea with his binoculars. He'd taken up his post at the site nearer the trailhead. Kyle had gone along the beach to the west side of the bay to take the position with the better view out to sea to the east. Sydney was supposed to join Duncan as soon as she finished packing.

Under a morning overcast, everything was wet and chilly. Duncan could hear the distant surf washing in against the sand beach at Nissen Bight beyond the small headland behind him. In spite of their intent to avoid confrontation with the Independence Leaguers, he couldn't help but feel anxious. Although it seemed unlikely, there was still time for the Leaguers to show. And somehow, that thought was more unsettling now than it had been two days ago. Even though they were committed to their promise to make their phone call and keep their distance.

A couple of hikers showed up at the trailhead around 8:00 a.m. Little did the hikers know that two sets of binoculars were focused on them, watching their every move. They unshouldered their packs and sat on a log. After a short rest and a drink out of a shared bottle of water, they got up and headed back inland toward the main trail.

As the hikers disappeared, Duncan decided he could use something to drink himself. Where was that thermos of coffee Sydney had handed him as they were leaving? He reached into his pack and was surprised to come up with not one but two thermoses. Damn! He'd forgotten to give Kyle his coffee.

He looked around. It was still early. Kyle might want some coffee before the morning was over, and there were no boats anywhere in sight. He picked up the CB. "Kyle, you there?" he said.

After a moment Kyle responded, "Yep. Got nothing. How about you? Over."

"I got your coffee. Want some?"

"Sounds good."

"Meet me halfway, okay? Out."

Duncan grabbed the second thermos and walked along the quarter mile of curved rocky beach toward Kyle's position. He saw Kyle step out of the trees and head toward him.

"Thanks," Kyle said as they met midway and Duncan handed him the coffee. "This stuff isn't great, but it does help pass the time."

"When we get back, we can get together again at Starbucks to celebrate."

The contrast between their present situation and the pleasant, safe, professional civility of Seattle's Columbia Center Starbucks made them both smile.

They were violating their agreed rule against standing in the open, but it felt safe enough at that early hour and with no boats or people anywhere in sight.

As Duncan turned to head back down the beach, he caught a glimpse of Sydney moving into the trees by their watching post a couple hundred yards beyond the trailhead. She must have finished packing and had come across the headland to join him. He wondered if she'd brought anything to snack on.

Seconds after she disappeared into the trees, three hikers stepped onto the shore at the trailhead. They were less than a hundred yards away, and he knew immediately that there was something different about them.

They weren't wearing your typical hiking gear purchased at Eddie Bauer or REI. Instead, they had on what looked like work clothes—jeans and camouflage jackets. The lead man was wearing what seemed to be a military issue pack. And the two others were carrying long-handled shovels.

Shovels! Jesus! That's when it hit him. It was them! They'd come by land instead of by boat. And early! With the five-hour hike to the Cape Scott trailhead, how could they have gotten here on foot so early?

Trying to remain calm, Duncan slowly turned back around, and forcing himself not to hurry, called out softly to Kyle. Kyle swung back to see what he wanted, and Duncan saw him stiffen. It was clear that he, too, sensed that the three men weren't ordinary hikers.

Then, glancing back, he saw that the three men were now headed toward them, coming along the beach, moving fast. It was too late to run. Would he and Kyle be able to convince them that they were innocent campers, out for a walk on the beach carrying a couple of thermoses of coffee?

He saw the gun at the same instant he heard a shot. A rock splintered not three feet from where Kyle stood. They both froze and waited as the men drew near. Sydney would have heard that shot and might already have her binoculars trained on them. He hoped like hell that she stayed well out of sight.

"Well, what do you know," said the older of the three men. "I've got to admit, I kinda looked forward to running into you here."

Duncan's mind was racing, struggling to come up with something to say that might convince the three men that he and Kyle were just campers.

The older man just shook his head. "Don't bother, Mr. Carmichael. I'd know you anywhere. Your law firm has a great website, by the way. Very impressive."

The two other men had handguns out. One was pointed at Kyle, the other at Duncan. "What now, boss?" said one of the younger men.

The older man gave it some thought. "You two alone?" When neither Duncan nor Kyle answered, the man answered for them. "Yeah, I guess you are. Who the hell else would be dumb enough to come all this way looking for 45-year-old rifles, right?"

The leader turned toward one of his men. "Get on the radio. Call for the boat. We came a long way for this. And these two wouldn't be here if we were wrong." He turned toward Kyle. "Who are you?" he asked.

"Just a friend."

"Unfortunate for you. Ought to have more sense. Stick to whatever ghetto you grew up in." He turned back to Duncan. "I'm betting you two already know where they are, so save us a lot of grief and take us there."

When Duncan hesitated, one of the younger men stepped forward and poked him in the ribs with his gun. "Right now. Got that, shitheads?"

Duncan was trying to decide if they could buy time by claiming they hadn't found the rifles yet, but he wasn't sure that was wise. If they didn't know anything, then what use were they to these men?

"How did you get here so early?" Kyle asked. He'd apparently decided it was useless to try to bluff. His question may have also been designed to prevent Duncan from doing something stupid. Maybe also a delay tactic. Or just curiosity.

The older man laughed. Ignoring Kyle and speaking to Duncan, he said, "Hasn't your boy here ever heard of airplanes? We sure as hell weren't going to hike in."

Duncan glanced at Kyle who had ignored the racist jibe. Then he remembered. Dammit, Constable Brown had told them that in good weather it was possible to land a floatplane on nearby Hansen Lagoon. But they hadn't seriously considered the possibility that part of the Independence League contingent might come in early by air to find the weapons before calling in a boat to carry them away. Now it made obvious sense.

It seemed likely that he and Kyle would pay for that mistake.

"Which way?" the older man asked. "Let's get a move on."

Reluctantly Duncan and Kyle headed in the direction of the cache. The RCMP boat wouldn't be there until mid to late afternoon. It would take a while for these men to dig up the cache and ferry it out to a boat that may not have yet left Port Hardy. There was a good chance the two groups would overlap. Somehow, they needed to stay alive long enough . . .

"Look, I . . .," Duncan began.

"Just shut the fuck up," the older man ordered. "You two show us where those weapons are or one or both of you is going to end up dead. You got that?" The man was using his left hand rather awkwardly as he motioned them forward.

The whole scene was painfully familiar to Duncan. Here he was, caught up in a nearly perfect repeat of the situation he'd been in 45 years earlier. And now he'd put Kyle's life in jeopardy as well.

"The RCMP will be here any time now," Kyle said, his voice a lot calmer than Duncan felt. "If you leave now, there's a good chance you could get away."

The older man grinned. "Nice try. But I very much doubt that. Unless you have a phone in that thermos?" The three men laughed.

"They're coming by this morning to see what we've found," Kyle said, trying to sound convincing.

"Nah. If they knew there were guns buried here, there'd be cops crawling all over this place. That's why we came to have a look before bringing the boat in." He motioned them forward. "Keep moving. Don't stop until you have something to show us."

Duncan was kicking himself for not anticipating this. It was so obvious. He'd been unforgivably sloppy. Again!

They slowly made their way east along the rocky shore. Duncan couldn't think of any way to avoid showing these men where the cache of arms was buried. The question was, how were they to stay alive afterward? They needed to stall. Maybe the RCMP boat would be early. Or maybe, after they recovered the guns, their captors would be satisfied and leave them tied up somewhere.

Sure! And maybe they'd lay out blankets and have a nice picnic while they waited for the boat to arrive! No, he and Kyle were witnesses. At this point, the *only* witnesses. They were going to die this morning. He had no doubt whatever.

Duncan was in the lead with Kyle close behind. The three, armed Independence Leaguers brought up the rear several yards back. They passed the trailhead and continued up the beach to the area where they'd found the buried cache of arms. When they arrived, he paused and looked at Kyle who was standing a few yards to the side. Kyle just shrugged and nodded in the direction of the weapons. They didn't have much choice.

With his foot, Duncan kicked aside some of the sod they'd replaced and exposed a piece of the black plastic tarp that covered the weapons.

"Holy shit," said one of the two men. All three moved forward to take a closer look.

Duncan stepped back to stand beside Kyle as the two "soldiers" pushed aside the sod, soil, and loose brush. Then they peeled back the battered tarp that covered the U.S. Army crates.

The older man had drawn his own weapon and held it unwaveringly on Kyle and Duncan. As it became completely clear that they had found the cache of aging M-16s, Duncan noted a change in the man's face. Their fate was written there as his resolve hardened. He and Kyle were about to die. The only question was when and how.

"Freeze assholes!"

Duncan couldn't believe his eyes. It was Sydney. She'd stepped from behind some thick brush and was moving toward them, right there in the open. She was holding an M-16.

Startled, everyone froze . . ., for a moment. Then the Independence Leaguers, all three, spun in her direction, guns extended.

There was the deafening clatter of automatic gunfire, an ear-splitting, violent burst of sound that lasted for several seconds.

And then silence.

It took Duncan a moment to register the fact that he hadn't been hit and that Sydney was still standing. He turned and saw that Kyle was okay too.

But all three of the men behind them were on the ground, writhing and moaning. Duncan saw blood seeping from multiple wounds, mostly to their legs.

Sydney walked toward them. She carried the M-16 rifle they'd reassembled as if she'd been born to it. She kept it tightly trained on the three men on the ground. "Duncan," she said calmly, as she approached. "Would you kindly secure their weapons?"

Kyle was staring at the wounded men as if having a hard time taking in what had just happened. Then he turned to Sydney with a huge, admiring grin.

"Kyle, did you call for help?" Sydney asked.

"Nope," he said. "I guess you got this, right?"

She nodded, but her concentration never wavered.

"The phone is back at my post," he said, and then hurried off in that direction.

"When you call, you might mention that we need a medical evacuation," Sydney called after him. "I think these boys may require some urgent care."

Duncan carefully kicked away and then picked up the handgun that moments before had been the apparatus of their death. Keeping out of Sydney's line of fire, he also confiscated the two handguns on the ground near the other men. As he backed away, he turned toward Sydney. There she stood, confidently holding an M-16 rifle. The look in her eyes was identical to the look he recalled from forty-five years earlier on the night she'd stepped out from the *Spindrift*'s cabin after ramming the packer at Esperanza Inlet. She was older and grayer now. But there was no doubt that this was the very same Sydney Warren in every other conceivable way.

She looked back at him and smiled tightly. "Let's not make this a habit," she said.

The tense shock of adrenaline was washed away by admiration, relief, and humor.

"'Freeze assholes?'" he said shaking his head. And then, spreading his hands, "I know, I know. You've . . ."

". . . always wanted to say that," she completed.

Their exchange was interrupted by one of the younger men yelling at them. "Why the fuck did you do that?" He sounded aggrieved and surprised. "Jesus Christ. You shot me."

Duncan wanted to laugh outright. But neither he nor Sydney bothered to reply. He could, however, tell that Sydney was starting to feel the impact of what she had done. She had turned a bit pale and her hands weren't quite as steady as they had been moments earlier.

The other younger man was trying to sit up, without much success.

The older man was lying on his side with his face down, awkwardly holding his thigh, and still breathing.

"We'd better try to help them with some first aid," Duncan said. "But before we do that, there's something you need to see." He reached down, took hold of a shoulder, and gently but firmly rolled the older man over to give Sydney a look at his face.

She stared for several long seconds. "You're kidding me!"

"There's something else, as well," he said. "I noticed he's favoring his left arm. So, in case you're feeling at all bad about shooting him . . ."

Duncan waited for what he'd said to sink in. He vividly recalled that day, a couple months earlier, when he'd spotted her out there in the center of 5th Avenue, kneeling beside that injured fellow protestor, calmly binding his wounds. That had been mere moments after she had been under active, life-threatening gunfire.

She paused a moment in thought. Then she said, "Favoring his left arm, huh?" She pointed the barrel of her M-16 at the man's bleeding leg. "Hmm. Well . . ., I'd say they shouldn't have much trouble getting a blood sample to match what they found on the pavement after the shooting at that protest last summer, you think?"

"No trouble at all," he replied.

The face staring back at them was much older, heavily lined, and somewhat jowly. The eyes were deeper and the hair was grayer. But there was no doubt.

It was their former client, Arnie Beck.

CHAPTER 55

Saturday evening in late September
Magnolia District, NW Seattle
The private home of Kate and Duncan Carmichael

The view from the front deck of the Carmichaels' Magnolia Bluff home was spectacular. The last warm rays of a setting sun backlit the distant peaks of the Olympic Mountains and glinted off Puget Sound below like a sprinkle of diamonds. The five good friends sat comfortably together. All of them had wine glasses in their hands and Kate Carmichael's pesto pasta settling nicely in their stomachs. It was one of those idyllic October evenings that Pacific Northwesterners cherish, a last soft breath of summer.

"So, I have a confession to make," Duncan said. "I wrote a small check yesterday. A contribution to Frank Merrill's Senate Exploratory Committee." He smiled in anticipation of the deep groans from Kyle and Sydney and an indulgent sigh from his wife.

"He's a good guy," Duncan added. "And a moderate. We need more like him."

"I'm not sure there's such a thing as a moderate conservative these days," Kyle countered. "He'll be voting with the rest of that caucus if he ends up in the Senate."

Duncan nodded in Sydney's direction. "Didn't you tell me that he recently voted through a new appropriation for battered women? That sounds pretty mainstream to me."

"Window dressing," Kyle complained. "You know that, right? He's just building his legend. Manufacturing moderate credentials so he can win in liberal Washington State. In fact, I assume you know he has enthusiastic support from the party's right-wing—and that isn't an accident. I doubt he'll have a significant primary opponent because even the extremists know he's their only real hope in a general election here."

Kate broke into the exchange by lightheartedly admonishing her husband to: "Stop needling your friends, Duncan." She stood up to refill wine glasses and added, "We're supposed to be celebrating. You all recently accomplished something amazing. You closed down a criminal conspiracy that's been hanging out there for decades. Kept a bunch of automatic rifles off the streets. Probably saved a lot of lives. Put the bad guys behind bars. So, hey, take a break, Relax and congratulate yourselves."

She put the wine bottle down. "Who's interested in a slice of Chocolate Decadence?" Enthusiastic yeses and affirmative nods quickly replaced the political bickering.

As Duncan got up to help his wife with the cake, he saw Kyle reach over, pick up Sydney's phone from one of their outdoor side tables and begin to scroll again through the pictures Sydney had shown them a few minutes earlier—the ones she'd taken on their recent trip to Port Hardy and Fisherman Bay.

By the time Carmichael returned with the dessert, Kyle was staring intently at one of the pictures and looking deeply puzzled.

"Sydney? Duncan?" Kyle said. "Um, back in '78, when that ship first showed up in Canada with the arms . . .?"

Duncan handed him his cake and a small fork. "Yeah."

"You guys saw it, right? The ship itself?"

He and Sydney nodded.

Kyle held up Sydney's phone and pointed to one of her pictures. He'd expanded the photo to zoom in on the corner of a heavy dark plastic tarp that had been wrapped around some of the buried crates of rifles. "There," he said. "Was that the name of the ship? The one that brought the arms over from the Philippines. The one you guys intercepted that day back in '78?"

The ship's name had been stenciled in white onto the heavy black plastic tarp. "Yeah," Sydney said. "That's it. The *Isabela*. Homeport, Colón in Panama. Van Damme's ship."

"What is it, Kyle? What are you getting at?" Duncan asked.

Kate came out carrying another couple of dessert plates. Upon seeing the group huddled intently around Kyle's chair and studying Sydney's phone, she set down the plates and joined them.

"Damn," Kyle said. "When we were there at Fisherman Bay, I never noticed this. And I've kept asking myself: why now? That shipment was buried there for forty-five years, right? What changed? Why, after all this time, was removing it suddenly worth the risk? Somehow, I can't imagine that they had some sudden need for those rifles. Frankly I think it's a miracle that they turned out to be serviceable after all these years. So what else was happening to make them change their plans?"

"Well, Truman Beck died in prison this past spring," Duncan said. "He was the one who probably saved those old charts. Maybe in anticipation of dying he passed them along to his son or someone else whose interest was piqued. Or someone came across them in his effects. The catalyst could have been as straightforward as that."

"But he was in prison, right? It's not like he'd had a bunch of charts hidden away in his cell. They'd have been at home with his family. He was sick for months. If he'd lived, he would have been out just a couple of years from now. Wouldn't you think he'd have acted before, or passed this information and the charts along to someone—his son or his colleagues—a long time ago?"

"Maybe," Duncan said. "Or, maybe the opposite. Maybe he was waiting until he got out. Could have been saving them all these years to fund his post-prison retirement."

"There's still another possibility," Sydney said. "Remember, Truman and his son were estranged. Truman blamed Arnie for everything that went wrong back then. Maybe he had a falling out with colleagues after what happened. Their original plan to get the guns failed, and the Independence League became a target for law enforcement."

"But why is the ship's name so important?" Duncan asked.

"It's Merrill," Kyle said, scowling. "Frank Merrill."

Everyone fell silent and stared at Kyle.

"*Isabela* is the name of the ship that Frank Merrill commandeered to save all those Vietnamese refugees fleeing Saigon back in 1975 at the end of the war."

There was a stunned silence.

"You're kidding," Sydney said.

"How would you know that?" Duncan asked.

"I saw it. Not six months ago."

"I don't understand," Sydney said.

"In his Issaquah office. I was there last fall to lobby him on behalf of our Mercer Island City Council. On the sanctuary cities issue. He had a framed picture on the wall behind his desk. Of *that* ship. He was proud of it. He had framed this old *Navy Times* article with a press shot originally taken at Subic Bay when the ship was unloading its refugee passengers. In the photo, the ship's name was right there on the stern. *Isabela.* It's the *same goddamned ship.*"

Now Sydney was shaking her head. "I was there. Just a couple of months ago," she said. "In his office. I didn't see any picture on the wall."

"Proves my point," Kyle responded. "He's cleaning up his act. Protecting himself."

They were all silent for a moment as they took this in.

"Why now?" Kate asked, mirroring Kyle's earlier question.

"His Senate race," Kyle said in unison with Sydney.

"It makes sense," Duncan added reluctantly. "When they were grilling me on the packer that night at Rosa Island, van Damme admitted his actions in the Beck case were designed to provide Beck with reversible error. And remember how during the investigation each time one or another of the legal maneuvers or obstructions went away, another took its place? Even then, I was a bit surprised that van Damme, a non-lawyer, could have come up with all of those carefully calibrated legal strategies on his own. I bet Frank Merrill was advising him right along."

He paused in thought. "I also don't believe there were all that many Americans in Saigon in the last days before it fell. Merrill was a JAGC officer. Van Damme was a Navy liaison. They were both at the U.S. Embassy. They surely knew each other. If van Damme needed help with his shipment, Frank could have been a natural ally—even if he was only a lawyer."

"So, you're saying Frank Merrill willingly joined van Damme's criminal enterprise? For what? Some kind of financial payoff?"

"That or, maybe he was asked to see to the *Isabela's* departure without knowing the full nature of the cargo," Kyle's wife, Mary Lynne suggested. "By the time he learns what's up, it's too late to pull out. Or maybe he's just too loyal to snitch on his friend."

"I bet those weapons were on board the *Isabela* the day that picture was taken, when those refugees disembarked at Subic. Given everything that was happening, I'd say it was likely that nobody bothered to check out its cargo before sending the civilian vessel on its way to clear badly needed dock space at a critical moment in history." Sydney looked to Duncan for confirmation.

He nodded. "That also explains something I've wondered about over the years, how Frank, despite being just a lowly JAGC officer, was still able to somehow magically 'commandeer' this private vessel and save those refugees. He probably already owned it. Who knows, maybe they didn't really have any choice about boarding the refugees. Or maybe, from Frank or van Damme's perspective, the refugees were cover for what they were actually up to. Hard to be sure."

Kyle nodded. "Seems plausible to me."

"Or who knows, maybe he really was some kind of hero," Mary Lynn suggested. "Did the right thing while in the middle of doing the wrong one."

There was a long moment of silence while the group digested this and the rest of the speculation. Meanwhile, Kate laid out the remaining desserts and everybody took their seats again.

They'd all taken a bite or two when Mary Lynne contributed another thought. "I can understand why Merrill wouldn't have wanted those buried weapons to surface again, but wouldn't his involvement in that arms shipment have come up long before now? At this point, he's been elected five or six times to the House of Representatives. Doesn't that already involve an awful lot of, um, public scrutiny?"

Kyle shook his head. "Nah. Think about it. The initial coverage of this event was all positive. Merrill was an American hero at a time when one was sorely needed. Nobody cared about the ship. Then, when the ship was finally captured three years later, it happened in Canada. Probably never even made the U.S. news. And it was, what, twenty years after that before Merrill first ran for Congress. He probably considered it ancient history. Didn't figure anyone would put it all together after all that time."

"They did play up the hero thing though," Duncan commented. "You'd think opposition investigators might have dug up something about it. Or that Merrill would have been more worried about potential discovery and not have made it into such a big campaign credential."

"People have short memories," Kyle said. "I never would have remembered it myself if I hadn't noticed that photo on Merrill's wall a few months back. And then seen the ship's name here on Sydney's phone. Researchers don't always look as closely at details like this as you might think. And politicians tend to believe their own BS.

"When I ran for City Council, even though it was a small-time race, I retained a political consultant to help me get off on the right foot. A knowledgeable guy. He asked me about my history. If I had any secrets that might come back to haunt me. Stuff my opponent might dig up in opposition research."

Kyle smiled before continuing. "I told him that I'd spent an active decade with the U.S. Central Intelligence Agency, so, 'yes' there definitely were secrets. But I wasn't going to be answering questions about any of them."

Duncan laughed at that. "That must have set him back on his heels."

Kyle nodded. "He said that kind of admission was a first for him.

Told me that's a question he'd asked every client he'd ever worked for. And there'd been scores. It's something of an inside joke in his profession: they *always* ask. And they *always* get the same response."

"What's that?" Sydney asked.

"They lie," Kyle said. "They always lie."

CHAPTER 56

Late September
Preston-Martin Building, Seattle
Law Offices of Warren and Carmichael

Sydney came in unannounced and sat in Duncan's favorite chair in the corner of his office. Its worn brown leather reminded her of something you'd have expected to find in a men's club in the early 1900s. All that was needed to complete the picture would have been an ashtray sporting an expensive cigar and a folded newspaper. She suspected Duncan napped in the comfy chair when no one was around.

He looked up and smiled.

"I've been thinking . . .," she began as she settled back and made herself comfortable.

"Always a dangerous sign." He, too, leaned back, awaiting the reason for her visit.

"I'm still getting my mind around all of this stuff about Frank Merrill."

He nodded.

"The way I've got it pieced together, Merrill had to have known about the contents of the cargo loaded aboard the *Isabela* that day he sailed it out of Saigon. Whether he was an unwitting accomplice initially is beside the point. Once that ship took off, he became a partner in the operation."

"I agree."

"The press coverage upon their arrival in Subic must have thrown him," Sydney said.

"But being labeled a hero for saving those escaping Vietnamese from capture by the North Vietnamese Army—that had to feel awfully good."

"Uh huh. The hubris of military command. Like the politician he is, he probably couldn't help but believe his own bullshit."

Duncan laughed. "You're never going to let up on us old Navy men, I guess." Then he got serious. "I've gone over this a million times in my head, too. Merrill was damned lucky that all those hundreds of refugees were the story. Otherwise, officials would have checked the cargo."

"Without the refugees, he probably wouldn't have gone in there at all," she suggested.

"He was certainly lucky. Even so, the military's compulsive record-keeping did set him up for eventual discovery. The U.S. Navy's port management officials at Naval Base, Subic followed procedure by recording the arrival and subsequent departure of the civilian cargo vessel, *Isabela*, noting that it was homeported and documented in Colón, Panama. That was a record trail neither Merrill nor van Damme could ever erase."

"And don't forget that the Canadian Coast Guard carefully documented their interdiction of illegally imported arms three years later. That, too, was public record."

"Again, he was damned lucky those events happened seven thousand miles, in two very different countries, and three years apart."

In the days following the gathering at his home, Duncan couldn't resist poking into the old Canadian and U.S. arms prosecution to see if Merrill's name popped up. The court records for Truman Beck's 1979 arms smuggling case before the Provincial Courts in Vancouver, B.C.

listed a barrister by the name of Gavin Carter as Truman Beck's Canadian attorney. Carter was long retired, but Duncan ran down a phone number for him and gave him a call.

Carter's recollection of the Beck case was crystal clear. "Oh yeah," he said. "I remember that guy. Merrill, you say. Yeah, he was U.S. Navy JAGC as I recall. He was one of Beck's more loyal supporters. At one point we considered calling him as a character witness in the extradition. But it turned out to be pointless."

The Canadian neo-Nazi crew of that second packer would surely have told their leaders about the buried weapons cache and have passed along the charts and waypoints for its location before going dark. And the charts and information seemed likely to have made its way back to Truman Beck. Through a friend in the U.S. Attorney's office, Duncan learned that Merrill had visited Beck in jail on a few occasions over the years. That, in Duncan's view, was the final proof of their criminal connection—why else would Merrill have had sufficient cause to visit Truman Beck in prison.

Truman Beck, in turn, had apparently kept that secret, even from his own son. Perhaps he considered it leverage—a treasured remnant of power to be wielded from his residence in a federal prison. Or, if as they suspected, the arms were intended to ease his future retirement, he could have lost interest in them as his final illness worsened.

When he'd learned that Frank Merrill, one of his few loyal confederates and supporters was planning a run for the U.S. Senate, Beck would have immediately appreciated the potential importance of his secret to Merrill's campaign and could have decided to make use of it.

It must have come as a huge and unpleasant surprise to Frank Merrill when he learned that his much-lauded post-Vietnam refugee escapade could so easily be connected to convicted smuggler Truman Beck and to the disgraced Admiral Clifford van Damme. And it would have been an even bigger and deeply ironic surprise for the Independence League's new leader Arnie Beck when Arnie's one-time prosecutor, Frank Merrill, reached out to him for help in removing that arms cache in order to make sure no one else would ever find it. Regardless of their history, Arnie had every reason to cement his relationship with a future U.S. Senator.

And, what an unnerving setback it must have been for Merrill when that chartered yacht went aground, and the yacht's Marine Insurer assigned its subrogation claim to the law firm headed by none other than Duncan Carmichael and Sydney Warren.

For Arnie Beck to have been acting on his own in bugging Sydney and Duncan's law firm was hard to imagine. Merrill, on the other hand, had the knowledge and means to understand what had to be done. He knew the insurance claims investigator needed to settle the case immediately. And he knew he had to see that case file if he was to know what Carmichael and Warren might come to know. Fortunately for him, he had the connections with law enforcement that allowed him to gain access to high-tech electronic surveillance equipment—the infamous "M&Ms."

Unfortunately, those intrusive acts turned out to be big mistakes that stimulated interest where none had existed before.

Even so, no one in the current day political press had connected the dots. Not until a few days after that social gathering at the Carmichael home. That's when an anonymous phone call was received by a hungry reporter with King 5 News.

A closer look might have shown that the call had come from a burner phone paid for in cash and bought from a store located just down the street from the Seattle offices of Marshall Security and Investigations. But nobody bothered to trace it. And, with that single phone call, Frank Merrill's political demise was set in motion. Once his easily documented connection with the arms shipment on the *Isabela* was revealed, the story went viral.

In an instant, he was political history.

~

The three Independence Leaguers injured by Sydney's M-16 fire that day at Fisherman Bay, the aging Arnie Beck and his two "soldiers," recovered from their gunshot wounds. But they remained silent regarding their purpose for being there.

Like his father before him, Arnie Beck was ultimately extradited back to the U.S. where, based largely on DNA evidence, he was convicted of murder in connection with the Seattle protest shooting. He avoided Canadian arms charges. But, ironically, he was sentenced to serve out his last days in the very same prison and facing the very same fate as had his father before him.

Beck's two "soldiers" turned out to be Canadian citizens, one of whom admitted to his attorney that he'd been aboard that small cruiser that had gone aground in June. Neither the crown prosecutor nor the RCMP ever suspected that earlier connection. Both men were charged with unregistered firearms possession and assault and intimidation. In their statements, they denied those charges, claiming that *they* were the victims. That they'd been attacked, without provocation, by a crazy old American woman armed with an ancient M-16 rifle her possession of which was, itself, a crime!

On the faith of their story, they were both granted pretrial bail and both promptly disappeared.

Epilogue

0200, Sunday, February 5, 1978
Sand Point Naval Station, Seattle
Enlisted Men's Barracks One

Petty Officer Third Class Steven Jerome sank slowly to the floor beside the urinal. As his last faint breaths of life expired into the chill night air, he managed one brief wondering look in the direction of the man who'd stabbed him.

In that final moment, just before disappearing through the rear barracks door, the killer turned back into the room and screamed one word, a viciously offensive racial slur. A dim band of outside lighting shining through the nearby frosted windows moved across the killer's face as he turned to flee.

Jerome was not surprised.

It was the face of Arnie Beck.

END

Military withdrawal from an active war zone can be a tricky business. According to the New York Times, more than a billion dollars in American military equipment was lost or left behind in the fall of Saigon on April 30, 1975. (Six billion in today's dollars – comparable with what was left behind in Afghanistan.)

That Vietnam episode was the inspiration for this book.

While most of the events and the people in this book are fictional, the settings are real. Sand Point in North Seattle lies along the western shore of Lake Washington. During World War II it was a busy place with as many as 8,000 military personnel. After the war, its usefulness diminished, and in 1970 it was decommissioned as an active Naval Air Station. Up until 1979, however, Sand Point continued to serve as a "Naval Support Activity" housing the headquarters of the Commandant, Thirteenth Naval District and its associated "Law Center." Author Don Stuart was stationed there as a Navy JAGC officer in 1970-72. At the time, the Naval Correctional Facility (Navy Brig) was located at a U.S. Navy facility at Smith Cove in the Interbay area of Seattle. That facility, too, later closed and its functions moved elsewhere.

In 1995 the Sand Point property was finally given to the City of

Seattle and ultimately became what is today: the beloved Magnuson Park.

Much of this book, is also set at remote sites along the Pacific Ocean coast of British Columbia, Canada. These settings, too, are authentic. In their years of pleasure cruising and commercial fishing, authors Charlotte Stuart and Don Stuart visited or voyaged through the places mentioned and have endeavored to accurately describe them as they were at the time. Many of them continue to be magical places well deserving of a visit and of a moment of respect for the natural power they still retain.

CHARLOTTE STUART

Charlotte Stuart, PhD got her start in academia. She left a tenured faculty position to spend a year with her husband, Don, cruising the Pacific coastal waters of the U.S. and Canada. That inspired the two of them to purchase a 47' sailing boat bare hull and to build a commercial salmon troller that they fished in Southeast Alaska for nine years. Charlotte later became a partner in a management consulting group and then a VP of HR and Training for a national credit union. She draws upon her work as a corporate VP and a business consultant and from her years with non-profit volunteerism to create the character and voice of Sydney Warren, the ACLU lawyer who takes on a case in the challenging world of military justice.

Charlotte's books have placed or made finals in various competitions, including: 1st Place in the Chanticleer International Mystery &

Mayhem Book Series Award, Global Book Award Gold, Global eBook Gold, Reader Views Silver, Book Fest 2nd Place, and a finalist in Foreword Indies, Killer Nashville's Silver Falchion, IBA (International Book Awards), and Eric Hoffer Awards.

Charlotte lives and writes on Vashon Island in the Pacific Northwest. She is the past president of the Puget Sound Sisters in Crime and a member of the Mystery Writers of America and the International Thriller Writers. See her website at charlottestuart.com.

Her books include:

Fiction:

- *Survival Can be Deadly: A Discount Detective Mystery* (Walrus Publishing – an imprint of Amphorae Publishing Group, 2019)
- *Campaigning Can be Deadly: A Discount Detective Mystery* (Walrus Publishing – an imprint of Amphorae Publishing Group, 2020)
- *Shopping Can be Deadly: A Discount Detective Mystery* (Walrus Publishing – an imprint of Amphorae Publishing Group, 2021)
- *Moonlight Can be Deadly: A Discount Detective Mystery* (Walrus Publishing – an imprint of Amphorae Publishing Group, 2022)
- *Unicorns Can be Deadly: A Discount Detective Mystery* (Walrus Publishing – an imprint of Amphorae Publishing Group, for release in 2025)
- *Bogged Down: A Vashon Island Mystery* (Taylor and Seale Publishing, 2020)
- *Why Me? Chimeras, Conundrums, and Dead Goldfish: A Macavity & Me Mystery* (Taylor and Seale Publishing, 2019)
- *Who Me? Fog Bows, Fraud, and Aphrodite: A Macavity & Me Mystery* (Taylor and Seale Publishing, 2021)

- *Not Me! Speluncaphobia, Secrets, and Hidden Treasure: A Macavity & Me Mystery* (Taylor and Seale Publishing, 2022)
- *In$ured to the Hilt: A John Smith Mystery* (Level Best Books, 2023)
- *In$urance to Die For: A John Smith Mystery* (Level Best Books, 2024)
- *In$ured for Life--and Death: Delia's Demise: A John Smith Mystery* (Level Best Books, for release in 2025)
- *Raven's Grave* (Vine Leaves Press, 2023)

Non-Fiction:

- *Disastrous Interviews: The Comic, Tragic & Just Plain Ugly* (Charlotte L. Stuart, 2013)

Don Stuart

Don Stuart, JD was a U.S. Navy JAGC officer during the Vietnam War (1968-72) and later a partner in a Seattle law firm. Don and his wife Charlotte quit their professional jobs to cruise the Pacific coastal waters of the U.S. and Canada and then personally built a 47' commercial salmon troller and, during the 1980s, earned their living fishing in Southeast Alaska. Don later became a non-profit manager for the commercial fishing industry, then for conservation districts, and finally for a national organization working for agriculture and the environment. In that work he gained 20 years' experience as a legislative lobbyist. He draws upon his years trying court-martial cases in the U.S. Navy and in the practice of law for his depiction of JAGC Lieutenant Duncan Carmichael whose assignment to the criminal defense of an unlikable client requires working with independent-minded civilian ACLU volunteer lawyer Sydney Warren.

Don's books have earned 1st place in the BookFest Award, the Incipere Award for Exceptional Writing, and the Pinnacle Book Achievement Award. He's received 2nd and 3rd place or a Bronze Medal in the Outstanding Creator Book Awards and Global Book Awards. And he was a Finalist, Top Pick, Short Listed, Distinguished Favorite, or Recommended Read in the Next Generation Indie Book Awards, Killer Nashville Best Books, Cygnus Book Awards, Author Shout, New York City Big Book Award and the Eric Hoffer Book Awards' Montaigne Medal.

Don lives and writes on Vashon Island in the Pacific Northwest. See his website at donstuart.net.

His books include:

Fiction:

- *Final Adjournment: A Washington Statehouse Mystery* (Epicenter Press, 2017)
- *Suspension of the Rules: A Washington Statehouse Mystery* (Northwest Corner Books—an imprint of Epicenter Press, 2021)
- *Censure and Repeal: A Washington Statehouse Mystery* (Northwest Corner Books—an imprint of Epicenter Press, 2024)
- *Darwin's Dilemma: A Story of Humans, AIs, and the Future of Intelligence* (Quartermaster Press, 2023) – An interstellar confrontation between two superintelligent AIs with deeply conflicting points of view.
- *Secret Places: A Southeast Alaska Mystery* (Epicenter Press, to be released in early 2025)

Non-Fiction:

- *Barnyards and Birkenstocks: Why Farmers and Environmentalists Need Each Other* (Washington State University Press, 2014)
- *No Farms No Food: Uniting Farmers and Environmentalists to Transform American Agriculture* (Island Press, 2022)
- *Small Claims Court Guide for Washington: How to win your case* (Self Counsel Press, 1979, 1989)
- *CLEDEX: The Index to Continuing Legal Education in Washington* (CLEDEX Publications Inc., 1986-1991) (Originating author)

A Note from the Authors

We enjoyed doing this joint writing project together and hope you liked *Midnight for Justice*. We would deeply appreciate your feedback in the form of a rating and/or review on your favorite retailer or Goodreads. This is much more important than you might imagine. A sentence or two is all it takes to satisfy the retailer's voracious algorithm. We do know how valuable your time is, so we thank you in advance.